THE BEST OF TEMPTATION COLLECTION

Too hot to handle? Maybe a little,
but this 2-in-1 collection of sassy, sexy romances
will have you captivated from page one.

Filled with steamy nights and sizzling days,
these classic stories explore what happens when
a fun, flirty woman meets an irresistible man.
The result of such chemistry is often explosive,
usually unexpected and always unforgettable!
We're sure you'll agree....

These tempting tales prove that sometimes reality
can be even better than your most private fantasies!

STEPHANIE BOND

New York Times bestselling author Stephanie Bond grew up in eastern Kentucky, but traveled to distant lands through reading Harlequin romance novels. Years later, the writing bug bit her, and once again she turned to romance. Her writing has allowed her to travel in person to distant lands to teach workshops and promote her novels. She's written more than forty projects for Harlequin. To learn more about Stephanie Bond and her novels, visit www.stephaniebond.com.

New York Times Bestselling Author

STEPHANIE BOND

About Last Night...

and

Too Hot to Sleep

HARLEQUIN®

THE BEST OF TEMPTATION COLLECTION

Recycling programs
for this product may
not exist in your area.

ISBN-13: 978-0-373-60626-9

ABOUT LAST NIGHT... AND TOO HOT TO SLEEP

Copyright © 2014 by Harlequin Books S.A.

The publisher acknowledges the copyright holder
of the individual works as follows:

ABOUT LAST NIGHT...
Copyright © 1999 by Stephanie Bond
TOO HOT TO SLEEP
Copyright © 2000 by Stephanie Bond

Printed in U.S.A.

CONTENTS

ABOUT LAST NIGHT…

CHAPTER ONE

"PINEAPPLE JUICE," Janine Murphy said, holding back her sister's light brown hair to scrutinize the two hickeys on her neck. Or was it one? She blinked, trying to focus through the effects of a half bottle of wine on an empty stomach—the piece of her own bachelorette party cake didn't really count. Two hours ago she'd eaten the exclamation points at the end of GOOD LUCK, JANINE!! But after reflecting on her and Steve's relationship most of the evening, she was beginning to think question marks would have been more appropriate.

"Drinking pineapple juice will make hickeys go away?" Marie met her gaze in the dresser mirror, her eyebrows high.

Janine nodded and the movement sent showers of sparks behind her eyes. She wet her lips and spoke carefully around her thickened tongue. "The vitamin D helps the broken blood vessels heal."

Marie screwed up her face. "When you put it that way, it's kind of gross."

"Good," Janine said, letting Marie's hair fall back in place. "Because it *looks* kind of gross. You're not in high school anymore. Besides, hickeys can be dangerous."

Her sister laughed. "What can I say? Greg's an animal."

Envy surged in Janine's chest. She'd been living vicariously through Marie's sensual escapades for years, listening to her adventures in between offering homeopathic treatments for bladder infections from too much friction, skin rashes from flavored body potions and strained muscles from unnatural positions. "Well, you better tell Greg to stay away from your jugular with those Mick Jagger lips of his."

"Always the doctor," Marie said with a wry smile.

"Physican's ass..." She stopped and they giggled at her words. "Physician's assistant," she corrected primly, then fell back on her bed where they were sitting amidst stacks of gifts. Marie fell back too, toppling boxes, and they broke into gales of laughter.

Janine sighed and toyed with her empty wineglass. "Thanks for arranging the party, sis. It was fun."

"You're welcome," Marie said. "But don't lie. These kinds of things are always a roaring bore for the guest of honor."

She laughed—her older sister was nothing if not honest. Instead of basking in the glow of the spotlight, Janine had spent the evening nursing a bottle of zinfandel, listening to a roomful of women talk about their fabulous sex lives. Someone had started a round robin of, "What was your most memorable encounter?" and when her turn came, she'd recounted a fantasy as if it had actually happened. She'd felt a little guilty about lying, but somehow, the middle of a raucous bachelorette party didn't strike her as the best place to divulge the fact that she was a virgin. Not even Marie knew.

Janine sipped her wine and reflected on her chaste history. Her virginity certainly wasn't a source of personal embarrassment. On the other hand, she didn't deserve to be pinned with the good-girl-of-the-year ribbon—given the right man and the right circumstances, she imagined she would have indulged as enthusiastically as the next person. She'd simply…never gotten around to having sex. In high school she'd been too shy to attract a boyfriend. In her ten grueling years of part-time college and med school, she'd been too busy working and studying to be a social butterfly. And afterward…well, afterward, she'd met Steve.

"I just wish you had let me hire some live entertainment," her sister said, breaking into her thoughts.

Janine flushed, relenting silently that her sense of modesty *was* perhaps above average. "You know that's not my style."

Marie scoffed. "After that story about doing it on a penthouse balcony?"

"Oh, that." Janine smiled sheepishly. "I, um, might have stretched the truth a tad."

"How much?"

"Like a piece of warm taffy."

Her sister laughed. "You have a great imagination—that part about you dropping a shoe really had me going."

The details were specific because she'd relived the hot summer-night scene in her head so many times. She suspected her claustrophobia made her fantasize about open spaces, and she suspected her celibacy made her fantasize, period.

"And I thought your penis was pretty impressive," Marie continued, her lips pursed.

"Thanks," Janine said a bit wistfully. "I didn't think it was half-bad myself." Marie's brainchild of seeing who could sculpt the best penis out of a Popsicle before it melted had been a big hit, especially after the wine had started flowing.

"I guess Steve was your inspiration."

Janine pushed her long hair behind her ears to avoid eye contact. "I got an A in anatomy."

Marie's eyes lit with curiosity. "Oh? Is the infamous plastic surgeon's operating equipment lacking?"

For all she knew, Steve's equipment could be as blue as her Popsicle prizewinner, but she decided to cover. "Marie, I'm not going to discuss my future husband's physical assets."

Marie pouted, then assumed a dreamy look, already distracted. "Can you believe that in less than forty-eight hours you'll be a married woman?"

She stared at the ring on her left hand, the cluster of huge diamonds perched atop a wide platinum band—a priceless heirloom that once belonged to Steve's grandmother. "Yeah, married." She wished the light-headed anticipation and breathless impatience she'd read about in *Bride* magazine would sweep down and roll away the stone of anguish in her stomach. Wasn't cold feet a malady for the groom?

Marie held up a troll doll wearing a bridal gown. "Ugh. Who gave you this?"

"Lisa. It's kind of scary, don't you think?"

"Well, she's still bitter over her divorce. She told me

she ran her husband's Armani suits through the wood shredder and mulched her azalea bushes. Cold, huh?"

"Brrr."

"Heeeey, what about this sexy little number?"

She had to hold her temple when she turned her head. Upon seeing the pink and black bustier and garter belt, she frowned. "Sandy."

Marie pushed herself to her feet, holding the outfit in front of her curvaceous figure, and posed in the mirror. "Why the attitude? I think it's hot."

Propping herself up on her elbow, Janine twirled a strand of honey-colored hair around her finger. Her split ends needed to be trimmed before the rehearsal dinner tomorrow—how would she be able to fit in an appointment? "It might have something to do with the fact that she assured me pink was Steve's favorite color on a woman."

Marie's mouth formed a silent O. "Well, she's his receptionist. She should know, I suppose."

"*I* didn't know," Janine murmured, feeling ridiculously close to tears.

"Oh, come on. You don't think there's anything going on between Steve and that bimbo, do you?"

She shook her head. "Honestly, I don't think he has enough sex drive to have an affair." Her fingers flew to her mouth. Had she actually said that?

Marie's eyes flew wide. "Oh? You should get drunk more often." She bounced on the corner of the bed, scattering more boxes. "Do tell."

Janine hesitated, wondering how much of her musings could be attributed to last-minute jitters.

"Come on," Marie urged. "I gathered that you and

Steve don't exactly set the sheets on fire, but I figured it wasn't all that important to you."

"Should it be?"

"What?"

"Important to me. Sex, I mean."

Marie's eyes widened. "You're asking *me?*"

She smirked. "Try to be objective, sis. Haven't you ever had a good relationship without great sex?"

"Let me think—no."

"You're a big help."

"Okay, I'm sorry." She crossed her arms and donned a serious expression. "What seems to be the problem? Foreplay? Duration? Frequency?"

"Frequency would cover it, I think."

"Hey, lots of couples abstain for several weeks before the wedding to, you know—" she pedaled the air with her fists "—shake things up a little."

"We've abstained for longer than a few weeks."

"How long?"

"A year."

Marie's eyes bulged and she guffawed. "No, really."

"Really."

"But you've only known the man for a year!"

"Precisely."

Her sister's head jutted forward. "You've *never* had sex with Steve?"

"Bingo."

"Unbelievable!" Jumping to her feet, Marie began pacing and waving her arms. "How come you never said anything?"

At the moment she was wishing she *still* hadn't said anything, and now she darn sure wasn't going to admit she was a virgin on top of everything else. "I started to mention it several times, but I was just too...I don't know—embarrassed, I guess."

"So have you two ever talked about it?"

"I've brought up the subject lots of times, but he only said that he wanted to wait until we're married."

"Which explains why he proposed so quickly."

Janine frowned.

"And the fact that he loves you, of course," Marie added hastily. "Maybe you need to be more aggressive. You know, take the bull by the horns, so to speak."

She reflected on the few awkward episodes when she'd tried to make her physical needs known to Steve. "I've tried everything short of throwing myself at him."

"Hmm. Maybe he's truly trying to be chivalrous."

She pursed her lips and nodded. "And I'm glad he respects me. But it's more than not having sex. He gets angry when I bring it up, and he shuts me out. Sometimes he doesn't call for days afterward."

Marie let out a low whistle. "Sounds like he might have some hang-ups. Maybe he's burnt out from fixing all those breasts and butts and lips and chins."

"Maybe," she agreed.

"Well, you know he's a full-fledged hetero—Steve's other girlfriends weren't known for their, ahem, virtuous restraint."

Janine closed her eyes, suddenly sick to her stomach. "That's what worries me. I've heard him say there are two kinds of women—the ones you sleep with and the ones you marry."

Marie winced. "Uh-oh. Therapy alert."

Janine nodded, blinking back tears.

"So if you're worried, why did you say yes?"

She inhaled, then sat cross-legged. "Good question. I think I need another glass of wine."

Marie obliged, filling her lipstick-smudged glass from the bottle sitting on the dresser. "No more for me, I'm going over to Greg's later."

Janine swallowed a mouthful of the sweet liquid, savoring the slight tingle as it slid down her throat. "Why did I say yes? Because Steve is great-looking and he has a terrific future, and he's charming and he likes the same things I do."

"Harvesting herbs and practicing yoga?" Marie looked dubious.

"Okay, not *every thing* I like to do, but we're good together—you said so yourself."

"Uh-uh," her sister denied with a finger wag. "I said you *look* good together—blond and blue-eyed, you the flower child, he the Valley guy. But that doesn't mean you're *good* together."

This conversation was not making her feel better. No one at the clinic was more surprised than she when Steve Larsen, the hunky surgeon who had every woman in white shoes worked into a lather, had asked her out. Frankly, she'd anticipated losing her virginity rather quickly to the ladies' man with the notorious reputation, but instead, he had scrupulously avoided intimate contact.

"Steve's a gentleman," she murmured.

"Janine!" Marie said, exasperated. "You shouldn't marry the guy just because you think he's nice. Are you sure you want to spend the rest of your life with Steve Larsen?"

She'd lain awake last night asking herself the same question, wallowing in her concerns, trying to sort through her overblown fantasies of passionate love and what appeared to be a less interesting reality. "His life and his family are just so…fascinating."

"You're fascinating," Marie insisted.

"I thought I was the one drinking. Sis, I have the most boring life of any person I know."

Marie lifted her hands. "I'm sure there are exciting things going on at the clinic all the time."

"Oh, yeah, flu season gives me goose bumps."

Marie crossed her arms. "Okay, I'll bite—what would you consider exciting?"

Janine studied the ceiling, smiling in lazy wishful thinking. "I'd like to be caught up in a passionate relationship with Steve—you know, where we can't keep our hands off each other. I want…something irrational. Illogical. And highly irregular."

Her sister sighed. "Don't we all? If you're having second thoughts, you need to be proactive. Look in the mirror, Janine. In case no one's told you, you don't have to settle."

"Spoken like a true sister," she teased, but panic swirled in her stomach. She gripped her glass tighter. "And I don't feel like I'm settling…most of the time. I love Steve, and I know sex isn't everything, but what if he and I aren't physically compatible?"

Marie angled her head. "Couples can work through those things, although Steve doesn't strike me as the kind of guy who would agree to see a counselor."

"You got that right." Steve prided himself on having his life together, from his thriving cosmetic surgery practice to his low golf handicap.

Marie quirked her mouth from side to side. "You're not married yet. There's still time."

Janine laughed miserably. "Right, I can just see telling Mother I'm canceling the wedding because Steve won't have sex with me."

"No, I mean you still have time to find out if the two of you are sexually compatible." Her mouth curved into a mischievous smile. "Where is Steve tonight?"

"The groomsmen gave him a bachelor party at the resort. He's spending the night there."

"Perfect! You said you'd tried everything short of throwing yourself at him, right?"

"Yeah," Janine offered, wary.

Marie held up the pink bustier and grinned. "I can't think of a better outfit to wear while throwing yourself at the man you're about to marry."

"But—" Her mind spun for a good reason to object, except she couldn't think of one.

"Try it on and see how it looks."

Janine stood and considered the outrageous getup while she sipped her wine. "I don't know if I can figure out all those hooks."

Her sister scoffed. "I have one of these things, although it's not nearly as nice." She glanced at the label and whistled. "Darn, Sandy must have dropped a pretty penny on this outfit."

"Steve obviously overpays her," Janine said, then immediately felt petty. Steve's receptionist wasn't to blame for the holes in their relationship. Maybe Marie was right—maybe she hadn't been vocal enough about her…needs.

"A little big," Marie observed, handing over the various pieces of the naughty ensemble, "but probably more comfortable this way."

Janine held up the lingerie, incongruous against her long, shapeless navy dress. A woman of twenty-nine had needs, after all.

"You're going to rock his world," Marie said over her shoulder.

She took her vitamins every day, she stayed fit, she read *Cosmo*…she could do this. Besides, she was a summer—pink was on her palette. "Okay, I'll do it."

Marie clapped her hands. "What a story for me to tell your daughter."

"Not until she's fifty, or I'm dead, whichever comes first."

MINUTES LATER, they were still struggling to get all the pieces in place. Marie grunted behind her and jerked the bustier tighter. "Inhale and hold it."

"I thought you said this was a little big," Janine gasped, afraid to exhale. "I think you detached a rib."

"For Steve's sake, I hope this thing is easier to remove than it is to get on." With a final yank, Marie straightened and backed away. "Where are those black heels you bought when we were at the mall a few months ago?" She walked to the closet.

"You mean those shoes you made me buy because they were such a great deal but they weren't such a great deal because I've never worn them?"

"Yeah."

"On the bottom shelf in the orange box."

Marie went to the closet, and emerged, triumphant. After Janine stepped into the shoes, she stared in the full-length mirror at the pink-and-black creation: the boned pink satin bustier pushed her breasts to incredible heights and left her shoulders bare above black ruffly trim. Black laces crisscrossed her back, and Marie had tied them off with a large bow at the top. The matching panties were cut high on the legs, veeing below her navel, and trimmed with more scratchy lace. The black garter belts connecting the bottom of the bustier with the top of her thigh-high black hose were drawn so tight, she was sure if they popped, she'd be maimed for life. "If I had a feather boa, I could walk onto the set of *Gunsmoke.*"

Behind her, Marie laughed. "You look awesome! You hide that fab figure of yours. Believe me, Steve won't know what hit him. You two will be so exhausted after tonight, you'll have to postpone the wedding."

Maybe it was the effects of the wine, but she had to admit she was feeling pretty sexy, albeit a little shaky, in her stiletto heels. "But what will I do?"

"I'll drop you off at the resort, and you can surprise him."

She looked down. "I'll be arrested if I walk into the hotel like this."

Her sister went back to the closet and returned carrying a black all-weather coat. "Here."

Janine shrugged into the coat and belted it.

"See—perfectly innocent," Marie said. "No one will ever know that beneath the coat is a red-hot siren getting ready to sound."

"But what will I do for clothes tomorrow?"

"Are you serious? You two won't leave that room. Don't worry, I'll come early and bring your outfit for the rehearsal dinner. Now let's get going before you lose your nerve."

Janine grabbed Marie's arm. "I think I'd better call him first."

"But this is supposed to be a surprise!"

"But what if he isn't there? I mean, what if the guys stay out late?" She fished a thick phone book from a deep drawer in the nightstand.

Marie checked her watch. "It's after midnight, and it'll take us thirty minutes to get to the resort."

"But if they went out, the bars are still open."

Her sister sighed. "Okay, but no talking—if he answers, just hang up."

"Agreed," she said, dialing. An operator answered after a few rings and transferred her to Steve's room. When the phone started ringing, for the briefest second she hoped he wouldn't answer, to let her off the hook. She *was* a little tipsy, after all, and things would most likely make sense again in the morning. Their relationship was strong and their sex life would probably be great after they were married.

But on the third ring, he picked up the phone. "Hello?" he mumbled, obviously roused from sleep.

A thrill skittered through her at the sound of his smoky voice. He wasn't out at the strip clubs with the guys after all—not that she'd been worried.

"Hello?" he repeated.

She smiled into the phone, then hung up quietly, considerably cheered and suddenly anticipating her little adventure. They would make love all night, and in the morning she would laugh at her fears. She stood and swung her purse over her shoulder, then grinned at Marie. "Let's go."

But while climbing into her sister's car—she practically had to lie down to keep the boned bustier from piercing her—she did have one last thought. "Marie, what if this stunt doesn't work?"

Her sister started the engine and flashed her a smile in the dark. "Whatever happens, Janine, this night could determine the direction of the rest of your life."

DEREK STILLMAN MUMBLED a curse and rolled over to replace the handset. He missed the receiver and the phone thudded to the floor, but his head ached so much he didn't move to replace it. Just his luck that he'd finally gotten to sleep and someone had called to wake him and breathe into the receiver. He lay staring at the ceiling, wishing, not for the first time, he were still in Kentucky. There was something about feeling like hell that made a person homesick, especially when he hadn't wanted to make the trip to Atlanta in the first place.

The caller had probably been Steve, he thought. Maybe checking in to see how he was feeling. A second later he changed his mind—his buddy was too wrapped up in enjoying a last night of freedom to be concerned about him. He sneezed, then fisted his hands against the mattress. Confound his brother, Jack! In college Jack had been closer to Steve than he, but since Jack had dropped out of sight for the past couple of months, Derek had felt obligated to stand in as best man when Steve had asked him. Once again, he was left to pick up his younger brother's slack.

He inhaled cautiously because his head felt close to bursting. He'd obviously picked up a bug while traveling, which only added insult to injury. On top of everything else, the timing to be away from the advertising firm couldn't be worse—he was vying for the business of a client large enough to swing the company well into the black, but he needed an innovative campaign for their product, and soon. If ever he could use Jack, it was now, since he'd always been the more creative one. Derek was certain their father had established the Stillman & Sons Agency with the thought in mind to try to keep Jack busy and out of trouble, but so far, the plan had failed.

Hot and irritable, Derek swung his legs over the side of the bed and felt his way toward the bathroom for a glass of water. His throat was so parched, he could barely swallow. He banged his shin on a hard suitcase, either his or Steve's, he wasn't sure which. If his trip hadn't been enough of an ordeal, he'd arrived late at the hotel and they'd already given away his room. Since Steve was planning to be out all night partying, he'd offered Derek his room, and since Derek had felt too ill to join the rowdy group for the bachelor party, he'd accepted.

The tap water was tepid, but it was wet and gave his throat momentary relief. He drank deeply, then stumbled back to bed, knowing he wouldn't be sleeping again soon.

Too bad he hadn't come down with something at home. Then he would've had a legitimate excuse to skip the ceremony. He thought of Steve and grunted in sympathy. *Marriage.* Why on earth would anyone want to get married these days anyway? What kind of fool would stake his freedom on a bet where the odds were two failures out of every three? Wasn't life complicated enough without throwing something else into the mix?

They were all confirmed bachelors—he, Jack and Steve. Steve was the womanizer; Jack, the scoundrel; and he, the loner. He couldn't imagine what kind of woman had managed to catch Steve Larsen's eye and keep it. The only comment his buddy had made about his fiancée was that she was sweet, but anyone who could convince Steve to set aside his philandering ways had to be a veritable angel.

Achy and scratchy, he lay awake for several more minutes before he started to doze off. Oddly, his head was full of visions of angels—blond and white-robed, pure and innocent. A side effect of the over-the-counter medication, he reasoned drowsily.

CHAPTER TWO

"I'M SORRY, ma'am, but I can't give you a key to Mr. Larsen's room without his permission." The young male clerk gave Janine an apologetic look, but shook his head.

Janine bit down on her lower lip to assuage her growing panic. What had she gotten herself into? Marie was long gone and said she was going to stop by Greg's on the way home. Janine would have to call a cab to get a ride back to the apartment they shared. Which would be fine except she'd left her purse in Marie's car, and she had no money or apartment key on her person.

And beneath the raincoat, had very little *clothing* on her person.

"Okay, call him," she relented. It would still be a surprise, just not as dramatic.

The clerk obliged, then looked up from the phone. "The line's busy, ma'am."

She frowned. Who could Steve be talking to at one in the morning? A sliver of concern skittered up her spine, but she manufactured a persuasive smile. "He's probably trying to call *me*. If you'll give me his room number, I'll just walk on up."

"I'm afraid that's against hotel policy, ma'am." The

teenager ran a finger around his collar, and he looked flushed.

Sizing up her options, she leaned forward on the counter, making sure the coat gaped just enough for a glimpse of the pink bustier. She looked at his name tag. "Um, Ben—may I call you Ben?"

He nodded, his gaze riveted on the opening in her coat.

"Ben, Mr. Larsen is my fiancé, and we're getting married here on Saturday. I dropped by to, um, surprise him, and I'd hate to tell him that you're the one who wouldn't let me up to his room."

Ben swallowed. "I'll call his room a-g-gain." He picked up the phone and dialed, then gave her a weak smile. "Still busy."

She assumed a wounded expression, and leaned closer. "Ben, can't you make an exception, just this one teensy-weensy time?"

"Is there a problem here, Ben?"

Janine turned her head to see a tall blond man wearing a hotel sport coat standing a few steps away.

The young man straightened. "No, Mr. Oliver. This lady needs to see a guest, but the line is busy."

The blond man's clear blue eyes seemed to miss nothing as his gaze flitted over her, then he turned to Ben, obviously his employee. "Ben, there seems to be a bug going around and you look a little feverish. Why don't you take a break and I'll help our guest."

Ben scooted away and Mr. Oliver took his place behind the counter. "Good evening, ma'am. I'm Manny Oliver, the general manager. How can I help you?" His smile was genuine, and his voice friendly. She immediately liked him and her first thought was that he was as sharp as a tack. She hoped she didn't look drunk.

"I'm Janine Murphy and I came to visit my fiancé, Steve Larsen. We're having our rehearsal dinner here tomorrow—I mean, tonight, and our wedding in your gazebo on Saturday."

He nodded. "Congratulations. I'm familiar with the arrangements. Now, let me see what I can do for you." He consulted a computer, then picked up the phone and dialed. A few seconds later, he returned the handset. "Mr. Larsen's phone is still busy, but I'd be glad to walk up and knock on his door to let him know you're here."

The best she could manage was a half smile.

Mr. Oliver leaned on the counter, an amused expression on his smooth face. "Why do I have the feeling there's more to this story?" He nodded to her gapped coat.

Janine pulled her coat lapels closed. "I…I thought I would surprise him. He's staying here tonight because his house is full of relatives and his groomsmen were taking him out for his bachelor party."

He checked his watch. "And he's back already?"

She nodded. "I called before I left, and he answered the phone."

"So he *does* know you're coming?"

"No, I hung up. This is supposed to be a surprise."

He pursed his lips and mirth lit his eyes. "You've never done anything like this before, have you?"

Janine winced. "No, but after a half bottle of wine, it seemed like a good idea when my sister suggested it."

Suddenly he laughed and shook his head. "You remind me of some friends of mine."

"Is that good?"

Pure affection shone on his face. "Very."

"So you'll give me his room key?"

He stroked his chin as he studied her. "Ms. Murphy, even though it's none of my business, I have to ask because you seem like a nice woman." He lowered his chin and his voice. "Don't you think it's a little risky to surprise a man on the night of his bachelor party?"

"But he was asleep when I called," she said.

He pressed his lips together and lifted his eyebrows, then stared at her until realization dawned on her.

"Oh, Steve wouldn't," she said, shaking her head.

"Alcohol can make a person do things they wouldn't ordinarily do," he said, giving her a pointed look. Then he patted her hand. "My advice would be to save it for the honeymoon, doll."

She wasn't sure where the tears came from, but suddenly a box of tissues materialized and the man was dabbing at her face.

"You'd better switch to waterproof mascara before the ceremony," he chided gently, and she had the feeling he'd wiped away many a tear. "Did I say something wrong?"

"N-no," she said, sniffling. "It's just that...well, I don't want to wait for the honeymoon—that's sort of why I came here."

His eyes widened slightly. "Oh. Well, now I understand your persistence."

"So you'll give me a key?"

Mr. Oliver chewed on his lower lip for a few seconds. "What will you do if you walk in and find him in bed with someone else?"

She blew her nose, marveling she could be so frank with a stranger. "I'd thank my lucky stars and you that I found out before it's too late."

"No bloodshed?"

Janine laughed. "I'm not armed."

"Not true, I saw those stilettos." He reached under the counter and slid an electronic key across the counter. "Top floor, room 855. Good luck."

"Thank you, Mr. Oliver." She smiled, then turned on her heel, somewhat unsteadily, and headed toward the stairs. With her claustrophobia, she avoided elevators, and the long climb upward gave her time to anticipate Steve's reaction. Maybe she should simply open the door and slide into bed with him. After all, this was her chance to let it all hang out, and to find out if Steve would continue to draw sexual boundaries for their marriage.

By the time she reached the eighth floor, her heart was pounding from nervousness and exertion. A blister was raising on her left heel, and her breasts were chafed. Being sexually assertive was hard work, and darned uncomfortable. She stopped to refresh her pink lipstick under the harsh light of a hallway fixture, and didn't recognize herself in the compact mirror. Her angular face was a little blurry around the edges, a lingering effect of her wine buzz, she assumed. Blatant desire softened her blue eyes, intense apprehension colored her cheeks and rapid respiration flared her nostrils. One look at her face—plus the fact that she was trussed up like a pink bird—and even a fence post couldn't mistake her intention.

Janine drew color onto her mouth with a shaky

hand, then gave herself a pep talk while she located his room. Her knees were knocking as she inserted the electronic key, but the flashing green light seemed to say "go": Go after what you want, go for the gusto, go for an all-nighter.

So, with a deep breath—as much as she could muster in the binding bustier—Janine pushed open the door, limped inside and closed the door behind her.

THE SQUEAK OF HINGES stirred Derek from his angelic musings, and the click of the door closing garnered one open eye. Steve's conscience must have kicked in; apparently he was back earlier than he'd planned. Derek faced the wall opposite the door, and he didn't feel inclined to move. Steve could take the floor. He felt grumpily entitled to a half night's rest in an actual bed for making the darned trip south.

Suddenly the mattress moved, as if his buddy had sat down on the other side. Removing his shoes, Derek guessed. Indeed, he heard the rustle of him undressing. But then the weight of the body rolled close to him.

"Hey, honey," a woman whispered a split second before a slim arm snaked around his waist. "Tonight's the night."

Whoever she was, she had burrowed under the covers with him. Shock and confusion paralyzed him and, for a moment, he convinced himself that he was still dreaming.

"I just can't wait any longer," the woman said, suddenly shifting her body weight on top of him. "I need to know now if we're good together."

Through his medicated fog, he realized the woman

was straddling him. In the darkened room, he could make out only a brief silhouette. He opened his mouth to protest, but mere grunts emerged from his constricted throat. Small, cool hands ran over his chest and his next realization was that he was being kissed— soundly. Moist lips moved upon his while a wine-dipped tongue plundered his unsuspecting mouth. A curtain of fragrant hair swept down to brush both his cheeks. His body responded instantly, even as he strained to raise himself.

Everywhere he touched, a tempting curve fit his hand. Curiosity finally won out, and he skimmed his hands over the mystery woman's body, letting the kiss happen. He'd nearly forgotten the rapture of warm, soft flesh pressed against him. He was midstroke into arching his erection against her when sanity and wakefulness returned. Extending his left hand to the side, he fumbled for the lamp switch. With a click, light flooded the room, blinding him.

He caught a glimpse of long, long blond hair and something pink before the woman drew away and screamed like a banshee. Derek caught her by the arms, strictly for self-defense, and as she tried to wrench from his grip, his vision cleared, if not his brain.

The woman was slender and dark-complexioned with wide eyes and so much hair it had to be a wig. And she was practically bursting out of some sexy getup he'd seen only in magazines that came in his brother's mail. She floundered against him, flaming the fire of his straining arousal. It appeared the woman liked to struggle, but since that was a scene he did not get into, he released her to take the wind out of her sails.

She scrambled off the bed in one motion, and ran for the farthest corner, where she hovered like a spooked animal, arms laughingly crossed over her privates. Derek's skin tingled from the scrape of her fingernails, but at least she had stopped screaming.

They stared at each other for several seconds, giving Derek time to size her up. She was around five-eight or -nine, although her black spike heels accounted for some of her height. Despite her stature, the first thing that came to mind was that she was elfin—petite, chiseled features and lean limbs, with stick-straight blond hair parted in the middle. The naughty outfit accentuated her amazing figure—her breasts were high, her waist slight, her hips rounded. Between the wig and the getup, she had to be a hooker the guys had bought for Steve.

"I thought this was Steve Larsen's room," she gasped, inching her way along the wall in the direction of the door, her gaze on a black raincoat draped over the foot of the bed.

She was a hooker who knew Steve well enough to recognize him, which didn't surprise him. "This *is* Steve's room," he said, and she stopped. Pressing a finger against the pressure in his sinuses, he pushed himself to his feet. As silly as standing around in his boxers in front of the woman seemed, having a conversation with her while lying in bed seemed even more absurd, especially since she herself was in her skivvies.

"Stay right there!" She pointed a finger at him as

if a laser beam might emerge from her fingernail at will. "Who are you?"

Derek put his hands on his hips, irritated to be awakened and not amused by the idea that the woman had come to Steve's room for an eleventh-hour fling before his wedding. "Since Steve gave me his room for the night," he asserted, "maybe you should tell me who *you* are."

She shoved her hair out of her eyes, and her chest moved up and down in the pink thing that resembled a corset. She seemed very close to spilling over the underwire cups, and he felt his body start to respond again. The woman was one incredibly sexy female.

"I'm J-Janine Murphy, Steve's fiancée."

Derek swallowed and abruptly reined in his libido. He realized he'd been cynical in his assumption about the reason for this woman's presence in Steve's room—blame it on years of witnessing his brother's shenanigans. Not many things surprised him these days, but her declaration shook him. *This* was the woman who'd snared Steve? So much for his theory of her being a missionary type. But he had to hand it to her—the woman's costume made it clear she knew how to communicate on Steve's level. Guilt zigzagged through his chest when he acknowledged he'd been affected by her himself—he, the man of steel, who prided himself on discretion and restraint.

He stared at his friend's bride-to-be and realized this was about the most awkward predicament he'd ever landed himself in. And, he thought wryly, par for the course of his life lately—in a hotel room with a gorgeous half-naked woman, and she was totally, ut-

terly and indubitably off limits. Derek's dry laugh was
meant to express his frustration at the accumulation
of injustices of the past few months, but the woman
was clearly offended.

"What's so funny?"

He pursed his mouth. "Well, now...Janine...this *is*
a bit awkward." Picking up her coat, he slowly walked
toward her, using the gesture of courtesy to help shield
his appallingly determined arousal. "I'm Derek Stillman. Your best man."

CHAPTER THREE

JANINE FROZE, although her insides heaved upward. "My b-best man?" *Oh, please, dear God, take me now—no wait, let me change clothes first.* The stranger's smug expression mortified her, but at least he'd carried her coat to her, which she snatched and held over herself.

"Technically speaking," he said, curling his fingers around one wrist and holding his hands low over his crotch, "I guess I'm *Steve's* best man."

She snapped her gaze back to his and squinted at him in the low lighting. She was certain she'd never met him before, although granted, people looked different with their clothes off. He was a big man—even in her preposterous shoes, he towered over her. His dark hair was cropped close at the sides and back, with the top just long enough to stick up after sleeping. His face was broad and pleasing, with a strong jaw, distinct cheekbones and an athletically altered nose which now appeared red and irritated. On his mouth was the telltale stain of her pink lipstick and she cringed, recalling the way she'd kissed the perfect stranger. But on the list of kissing transgressions, surely kissing your fiancé's best man was worse than kissing a perfect stranger... Her brain was too fuzzy to work it all out—she'd have to ask Marie.

But one realization did strike her with jarring clarity: she hadn't even realized she wasn't kissing Steve.

With that sobering thought, Janine refused to look lower than Derek's wide shoulders, although she vividly remembered the mat of hair she'd run her fingers through while straddling the man. She wasn't even sure Steve *had* hair on his chest. A wave of dizziness hit her and she realized the bustier was probably limiting her oxygen supply. "You…" *Are the most physically appealing man I've ever laid eyes on.* "You must be Jack's brother."

The man's mouth tightened almost imperceptibly. "Yes."

"You went to college with Steve?"

He nodded, and she noticed his eyes were the deepest brown—quite intense with his dark coloring.

"Um…" She glanced around, spying Steve's suitcase sitting next to a writing desk. "Where *is* Steve?"

"At his bachelor party."

Not a man of many words, this one. "Why aren't you with him?"

"I wasn't—that is, I'm not—feeling well."

She peered closer, taking in his drooping eyes. "Do you have a cold?"

"I suppose."

"What are you taking for it?"

His eyebrows knitted in question.

"I'm a physician's assistant."

He looked thoroughly unimpressed. "I'm taking some stuff I picked up in the gift shop."

He reached for a handkerchief on the nightstand next to the bed, then sneezed twice, each time causing his flat abdominal muscles to contract above the waistband of his pale blue boxers—strictly a medical observation of his general fitness level, she noted, which was important when prescribing treatment. "Bless you. You really should get some rest."

He turned watery eyes her way and smirked. "I was trying."

Her cheeks flamed. As if the mix-up were *her* mistake, as if she'd planned this fiasco. Flustered, she flung out her arm to indicate the dark walls of the room, but somehow ended up pointing to the bed where the covers lay as contorted as her thoughts. "What...when..." She jerked back her offending hand. "Why did Steve give you his room?"

"My flight was late, and I didn't have a room when I arrived. Steve said he wouldn't need—" He broke off and averted his gaze.

"Wouldn't need what, Mr. Stillman?"

Glancing back, he massaged the bridge of his nose and winced. "Don't you think we can drop the formalities since we're both in our underwear?"

At his sarcastic tone, anger drove out any vestiges of fear that lingered, since she didn't appear to be in imminent danger of anything other than dying of humiliation. Still, she forced herself to speak in a calm tone to Steve's best man. "Okay. *Derek,* Steve wouldn't need what?"

He wiped his mouth with the back of his hand, then frowned at the streak of pink lipstick. Janine squirmed when he looked to her. "He said he wouldn't be needing the room—I suppose the guys were going to party all night." His gaze fell to her shoes and one corner of his mouth drew back. "I take it he wasn't expecting you."

She summoned the dredges of her pride and lifted her chin. "It was supposed to be a surprise."

"Trust me, it was," he said, then retrieved a pair of wrinkled jeans from the arm of a chair.

Distracted by the fluid motion of his body performing the simple act of getting dressed, she almost lost her own opportunity to don her coat in relative privacy. But she quickly recovered, and by the time he'd pulled on the jeans and a gray University of Kentucky sweatshirt, she had buttoned the coat up to her chin and knotted the belt twice. With his back to her, he used the palm of his hand and pushed his chin first right, then left, to the tune of two loud pops of his neck bones.

"You really shouldn't do that," she admonished. "It could...be...danger...ous..." She trailed off when he looked up, his lips pursed, his expression perturbed. Janine swallowed. "M-maybe I should call Steve on his cell phone."

He nodded curtly and walked past her into the bathroom without making eye contact. A few seconds later the muffled sound of the sink water splashing on floated out from behind the closed door.

With her heart in her throat, Janine trotted to the nightstand, then followed the phone cord to the handset that lay under the bed. Now she knew why the line had been busy, and with shock realized that smoky voice on the other end when she'd called from home had been none other than Derek Stillman's. She bit the inside of her cheek. What a fine mess she'd gotten herself into. Steve's surprise was ruined, and she'd never live down this scene. She sat on the floor, her finger hovering over the buttons. Maybe she should just call a cab and vamoose, after swearing Derek to secrecy. Assuming she could trust the man. He seemed pretty surly for someone who was supposed to be a friend of Steve's.

Her fingers shook as she punched in the number of her sister's boyfriend's place, but no one answered and Greg didn't believe in answering machines. She called twice more, allowing the phone to ring several times, to no avail. Next she called her and her sister's apartment, but Marie was either in transit, or still at Greg's—probably indulging in something wonderfully wicked. When the machine picked up, she left a quick message for Marie to stay put until she called again.

Janine hung up and glanced over her shoulder at the closed bathroom door, still tingling over the accidental encounter with the unsettling stranger. Talk about crawling into the wrong bed—Goldilocks had officially been unseated. To top it off, Derek had shrugged off the sexualized situation with a laugh, while she'd been shaken to her spleen, not just by her unbelievable gaff, but by her base response to the man's physique.

To curtail her line of thinking, she punched in Steve's cell-phone number, willing words to her mouth to explain the awkward situation in the best possible light. Steve might get a big kick out of the mix-up and return to the hotel right away. She brightened, thinking the night had a chance to be salvaged, if they could shuffle the best man to another room, that is. After Steve's phone rang three times, he answered over a buzz of background noise. "Hello?"

"Hi, this is Janine," she said, fighting a twinge of

jealousy that Steve was probably out ogling naked women. The fact that she'd been ogling his friend didn't count because she hadn't gone looking for it, and besides, Derek hadn't been naked. Completely. And she hadn't tipped him.

The background noise cleared suddenly, then he said, "Janine, look over your shoulder."

Perplexed, she did, and scowled when she saw Derek standing in the room, talking into a cellular phone.

"Steve left his phone in the bathroom," he said, his voice sounding in her ear. His mouth was pulled back in a sham of a smile.

She replaced the handset with a bang. "That's not funny."

He pressed a button on the phone and pushed down the antenna. "No. Not as funny as the fact that you can't recognize the voice of the man you're going to marry."

Annoyed, she flailed to her feet and was rewarded with a head rush, plus a stabbing pain in her heel that indicated she had burst the blister there. "You sound like him," she insisted. Only to tell the truth, Derek's voice was deeper and his speech slower, more relaxed.

Derek's jaw tightened, but when he spoke, his voice was casual. "I'm nothing like Steve."

An odd thing to say for someone who was supposed to be Steve's friend, but he was right. Steve was gregarious, carefree. Derek carried himself as if the weight of the world yoked those wide shoulders, and she wondered fleetingly if he had a wife, children, pets.

He held up a pager. "This was in the bathroom too."

Her shoulders fell in defeat. It was obvious Steve hadn't wanted to be bothered tonight. "Do you know where he went?"

He shook his head and shoved his feet into tan-colored loafers. "Sorry."

She frowned as he strapped on his watch, then stuffed a wallet into the pocket of his jeans. When he picked up a small suitcase and a computer bag, then headed toward the door, her stomach lurched. "Where are you going?"

He nodded toward the door with nonchalance. "To get another room."

Humiliated or not, she couldn't help feeling panicky at the thought of Derek leaving. What must he think of her? What would he tell Steve? "But I…I thought you said the hotel was out of rooms."

Derek shrugged. "There has to be an empty bed somewhere in this place, and no offense, but I feel lousy and I need to get some sleep."

"*I'll* leave," she said quickly, walking toward the door. "I'll call my ride from the lobby."

He held out a hand like a stop sign and laughed without mirth. "Oh, no. Steve would never forgive me. The place is all yours." He put his hand on the door-knob and turned it.

"But—"

"It was, um—" he swept her figure head to toe, and for the first time, genuine amusement lit his dark eyes "—*interesting* meeting you." Then he opened the door and strode out.

CHAPTER FOUR

DEREK MARVELED at the turn of events as he stumbled toward the elevator. Whew! Steve had one kinky nut of a fiancée on his hands, that much was certain. His buddy's and his brother's escapades with women never ceased to amaze him, and every time he felt the least bit jealous of their ability to attract the most outrageous litter of sex kittens, he reminded himself that their lives were roller coasters and his life was a…a…

He frowned and rubbed his temple to focus his train of thought. Searching for a metaphor to symbolize his solid, responsible position in the amusement park of life, the best he could come up with was…a chaperone. God, he felt older than his thirty-five years.

Thankfully the elevator arrived, rousing him from his unsettling contemplation. On the ride to the lobby he snorted at the memory of Janine Murphy straddling him, thinking he was Steve. Tomorrow when he felt better, he was sure he'd have a belly laugh over the case of mistaken identity, but for now he knew he desperately needed sleep. He glanced at his watch and groaned. Almost two in the morning, which meant he'd been awake for nearly forty-eight hours, thanks to Donald Phillips. And Steve Larsen. Oh, and Pinky Tuscadero.

Back in Lexington, Donald Phillips was one of the largest producers of honey in the Southeast. Dissatisfied with his product sales, Phillips had decided to shop around for a new advertising firm, and Stillman & Sons, which at the moment consisted solely of himself, was being given the opportunity to swipe the account from a larger competitor. But Derek was having one little problem: inventing a campaign designed to entice consumers to buy more honey. *Honey,* for crissake—a sweet condiment best known in the South for spreading on toast and biscuits; consequently, market growth was not projected to be explosive.

Computers and wireless phones and home stereo systems were flying off the shelves. Branded sportswear and gourmet appliances and exercise-equipment sales were booming. Large vehicles and exotic vacations and swimming pools were experiencing a huge resurgence. With all the sexy, progressive products in the world, he was chasing a darned *honey* account to save the family business.

When the elevator dinged and the door slid open, his exhaustion nearly immobilized him, but he managed to drag himself and his bags across the red thick-piled carpet to the empty reservations counter. Just his luck that everyone was taking a break. He looked for a bell to ring, but he guessed the hotel was a little too classy for ringers. Live flower arrangements the size of a person graced the enormous mahogany counter shiny enough to reflect his image—in his opinion, just another overdone element of the posh resort whose decorating philosophy seemed to be "Size *does* matter."

He wondered briefly how much green the bride and

groom were dropping for the wedding. Between the rehearsal dinner, the ceremony and the reception, all of which were supposed to take place at the resort, he suspected his buddy would have to perform an extra face-lift or two to foot the bill. Derek scoffed, shaking his head. Marriage—bah. He gave his pal and the Murphy woman six months, tops.

"Hello?" he called, trying to tamp down his impatience. He was not above stretching out behind the counter to sleep if he had to.

A door opened on the other side of the elevators, and his mood plunged when Pinky herself emerged from the stairwell, pale and limping, hair everywhere, coat flapping. "Oh, brother," he muttered. The last thing he needed was to spend one more minute with the leggy siren.

Stepping up next to him, she said, "Derek, I insist you take the room."

One look into her blue eyes gave him a glimpse of Steve's future—the woman would be a handful, even for Steve. He might have felt sorry for his pal, but, he reasoned perversely, the man who had led such a charmed life to date probably deserved a little grief. "Janine, go back upstairs."

She frowned and planted her hands on her hips. "I thought people from the country were supposed to be polite."

His ire climbed, then he drawled, "I get testy when I run out of hayseed to chaw on."

Her eyebrows came together and she crossed her arms, sending a waft of her citrusy perfume to tickle his nose. "What's that smart remark supposed to mean?"

He did not need this, this, this...aggravation, not when his body hummed of fatigue, stress and lingering lust. Derek felt his patience snap like a dry twig. He leaned forward and spoke quietly through clenched teeth. "I'll tell you what it means, Pinky. It means I left my firm in the middle of a very important project to fly here and stand in for my runaway brother in a ceremony I don't even believe in, only to catch some kind of plague and have my reservation canceled and have my sleep interrupted by a stranger crawling into my bed!"

She blinked. "Do you have blood pressure problems?"

Heat suffused his face and he felt precariously close to blowing a gasket. She and Steve deserved each other, and they'd never miss him. So after one calming breath, he saluted her. "I'm going home. Please give Steve my regrets." He turned, then added over his shoulder, "And my condolences."

He picked up his suitcase, then headed toward the main lobby, not a bit surprised to hear her trotting two steps behind him. "Wait, you can't go!"

"Watch me," he growled.

"I'm sorry—you can have the room."

Derek lengthened his stride.

"After all, you made the trip down here..."

As he approached the lobby area, a buzz of voices rose above the saxophone Muzak, reminding him of bees. But then again, he did have honey on the brain. Good grief, he needed sleep.

"And you're not feeling well," she rattled on. "Blah, blah, blah..."

The buzz increased as he rounded the corner. He stopped abruptly at the sight before him, and she slammed into him from behind, jarring his aching head.

"Oh, I'm sorry," she gasped. "I didn't realize—"

"Can you be quiet?" He pulled her by the arm to stand alongside him, too distracted by the scene to worry about her tender feelings.

The step-down lobby of the hotel was swarming with people, some in their pajamas sitting in chairs or lying on couches, others in lab coats, tending to the guests, others in security uniforms, hovering.

"What the hell?" he murmured.

"They're medics," Janine said. "Something's wrong." She walked over and knelt in front of a young man in a hotel uniform sitting in a chair looking feverish and limp. While her lips moved, Janine put a hand on the youth's forehead and took his pulse. The coat she wore fell open below the last button, revealing splendid legs encased in those black hose, and bringing to mind other vivid details about what lay hidden beneath the coat. She tossed the mane of blond hair he'd come to suspect was real over one shoulder, evoking memories of its silkiness sliding over his chest and face.

Recognizing the dead-end street he was traveling, Derek shook himself mentally and strained to remember what she said she did for a living. A nurse? A nurse's aide? No, a physician's assistant. Except the woman seemed way too flaky to oversee someone else's welfare.

She rose and patted the young man on the arm, then returned.

"What's wrong?" he asked.

Janine shrugged. "No one knows. Several employees and guests have come down with flulike symptoms, so they called for medical assistance."

The remains of pink color shimmered on her full mouth…a mouth that had been kissing him not too long ago. His groin tightened. "Is it serious?"

She shook her head. "It doesn't seem to be. My guess is a bad white sauce served in the restaurant, or something like that." Then she stopped and angled her head at him. "Wait a minute—when did *you* start feeling bad?"

He shrugged. "When I got here, there was a mixup on my reservation, so I hung around the lobby for a while until Steve arrived. I remember asking the clerk for directions to the gift shop to buy some cold medicine before I walked up to Steve's room."

She stepped closer and tiptoed to place her small hand on his forehead. He flinched in surprise, but relented. Her eyes were the same deep color of blue as his mother's favorite pansies. The best part of winter, she always said. His pulse kicked higher. He had to get out of here, fast.

"You're a little warm," she announced, her forehead slightly creased. "But not anything alarming."

He stepped around her, his eye on the revolving exit door on the far side of the lobby. Outside sat a yellow taxi, his escape hatch. "Listen, I'm going to grab that cab to the airport. I'll see ya, Pinky. Have a happy marriage and all that jazz." *And good riddance.*

"But wait, don't you want to see a doctor?"

He shook his head as he turned to go. "Nope."

She grabbed his arm. "Derek, what are you going to tell Steve...about tonight?"

He took in her wide eyes and her parted lips and for a minute he wondered if she knew what kind of man she was marrying. She seemed so innocent. Then he laughed at himself—dressing up in naughty lingerie and coming to the hotel to please Steve was not the act of an innocent. Besides, for all he knew, Steve *had* changed and would be a faithful husband. On the other hand, sometimes women knew their boyfriends were philanderers and didn't care, or liked the freedom it afforded them. Steve was probably well on his way to becoming a wealthy man, and money could make people overlook a variety of indiscretions. Either way, it was none of his business. He wet his parched lips. "What do you want me to tell him?"

She averted her eyes, and he could see the wheels turning in her pretty head. When she glanced back, she looked hopeful. "Nothing?"

He smirked. Nothing like honesty to get a marriage started off on the right foot. "You got it, Pinky. Nothing happened. We ran into each other in the lobby as I was leaving."

"Okay." Her smile was tentative as he increased the distance between them. "Well, goodbye," she said, then waved awkwardly.

He nodded. "I'll leave Steve a message when I get to the airport and I'll touch base with him next week."

"We'll be in Paris for two weeks," she called.

"Better him than me," he said, knowing she couldn't hear him. He waved and smiled as if he'd said something inanely nice, then turned and strode toward the exit, his steps hurried. He couldn't wait to feel bluegrass under his feet again. Steve and Jack could have the high life and the high-maintenance women. Right now he'd settle for a honey of a good advertising idea.

And a good night's sleep to banish the memory of Steve's bride in his bed.

WITH MIXED FEELINGS swirling in her chest, Janine watched Derek's broad-shouldered frame walk out the door. She was off the hook. She could leave now and Steve would never know she'd been there. Derek had said he wouldn't mention the incident, and for some odd reason, she believed him. His seriousness had struck her—he was a man with a lot of responsibility. What had he said? That he'd left at a busy time to attend a ceremony he didn't believe in?

Actually, she should be feeling nothing but giddy relief. Instead, she had the most unsettling sensation that something…important…had just slipped through her fingers…

Janine shook herself back to the present. She still had tomorrow night—technically, tonight—after the rehearsal dinner to broach the issue of having sex with Steve. Leaning over to massage her heel, she acknowledged she might have to regroup and come up with a different outfit, but Marie would think of something.

She headed toward the pay phones, threading her way through the people in the lobby. She was tempted to offer assistance to the medics, but they seemed to have everything under control, and she was still feeling the effects of the wine. Tomorrow morning—correction, in a few hours—she'd call that nice Mr. Oliver to make certain the problem had been resolved. The last thing she needed was to have the entire wedding party food-poisoned at the rehearsal dinner. Her mother was already on the verge of a nervous breakdown.

She picked up the phone and redialed the apartment using her memorized calling-card number. Her sister answered on the first ring.

"Marie, thank God you're home."

"I just walked in the door. I stopped on the way home to pick up pineapple juice. Why aren't you, um, *busy?*"

"Because Steve's not here."

"What? But he answered the phone when you called."

"No, his *best man* answered the phone. Steve gave the guy his room because the man was sick and didn't feel like going out with everyone else." She waited for the revelation to sink in and was rewarded with a gasp.

"You mean, you greeted the best man wearing that pink getup?"

Janine relived her humiliation yet again. "Noooooo. I mean, I crawled into bed with the best man wearing this pink getup."

For once, she had achieved the impossible—Marie was struck speechless.

"Marie, are you there?"

"Are you saying—" her sister make a strangled noise "—that you put a stroke on the best man?"

"No!" she snapped. "We sort of realized the mistake, Marie."

"At what point?"

Janine remembered the kiss and experienced her first all-body blush—not completely unpleasant—then leaned against the enclosure. "My virtue is intact."

"Unbelievable! See, exciting things do happen to you."

"Really? *Humiliating* was the first word that came to my mind."

"Isn't your best man that dreamy Jack Stillman?"

"He was. But Jack disappeared, so Steve asked Jack's brother, Derek, to stand in."

"Is he gorgeous too? And single?"

Her head had started to throb again. "Marie, I didn't call to discuss the Stillman gene pool. I called to see if you would come to pick me up. I left my purse under the front seat of your car and I have no money and no key."

"Well, sure I'll come back, but don't you want to wait for Steve?"

"I don't think so." She wasn't sure she could go through with her plan to seduce Steve with the memory of another man's mouth on hers so fresh in her mind.

"You lost your buzz, ergo your nerve."

"Well—"

"Janine, if you come home, you won't be any closer to the answer you went for."

The sick feeling of anguish settled in her stomach again, but she appreciated her sister's objectivity, quirky as it was. "You're right, but Derek said the guys are supposed to be out all night."

"Okay, so you wait in Steve's room until morning." Marie laughed. "That is, unless you think he won't do it in the daylight."

Janine tried to smile, but she felt too disjointed to respond.

"Oh, wait," her sister said. "You said that the best man is staying in Steve's room."

"No," Janine said morosely. "He left."

"Left to go to another hotel?"

"No," she said, swinging her gaze toward the revolving door. Flashing lights outside the front entrance caught her attention. Two ambulances and several police cars had arrived, along with a van that bore a familiar insignia: the Centers for Disease Control. A knot of people stood outside, as if in conference, and she recognized the general manager she'd been talking to earlier as one them. The revolving door turned and, to her amazement, Derek walked back in, his expression as dark as a thundercloud.

"He's back," she said into the phone.

"Steve?"

"No, Derek. Hang on a minute, sis. Something is happening in the lobby." With every turn of the door, more and more suited and uniformed personnel filtered into the lobby of the hotel. Mr. Oliver walked in, and his smooth face seemed especially serious.

A terrible sense of foreboding enveloped her. Janine waved at Derek and motioned him toward her. He seemed none too pleased to see her again, but he did walk toward where she stood, his gait long and agitated.

"What's going on?" she whispered.

Derek gestured in the air above his head. "I don't know. A deputy said I couldn't leave and asked me to come back inside."

A man in a dark suit and no tie lifted a small bullhorn to his mouth. "Could I have your attention, please?"

The lobby quieted, and for the first time, Janine realized just how crowded the expansive space had become. Her lungs squeezed and she breathed as steadily as she could, trying to hedge the feeling of claustrophobia. Standing next to Derek didn't help because his big body crowded her personal space. She stepped as far away from him as the metal phone cord would allow, which garnered her a sharp look from his brown eyes. With much effort, she resisted the urge to explain and gave the doctor her full attention.

The man had paused for effect, sweeping his gaze over the room. "My name is Dr. Marco Pedro, and I'm with the Centers for Disease Control here in Atlanta. As you can see, several dozen people have been stricken with an illness we are still trying to identify. With a recent outbreak of E. coli contagion on the west side of town, we can't be too careful."

Janine's knees weakened with dread. Because of her medical training, she knew what the man's next words would be.

"So, until further notice," Dr. Pedro continued, "guests cannot leave the premises. Every individual in this facility is officially under quarantine."

CHAPTER FIVE

JANINE'S HEART dropped to her stomach. "A quarantine?" she whispered. *This can't be happening.* Next to her, Derek muttered a healthy oath that corresponded with the collective groan that went up throughout the lobby.

"Janine," Marie said in her ear. "What's going on?"

"The CDC just put the place under quarantine," she croaked. "I'll call you back." Then she hung up the phone unceremoniously.

"Was that Steve?" Derek asked.

"No, my sister," she replied, distracted by the uproar.

Angry guests were on their feet, firing questions at the doctor:

"For how long?"

"But I have to leave tomorrow!"

"Am I dying?"

Dr. Pedro held up his hands. "One at a time. We will answer your questions as soon as possible. The symptoms at this time don't appear to be life-threatening. For obvious reasons, we don't know how long the quarantine will last, but I estimate you'll be detained for at least forty-eight hours."

"Oh no," Janine murmured, and the lobby erupted

into more chaos. A few people tried to make a run for the exits, but security guards had already been posted. Her heart tripped faster when she realized she was confined to the building, and might be for some time—a claustrophobe's nightmare.

"There is no need to panic," the doctor continued in a raised, but soothing voice. "Believe me, ladies and gentleman, the quarantine is for your own protection and for the protection of the people outside these walls with whom you would otherwise come into contact."

As a health professional, Janine knew her first concern should be her own welfare and the safety of those around her, but as a bride-to-be, her thoughts turned to wedding invitations, ceremony programs and honeymoon reservations, all with a big red Cancel stamped on them. She swayed and reached for something to steady herself, meeting soft cotton and solid muscle.

"Easy," Derek said, righting her. "Are you okay?"

"Yes." She swallowed. "But my mother is going to have a stroke. We'll have to postpone the wedding."

One corner of his mouth slid back. "Gee, and the rest of us only have to worry about a slow, painful death from a mysterious disease."

Remorseful, she opened her mouth to recant, but the doctor spoke again.

"Please, everyone return to your rooms immediately. If you need assistance, ask anyone who is wearing a white coat or a yellow armband. If you develop symptoms, call the front desk and leave a message, a doctor or nurse will be with you soon. Medical personnel will be canvassing the hotel room by room to ensure no potential case is overlooked. We'll keep ev-

eryone updated as the situation progresses. We'd like
to have this area cleared. After that, do not leave your
room unless you are given permission by a person
wearing a yellow armband."

Now she knew what it felt like to be hit by a truck
and live, Janine decided. So many emotions bombarded her, she didn't know what to feel first—out-
rage that her life would have to be rescheduled, fear
that she'd been exposed to a dangerous contaminant,
or panic that she was expected to spend at least the
next forty-eight hours in close quarters with a virtual
stranger. A virtual stranger who had been vocal about
the fact that he didn't want to be here at all.

A sentiment now reinforced by his brooding expression. His jaw was dark from the shadow of his beard,
his eyes bloodshot and his nose irritated.

"You look terrible," she said without thinking.

The sarcastic glance he shot her way made even her
creeping panties seem comfortable by comparison. In
a dismissive move, he picked up his suitcase and joined
the throng moving toward the elevator and the stairs.

"I'll be right behind you," she said. "I'm going to
leave my name with the doctors just in case they can
use my help." She was trying desperately not to think
about the fact that she and Derek might be sharing
a room for the rest of the night. Or the little issue of
having no money, no ID, no toiletries, no makeup, no
clothes, no shoes and no underwear save the costume
beneath her coat.

His only acknowledgment that he'd heard her was
the barest of nods. Janine frowned at his back, then
turned to approach Dr. Pedro.

A crowd of guests had gathered around him, some angry, some concerned, all asking questions. The doctor spoke succinctly in a calming voice, assuring the knot of people that quarantine procedures would be distributed to every room, then asked them to clear the lobby as soon as possible. She touched the arm of a woman who appeared to be the doctor's assistant and asked if she could have a word with the doctor about a professional matter. The woman nodded and made her way toward him.

"Ms. Murphy, our paths cross again."

She swung around to see the general manager approaching her, a hint of a smile hiding the worry she knew lingered under his calm surface. "I trust you found room 855?"

"Um, yes."

He looked as if he was curious about the outcome, but was too much of a gentleman to ask.

She cleared her throat. "Mr. Oliver, I was hoping you would speak to the doctor on my behalf."

"On your behalf?"

"Well, since you can verify I arrived at the resort less than an hour ago—" she splayed her hands "—I was hoping you could arrange for me to leave."

He poked his tongue into his cheek. "Leave? If I remember correctly, when I first saw you, you were having a nose-to-nose conversation with Ben, who is now quite ill."

She leaned forward and whispered, "I'm also extremely claustrophobic."

A slight frown creased his forehead. "I suppose

I could consult the doctor about your situation, Ms. Murphy, but what about your fiancé?"

"He, um, wasn't in the room after all."

He pulled a notebook from his pocket. "We have to account for all guests—I'll make a note that the room is empty."

She told herself she should keep her mouth shut, but Derek *was* ill and, therefore, probably needed to be kept under surveillance. Her medical ethics kicked in, and she sighed. "Actually, there was another gentleman in the room."

Mr. Oliver's blue eyes widened. "Oh?"

At that moment, the doctor walked up, nodding to Mr. Oliver, then to Janine. "My assistant said you wished to speak to me."

She tried on her professional face, wondering how disheveled she appeared. "Dr. Pedro, my name is Janine Murphy. I'm a P.A. here in Atlanta, and I wanted to offer my services in case you find yourself short of personnel."

He was a pleasant-looking man who seemed unruffled in the midst of the pandemonium. "It's kind of you to offer, Ms. Murphy, but we're fully staffed. Are you feeling well?"

She was sick to her stomach with worry, not to mention a little hungover, but she nodded. "Yes, and Mr. Oliver can verify I haven't been at the resort very long, so if you don't think you'll need my help, I was wondering if you might see your way to release me from the quarantine."

Dr. Pedro gave her a regretful smile. "Ms. Murphy, because of your medical training, you understand why

I can't release you, but if you don't fall ill and a lot of other guests do, indeed we might need your help. I assume you have your license with you?"

Too late, she remembered she didn't have her purse, in which she kept a card-size copy of her license. "Um, no, I'm sorry, I don't have my license with me."

"If you have other ID on you, my assistant can verify your credentials over the phone."

Her shoulders fell. "Actually, I don't have ID with me, either." She conjured up a laugh. "You see, my sister dropped me off to visit my fiancé. I, um, hadn't planned an extended visit." Her temperature raised with every mortifying word that seemed determined to spill out of her mouth for both men to hear.

The dark-haired man's gaze dropped to her black high heels for a split second, then he lifted one bushy eyebrow. "I see. And how are both of you feeling?"

She squirmed and manufactured a you're-not-going-to-believe-this laugh. "Well, it turned out that my fiancé isn't here after all. He let another man have his room for the night. His best man. Our best man, that is. For the wedding."

Mr. Oliver pursed his mouth, and put pen to paper. "The man's name?"

"D-Derek Stillman."

An amused smile crossed his face. "Is that with two D's?"

The doctor looked completely lost. "Forgive me, but I'm a very busy man—"

"Wait, Dr. Pedro." Janine looked behind her, relieved to see Derek was definitely out of earshot, then turned back and encompassed both men with the smile she'd been practicing for her wedding photos. "Perhaps I could at least get a separate room." When the doctor hesitated, she added, "I barely know the man, and he's exhibiting symptoms." *Two of many reasons for separate quarters.*

Dr. Pedro made a sympathetic sound, then looked to Mr. Oliver. "Do you have any empty rooms?"

The general manager shook his head.

The doctor shrugged. "I'm sorry, Ms. Murphy."

"Perhaps I can stay with the medics," she urged, grasping.

Her face must have reflected her distress because his face softened into an indulgent smile. "No, but maybe we can arrange to place you with a female guest who isn't exhibiting symptoms and who hasn't been exposed to someone who is."

She smiled, enormously cheered.

"Unless you've already spent time in the man's room."

Her smile dropped while Mr. Oliver's eyebrows climbed. She considered lying, then glanced back to the doctor and nodded miserably.

"For how long?"

"About thirty minutes, total."

He pursed his lips. "That's not so bad."

Hope resurrected, she smiled.

"But how close was your contact?"

Her smile dropped again. "Fairly close. I checked to see if he had a fever." *Among other things.*

The manager must have read her wicked mind, because his lips twitched with suppressed mirth.

"Well, if that's all—" the doctor began.

"No," she broke in, exasperated with herself, but knowing she had to tell the truth. "Actually, I k-kissed him."

Both men blinked.

"Completely by accident," she assured them hastily. "I thought he was my fiancé." She sounded like a raving idiot, but she couldn't seem to stop, as if she needed to purge herself.

Dr. Pedro's eyes widened. "Are the men identical twins?"

"N-no, but it was very dark."

Looking completely baffled, he cleared his throat. "Ms. Murphy, if you've already been exposed, you simply must stay in the room." He turned to the general manager. "Moving guests would make it impossible to identify whether the problem is isolated to certain areas of the hotel."

Mr. Oliver nodded solemnly. "I'll make certain my staff is aware."

The man turned back to Janine. "I hope you understand, Ms. Murphy, why I cannot compromise the quarantine. I'm sorry if these circumstances put you in a delicate situation."

She nodded, backing away, wishing a tornado would rise up behind her and spirit her away to Kansas. "Thank you for your time, Dr. Pedro. And please let me know if I can be of service somehow." As if he would ask her now. He probably thought she was an escapee from the state loony bin. *She* certainly would if she were in his shoes. And right now she'd trade shoes with just about anyone in the building.

He nodded, his expression wary. "I'll examine your, um, *friend* myself as soon as possible."

"Thanks," she said, then felt compelled to add, "but he's not a friend, he's just my best man."

He stared at her as if she might be dangerous.

Janine managed a tight smile for Mr. Oliver and turned to join the exiting crowd. Maybe she had already contracted the mysterious disease and didn't realize it. How else could she explain her leaking brain cells and runaway mouth? Of course, exhaustion could have something to do with her state of mind, she reasoned as she waited at the end of the line to climb the stairs to the eighth floor. Stairwells were confining even without the swell of bodies to deal with, so she hung back.

When she leaned against the wall, she spotted a curtained door at the end of the perpendicular hallway. There had to be a way out of this place, she decided suddenly, then squared her shoulders. It was dark, she was wearing black...she could walk the half mile to the convenience store on the main road and call Marie.

After making sure no one was watching, she slipped down the hallway and opened the curtain an inch. The solitary office was neat and whimsical, but the best part was that the neat, whimsical person had left open one of the three high windows. The cool night air beckoned. She could climb up and over the windowsill, then drop the eight feet or so to the ground and be gone in a matter of minutes.

Stacking a sturdy stool on a chair beneath the window gave her enough height to reach freedom. Cursing her bulky coat, she carefully climbed up and steadied herself on the stool, then reached up and grasped the sill. While propelling herself up on her elbows, she kicked over the stool, which crashed to the floor, taking the chair with it. Janine looked down and made a face. Nowhere to go now but up unless she wanted to drop back to the marble floor. *Ouch.*

But going up wasn't as easy as she'd thought, because she'd overestimated her upper-body strength. After a few seconds, she'd managed to chin herself up to the sill, only to drop back and hang by her hands when her arms gave out. Then both high heels dropped to the floor, leaving her hanging shoeless, suspended between the window and the floor, too weak to go up, and too fond of her anklebones to go down. On hindsight, maybe trying to escape hadn't been one of her brighter ideas.

"Well, if it isn't Ms. Murphy," a man said behind her. She craned around, hanging on for dear life, to see Mr. Oliver standing in the middle of the room, his arms crossed.

She gave him her most dazzling smile. "Hi."

"You neglected to tell me and the good doctor that you were also Bat Girl."

"Um, it slipped my mind."

"Do you need a hand back to earth?"

She nodded, her chin rubbing against the wall. "That would be good."

He was tall, and had no problem assuming her weight from below. When he set her back on her feet, he gave her the tolerant look of an older, wiser brother. "Have we learned our lesson?"

Rubbing her arms, she nodded, then picked up her high heels. "I think I'll be going back to my room now."

He nodded. "Sweet dreams."

She found her way back to the stairwell, stinging from her failed jailbreak, and dragged herself up the flights of stairs. At last she reached the eighth floor and retraced her steps to room 855, surprised to see Derek waiting in the hall, his face a mask of concern. "Where did you go?"

Janine frowned at his impatient tone, not about to admit she'd been caught trying to escape. "I told you I was going to talk to the doctor."

"Oh, right," he said, his voice contrite. He pushed his hand through his hair. "Sorry, I'm a little punchy, I think." Then he turned and extended his right hand to her. A peace offering, she thought, absurdly pleased. She smiled and put her small hand in his for a friendly squeeze, and her heart pitched to the side. "I hope we can be friends when this is over, Derek."

But his smile seemed a bit dim. "That seems highly unlikely, Pinky." He extracted his hand and wriggled his fingers. "The room key?"

"Oh." Her cheeks flamed at mistaking his gesture. Was she destined to forever embarrass herself in front of this man? She shoved her hands into her pockets, hoping she might also find money she'd left the last time she'd worn the coat. One pocket produced a quarter and two pennies and a half a pack of chewing gum. From the other she pulled an ancient tube of lipstick and—she stared, incredulous—a brand-new strip of lubricated condoms. *Marie.* She groaned inwardly and slid her gaze sideways to see if Derek had noticed. He had.

"All the necessities, I see."

"But these aren't mine," she began.

"Okay, okay—whatever. Just…give me…the key." His smile was pleading and his hands were shaking. "Please, can you do that? No talking, just the key."

She swallowed and fished deeper in her pocket to remove a parking ticket, a lone glove, and finally, the room key, which he plucked from her hand.

"Where's *your* key?" she asked tartly as she returned the trinkets to her pockets. Then, remembering she sometimes stuffed cash in the inner pockets, she turned away, unbuttoned her coat and reached inside. Dammit—nothing.

"I didn't think I would need a key, so Steve took it with him."

Which made Janine wish she hadn't even asked, because Steve's name triggered another avalanche of emotions—dread, shame, remorse. She closed her eyes and moaned. Not in her wildest dreams could she imagine what else could go wrong.

"Janine Murphy, isn't it?"

She whirled and stared blankly at the attractive woman walking by in designer pajamas.

"Maureen Jiles, sales rep for Xcita Pharmaceuticals," the woman said.

Her memory clicked in, and she pulled a smile from somewhere, realizing she knew the woman from the clinic. Maureen Jiles was the buzz of the doctors' lounge—with her exotic looks and plunging necklines, she couldn't have been more suited to peddling one of the industry's new impotence drugs. And judging by the way she was eyeing Derek and licking her chops, her reputation as a man-eater had been well earned.

Janine bristled, not because the woman was ogling Derek, of course, but because she apparently ogled every man. "Maureen. Sure I remember."

"You were going to marry that yummy plastic surgeon, weren't you?" As she spoke, the woman perused Janine's outfit beneath the gaping coat, from her shiny bustier to her black-stockinged feet.

Janine nodded and jerked her coat closed, then leaned over to slip on her shoes despite her aching, raw heel. "The day after tomorrow here at the resort," she said, smiling wide. "Well, isn't this quarantine the most crazy turn of events?"

But Maureen had eyes only for Derek. "Oh, I don't mind being confined...with the right person. Janine, aren't you going to introduce me to your friend?"

"Derek Stillman," he said, stepping forward.

"And we're not friends," they said in unison.

Maureen looked back and forth between them.

"He's my best man," Janine offered.

Maureen's eyebrows drew together.

"And if you ladies don't mind," Derek said in a tired voice, "I'd like to go to bed now." He nodded to Maureen, then picked up his bags and disappeared inside the room.

"He's ill," Janine offered in the ensuing silence, then lowered her voice to add, "and probably very contagious."

The woman made a sympathetic sound. "Too bad. So why are *you* at the resort?"

"Oh, you know, taking care of last-minute wedding details," she sang. "Are you staying on this floor?"

"I'm right here," the woman said, gesturing to the door directly across from theirs.

Her empty stomach lurched. "Oh. That's...lovely."

"Where is your room?"

The door behind Janine opened and Derek appeared. He was naked to the waist, and barefoot. Splendidly so. "Here's the key," he said. "I'm going to take a shower."

Janine took the key he shoved into her hand and stood rooted to the floor after the door closed again. Interminable seconds later, she lifted her gaze to find Maureen's eyebrows up to her hairline. Everyone she worked with, including Steve's associates, would know about the sleeping arrangements in a matter of hours unless she thought of something fast.

"It's n-not what you think," she said hurriedly. "I came to see my fiancé, b-but he planned to be out all night for his bachelor party, and he'd given his room to Derek b-because he wasn't feeling well, and now there aren't any rooms available, and, well..." She swallowed, desperate. "Derek is gay."

Maureen's smile fell and she grunted in frustration. "All the cute ones are!"

Janine sighed and shook her head. "I know."

Dejected, the woman turned and unlocked her door. "Well, good night, I guess."

She gave her neighbor a fluttery little wave. When Maureen's door closed, Janine leaned heavily against the wall, mulling over the events of the past—she checked her watch—*three* hours? Geez, it seemed a lifetime had passed since she and Marie were in her bedroom, joking, planning her sexy adventure.

Whatever happens, Janine, this night could determine the direction of the rest of your life.

Janine sighed again. She'd always had a terrible sense of direction.

Numbly, she turned and faced the door, her mind reeling. She couldn't bring herself to go in because even after everything that had happened, she had the strangest feeling that things would only get worse before they got better. She wasn't sure how long she'd stood there before a security guard came by and asked that she return to her room to keep the hallways clear.

She nodded and inserted the key, then opened the door and walked inside. Derek stood by the phone with a towel around his hips, his skin glistening, his hair wet and smoothed back. Her pulse kicked up in appreciation, but she acknowledged that her body was so shell-shocked, it no longer knew how to respond appropriately. She was suddenly so tired, she wanted to drop on the spot and curl into a fetal position.

Derek looked up and held the phone out to her. "It's for you."

"At three o'clock in the morning? Who is it?" she asked wearily, taking the handset, thinking Marie had tracked her down for more details.

He shrugged and stretched out on the bed, still wearing the towel. "She says she's your mother."

CHAPTER SIX

DEREK HAD HEARD of being too tired to sleep, but he thought he might have reached the point where he was too tired even to breathe. He lay still on the bed, eyes closed, waiting for a burst of energy that would allow his lungs to expand. Meanwhile, he listened to the perpetually frazzled Janine murmur and moan and otherwise fret up her nerve to speak to her mother. Unfortunately for him, hearing was the only one of five senses that required no energy whatsoever.

"Mom?" Her voice squeaked like a cartoon character's. "I'm fine—yes, I'm sure. I just walked back into the room. Uh-huh."

She must have a decent relationship with her mother, he noted, else she wouldn't be so eager to reassure her.

"How did you know I was here? Oh, I forgot about your police scanner. You called Marie? And she told you I was here. Ah. Hmm? Yes, we're definitely under a quarantine." She cleared her throat. "Yes, we might have to consider p-postponing the wedding."

A staticy screech sounded through the phone. He opened one eye to find her holding the handset away from her ear. When the noise subsided, she pulled it closer. "Mom, I said 'might.' I'll know more in a few hours. Right now I really need to go to bed."

An unfocused thrill rumbled through his beleaguered body at her words—a base reaction to a woman's voice, he reasoned. Any woman's voice.

Her gaze lowered to meet his, and she blanched. "I m-mean, I really need to get some rest, Mom. Not necessarily in bed. A person doesn't have to be *in bed* in order to rest. Hmm?" Her eyes darted around. "The man who answered?"

He might have laughed at her predicament if he'd had the energy. As it was, he was having trouble keeping the one eyelid half-open.

She was staring at him, chewing on her lower lip. "That was, um, the, um…"

"Best man?" he prompted, barely moving his lips.

She scowled and turned her back. "That was the… be—ll man. Yes, the bellman."

He wondered briefly what the bellman's job paid and how it compared to advertising.

"Why am I here?" Another fake laugh, except this one sounded a tad hysterical. "I'll tell you all about it later, okay?" She bent over, still talking as she moved the handset closer to the receiver. "Good night, Mom. Okay…okay…okay…bye." She jammed the phone home with a sigh, now the only sound in the room the faint whir of the air conditioner, which he'd turned up. He closed his one eye. Man, was it hot down here in Atlanta.

"I assume you requested a cot."

His eyes flew open at the accusing tone in her voice. She still wore that black raincoat, rendered even more ridiculous because he knew what lay beneath it. Her arms were crossed, and with her blond hair falling in her eyes, she looked like a cross between Rapunzel and Columbo.

He closed his eyes again to summon enough strength to speak. "Yes."

He'd nearly drifted off to sleep when she broke in again. "And are they sending one up?"

Sigh. "No."

"Why not?"

She was like a pesky fly, and he was too tired to flick his tail. "They were out," he mumbled.

The haze of sleep was claiming him again.

"Okay, you can get up."

He jerked awake and cast his weary gaze in her direction. "Excuse me?"

"I said you can get up."

He scoffed—a tremendous feat—and shook his head.

"I'm not about to share this bed with you," she said, her voice laced with indignance.

"Relax, Pinky," he muttered, then yawned. "Even if you were my type, which you're not, I'm too tired to take advantage of you."

"If…think…sleeping…you…another think coming."

He squinted at her because her voice faded in and out. "Suit yourself." It was her fault he was in this worsening mess, her fault he was in Atlanta, period. Hers and his brother's, dammit. At the moment, he wasn't sure which of them he resented more. He would sleep on it, Derek decided.

JANINE WASN'T CERTAIN he'd fallen asleep until one of his pectoral muscles twitched, causing her to jump. She pressed her lips together in anger. Surely the man didn't expect her to crawl into bed with him. She swallowed. Again.

As if he'd sensed her thoughts, he groaned in his sleep and rolled on his side to face her, hugging the pillow under his head with a bent arm. The cream-colored towel around his waist parted slightly, revealing corded thighs covered with dark hair and the faintest almost-maybe-could-be glimpse of his sex. A pang of desire struck her low—or had her corset simply ruptured? Feeling like the most naughty of little girls, she strained for a better look, but when he shifted again and the towel fell away completely, she squeezed her eyes shut and whirled to face the wall.

Yesterday she was a yearning bride-to-be, and today she was peeping at sleeping naked men. She was going to hell, she just knew it.

Bone-deep weariness claimed her and she scanned the room for another place to lie down. She hadn't realized how opulent the room was, and now she crinkled her nose at the decor, designed more for southern aesthetics than functionality. Being on the top floor, the room boasted a cathedral ceiling and a garish chandelier with fringed minishades over the lights. Several bouquets of flowers were situated around the room, emitting a cloying sweetness. The walls were a deep burgundy with a nondescript tone-on-tone design, broken up with a jutting off-white chair rail. To her left, a large pale-painted writing desk with curlicued legs and gilded accents sat at an angle. She walked over and tested it for strength, but didn't like the looks of the distance to the hard parquet floor, at least not the way her luck had been running.

A bulky armoire in the same gaudy style contained a television and colorful tourist guides. A wooden valet sat next to it, draped with Derek's jeans and sweatshirt, white socks balled on the floor. Janine stared, struck by the innocent intimacy of those socks.

Past the door, a padded straight-back chair sat mocking her with its stiffness. Next came a fat, curvy dresser with a mirror, which, to her chagrin, reflected Derek's partially nude figure reclining in the comfy-looking bed. Sprawled amongst the sheets, he seemed even larger than when standing. He looked absurdly out of place, broad shoulders and long limbs against the ornate headboard, his feet practically hanging over the end of the mattress.

Despite his massive form, the other side of the bed appeared plenty large enough for her. Perhaps if she slept on top of the covers and put some kind of divider between them—What was she thinking? She'd be better off bedding down on the loopy cotton rug situated outside the bathroom door, a small island against the dark parquet floor. Wanting to wash her face, Janine kicked off her shoes and limped past Steve's and Derek's suitcases to the oversize bathroom. She squinted beneath the flickering pinkish light over the vanity, but reveled in the feel of the cool tile against her fiery feet.

The luxurious moss green bathroom—also vaulted—featured a large vanity area, a padded stool, an electric towel warmer and a skylight over the large tub. The wall seemed curtained with thick cream-colored towels, one

conspicuously missing from the long chrome rack—
the one now wrapped around Derek, she presumed.

One look in the mirror brought a flood of exhausted
and humiliated tears to her eyes. She looked as though
she'd been—what was the saying, *rode hard and put
up wet?* Her hair lay, or rather, stood, in disarray—
big yellow loops out of place, and a rat's nest at the
nape of her neck. Black flecks of mascara dotted her
cheeks. The rest of her makeup had faded, leaving her
skin streaked and blotchy. Her head hurt and her body
ached and her pride smarted. And she had to get out
of this unbearable costume.

She lowered herself to the stool in front of the vanity, surveying her ragged hose, frowning at her short-
lived fantasy of Steve leisurely rolling them down over
her knees, calves, ankles. She removed the thigh-highs
with a series of frustrating yanks and tossed them into
a little shell-shaped wastebasket. After much tugging
and cursing, she was finally able to loosen the lac-
ings of the bustier. Her ribs ached from their sudden
release, and she inhaled deeply enough to tempt hy-
perventilation. Janine tossed the offending piece of
lingerie onto the vanity and scrubbed her face, then
contemplated dragging herself back into the bedroom
to take up residence on the skimpy little rug.

Irritation at Derek Stillman welled in her chest—
if it weren't for him, she wouldn't be in this mess. If
he hadn't answered the phone when she called, she
would've stayed at her apartment, and none of this
would have happened. And if he were half a gentleman, he would've slept on the floor and given her the

bed. When Steve heard about this, he'd undoubtedly find yet another best man.

Steve.

She moaned and lowered her head, shoving her fingers deep into her hair. How was she going to explain this situation to Steve? Steve, with his family's ultra-conservative sensibilities? Tears of misery streamed down her cheeks.

After a good hiccuping cry, Janine sniffed and pushed herself to her feet, then buttoned her coat over the ludicrous pink panties. Everything would look better in the light of day, she told herself, then glanced in the mirror. Well, everything except her hair, maybe.

Meanwhile, she was loath to go back into the bedroom with that, that…big uncouth man-person. She lifted her head, and through bleary eyes saw the huge Jacuzzi-style bathtub and brightened. Why not?

It was certainly big enough to sleep in, and if she lined it with towels… She jumped up and spread several of the thick towels in the bottom of the tub, telling herself it would sound much better if she could tell Steve that she and Derek slept in separate rooms. And she had to admit, she hadn't discounted the possibility of acquiring Derek's illness—whatever it was—if they shared the same air. She turned off the light and closed the door, then climbed into the deep tub, feeling only slightly foolish. After the events of the past few hours, everything was relative.

The air hung damp around her, remnants of Derek's shower. The scent of soap teased her nostrils, evoking thoughts of the intriguing man lying in the next room. She wondered suddenly if he was married, or engaged, or otherwise attached. Because for some reason, the thought of her, Steve, Derek and someone else all lying awake thinking about each other seemed very funny. A split second later, she sobered.

Steve wasn't thinking about her—he was obviously still out celebrating his last few hours of freedom, while she was bunking down in a bathtub. A sliver of resentment slid up her spine, but was quickly overpowered by the onset of claustrophobia sloping in around her. Janine concentrated on the stars through the skylight above her until the panicky sensation subsided.

She snuggled farther into the pallet of towels, smoothing out a lump under her left hip, then admitted the tub was more comfortable than she'd expected. Janine sighed, trying to mine a nugget of philosophical wisdom from her predicament, concluding instead she was living an *I Love Lucy* episode.

She fell asleep with a vision of her and Steve in black and white, toothpaste smiles, hair perfectly coifed...and sleeping in twin beds.

CHAPTER SEVEN

WHEN DEREK STARTED AWAKE, several seconds passed before he remembered he was in Atlanta at the resort where Steve was to be married on Saturday. Other memories of the previous night were too ludicrous to believe. When he lifted his heavy, aching head to find he was alone in the room, he nearly laughed aloud with relief. Those were some strong pills he'd taken for his cold. For a while there— Derek chuckled despite his headache. *No way.*

From the filtered light coming through the floor-to-ceiling windows to his left, he estimated the time to be around 6:00 a.m. Typically, he'd be rolling out of bed for a bike ride, weather willing, or a run on the dilapidated treadmill that sat less than five steps from his bed. Then he'd shower and arrive at the office by seven-fifteen.

But at the moment, he needed more cold medicine, hallucinogen or not. He pushed himself out of bed gingerly, tossing the still-damp towel twined around his legs to the floor. Holding his head so it wouldn't explode, and swallowing to moisten his dry throat, he stumbled through the semidarkness to the bath-room and pushed open the door. By the illumination of the skylight, he felt along the vanity for the box of cold medicine, but instead came up with a perplexing object, flat and flexible, with ties and mysterious textures.

Bewildered, he groped for the light switch and flooded the room with light. He blinked at the pink-and-black thingamajig in his hand for an entire second before a shriek sounded behind him. Derek swung around to see a person sit up in the bathtub, and when he registered the dark coat and the blond hair, he grasped the horrifying fact that he hadn't been hallucinating after all. Gripping both sides of the tub as if she were in a sinking lifeboat, Pinky looked at him and screamed.

As if he'd taken a bite from the forbidden fruit, Derek suddenly realized he was naked. He thrust the top of her costume over his privates, straining from their morning call, and backed up against the counter. "What the devil are you doing in the bathtub?" he thundered, grimacing at the pain in his temples.

She pushed a mop of hair out of her eyes. "Sleeping."

The woman was a bona fide nutcase. "I can see that," he said calmly. "But why are you sleeping *in the bathtub?*"

"Because," she mumbled, "you were in the bed." She spit hair out of her mouth. "I can see your butt in the mirror."

He clenched and opened his mouth to say something he hadn't yet thought of, but the phone rang. Backing out of the bathroom, Derek sneezed twice on his way to answer the phone. He flung the corset on the bed and managed to grab a handkerchief before he yanked up the handset. "Hello?"

"Hey, man, what's going on over there?" Steve Larsen's voice sounded concerned, but a little indistinct, as if his last drink was not in the too-distant past. "I came back to the hotel a few minutes ago and they wouldn't let me past the gate. Something about a quarantine?"

Derek stretched the phone cord to reach his jeans on the valet. He jerked them on as he answered Steve. "Yeah, several of the guests have come down with something, and the CDC put the entire facility under quarantine."

"That's nuts. For how long?"

He sat on the bed and leaned forward to cradle his head in his hands. "The top guy said at least forty-eight hours."

Steve cursed. "Which means we'll have to postpone the rehearsal and the dinner for tonight. Maybe even the wedding." He swore again, this one causing Derek to wince. "My mother is going to be irate, and I don't know how I'm going to break it to Janine."

The topic of their conversation walked into the room. With her bare legs and feet sticking out below her wrinkled black raincoat, she resembled a bag lady. A very fetching bag lady, Derek realized with a start. "Steve," he said, loudly enough to gain her attention. "Janine already knows about the quarantine."

"What? How does Janine know?" Steve asked. "Wait a minute—how do *you* know that Janine knows?"

Derek watched her face crumble with dread as he mulled over how best to break the news to his friend. She bit her lower lip, beseeching him to…what? "She's here at the hotel," he said, nausea rolling in his stomach. Only his brother, Jack, made him feel this way: protective, yet taken advantage of. He hated it.

"At the hotel?" Steve shouted. "Where? How?"

Janine Murphy, Derek decided, was a big girl who'd gotten them both into a big mess and she and her big blue eyes could take responsibility for it. "She's...I'll have her call you when I see her," he finished lamely, ridiculously warmed at the expression of gratitude on her face. "Are you at your place?"

"I'm at a friend's," Steve said. "But I'm going to my folks' to break the news to my mom before she hears it on television."

"Television?"

"There were at least four TV crews in front of the hotel," Steve offered. "And so many uniforms we thought a bomb had gone off. By the way, what's Janine doing at the hotel?"

For a few seconds, he panicked. "Looking for you, I suppose." Derek strained to remember what she'd said when she'd crawled on top of him, but he'd been kind of distracted at the time by her roaming hands.

"So where did you run into her?"

"We...saw each other in the lobby," he hedged, looking to her for affirmation. She nodded. And it wasn't exactly a lie, though he hated covering for the minx.

"She's a sweetheart, isn't she?" Steve asked. "I know she doesn't exactly stand out when she enters a room," he continued, causing Derek to raise his eyebrows. "You probably noticed she's kind of a nature girl."

The image of Janine in that very unnatural pink getup was seared on his brain. "Um, no, I didn't notice that," he said wryly, certain his sarcasm was lost on his hungover friend. Janine frowned and scratched her bare foot with her toe.

Steve laughed, then lowered his voice in a conspiratorial tone. "But underneath those tentlike clothes, Janine has a nice bod."

"She sure does," Derek said without thinking, then coughed and added, "She sure does seem like a nice girl, I mean."

Her eyes widened and a hint of a smile warmed her lips. He wanted to shake his head to let her know he was only talking for Steve's sake, but once again, he didn't have the heart to hurt her feelings.

"You sound horrible, man. Do you have whatever is going around at the resort?"

"Maybe," Derek admitted.

"Well, do me a favor and don't touch any of my stuff."

Steve's casual guffaw irritated him. Derek surveyed Pinky's elfin frame, tempted to inform Steve just how much of his "stuff" he'd already touched.

"And do me another favor," Steve added. "Keep an eye on Janine for me, would you?"

Derek pursed his mouth. "That should be easy."

"If you know what room she's in, I'll call her myself," Steve said. "Or I'll check with the desk."

"Um, no." Derek rushed to stop him. "She's staying with…" He rolled his hand to indicate he needed help.

She put her fingers in her ears, then pinched together the fingers of her right hand and started punching the air.

"She's staying with the operator," he said, but Janine stopped, disgusted with his guess.

He splayed his hands, at a loss. She mouthed something emphatic several times before he covered the phone. "What?"

"I'm with the doctors, Einstein," she hissed. "This—"

she repeated the motion "—is using a stethoscope, not a switchboard!"

He frowned, then uncovered the phone. "I mean, she's staying with the medics...on the slim chance she can help."

His words garnered another dark look from Janine, but Steve seemed convinced. "Oh. Will you see her?"

"I'd say that's a safe bet," Derek said, his tone dry.

"Just tell her to call me." Steve said, then laughed without humor. "I'm sorry as hell you got caught in this mess, man. By all rights, it should be Jack holed up with the plague, eh?"

"Just one more reason to kick his ass when I see him," Derek grumbled, then said goodbye and hung up.

For a few seconds, neither he nor Janine spoke. Fatigue pulled at his shoulders so he stretched his arms high, then he rubbed his eyes with his fists.

"You really shouldn't do that."

He stopped. "Shouldn't do what?"

"Rub your eyes like that," she said. "You could scratch your corneas."

Derek stared at her, feeling luckier and luckier to be unencumbered by a female. "You," he said, pointing a finger, "be quiet."

She blanched, then he was horrified to see tears pool in her eyes. "Oh, no," he said, holding up his hands. "Don't cry." A big tear slid down her cheek and he groaned. "Ah, for the love of Pete," he begged, feeling like a heel. "*Please* don't cry. I shouldn't have snapped at you."

"I'm s-sorry," she whispered. "It's the wedding, and, and, and now this q-quarantine..."

"Are you feeling ill?" He'd hate to think he'd given her whatever he had. Derek bit down on the inside of his cheek—there he went again, caring.

"I don't think so," she said, her lower lip trembling.

He stood and walked over to her, then gently clasped her shoulders and turned her around to face the bathroom. "Why don't you take a nice, long bath?" he said in the voice he saved for his most neurotic clients. "I'm sure you'll feel much better."

She nodded mutely and disappeared behind the closed door. The water splashed on and, too late, he realized his cold medicine was still on the vanity. Derek blew his nose, then lowered himself to the floor for twenty-seven push-ups before he had to stop and sneeze again. He gave up and pulled an accordion file marked Phillips Honey from the bag he'd repacked, along with three pint-size clear plastic containers of Phillips's products: nearly transparent wildwood honey, pale yellow honey butter and a mahogany-colored sourwood honey with a chunk of the waxy honeycomb imbedded in its murky depths.

Derek stared at the honey, willing a brilliant idea to leap to his blank pad of paper. After a few seconds without a revelation, he numbered lines on the pad from one to twenty. He would start with trite ideas, but sometimes when he reached the end of the list, something fresh would occur to him. *A honey of a taste. How sweet it is.* He kept glancing toward the bathroom, wondering what she was doing in there. *Sweet, sweet surrender.* He tossed down his pen in disgust.

Picking up the container of light honey, he rolled it between his hands to warm and loosen the contents, then opened the flip-top lid and squeezed a tiny dollop onto his finger. He smelled the translucent stickiness, jotting down notes about the aroma—sweet but pungent and a little wild. He tasted the honey, sucking it from his finger, allowing it to dissolve in his mouth, wondering why, instead of images of warm biscuits, the nutty sweet flavor of the honey evoked images of the woman bathing in the next room. Probably because she was a nut, he reasoned, then massaged his aching temples.

A knock on the door interrupted his rambling thoughts. Derek pulled his sweatshirt over his head and ran a hand through his hair, then checked the peephole to see two sets of suited shoulders. He opened the door to Dr. Pedro and a tall blond man who introduced himself as the general manager. The doctor carried a black leather bag, and the manager sported a clipboard that held down a one-inch stack of papers. Both men appeared weary, their eyes bloodshot.

"Mr. Stillman," the doctor said. "I understand you're not feeling well. I need to examine you, draw some blood and record your symptoms."

Derek invited them inside. The general manager hung back, then peered around warily as he entered. "Isn't Janine Murphy in this room?"

A strange sound emerged from the bathroom. The men stopped and Derek identified the low noise as the world's worst rendition of "You Light Up My Life." He looked at Mr. Oliver and nodded toward the closed door. "Janine." When she hit a particularly off-key note, he felt compelled to add, "I don't really know her."

The doctor offered him a tight smile. "She informed us of your, um, unusual circumstances." While Derek pondered *that* conversation, the shorter man pulled the straight-back chair toward the foot of the bed. "Shall we get started?"

Derek sat in the chair and allowed the doctor to take his vital signs. "What's the status of the quarantine?"

"Still on," the man muttered, while peering into Derek's ears with a lighted instrument. He made notes on a pad of yellow forms.

"Have you identified the illness?"

"Yes," the doctor replied. "But not the source. Open your mouth and say 'ah.'"

Derek obeyed, realizing he'd have to drag answers out of the man. Meanwhile, he watched Mr. Oliver pivot and take in details of the room. The man stopped, his gaze on the pink-and-black bustier lying on top of the bedcovers where Derek had tossed it after using it as a shield. With an inward groan, Derek resisted the urge to jump up and discard the misleading evidence. Mr. Oliver's perusal continued, this time stopping to stare at the stash of honey on the nightstand. One of the manager's eyebrows arched and he slid a glance toward Derek. Great, Derek thought in exasperation. *He thinks I'm doing kinky things with that woman braying in the bathroom.*

"Your throat is irritated," the doctor announced.

Derek gagged on the tongue depressor, then pulled away and swallowed. "I could have told you that."

"When did you arrive at the hotel?"

"Yesterday, around three o'clock."

"When did you first start exhibiting symptoms?"

"Around five o'clock, I guess."

"Describe your symptoms."

Derek shrugged. "Congestion, sore throat."

"Body aches?" the doctor prompted.

He nodded. "Some."

"Vomiting?"

"No."

"Diarrhea?"

"No."

Mr. Oliver stepped forward. "Did you eat in the hotel restaurant?"

He nodded.

"When and what did you eat?" the manager continued.

"A burger and fries, around four o'clock."

"What did you have to drink?" Dr. Pedro cut in.

"Water and coffee."

"Decaf?"

"No, I was tired and needed the boost."

"Have you eaten anything else since you arrived?" the doctor asked.

Derek shook his head.

"Honey, perhaps?" The general manager nodded toward the nightstand with an amused expression.

He frowned. "Only a taste. And just this morning."

"What else?" Dr. Pedro asked, scribbling.

"Some over-the-counter medicine I picked up in the gift shop."

"I'll need to see it."

Derek jerked his thumb toward the bathroom where Pinky continued her teeth-grating performance. "It's in there."

The doctor gestured toward the bathroom. "Is Ms. Murphy ailing?"

"Sure sounds like it, doesn't it?" Derek asked wryly, then rose. "Give me a minute or two." He walked over to the bathroom door and rapped loudly. The singing, thank goodness, stopped, although he could still hear the hum of the Jacuzzi and the gurgle of bubbling water.

"Who is it?" she called.

He rolled his eyes. "Derek. I need to get my medication."

"Just a minute." A rustling noise sounded through the door. "You can come in."

With a backward glance to their visitors, who seemed rapt, he opened the door and leaned inside, patting the vanity.

Behind the closed shower curtain, Janine held her breath as he rummaged on the vanity for what seemed like an eternity. Finally she moved the curtain aside mere inches to peer out. He was leaning inside the room, stretching his arm across the counter, but unable to reach the bright orange box at the far end.

"I said you could come in," she repeated, although grateful for his attempt at discretion.

Wordlessly, he stepped into the room to grab the box, then caught her gaze in the mirror.

For a few seconds, they were frozen in place. An erotic tingle skipped across her skin, sending chills over her shoulders and knees—the only part of her not submerged in the bubble bath. Even fully dressed, the man emitted a powerful sexual energy that spoke to her. His hands, his arms, his shoulders, his face—all of him radiated a strength and masculinity that stirred her insides in the most confounding way, which might explain why her normal levelheadedness had abandoned her, and clumsiness had taken its place.

"Found it," he said suddenly with a tight smile, holding up the box.

"Good," she said inanely, supremely aware that only a paper-thin curtain shielded her nudity from his eyes.

"Um, the doctor and the general manager of the hotel are here," he said, nodding toward the door. His grin was unexpected. "You might want to keep it down, or at least come up with a new song."

Her cheeks warmed and she returned a sheepish smile. "I didn't realize anyone could hear me."

"They want to know if you're feeling okay."

She nodded, suddenly wanting the other men to leave and wanting their conversation to continue. "Has the quarantine been lifted?"

"Nope. Looks like we're stuck here together for the day."

An unbidden thrill zipped through her. She studied Derek's face for his reaction to the news, but his expression remained unreadable, although he began to tap the box of medication against his other hand.

"Guess we'll have to make the best of it," he added lightly.

Her breasts tightened and she curled her fingers into such a tight fist, her nails bit into her palm. Could he hear her heart beating?

Suddenly he straightened. "I'd better get back to the doctor and the manager."

"I'll be out soon," she felt compelled to murmur as he headed toward the door.

He hesitated, his hand on the doorknob. "Take your time," he said, although his voice sounded hoarse.

When the door closed behind him, Janine leaned back against the smooth surface of the tub and allowed a pressing smile to emerge. Sliding deeper into the water, she ran her hands over her body. She raised her right leg and watched the suds drip from the end of her bright pink-polished toe. Without too much difficulty she could imagine Derek facing her on the other end of the tub, naked and slippery, their legs entwined. She lazily lowered her toe to the shiny chrome faucet and outlined the square opening. Feeling uncharacteristically wanton, she cupped her breasts, reveling in the textures—silky smooth and achingly hard. Long-denied sensations seized her, and she gave in to the lull of the warm bubbling water. After a moment's hesitation, she closed her eyes and slipped a washcloth to the apex of her thighs.

Holding it from corner to corner, she drew the wet nubby cloth over the folds of her flesh, sighing as tremors delivered wonderful, quivering sensations to her extremities. This was how she wanted him to touch her, with gentle, firm strokes, knowing when to take his time and…and…and…*when to speed up*. She pressed her lips together to stifle the moans of pleasure that vibrated in the back of her throat. As the waves of release diminished, she sank farther into the luxuriously warm water to enjoy the lingering hum. *Oh, Derek…*

DEREK TORE HIS GAZE from the closed bathroom door and tried to concentrate on the doctor's words. The only part of Janine he'd seen was her face, surrounded by hunks of wet blond hair, but with little imagination he could picture her slender body on the other side of that shower curtain, buoyed by the water. He ground his teeth against the image, then realized the doctor had said something and was waiting for a reply.

"Excuse me?" He put a finger to his temple to feign the distraction of a headache.

Dr. Pedro smiled as he scrutinized the box of medication Derek had handed to him. "I said I'm glad Ms. Murphy is still feeling well."

"Oh, yeah, right." With a swift mental kick, Derek reminded himself that while they were in the middle of a serious medical situation, *he* was obsessing over his unexplainable attraction to Steve's bride. With sheer determination, he pushed all thoughts of the woman from his mind.

Dr. Pedro directed Derek to keep taking the medicine for his symptoms. Afterward he quickly drew a blood sample from Derek's forearm, then stood to leave. "If your, um, friend starts exhibiting symptoms, please call the front desk and I'll be notified."

Mr. Oliver extended a sheet of green paper. "These are a few guidelines concerning movement about the property during the quarantine, how your meals will be delivered, how information will be disseminated, et cetera."

Derek exhaled noisily, then accepted the sheet. "How serious is this situation?"

Dr. Pedro's mouth turned down. "We had to transport three people to the hospital this morning, but we're optimistic they'll respond to an antibiotic IV."

Derek sobered. "How long will we be confined?"

"Until the source of the bacteria is detected, the method of contagion identified and the incubation period has passed."

"Worst-case scenario?" he asked.

The doctor shrugged. "Two weeks."

Derek felt a little rubbery in the knees. "I have to sit down." He dropped to the side of the bed, reeling. He was going to have to resist Janine for two weeks? Plus, in two weeks the Phillips Honey account would be long gone, and possibly his company's viability. *Jack, where the hell are you?*

"But that's worst-case scenario," Dr. Pedro added. The men walked toward the door, the general manager saying something about free phone calls. When the door closed, he lay back on the bed, holding his head and wondering if the situation could possibly get more bizarre.

"Derek?" Janine yelled from the bathroom. "Derek!" Her voice held a note of panic that roused him to his feet in one second flat.

He raced to the door and pressed his cheek against the smooth surface. "What's wrong?"

"I'm stuck."

Derek frowned. "What do you mean, you're stuck?"

"I mean my big toe…it's stuck in the bathtub faucet. Help me!"

CHAPTER EIGHT

WARM SUDSY WATER lapped at her mortified ears. Janine stared down at the end of the tub where her leg arched up out of the water—bent at the knee, dripping foam, and ending in a union with the shiny gold faucet. Trapped toe-knuckle deep into the opening of the chrome fixture, her big toe was as red as a cherry tomato from several minutes of futile tugging—a fitting end to her outrageous behavior, she decided. For fantasizing about another man, she was now trapped in this bathroom, a realization that did not sit well with her preference for open spaces. Her heartbeat thudded in her ears.

She hadn't heard the door open, but suddenly Derek's big body was silhouetted through the shower curtain.

"Janine, from the other side of the door it sounded like you said—"

"My big toe is stuck in the bathtub faucet."

He scoffed. "That's impossible."

"I beg to differ," she said miserably, then moved the curtain aside to peep out, and up. "Are you going to help me or not?"

The man looked harried. And not well. Guilt barbed through her. She should be looking after him instead of getting into scrapes. At the moment, however, she had no choice but to don the most pitiful expression she could conjure up.

It must have worked because Derek threw his hands in the air. "What do you want me to do?"

"Hand me a towel so I can cover myself, then try to get my toe unstuck."

He looked up, as if appealing to a higher power, then sighed and handed her a towel.

"Thank you." She dunked the thick towel under the water, dissolving mounds of bubbles, and spread it over her nakedness. But her heart thumped wildly at the thought of Derek seeing her yet again in a state of near undress, especially when she was so recently sated on thoughts of him. "Okay, I'm ready."

His large fingers curled around the edge of the shower curtain, and he pushed it aside slowly. The cool air hit her bits of exposed skin and sent a chill down her neck. She shivered, an all-over body shimmy, although she conceded she couldn't blame her reaction entirely on the elements. The man was huge, especially from her angle, his proportions nearly those of a professional athlete. A memory surfaced that Steve had once told her he had a pal who had played college football. Perhaps he'd meant Derek.

He ran a hand down over his face and looked at her through his fingers. "*What* is a person thinking when she shoves her toe up a faucet?"

Janine averted her eyes. She certainly couldn't tell him what she'd been doing. "I wasn't thinking."

"Obviously," he said, his expression bewildered. He slid the curtain to the wall, then lowered himself to one knee.

She felt at a terrible disadvantage at this lower level, not to mention naked and submerged. The towel covered her, but clung to her figure in a manner that belied its purpose. Of course, it didn't matter, since the man seemed completely unfazed. He leaned close to the faucet, so close she could feel his breath on her bare leg. Thank goodness she'd shaved them earlier.

He swept a soap wrapper and an empty miniature shampoo bottle from the side of the tub into the trash to clear a spot, then picked up the dripping metal razor and gave her a pointed look. "You used my razor?"

She bit her lower lip. "To shave my legs. I thought it was Steve's."

His jaw tightened as he set aside the razor. "It isn't."

He didn't have a girlfriend, she realized suddenly. At least not a live-in. Not even a lady friend who occasionally spent the night, else he would be used to sharing his razor. Then she frowned. Not that she'd ever used Steve's.

"Would you please turn off the motor so I can think?" he asked, his voice strained.

"I can't reach the switch," she said, pointing over his shoulder.

He stabbed the button in the corner of the tub ledge and the rumbling motor died abruptly, taking the soothing bubbles with it. Suddenly the room fell so quiet, she could hear the calling of birds outside the skylight, where daybreak was well under way. The eve of her supposed wedding day. She felt light-headed and realized she hadn't eaten in hours. And Derek's imposing nearness was tripping her claustrophobic tendencies.

He gripped the side of the tub and perused her foot from all directions, then he glanced back at her. "Can't you just pull it out?"

She scratched her nose, realizing too late her hand was covered with suds. Sputtering the bubbles away from her mouth, she said, "If I could, I wouldn't have called you."

He pursed his mouth, then said, "I'm not a plumber."

"Do something," she pleaded. "The water's getting cold, and I'm shriveling up."

"Really? Gee, and you've only been in here for an hour."

She frowned at his teasing. "You were the one who suggested I take a long, hot bath."

He laughed, then turned his attention back to her foot. "Except I don't recall suggesting that you insert your toe into the metal pipe coming out of the wall."

She pressed her lips together and braced for his touch. He clasped her foot gently, but firmly, and his fingers sent arrows of tingly sensations exploding up her leg, reminiscent of her climax. She grunted and he looked over his shoulder.

"My leg is asleep," she explained.

He isolated his grip to the base of her toe, wriggling it side to side. The inside lip of the faucet dug into her tender skin.

"Ouch! Not so hard."

"I'm sorry," he said, seemingly at a loss for what to do next. "I need something slick to lubricate your toe." He looked around. "Where's the soap?"

Janine lifted her hand and held her thumb and forefinger close together. "You mean that little bitty bar of soap the hotel provided?"

Derek nodded.

A flush warmed her cool cheeks. "I used it all."

He flicked a dubious glance over her towel-covered body. Maybe he thought she didn't look clean enough to have used an entire bar of soap. Her skin tingled, and not from her leg being asleep.

"Shampoo?" he asked.

She lifted a shaky finger to point to her hair, wet and plastered to her head. "I have a lot of hair."

A wry frown tugged at his mouth. "I can see that."

"Don't you have soap or shampoo in your toiletry bag?" she asked, pointing to the black case on the vanity she'd mistaken for Steve's.

He shook his head. "I travel light and expect hotels to have those things." Then he snapped his fingers. "But I do have shaving cream."

Janine smiled sheepishly and reached behind her to hand him the empty travel-size can of shaving cream. "You were almost out anyway," she offered in her defense.

He depressed the button to the sound of hissing emptiness. The side of his cheek bulged from his probing tongue. He rimmed the can into the trash, then pushed himself to his feet. "Maybe Steve will have something in his bag."

The bathroom seemed cavernous in his absence, and she wondered briefly how Steve would have handled this predicament. With much less good humor, she suspected, and the realization bothered her.

Derek returned with Steve's black bag, set it on the

vanity and ransacked it for several minutes. "Nothing," he said, defeated. "I'll call the front desk and have something sent up."

The water had taken on a distinct chill, the last cloud of bubbles were fizzing away and her leg was beginning to throb. "Tell them to hurry," she called.

But a few minutes later, he was back in the doorway. "The line is still busy. I'll have to go downstairs."

"I thought we weren't supposed to leave our rooms."

He smirked and gestured toward her foot. "I'll leave it up to you, but I'd say this constitutes an emergency."

"Don't you have *anything* in your bag that would do? Hair gel? Lotion?"

"Nope."

"Petroleum jelly? Body oil?"

He shook his head.

"What would happen if you turned on the faucet?"

A tolerant smile curved one side of his mouth. "Believe me, you don't want to do that. But I can let out the water if you're cold."

"I think the water is helping to support my weight."

His gaze swept over her again. "What weight? I thought you southern women were supposed to have a little meat on your bones."

She scowled. "*Do* you mind? I thought you were going to help. Don't you have anything that might work?"

"I told you, I—" He stopped and his dark eyebrows drew together, then his mouth quirked.

"What?"

He shook his head, as if he'd dismissed the thought. "Never mind."

"No, what is it? Tell me!"

"It wouldn't work."

"For crissake, Derek, spit it out!"

"Honey butter."

"What?"

"I have a pint of honey butter."

Janine angled her head at him. "Are you feeling worse?"

He rubbed his eyes with thumb and forefinger. "Yes."

"You really shouldn't do that."

He stopped rubbing, gave her a silencing glance, then whirled and disappeared into the bedroom.

She stretched her neck, but he'd moved out of her line of vision. Had he said honey butter? The man was incoherent, she decided, but her worry over his deteriorating symptoms was overridden by her immediate concern of being left alone to die a slow death in this bathtub. She laid her head back and stared at the skylight. At least the view would be nice.

But Derek returned in a few seconds with a small container in his hand, reading the label. "This stuff has butter in it, so maybe it'll work."

Janine eyed the container with surprise. "Where did you get it?"

"I brought it with me."

Okay, maybe he wasn't incoherent, just strange. "And do you always travel with a stash of condiments?"

His smirk defined the laugh lines around his mouth. She guessed his age to be thirty-five or -six, a bit older than Steve. "It's a long story. Let's just hope this works."

He knelt again, and she was struck by the sheer maleness of him—the pleasing way the knobby muscle of his shoulder rose from the collar of the sweatshirt and melded into the cord of his neck, the sheen of his hair, close-cropped but as thick as a pelt, the large, well-formed features of his face. And his hands...

Janine shivered again. Square and strong and capable. Mentally she compared them to Steve's, which were slender and beautiful—a surgeon's hands—and wondered what Derek did for a living. But in the next second, she was distracted because those hands were on the verge of smearing a gob of pale yellow goo on her toe. His concentration seemed so dogged, she was overcome by a sense of being taken care of. And it occurred to her that he still hadn't questioned her about her surprise appearance last night. He probably thought she was some kind of sex-crazed kitten, when, in truth, she was a sex-*starved* kitten—er, woman.

He made a disgusted sound in his throat. "People actually eat this stuff?"

"Listen, Derek," she murmured, then cleared her throat. "About last night...*ahhhhhh.*" She couldn't help it—the combination of his hands on her foot, the slippery substance he smeared on her skin and the tingly numbness of her leg made her body twitch and surge.

He seemed not to notice and continued to slather the area around her toe.

"You're probably wondering why I showed up here wearing that, um, costume."

Derek grunted and worked her toe back and forth.

"You see, it was a little joke between me and Steve."
She manufactured a laugh, but dipped her chin and accidentally swallowed a mouthful of cool soapy water,
then came up sputtering.

He looked over his shoulder, then shook his head
as if considering whether to hold her under until she
stopped flopping. God, what about this man turned her
into such a klutz? After shoving his sweatshirt sleeve
up past his biceps, he plunged his hand into the water
and she heard the dull thunk of the pulled plug before
he returned to his greasy task.

The water level began to lower, tickling her as it
drained away, and making her feel even more exposed.
The towel covered her from neck to knees, but just
knowing that the only thing that stood between Derek
and her birthday suit was a layer of wet terry cloth left
a disturbance in her stomach. When the silence became unbearable, she picked up where she'd left off.
"Like I was saying, Steve and I are always joshing
each other." She laughed. "Josh, josh, josh. You know
how couples are," she said, hoping she didn't sound
as inane as she felt.

Derek's arm moved back and forth as he worked
to loosen her toe, then suddenly her foot jerked back,
and she was free.

"Oh, thank you," she said, weak with both relief
and immobility. "I was afraid we'd have to call the
fire department."

Wiping his hands on a towel, he gave her a whisper of a smile. "Do you need a hand getting up?" She
did, but she knew she'd never be able to keep herself
covered in the process. He must have read her mind

because he added, "Don't worry, Pinky, I'll close my eyes."

For some reason, she liked the ridiculous nickname. "Okay." Janine raised her arms for him to clasp, then he closed his eyes and lifted her to her feet as easily as if she were a piece of fluff. Water sluiced from her hair, her body and the towel, which she tried to keep close to her with her elbows, to no avail. The towel fell to the bottom of the tub, and when she put her weight on her foot, it slipped out from under her. She shrieked and Derek responded by scooping an arm around her waist to steady her, jamming her up against his body. Desire bolted through her, although he kept his hands in innocent places. Concern rode over his features, but true to his word, his eyes remained closed.

She clung to his arms—his sleeves really, which were the first handholds she'd been able to grab. Even with her toes dangling a couple of inches off the ground, the top of her head reached only to his collarbone. The soft cotton of his sweatshirt soaked up the water from her breasts pressed against him, and the skin below her navel stung from proximity to the metal button on his jeans. His fingers curved around her waist, hot and powerfully strong, and the male scent of his skin filled her nostrils. Janine's lips parted, and in that instant, crazily, she wanted more than anything for this man to kiss her. Kiss her so she could be indignant, outraged, even insulted that he would think that she, on the verge of being married, would entertain being kissed by someone other than, um…she winced…oh, yeah—Steve.

"Are you okay?" he asked, his eyes still closed.

Other than waterlogged and adrenaline-shot? "I think so," she managed to say. "Just let me down slowly."

Derek swallowed, wondering if she could feel and hear his heart thudding like a randy fifteen-year-old's. Against screaming instincts, he kept his eyes closed. He'd been too long without a woman, he decided, if he could be so easily affected by the accident-prone wife-to-be of a friend. The same woman, he reminded himself, who was responsible for him being detained, sleep-deprived, inconvenienced and very, very wet.

Doing as he was told, he set her down slowly, although it meant her nude body slid down the length of his straining one. The ends of her wet hair tickled his hands as he lowered her, and he held her waist until she had her footing.

"I think I can stand on my own now," she murmured, but he was reluctant to let go. His thumbs rested on the firm slick skin around her navel, and his fingers brushed the small of her back. She was willowy, and lush, like a long-stemmed flower, and it was all he could do not to steal a glance of her in full bloom as he turned to exit the bathroom. She'd come to the hotel in that crazy getup to surprise Steve, and now he couldn't decide if his buddy was the luckiest man alive, or the most cursed.

Derek closed the door behind him, and exhaled mightily to regain control of his libido. He simply could *not* be physically attracted to the loony case in the bathroom, not if they were going to be in close quarters for the next several hours—possibly days—

and especially since she was about to marry a friend of his.

Suddenly some of the words Janine had murmured last night when she thought he was Steve flooded back to him. *I just can't wait any longer. I need to know now if we're good together.* Thunderstruck, he repeated the words to himself. Was it possible that his buddy was about to marry a woman he hadn't yet slept with? That she had come to the hotel with the intention of seducing her groom?

Derek groaned and ran his hand through his hair. If so, that meant the hormones of the shapely woman in the next room were probably raging as high as his. And something else was bothering him. He distinctly remembered seeing Steve rummage in a gray toiletry bag yesterday before he left, but now the bag was nowhere to be found. Derek had a feeling his buddy hadn't spent the night out partying with the other groomsmen.

And while admittedly, Janine Murphy seemed like the kind of woman who attracted trouble, she also struck him as being a little naive, sweetly vulnerable and completely sincere. As a determined bachelor, he was the last man qualified to give advice about getting married, but the very least she deserved was honesty and faithfulness from her partner.

Derek cursed as those protective feelings ballooned in his chest again. What kind of fool was he even to consider protecting Janine from the man she loved? Their relationship was none of his concern. And he had to admit that his newfound attraction to the woman, not to mention his medication, was probably coloring his judgment. So the only solution was to stay as far away from her as he could, while sharing a bedroom.

The bathroom door cracked and Janine's head appeared. "Derek?"

He turned, and his gut clenched. After his best efforts to resist a glance at her while wrestling in the bathroom, her nakedness was revealed in its splendor in the mirror over the vanity, clearly visible from his vantage point. He realized she was completely oblivious to the peep show, and he saw no reason to embarrass her by voicing his admiration for the brown beauty mark on her right hip. His body hardened instantly.

Her smile, conversely, resonated abject innocence. "I found only socks and gym shoes in Steve's bag. Do you have some clothes I can borrow?"

Derek swallowed hard and managed to nod. Janine beamed and closed the door, although he knew the imprint of her slender naked body wouldn't soon be erased from his mind.

Not generally a religious man, he nonetheless recognized his limits as a mortal and muttered a silent prayer for strength.

CHAPTER NINE

JANINE ADJUSTED her borrowed clothes. Derek's gray
sweatpants—the counterpart to his University of Kentucky sweatshirt, she assumed—swallowed her. Sans
underwear, the cotton fleece nuzzled her skin, which
was satiny smooth and warm from her prolonged bath.
Rolled cuffs helped shorten the pants while a draw-
string held the waistband just under her breasts. She
was forced to go braless until Marie or her mother
could drop off reinforcements. Derek's plain black
T-shirt fell to her knees, so she knotted it at her waist
to take up the slack. She gazed at her reflection and
nodded in satisfaction. The shapeless clothes were a
far cry from the costume she'd shown up wearing last
night, which was just the way she wanted it. After
an evening of prancing around like a Frederick's of
Hollywood reject, and after a morning of wrangling
naked in the bathroom, big and baggy was just the
look she needed to keep her body under wraps and her
urges under control. She sniffed a sleeve that fell past
her elbow, then pursed her lips in appreciation at the
mountain-fresh scent—the man used fabric softener,
so he had a sensitive side.

Either that or his mother still did his laundry.

The bathroom was equipped with a blow-dryer,

but she opted to detangle her wet hair with a small comb from Derek's toiletry bag—which she rinsed and dried carefully before replacing—to allow the long strands to dry naturally. She stared at her hair for several minutes, perusing the arrow-straight center part and waist-length style, knowing her hair was hopelessly out of date, while acknowledging it suited her. The color wasn't as blond as it used to be, but she felt no compulsion to lighten the honey-hued strands. And other than having to buy shampoo by the gallon, her long hair was low-maintenance, more often than not secured into a low ponytail with her favorite tortoiseshell clasp. For now, it would have to hang loose.

She wriggled her liberated big toe. Other than some tenderness and a few scratches in the pink nail polish—a gift pedicure from Marie—her toe seemed to have escaped permanent damage from the bathtub incident.

But her psyche, well, that was another story.

Derek Stillman had shaken her. For proof of that revelation, she needed to look no farther than her cheeks. Even in the absence of makeup or lotion, they bore an uncommon blush that marched across her nose and tingled with a fiery intensity. So she was attracted to the man. Okay, make that *wildly* attracted to the man. She had a simple explanation: Didn't it make sense that the sexual feelings she'd brought with her for Steve, she might now be projecting onto Derek?

No, came the resounding answer. It didn't make sense at all.

The body might be a fickle instrument, not caring who or what stimulated it, but the mind should be able to tell the difference between right and wrong. Carrying enough guilt on her shoulders to fill a cathedral ten minutes before Mass, she opened the bathroom door, hoping against hope that Derek would announce the quarantine had just been lifted. Or perhaps discover that her eyes had played tricks on her—her best man wasn't a great-looking, incredibly built specimen with whom she had to share four walls, but a homely, broken-down gnome who would take up residence *under* the bed if they had to spend another night together.

But Derek glanced up from his seat on the end of the bed and dispelled her hopes in one fell swoop with the concerned frown pulling at his appallingly handsome face.

"We're making headlines," he said, gesturing toward the television. Resisting the urge to sit next to him, she hovered a few steps away, riveted to the screen. The tag line on the bottom of the picture read: Quarantine Crisis, Green Stations Resort, Lake Lanier, Georgia. A grim-faced reporter wearing a yellow windbreaker, with a surgical mask dangling around his neck, stared into the camera as he delivered his report.

"A spokesperson for the Centers for Disease Control reports some form of Legionnaires' disease may have broken out among the guests at a resort near Lake Lanier, north of Atlanta, where a quarantine is in effect. An infirmary has been set up in the hotel workout facility to monitor and care for those who have fallen too ill to remain in their rooms, and other measures are being enacted to protect the many, many guests who were taken completely by surprise." The general manager appeared on-screen, holding a microphone with a gloved hand. The interview had been shot through a window.

"The resort enjoys a brisk business this time of the year," Mr. Oliver said. "So not surprisingly, we were booked solid. Including employees, we have around six hundred people inside the grounds, and we're going to do our best to make sure everyone is as comfortable as possible during the confinement period."

Dr. Pedro came on next, his setting similar to Mr. Oliver's. "As of about 5:00 a.m. this morning, approximately four dozen guests were exhibiting symptoms, with three of those cases serious enough to require hospitalization—" The clip of the doctor was cut short, obviously edited, and the reporter's dour face appeared once again.

"The resort has been inundated with calls and deliveries from relatives and well-wishers, but officials asked the media to inform the public that no objects, such as clothing, food or flowers, will be allowed inside the resort. Meals are being prepared in another facility and delivered under the supervision of the CDC." The man lowered his chin for dramatic effect. "Except for CDC personnel, *no one* is allowed to leave or enter the resort, unless, of course, a body needs to be moved to the hospital...or to the morgue." The reporter lifted the surgical mask to cover his mouth. "Reporting live from Lake Lanier. Now back to you in the studio."

Janine rolled her eyes and Derek scoffed, using the remote to turn down the volume. "According to that guy, we should be making out our wills."

She nodded. "I would've liked to hear what the doctor had to say that didn't make it into the news segment. Did he insinuate to you this morning that the situation is worse?"

"Just what you heard on TV. Three people in the hospital, although he said he didn't think their lives were at risk."

His voice was conversational and sincere, his demeanor fatigued. What was it about this man that made her want to touch him? His boy-next-door chivalry? His all-American looks? His aloof attitude? Despite being close to Steve's age, Derek seemed decades more mature. Worry lined his serious brown eyes. Was he more concerned about his health than he let on? She felt compelled to comfort him, to ease the wrinkles from his forehead. Angling her head, she circled to stand in front of him. "How are you feeling?"

"About the same," he said with a shrug.

"Still congested?"

He nodded.

She stepped forward and placed her hand on his forehead. With him sitting and her standing, they were nearly eye to eye. More like breast to eye, although she tried not to dwell on it. His skin felt smooth and taut, and she liked the silkiness of his short bangs against the pads of her fingers. His temperature felt normal, but hers had definitely risen a couple of degrees, even higher when she realized she was standing between his open knees.

Her gaze locked with his and awareness gripped her, electrifying her limbs and warming her midsection. His brown eyes were bottomless, and she realized with a start that she'd always equated dark eyes with thoughtfulness. And sincerity. And comfort. And sensuality.

"You don't have a fever," she whispered, then wet her dry lips. Her hand fell to the muscled ledge of his shoulder, a natural resting place, it seemed.

Something was happening, she could feel it. The energy emanating from his body pulled at her, and she had to go rigid to keep from swaying into him. But his face belied none of the sexual force vibrating between them. His mouth was set in a firm line and his eyes were alert. The only indication that he was affected by her nearness was the rapid rise and fall of his chest.

She lifted her hand to probe the soft area of his neck just beneath the curve of his jaw. He stiffened, but she pretended not to notice. She could best smooth over the awkward moment by continuing to check his vital signs. "Your pulse is elevated."

He exhaled. "I guess I can chalk it up to all the, um…"

"Excitement?" she finished.

"How's your toe?" he asked, effectively changing the subject.

She looked down at her small white feet situated between his two large ones, and experienced a queer sense of intimacy. "Fine," she said. "I never thanked you for rescuing me."

He returned her smile, which made her heart lurch crazily. "Glad to pinch-hit for Steve," he said. Then his smile evaporated and he added, "In that one particular instance."

At the mention of Steve's name, she relaxed, feeling firmly back on platonic footing. "Thanks, too, for the clothes. You're a lifesaver." Impulsively, she leaned forward and dropped a kiss on his cheek. Janine realized her mistake the second she drew away. Derek's mocha-colored eyes had grown glazed and heavy-lidded. The worry lines had fled, and his lips were open in silent invitation. Blatant desire chased reason from her mind. Acting purely on instinct, she lowered her lips to his for an experimental kiss. Just one, she promised herself. One last illicit kiss for comparison.

If indeed he hesitated, it wasn't for more than a heartbeat. His lips opened to welcome hers, and the tide of longing that swept over her left her breathless. Their tongues darted, danced and dueled in a coming together that could be described as anything *but* platonic.

Her knees weakened and she became aware that his hands were at her waist, and her arms around his neck. His taste was as foreign and delicious as exotic fruit, and she wanted to draw more of him into her mouth. Derek angled his head to deepen the kiss and she moaned in gratitude. Pulling her forward, he melded her body to his, and she was conscious of his hands sliding beneath her shirt. He splayed his hands over her shoulder blades, kneading her skin with his strong fingers in long, determined caresses that gave her a glimpse into his body rhythm.

She shivered and might have buckled had he not imprisoned her legs with his knees. Janine reveled in the strength and possession of his touch. She arched her back and rolled her shoulders, then slipped her hands inside his shirt and ran her hands over the smooth expanse of his back, kneading the firm muscle. His guttural sounds propelled her excitement to the highest plateau she'd ever endured. The world fell away around them, and Janine felt completely, utterly safe. She pressed her body against his, sure in the knowledge that he could fuel the flames licking at her body to an all-consuming fire, much more satisfying than her earlier release.

When he stiffened, her first instinct was to resist, but when she heard the knock at the door, she straightened and stepped back, disentangling herself from him. The look he gave her still smoldered from their heated kiss, but he wore his remorse just as plainly.

The full extent of her shameful participation flooded over her. She backed away and clapped a hand over her traitorous mouth, sucking air against her fingers to fill her quivering lungs. If her skin hadn't still burned from his touch, she might not have believed what had just transpired. Regret nearly paralyzed her. What had she done? What had she nearly allowed Derek to do?

He was watching her. She stared at him, at the body she could now call familiar, but she didn't know what to say. Janine suspected, however, that her face reflected her horror at her own behavior.

Another knock sounded at the door. Derek panned his hand over his face, then stood, visibly trying to shake off the effects of their encounter. Her gaze flew to the telltale bulge in his pants that he didn't attempt to hide as he limped a half circle in the room. Hair tousled, shirt askew, and hard for her...Derek Stillman was simply the most devastatingly appealing man she'd ever met. Best man, she corrected. *Her* best man.

She might as well run headlong into a train tunnel while the whistle sounded in her ears.

Realizing Derek was in no shape to answer the door, she cleared her throat and murmured, "I'll see who it is."

"Thanks," he said over his shoulder, his big hands riding his hips as he headed toward the bathroom.

Still reeling, she walked to the door and, through the peephole, saw the general manager standing in the hall. Shot with relief without really knowing why, she swung open the door. "Hello, Mr. Oliver."

A multishelved cart loaded with great-smelling covered trays flanked him. He took in her ill-fitting garb with only a blink and a smile. "Call me Manny, Ms. Murphy."

She felt warmed by the friendly tone in his voice. "Then call me Janine."

The blond man nodded. "Glad to see you're still with us. How are you feeling?"

Shoving a fall of hair away from her face, she pulled a smile from nowhere to hide her shaky emotions. "F-fine."

His penetrating blue gaze seemed all-knowing, but he didn't contradict her. "Mr., um, Stillman, isn't it?"

"Yes," she croaked.

"Mr. Stillman said this morning that you had no symptoms."

"That depends—is irrational behavior a symptom?"

He pursed his mouth, then shook his head slowly. "I don't recall, but I can mention it to the doctor."

She sighed. "Don't bother, I'm fine."

His eyes narrowed slightly, but he didn't skip a

beat. "Good. I've brought breakfast, not a typical resort meal, I can assure you, since our chefs didn't prepare the food, but not bad if you're hungry."

"I am."

The door across the hall opened and Ms. Jiles stepped out, perfectly coifed and wrapped in a coral-colored silk robe. "I heard voices."

At eight o'clock in the morning, the woman was stunning. Janine decided she must have slept in her makeup *and* sitting straight up. But she inclined her head politely. "Maureen Jiles, this is Manny Oliver, the general manager."

He smiled. "I'm delivering breakfast, ma'am."

"Something low-fat, I hope," she said in a voice reserved for lowly help.

"Yes, ma'am," Manny replied smoothly. "We have a vegetarian meal."

"That will do," she said, then turned back to Janine and smiled. "Is your friend Derek up and about?"

Is he ever. "Um, yes."

Maureen appeared to be chewing on her tongue as her face slowly erupted into a mischievous smile. "I thought about Derek all night. I love a good challenge, and I decided I'm not going to let his being gay get in the way."

Manny, setting a tray inside the Jiles woman's door, erupted into a fit of coughing.

Janine, stunned by Maureen's audacity, looked past the woman. "Are you okay, Manny?"

He nodded, facing her, and she could see he wasn't choking at all—he was laughing.

"So, Janine, do you have any suggestions for attracting a gay man?" Maureen asked, obviously warming up to her scheme.

Thrown off balance, Janine shook her head. "Since, to my knowledge, I've never dated a gay man, no, I can't say that I do."

Manny exited the woman's room. "Ms. Murphy, I'm sure Mr. Stillman will be wanting a vegetarian meal," he said, his mouth twitching. "Would you like a traditional breakfast for yourself?"

She sent him an exasperated look with her eyes. "Yes, thank you, one of each."

"And I have the magazine he requested." From a side rack of reading material, he produced a copy of *Victorian Age Decorating*.

Janine plucked the magazine out of his hand. "He will be pleased," she said, injecting a warning note into her voice.

Oblivious to their exchange, Maureen crossed her arms. "Does Derek cut hair? Because I could use a trim."

Manny cleared his throat. "Excuse me, Ms. Jiles, but guests are not supposed to be in each other's quarters."

Maureen stepped back into her room and harrumphed at Manny. "Probably want him for yourself." Then she closed the door with a bang.

Manny looked at her, his mouth drawn back in a wry grin. "Explain."

"It's simple," Janine said in a low voice, taking a tray from him and walking it inside. She glanced at the bathroom door to make sure Derek was out of earshot. "Maureen is a sales rep who calls on the clinic.

And she knows a lot of the same people I do. I had to think of something to keep the gossip down at work, so—" She glanced toward the closed bathroom door, then back to Manny. "I told her Derek is gay."

"Looks like it backfired," he observed. "She's determined to salvage the man."

One lie led to another, she realized. She set the tray on the writing desk and waited for Manny to set down the second one, her eyes tearing up. She was having a nervous breakdown, she was certain.

"Hey, come on now, it can't be that bad." Manny handed her a handkerchief, on which she blew her nose heartily.

"Manny," she whispered, "you see what a predicament I'm in here. No one can know I'm sharing a room with Derek."

"I'm sure all this will be over soon," he said in a soothing voice. "As long as you and Mr. Stillman agree to keep it quiet, who will be the wiser?"

"You're right," she said, sniffing. "It's just that I don't know how much more I can take."

"Is he hostile?" he asked, touching her arm, concern in his eyes.

"Oh, no," she said, waving off his concern. "It's not that." How could she explain her raging feelings about a man she barely knew to a man she barely knew? She gestured to her outfit. "It's the close quarters, no privacy—you know."

Manny studied her face, then gave her hand a comforting pat. "Janine, emotions run high during a crisis, and people can behave in ways that are out of character."

She hugged herself. "You think?"

He nodded. "You have a lot on your mind, with the wedding and all."

Janine sighed. "I guess we'll have to call the whole thing off."

He tipped his head to the side. "You mean postpone it, don't you?"

She straightened her shoulders. "Yes. Of course. Postpone the wedding, not call it off. Of course that's what I meant." A Freudian slip?

"Is there anything I can do to make this situation more bearable?"

"I need clothes and toiletries…and a cot would be nice."

He opened the desk drawer and removed a sheet of stationery and a pen. "We're completely out of cots, but write down whatever else you need and I'll see what I can confiscate from the gift shops."

"Thank you," she whispered, then jotted down a dozen or so items.

He gave her a brief wink before he left, and when the door closed, she felt so alone. Alone like a stone. And accident-prone.

She glanced toward the bathroom door. What was she going to say to Derek about the kiss? How was she going to explain that she was so overcome with lust that she was willing to indulge in a few hours of unfettered sex, despite her being about to exchange vows with a friend of his? What must he think of her? Probably no worse than she thought of herself, she decided, and walked to the bathroom door. Perhaps the words would come if she didn't have to talk to him face-to-face.

Janine rapped lightly on the door. "Derek? Derek, I'm so sorry for what just happened. The kiss was my fault, and I can't give you a good excuse, because I have no excuse." She sighed and leaned her cheek against the door. "Please know that I do love Steve, despite the abominable way I've behaved. If you feel compelled to tell him what happened, I'll understand and I'll accept full responsibility." She closed her eyes. "Thank goodness we stopped when we did."

When the silence on the other side of the door stretched on, she rapped again. "Derek?" No answer. "Derek?" she asked louder. Making a fist, she knocked harder. "Derek, answer me to let me know you're okay." Fingers of panic curled low in her stomach. What if he had grown more ill? What if he'd passed out and hit his head when he fell?

She turned the doorknob, relieved that it gave easily. After cracking the door open, she called his name again, but he didn't respond. Her heart pounded as she inched the door wider, but she didn't see his reflection in the mirror. Janine opened the door and stepped into the bathroom. The shower curtain was pushed back, just as she'd left it—he wasn't there. In fact, the huge mass of man was nowhere to be found.

CHAPTER TEN

THANK GOODNESS the tiny balcony was cast in the shade of the building at this early hour, because he needed to cool off. Derek leaned on the white wrought-iron railing and fought to collect himself, appreciating the view of walking paths, fountain and golf courses, and reproaching himself. He'd never acted so foolishly in his life. Women had never been high on his list of priorities—school, football, work, family and friendship had always taken precedence. Always.

At the age of fourteen, he'd lost his first girlfriend to his younger, but more debonair brother, Jack, and decided shortly thereafter that women weren't worth arguing over. He'd left the brightest flowers for both Jack and Steve, preferring to date quiet, uncomplicated girls who didn't consume him or his energy.

He still preferred the quiet ones. Which was why his infuriating attraction to Pinky—dammit—*Janine* so perplexed him. Not only was the woman the mistress of mischief, but she just happened to be engaged to a man who thought enough of Derek to ask him to be his best man.

Well, granted, he was second choice behind Jack, but still, the least he owed Steve was to keep his hands off his bride. No matter how adorably inept she was, the woman already had a protector—a rich doctor—so she certainly didn't need him, a struggling entrepreneur.

It was his near-celibate lifestyle of late, he decided. He'd been so caught up in trying to locate Jack, and with the goings-on at the ad agency, he hadn't indulged in much of a social life lately. Lenore, the woman he'd been seeing occasionally had moved on to greener pastures, and because he typically didn't believe in casual sex—too many crazies and too many diseases—he hadn't slept with a woman in months.

And the bizarre circumstances undoubtedly contributed to his behavior. The intimacy of the close quarters, and the highly sexual accidental encounters with Janine were enough to test any man's willpower. Plus, he had to admit, Janine was a looker with that mop of blond hair and her too-blue eyes. He grunted when the image of her body reflected in that mirror came to mind. Worse still, the silky texture of her skin was still imprinted on his hands. And that kiss...

The woman was a paradox. One minute she struck him as an innocent, the next, a tease. One minute he was running to help her, the next, he was running to escape from her. He massaged his temples and filled his lungs with morning-sweet air. Gradually, his head cleared and he was able to look at the situation logically. Even if he took Steve and the whole marriage variable out of the equation, Janine Murphy couldn't be more wrong for him or his way of life. She was messy, emotional and erratic. Fisting his hand, he pounded once on the railing with resolve, gratified by the slight echo of the iron vibrating and the dull pain that lingered in his hand. There was nothing like a little space and fresh air for perspective.

The sound of her raised voice inside the room caught his attention, and he jogged back to the sliding glass door. Apprehensive, he opened the door and pushed aside the curtain, then stepped into the room.

Janine whirled mid-yell, her eyes huge. "Oh, there you are. I was worried." Then she gestured vaguely, and added, "I mean, I was afraid you might be feeling bad. Sick, I mean. Feeling sick."

He steeled himself against the quickening in his loins at the sight of her all bundled up in his clothes. He'd have to toss them on the Goodwill pile when he returned to Kentucky. Jerking a thumb behind him, he said, "I stepped out onto the balcony."

She looked past him. "There's a balcony behind all those curtains?"

"Not much of one," he admitted, "but I needed some air." He pressed his lips together, trying to slough off the remnants of their kiss. "I'm sorry—"

"I'm sorry—" she said at the same time.

"—I had no business—"

"—I don't know what came over me—"

"—I mean, you and Steve—"

"—I'm getting married, after all—"

"—and I'm your best man—"

"—and you're my best man."

They stopped and she smiled. Begrudgingly, he returned a diluted version. He didn't know what her game was, or if she even had one, but he was *not* having fun. "We're both under a lot of stress right now,"

he said. "Let's try to get through this quarantine without doing something we'll regret, okay?"

She nodded. "My sentiments exactly."

Silence stretched like an elastic band between
them, and she wrung her hands. "Are you hungry?"
she asked, gesturing toward the desk. "Manny just
delivered breakfast."

"Manny?"

"The general manager."

His stomach rumbled in response. "I could eat."
Glad the initial awkwardness had passed, he crossed
to the desk and lifted a lid from one of the trays, but
scrutinized the assortment of fruit, yogurt and miniature bagels with distaste. "Not much here that'll stick
to your ribs."

She lifted the other lid to reveal eggs, sausage,
bacon and pancakes. "This one's yours."

Finally, something to smile about. "Coffee, too?
Excellent."

He pulled the straightback chair over for Janine,
then scooted the desk close enough to the bed for him
to sit. Faced with the task of having to make conversation over their meal, he used the remote to turn up
the television news station that appeared to be giving
the quarantine good coverage, replaying the clip of the
general manager and doctor every few minutes, and
speculating on how long the guests would be confined.

But no matter how hard he tried to concentrate on
the television, he couldn't shake the almost tangible
energy springing from the woman who sat across from
him, eating a banana of all things. Man, was he hot
for her. As soon as he finished eating, he was going

to take a long, cold shower. "Do you always eat like a bird?" he asked, although the words came out a little more tersely than he'd planned.

She chewed slowly, then swallowed and licked those fabulous lips of hers. "I'm a vegetarian." Pointing a finger at his plate, she added, "You, on the other hand, are courting heart disease with all those fat grams."

"I'm a big guy," he said, frowning. "I have big arteries."

Like she hadn't noticed he was big when they were grinding against each other, Janine thought, practically choking on her last bite of banana. Personally, she liked the way he ate, not wolfishly, but with a gusto that said he was a man who appreciated food, and lots of it. It suited him, the bigness, the heartiness, and hinted of other things he probably did with barely restrained energy. She averted her eyes from his hands and cleared her throat. "I remember Steve mentioning a friend of his who was a college football star. Was that you?"

Derek scoffed good-naturedly. "I played for UK, but Steve was probably referring to Jack. He was the star receiver. I was on special teams, not nearly as flashy a position."

She knew enough about football to know Derek spoke the truth about unsung positions on the field. "If you don't mind me asking, where *is* your brother, Jack?"

He swallowed, then drank deeply of the black coffee in his cup. "I don't have any idea," he said finally, in a tone that said he was accustomed to his brother's absence.

"Did he just...disappear?"

A nod, then, "Pretty much. He tends to drop out of sight when a crisis occurs at the office."

She hadn't even asked Derek what he did for a living. "The office?"

"We own an advertising agency in Lexington, Jack and I."

Janine tried to hide her surprise, but must have failed miserably because he laughed. "Actually, my father started the company, but I went to work there after I graduated. Then when Dad up and died on me a few years ago, I persuaded Jack to help me run things."

Her heart squeezed because she detected true affection in his voice when he mentioned his father. "I'm so sorry for your loss, Derek. Is your mother still living?"

A broad smile lit his face, transforming his features to roundness and light. "Absolutely. She still lives in the home where I was raised. I built a duplex for myself and Jack a few miles away so we could keep an eye on her."

"And so you could keep an eye on Jack?"

After a brief hesitation, he nodded, then made a clicking noise with his cheek. "But he still manages to slip away."

She sensed his frustration with his brother, who sounded like a rake. Derek's few words gave her insight into his life, and she pictured two boys growing up, the older, more serious sibling burdened with the responsibility of looking out for the younger, more unpredictable one. It sounded as if the mischievous Jack had led a charmed life at his brother's expense. "How long since you've heard from him?"

Derek scooped in another forkful of eggs, then squinted at the ceiling. "Two months? Yeah, it was right around tax time."

"And he's done this before?"

He nodded. "Lots of times. But he always comes back."

Intrigued by their obviously close yet adversarial relationship, she said, "And you always welcome him back."

Contrary to the response she expected, his mouth turned down and he shook his head. "Not this time, I don't think. He's been gone too long, and I'm tired of working eighty hours a week to cover for him."

"You're going to hire someone to take his place?"

Derek balled up a paper napkin and dropped it on his empty plate. "Depending on whether or not I land the account I'm working on, I might not have to worry about hiring anyone." His voice was calm, but a crease between his dark eyebrows betrayed his concern.

Setting down her bottled water, she asked, "You might close the family firm?"

He splayed his large hands. "I might have no choice. I've always managed the accounts, the scheduling, and supervised the day-to-day operations, but my father and Jack were the creative minds, and the artists." He smiled. "A person can only do so much with computer clip art."

"Can't you simply hire another artist?"

"Not and still pay Jack."

She angled her head at him. "But why would you still pay Jack?"

"A promise to my father," he said simply, and her

opinion of him catapulted. A man of his word—make that a *poor* man of his word.

"But how can Jack collect his paycheck if he's not around?"

"My mother keeps it for him and pays all his bills—his utilities, his health club membership—just as if he's going to walk back in the door tomorrow." He didn't seem bitter, just resigned.

A mother who doted on her prodigal son, Janine thought. Loath to state the obvious, but unable to help herself, Janine said, "It doesn't seem fair that you would have to sacrifice your livelihood because of your brother's selfishness."

He shrugged, moving mounds of muscle. "Life isn't fair. I'll be fine. I'm just glad I don't have a wife and family to provide for." He pointed to her left hand. "I guess Steve doesn't have to worry about those kinds of things."

She glanced down at her engagement ring, the diamonds huge and lustrous. Funny, but as beautiful as the heirloom was, she would've preferred that Steve give her something smaller, a ring he'd bought for her himself. Or one they'd purchased together. If truth be known, she was still in awe of Steve's family's money, and not entirely comfortable with the concept of being rich. Sure, Steve had worked hard to get through medical school, but a trust fund had covered his expenses, so when he completed his residency, he hadn't faced the enormous loans like most med students. And herself.

Steve lived in a nice home in Midtown, a very hip area. When they married, he would pay off her school loans, and their lives would be filled with relative luxury, as would their children's.

Assuming they actually had sex and conceived, that is.

"Steve always insisted on the very best," Derek said, pouring himself another cup of coffee.

Was he referring to the ring, she wondered, or to her? Warmth flooded her face. "I suppose I should call him and let him know what's going on," she said, then glanced up quickly. "Well, n-not *everything* that's going on."

One of his dark eyebrows arched as he sipped from the cup dwarfed by his fingers. "Nothing is going on," he said mildly, but enunciated each word.

"Right," she said, standing abruptly. "Nothing. Absolutely nothing. Which is what I'll tell him—that absolutely nothing is going on."

He pursed his mouth. "He has no reason to think otherwise."

"You're right," she said, walking to the phone. "After all, he thinks I'm staying with…what exactly did you tell him?"

"That you were staying with the medical personnel."

"Oh, right. Did Steve say he'd be at home? He took a few days off work for the wedding."

"He said he'd be at his parents'."

Janine exhaled, puffing out her cheeks. "I might as well get this over with." She dialed the number, and just as she expected, his mother answered the phone.

"Mrs. Larsen, this is Janine."

"Janine! Well, isn't this the most perfectly horrible

mess? I have every television on in the house watching for news of the quarantine, and Mr. Larsen is calling a friend of his at the CDC to arrange an immediate release for you."

Janine cleared her throat. "I appreciate Mr. Larsen's efforts," she said carefully, while something deep inside her resented the Larsens' attitude that every situation could be corrected simply by pulling a string. "But in my case at least, since I've been directly exposed to the illness, I seriously doubt that they'll make an exception."

Her future mother-in-law pshawed. "You'll learn soon how many doors the name Larsen will open for you in this town, my dear. Just let Mr. Larsen handle everything, especially since you're not really in a position to argue, are you?"

Janine frowned. "Excuse me?"

"Well, dear, if you hadn't gone to the hotel, then we simply could have moved the whole kit and caboodle to the club." She tsk-tsked. "If we can get you out by noon, we might still be able to make it work. Oh, Lord, give me strength, I'll be on the phone all day. Janine," she said, her tone suspicious, "why *did* you go to the resort?"

"To, um...to talk to Steve." Her prim-and-proper future mother-in-law was the last person she'd share her marital concerns with, especially since she was certain Steve had been conceived by immaculate conception. "Is Steve there, Mrs. Larsen?"

"Yes, I'll call him to the phone."

As the woman trilled in the background, Janine's

heart banged against her ribs. She heard the indistinct rumble of Steve's voice, then, "Janine?"

"Hi," she said, alarmed that his voice did not overwhelm her with the comfort she craved.

"Are you calling from the hotel?"

"Yes. The quarantine hasn't been lifted yet." A nerve rash pricked at the skin on her chest.

"I guess Derek told you I called earlier this morning."

"Um, yes." She glanced in her roommate's direction. He had risen quietly and was moving toward the bathroom, to give her privacy, no doubt. "Did you have a good time last night?"

"Sure," he said, but guilt tinged his voice. "Just guy stuff, you know."

She fought her rising anger. Had he spent all night watching strippers when he wouldn't even spend one *meaningful* night with her?

"But I know *your* party was rather spirited," he continued in a disapproving tone.

Janine frowned. "How could you know?"

He hesitated for a split second, then said, "Since Marie organized it, I don't have to stretch my imagination."

She smiled in concession. "Well, it was innocent fun. Everyone seemed to enjoy themselves."

"Janine," Steve said, lowering his voice. She could picture him turning his back to shield his voice from eavesdroppers. "What made you go to the resort in the first place?" Irritation, even anger, spiked his tone.

She chewed on her lower lip and glanced toward the bathroom. Derek had turned on the shower. The moment of truth had come, because Steve would never buy the story of her simply wanting to talk. "I thought it was time, Steve."

"Time for what?" His voice rose even higher.

Allowing the silence to speak for her, she sat on the bed and waited for realization to dawn.

"To sleep together?" he hissed.

Janine closed her eyes, since his incredulity was not a good sign. "Yes."

"Janine, we've talked about this—you know how I feel. I want to wait until we're married, and I thought you did, too."

"But Steve, if we're getting married tomorrow, why would one or two nights make a difference?"

"It does," he insisted, sounding as if he was gritting his teeth. "I thought you were a good girl, Janine. Don't disappoint me now."

Warning bells sounded in her ears. "A good girl? What's that supposed to mean?"

He sighed, clearly agitated. "You *know* what I mean. Someone who will do the family name proud."

She was stunned into silence. Panic clawed at her. "Janine?"

He hadn't said anything about love, respect or honor. Did he simply want a virgin to take on the good family name of Larsen? A lump lodged in her throat at her own gullibility.

"Janine?" Desperation laced his voice. "Janine, honey, you know I love you. By waiting until our honeymoon, I thought I was doing the honorable thing."

But she heard his words through a haze. The honorable thing—but for an honorable reason? Nausea rolled in her stomach. "Steve, I...I have to go."

"Dad will get you out of there soon, Janine," he said. "Then we can talk."

"Yes," she murmured. "We do need to talk, Steve."

"I'll call you after Dad makes the necessary phone calls," he said, back to his congenial self, their disagreement already smoothed over in his mind. "What room are you staying in?"

"Um, the health club has been turned into an infirmary," she replied truthfully, but evasively. "But it's a madhouse. If you need to talk to me, call and ask for the general manager, Manny Oliver. He knows how to reach me."

The shower in the next room shut off, and Derek's tuneless whistle reached her ears. She closed her eyes against the sexual pull leaking through the keyhole. *Not now.*

"Oh, and Janine, check in on Derek when you can," Steve said. "I feel better just knowing the two of you are there together."

CHAPTER ELEVEN

Dad is still working his contacts at the CDC.
Don't worry, this mess will be over soon.
Love, Steve

JANINE'S SHOULDERS DROPPED in relief as she stared at the handwritten note, then she raised a smile to the messenger standing beside her in the hallway.

Manny seemed surprised at her reaction. "Gee, the message didn't sound like such great news when I took it over the phone."

"Oh, but it is," she assured him.

Looking perplexed, he said, "But not if your fiancé is trying to get you out of here."

Janine glanced guiltily over her shoulder where she'd left the room door slightly ajar. She pulled the door closed and lowered her voice. "I, um…could use some time to sort through a few things."

He nodded thoughtfully, then crossed his arms. "Since I've been away from Atlanta for a couple of years, I didn't connect with the name Larsen at first. I checked the catering records to be sure—your future father-in-law is the vice-mayor."

She nodded. "Lance Larsen."

"The champion of the Morality Movement."

"Yes." The Morality Movement was a group of conservative individuals in Atlanta who had formed to banish prostitution and crack houses in a particularly seedy part of town. But once they'd made headway, the group had moved on to more controversial practices, and in the process, had propelled Lance Larsen to one of the most recognizable personalities in the city. Steve's father had run on the platform of being a family man with solid southern values, and had won the election by a nose.

"I know the man," Manny said, reclaiming her from her muse. "Very right wing. He and I clashed a time or two during rallies in my youth." He smiled, although the mirth didn't quite reach his eyes. "Is the son anything like the senior Mr. Larsen?"

Janine shook her head. "Steve has some of his father's traditional values, but he's much more openminded." But she stopped before the echo of her own words had died. Was Steve really more open-minded, or was it simply the persona he had perfected? "He's... a surgeon," she murmured, then caught Manny's gaze, which was crystal clear and reflected her own revelation. What did Steve being a surgeon have to do with anything that truly mattered?

But her new friend let her off the hook, his mouth softening into a smile. "A surgeon, huh? Sounds like a real catch."

She nodded slowly.

"And I understand now why you wouldn't want word of your accidental and unfortunate sleeping arrangements to get back to the Larsen family." He tilted his head and his eyes probed hers. "After all, they might jump to some crazy conclusion about you and Mr. Stillman."

Janine blinked once, twice. "Manny, I...I think I'm in over my head and I don't know what to do."

He exhaled, then smiled sadly and clasped her hand between both of his. "There's only one thing you *can* do when you're in over your head, sweetheart."

"What?" she whispered.

"You have to cut anchor." He nudged her chin up a fraction of an inch with his forefinger before giving her an encouraging wink, then turned on his heel.

"Manny," she called after him. He looked back, and she gestured to the shopping bag of goodies he'd brought her. "Thanks. For everything."

He inclined his fair head, then disappeared around the corner.

Janine hesitated long enough to scan the bright yellow tag on the doorknob which indicated an occupant remained symptomatic. From her point of view, she could see only one additional yellow tag, on a door at the end of the hall. She frowned at Maureen Jiles's empty doorknob. Apparently the woman was still kicking.

Uneasy about returning to the tension-fraught room, she nonetheless picked up the shopping bag and elbowed open the door. Derek glanced up from the desk where he'd been sitting for the past several hours, but immediately turned his attention back to his laptop computer screen.

Setting the shopping bag on the end of the bed, Janine strove to quiet the emotions warring within her. Since she'd talked to Steve this morning, she and Derek had retreated to separate areas of the room and, except for a few words exchanged when their lunch had been delivered, they had maintained conversational silence by mutual consent.

She'd passed the time playing solitaire and performing yoga exercises, exasperated to learn that when she stood on her head he was just as handsome upside down. She pretended to watch television, when in fact she'd absorbed little of what flashed across the screen. Instead, she had replayed in her mind scenes from her relationship with Steve, from meeting him on her first P.A. job to his romantic proposal six months later at the most exclusive restaurant in Atlanta. All told, she'd known him for one year.

Had she been so swept away by Steve's charming good looks and his position and name that she'd fallen in love with the image of him? A stone of disappointment thudded to the bottom of her stomach. Not disappointment in Steve, of course, but in herself. Was she so anxious to share her life with someone that she had sacrificed the chance of finding a man who, who…m*oved* her?

Involuntarily, her eyes slid to Derek, who looked cramped and uncomfortable sitting at the froufrou desk and jammed into the stiff chair. Frustration lined his face, and his dark hair looked mussed by repeated finger-combing. He winced, then ripped yet another sheet of paper from a legal pad, wadded it into a ball and tossed it toward the overflowing waste can at his knee. His face contorted, then he snagged a tissue from a box and sneezed twice, his shoulders shaking from the force. The crumpled tissue landed in the trash, displacing more yellow balls of paper. When he rubbed at his temples and groaned, a pang of sympathy zipped through her.

"You're feeling worse, aren't you?"

With head in hands, he glanced over at her, then closed his eyes and nodded.

"Have you been taking the antibiotics Dr. Pedro gave you?"

He nodded again without lifting his head.

She crossed to the desk, itching to touch him, but determined not to. "Are you running a fever?"

Straightening, Derek said, "No, my temperature is fine. It's the congestion that's so annoying." He massaged the bridge of his nose and winced.

Janine peered closer at his face, his red nose, his bloodshot eyes, and a thought struck her. "Derek, do you have allergies?"

His mouth worked side to side. "None that I know of."

She glanced around the room, at the vases of resort wildflowers on the desk, the dresser, the entertainment center. Thanks to her claustrophobia, every window was flung wide to allow a cool breeze to flow through the room. She walked to the balcony door and pushed aside the curtain, then squinted into the sun. Sure enough, tiny particles floated and zipped along on the wind. On the concrete floor of the small balcony, sticky yellow granules had accumulated in the corners. *Pollen.*

Every flower in Georgia was having sex—visitors' noses beware.

When she looked back to Derek, he was reaching for another tissue. And she was starting to think his symptoms were completely unrelated to those of the guests who were hospitalized. Circling the room, she closed and secured every window and glass door.

"I thought you said the open windows would help prevent your panic attacks," he said.

"Maybe so," she replied. "But we have to get the pollen out of this room, or you'll never feel better."

He scoffed. "I told you, I've never had allergies."

"Have you ever been to Atlanta in June?"

"No."

"Then there could be something seasonal in the air, or a combination of somethings, that might have triggered unknown allergies. Especially if your immunity is down from stress."

"Stress? What's that?"

She smirked and picked up the phone, then dialed the front desk. "Mr. Oliver, please. This is Janine Murphy." A minute or two passed, during which Derek leaned back in the chair and rubbed his eyes. "You really shouldn't do that," she admonished.

He stopped and frowned in her direction.

Manny's voice came on the line. "Janine?"

"Manny, hi. I need another favor."

"Anything within my power."

"Would you send someone up with a vacuum cleaner—I'll need all the attachments—and ask them to take away the vases of flowers that sit in the hall?"

"Sure thing. What's going on up there?"

"Well, I'm not certain, but I think Derek's symptoms are more related to our resident foliage than our resident bacteria."

"Allergies?"

"Maybe. His blood tests should be back by now, and would rule out the bacteria the other guests acquired. Would you ask Dr. Pedro to come back and reexamine him when he gets a chance?"

"Will do."

Janine thanked him and hung up the phone, then turned the air-conditioner fan on high.

Derek folded his hands behind his head and made an amused noise. "So you think I'm not afflicted with the plague after all?"

She directed a dry smile across the room. "Some people with allergies say it's almost as bad." With a vase of flowers in either hand, she headed toward the door.

He stood and crossed to open the door. Stepping into the hall, he turned and reached for the vases, but she pulled back. "I'm trying to help you here."

A noise sounded in the hall behind him. Janine peered out over top of the flowers to see Maureen Jiles bent at the waist, her shapely rear end stuck straight up in the air as she set a food tray on the floor. The woman straightened and beamed in Derek's direction. "Well, well, well. We meet again."

Janine frowned. "Meat" was more like it. Maureen's voluptuous curves were barely contained in a silver lamé bikini top. A sheer black wrap miniskirt laughingly covered the matching bottoms. Her deeply tanned legs were so long, they appeared to extend down through the carpeted floor. Her jet hair was held back from her face with a metallic headband, and her skin was so well greased, Janine marveled that the woman hadn't congealed. Next to the sun diva, Janine felt like a...well, a boy.

Beside her, Derek had apparently been struck dumb.

"I see you haven't yet fallen ill." Janine crinkled her nose against the leaf tickling her cheek, wondering how long Maureen had been standing butt-up in the hallway hoping Derek would open the door.

Maureen finally looked her way. "Surely you're not getting rid of all those lovely flowers!"

"Derek seems to be allergic," she replied.

"Would you like them for your room?" Derek asked, rankling Janine, although she couldn't identify why. After all, the flowers would otherwise be wasted.

Maureen's smile rivaled the Cheshire cat's as she devoured Derek with her eyes. "That would be lovely. Won't you bring them inside and help me arrange them?"

"I don't think we're supposed to be in each other's rooms," Janine interjected.

"Oh, just for a minute," the woman pleaded to Derek. "I'm having trouble with a stuck window."

He looked at Janine and shrugged. "Allergies aren't contagious."

"I could be wrong about the allergies," she whispered. Besides, there was no telling what kinds of creepy-crawlies he could catch from *Maureen.*

"But I'm *so* good at getting things unstuck," he whispered back, sounding like a teenage boy making excuses to help the divorcée across the street.

Janine frowned and shoved the vases into his hands. "Take your time."

He carried the vases into the woman's room while Janine stood rooted to the spot. Maureen gave her a little wave through the opening in the door before she closed it behind them.

Absurdly miffed, she marched back into the room, gathering up two more vases of flowers, then set them in front of the woman's door. Maureen's throaty laugh sounded, and Janine harrumphed. But unable to stem her curiosity, she leaned over and pressed her ear against the door.

The low rumble of Derek's voice floated to her, then Maureen's laugh, then his own surprisingly rich laugh. The phony—he'd barely cracked a smile since she'd met him, much less out and out laughed.

"It works better if you have a juice glass."

Janine jumped, then spun around to see Manny watching her with an amused expression, holding a vacuum cleaner.

She smoothed her hands down over her hips, displacing lots of baggy fabric. "I was just, um, checking to see if Ms. Jiles is okay."

Another burst of his and her laughter sounded from behind the door.

One side of Manny's mouth drew up. "She sounds fine to me."

Janine lifted her chin. "Well…good." With cheeks burning, she crossed to her own door that she'd left propped open, and awkwardly waved him inside. "You didn't have to bring up the vacuum yourself," she murmured.

He set the vacuum in the middle of the floor. "I might have sent someone from housekeeping, but there just isn't enough staff to go around."

A pang of regret stabbed her. "You probably haven't had a minute's peace since the quarantine was lowered."

"Not much," he admitted, then gave her a teasing grin. "But your little situation is the *most* entertaining distraction."

She shook her finger at him. "Don't be enjoying this, please."

This time he laughed, covering his mouth. "I'm sorry, Janine, I simply can't help it. This is such a feeling of déjà vu."

"Oh? You have another friend whose wedding was postponed when she was quarantined with her best man?"

"No, each of my female friends have gotten into their own little scrapes."

Untangling the hose-and-brush attachment, she gave him a wry look. "And where are they now?"

He ticked off on his long fingers. "Ellie is married with two impossibly gorgeous little girls, Pamela is married and her toddler son is a musical prodigy, and Cindy was married a couple of months ago—no kids yet."

Janine bent to the vacuum and unwound the cord, shooting him a dubious smile. "Are you saying you had something to do with all that marital bliss?"

"Well—" he splayed his hands "—I do have a perfect record to date."

"Then maybe you should rub my head," she said with a little sigh.

He laughed and helped her untangle the machinery. "May I ask if the robust Mr. Stillman has anything to do with you needing some time to sort things out?"

Fighting with the stiff cord, she broke a nail into the quick, then sucked on the end of her finger. "No."

"No? Or no, I shouldn't ask?"

Her heart galloped in her chest as she reconsidered her response. How much of her sudden uncertainty had to do with Steve's reaction to her final attempt to consummate their marriage, and how much of it had to do with her unexplainable attraction to Derek?

Misinterpreting her silence, Manny moved quietly toward the door.

"Manny."

He turned, his hand on the doorknob.

"Do you see something here that I don't?"

He pressed his lips together and his gaze floated around the perimeter of the room, then landed on her. "I see a woman who's willing to clean a room for a man who's being entertained across the hall." His smile softened his words. "You should at least consider retrieving the beast." Then he was gone.

Confounded by his words, she plugged in the vacuum and flipped the switch. She'd always enjoyed the monotonous, thought-blocking chore, but today as she decontaminated every surface within reach, her mind was far from blank. Images of Derek cavorting across the hall with Maureen kept rising to taunt her. So that was the sort of man he was, she sniffed. Common. Typical. Base. Chasing down any female within range. Their kiss had meant nothing to him, she realized. Not that it should, considering their respective relationships with Steve. But admittedly it galled her to think that what had been such a momentous lapse of character for her had left him quite unfazed.

Her naiveté didn't embarrass her—she would never be able to take sexual intimacy as lightly as most of the people in her generation seemed to, but she did recognize how her virginal perspective could put her at a slight disadvantage. After all, if any part of her decision to marry Steve was based on unrealized sexual curiosity, wasn't that just as misguided as rushing into a relationship founded purely on good sex?

Janine sighed and extended the reach on the brush she was running over the curtains. Would she even be having this bewildering conversation with herself if Steve's best man had been a chuffy married fellow instead of the "robust" Derek Stillman?

A tap on her shoulder would have sent her out of her shoes had she been wearing any. She whirled to see that Derek had returned, and he did not look happy. A flip of a switch reduced the noise of the vacuum to a fading whine.

"Gay?" he asked, arms crossed. "You told that woman I'm *gay?*"

She looked past him to the closed door. "I, um…it seemed like the prudent thing to say."

"The prudent thing to say?" His voice had risen a couple of octaves, and his face was the color of roasted tomatoes. "For whom?"

"Watch your blood pressure," she warned, bending to rewrap the cord. "I told Maureen you were gay for the sake of both our reputations—and for Steve's."

"Really?" He pursed his mouth, his body rigid. "Well, it seems to me that *your* reputation and *Steve's* reputation are safe, and now *I'm* a gay man."

She laughed at his histrionics. "I don't know what you're getting all worked up about—there's nothing wrong with being gay."

"Except," he said crisply, "I'm *not.*"

"Okay," she said, rolling the cleaner up against the wall. "So if you wanted to get it on with Maureen the Man-eater, then why didn't you just tell her you weren't gay?"

"Well, funny thing about denying you're gay after someone else has already told the person you *are* gay—" He threw his hands in the air. "They don't believe you!"

"So? The woman made it clear to me this morning that she's adopted a nondiscrimination policy. She doesn't care if you're gay."

"But I'm *not* gay!"

"But it doesn't matter to her!"

"Well, you know that's another funny thing," he said, pacing. "When a woman *thinks* you're gay, it kind of changes the dynamics."

"Well, excuse me," she said, irritated at herself for trying to make the room more comfortable for him. "If I'd known you were so hot for her, I would have gladly told her you were bisexual!"

"Whoa," he said, holding up his hand. "I am *not* bi. Okay? Repeat, I am *not* bi."

"I know that," she snapped.

"And I'm not *hot* for that, that, that...man predator. I just wanted to get away from *you* for a few minutes!"

Hurt, she stared openmouthed. "Well, it was a mini-vacation for me, too!"

Derek stalked across the room and dropped into the stiff chair in front of the desk, bewildered that this woman could so easily provoke him. He sighed, then pressed out his entwined fingers to the tune of ten cracking knuckles.

"You really shouldn't do that."

He pressed his lips together, then shot a weary look in her direction. "And why not?"

"It's not a natural movement for your body."

"Oh, but I suppose standing on your head *is* a natural movement."

She upended a shopping bag on the bed. "Several other species hang upside down, but none that I know of crack their knuckles."

Derek stared at her, his knuckle-cracked fingers itching to wring her tempting little neck. The woman was absolutely relentless, not to mention oblivious to how she affected him.

"I had Manny bring you some shaving cream," she said, waving a small can.

"I hope he brought *you* a razor," he said, slanting a frown across the room.

"You," she said, pointing, "are contrary."

At the sight of that little finger wagging, his blood pressure spiked again. "Well, excuse me," he said, tapping a key to bring his blank laptop screen back to life. "I'm sort of stuck in a quarantine in Atlanta, with a friend of mine's accident-prone bride, for God only knows how long, while a client in Kentucky sits patting his Flexisole wing tips." He shoved both hands into his hair, leaned his elbows on the desk and stared at the trio of bee by-products that were supposed to take his company into the millennium. "I'm a little stressed here," he croaked.

Suddenly his antagonist was behind him, her sweet breath on his neck. "You know, Derek," she murmured. "I just might be able to help."

CHAPTER TWELVE

JANINE COULD HELP his stress? Derek tensed for her touch. Part of him shouted he absolutely should *not* allow her to rub his shoulders, while the rest of him clamped down on his inner voice. Her right hand drifted past his ear and he fairly groaned in anticipation. But when she reached around to pluck up one of the containers of honey, he frowned and turned to face her.

She was studying the label, her lips pursing and unpursing. "Your client is Phillips Honey?"

"Potential client. You've heard of them?"

"Nope."

His shoulders fell. "Neither has anyone else."

"Bee-yoo-ti-ful honey?" she read, then made a face. "I hope that wasn't your idea."

Derek smiled and shook his head. "No. The CEO is shopping for a new ad agency."

"With a slogan like that, I can see why."

"I'm supposed to meet with him Monday. He's looking for a new label, a new slogan, a new campaign— the whole enchilada."

She shrugged. "So what's the problem?"

"Other than the fact that I might still be *here* on Monday?"

Janine nodded a little sheepishly.

"Well, excluding Winnie the Pooh, honey isn't exactly in demand these days."

"Oh?"

He gestured toward her. "Do *you* put honey on your toast in the morning?"

She shook her head. "Not typically."

"Drizzle it over homemade granola?"

"Nope."

"Dip your biscuits in a big warm pot of it?"

"Uh-uh."

"See? People our age simply aren't buying honey at the grocery store every week." His hand fell in defeat.

"You're right," she said. "I buy my honey at the health food store."

He swung back in surprise. "Really? So you do eat honey?"

"In various forms. I specialize in homeopathic medicine."

He squinted, searching for the connection.

Her smile was patient. "Treating symptoms with remedies from natural ingredients whenever possible. Honey is one of my favorites."

His interest piqued, he turned his chair around to face her. "To treat what?"

"Allergies, for one," she said, leaning forward to tap his nose with her finger.

The gesture struck him as almost domestic, and it warmed him absurdly.

"Bees make honey out of pollen," she continued, "and ingesting minute amounts of local pollen helps build immunity."

Dubious, he angled his head at her.

Janine sat on the bed facing him, still cradling the pint of honey in her hands. "It's the same concept that allergy shots are based on," she said simply.

He nodded slowly, but remained unconvinced. "So, what else is honey good for?"

Her pale eyebrows sprang up as she presumably searched her memory. "Minor arthritis pains, insomnia, superficial burns, skin irritations...among other things."

A red flag sprang up in his mind. "You mix up your own remedies and sell them to your patients?" Janine Murphy, Quack—the image wasn't much of a stretch.

A musical, appealing laugh rolled out. "No, I just encourage patients to read up on the benefits of natural foods. So instead of pushing honey as an indulgent, fattening topping for a big ol' plate of flour and lard, maybe Phillips should tap into its more healthful uses."

He held up the honey butter. "Like freeing stuck toes from bathtub faucets?"

The rosy tint on her cheeks made her look even more endearing, if possible. Derek felt an unnerving tingle of awareness that drove deep into his chest, shaking him. This mushrooming attraction to Janine was downright baffling. Certainly she was a great-looking woman, but he came into contact with attractive women on a daily basis, and he'd never before lost track of a conversation.

What *had* they been talking about?

He glanced down at the container in his hand. Oh, yeah, honey, the medicinal panacea for the new century. Derek cleared his throat, determined to focus. "Isn't it dangerous to make medical claims?"

She lifted one shoulder in a half shrug. "The medicinal uses for honey are as old as medicine itself. It should never be given to infants, and diabetics have to exercise restraint, but otherwise, it's perfectly safe. Some people swear by honey, just like some people swear by garlic or vinegar to boost general health." After averting her eyes, she added, "One male patient of mine insists that bee pollen and honey have improved his sex drive."

Derek had to swallow his guffaw. "And you?"

She nodded. "I have a teaspoon in my morning tea."

Derek swallowed. Even as his body responded to her nearness, his enthusiasm for Janine's ideas began to shrivel. He could picture himself in front of stodgy Donald Phillips, presenting his idea for a new slogan: Have Phillips Honey for Breakfast, Then Have *Your* Honey for Lunch.

Suddenly her eyes flew wide. "Not that it's improved *my* sex life," she added hastily. Her skin turned crimson as she clamped her mouth shut.

Despite his best efforts, Derek felt a smile wrap around his face. Perhaps honey was her secret. From the scant time they'd spent together, he'd learned two things about Pinky—she attracted trouble, and she oozed sex. From every tight little pore in her tight little bod. "Then I guess we're in trouble if we need a testimonial," he teased.

She pressed her lips together, eyes wide, looking as innocent as a pink bunny rabbit. Feeling like a lecherous old man, Derek shifted uncomfortably in his chair and cast about for a safer topic. "What do you think about the packaging?"

Janine smoothed a finger over the plain black-and-white label, working her mouth back and forth. "I like the simplicity, but it covers too much of the container."

He lifted an eyebrow.

"If the honey is pure, the color will sell it," she explained. "I like to see what I'm buying."

"Fine, but then where would we print all those new-fangled uses, Doc?"

"On the website," she said with nonchalance, then handed him the honey. Their fingers brushed, but she must not have felt the electricity because she stood and returned to sorting through the pile of items she'd dumped out of the shopping bag, as if nothing had transpired.

On the website...of course. Not that Phillips had a website, or even a desktop computer, for that matter, but someone had to drag the man out of the Dark Ages. Derek jotted down a few notes on the legal pad.

"And what about changing the name?"

He glanced up. "Excuse me?"

"The name," she said, tearing the tag off a pair of yellow flip-flops. "Phillips. It's not very buyer friendly, at least not for honey."

He stuck his tongue in his cheek, rolling around her observation. "But it's the man's name."

"What's his first name?"

"Donald."

She made a face. "What's his wife's name?"

Derek shrugged. "I have no idea."

"Daughters?"

He started to shake his head, then remembered that Phillips had bragged about his daughter's equestrian skills. Heather? No. Holly? No. "Hannah," he said as the name slid into place.

"Perfect," she said, dropping the brightly colored shoes to the floor and sliding her pink-tipped toes into them. Then she spread her arms as if presenting a prize. "Hannah's Honey."

Creativity flowed from her like water, and she seemed unaware of her talent. With a start, Derek realized who she reminded him of—Jack. Jack, who always needed rescuing from some scrape or another, yet somehow managed to escape unscathed. Jack, who could crank out more creative concepts in one day than Derek could eke out in a month. Jack, who was notorious for his ability to make a woman feel as if she were the most important person in the world, only to disappear before the morning paper hit the porch.

Did she know how she affected him? he wondered. Was her innocence simply a clever act? Was she the kind of woman who thrived on male attention, who flirted with danger? The kind of woman who would delight in seducing a friend of her fiancé's? His mouth tightened. Dammit, the woman probably knew just how adorable she looked swallowed up in his clothes, with clashing shoes and toenails.

Suddenly he realized she was waiting for his response. "I...I don't know how Phillips will feel about changing the name of his product line," he managed to say.

"If sales were booming, I assume he wouldn't be looking for a new agency," she said, holding a lavender Georgia on My Mind T-shirt over her chest. "A new name for the new millennium—what does he have to lose?"

He scoffed, extending his legs and crossing them at the ankles. "You make it sound so easy."

"Well, isn't it?"

"No," he insisted, a bit flustered. Leave it to someone outside the business world to overlook the nuances of wide-sweeping changes.

"I thought you said he was going to change the packaging anyway."

"It's not the same thing—"

The phone rang, and they both stared at it until the second ring had sounded.

"I could get it," she said. "But what if it's Steve?"

"I could get it," he said. "But what if it's your mother?"

Janine relented, leaned across the bed, then picked up the handset. "Hallooo," she said in her best Aunt Bea impression, fully intending to hand off the phone if Steve was on the other end.

"You *must* be sick if your voice is that distorted," Marie said, munching something fresh- and crunchy-sounding—maybe pineapple.

Mouthing to Derek that the phone was for her, she flopped onto the bed facedown. "No, I was trying to disguise my voice."

Crunch, crunch. "Why?"

She sighed. "Long story."

"Great, I just threw in a load of laundry, so I have plenty of time. I got your voice message that the wedding is off."

"Postponed," she corrected, perturbed.

"Whatever. I'm just glad to hear you're still alive. If you believe the news, everyone up there has the African flesh-eating disease."

Janine laughed. Marie could always lift her spirits. "No, it's not that bad, even though a few more guests have fallen ill. Dr. Pedro of the CDC told me the hospitalized patients are responding to antibiotics. I'm hoping we'll be out of here in another day or two."

"Speaking of we," Marie said, her voice rich with innuendo, "how's your roomie? I assume he's still there since Mother was concerned about some *bellman* in your room early this morning when she called."

"You didn't tell her, did you?"

"Of course not, and I made her promise not to call the room constantly."

Janine sighed. "Thanks."

"Well," Marie demanded. "How is Mr. Stillman?"

From beneath her lashes, Janine glanced to the desk where Derek had returned to his computer, tapping away. "Uninteresting," she said in a tone meant to stem further discussion on the subject.

"Is he still sick?"

"There's a good chance his symptoms are allergy-related instead of what the other guests have come down with."

"It has to be tough, sharing close quarters with a virtual stranger," her sister probed, crunching. "An attractive man and an attractive woman, at that."

With a last look at Derek's handsome profile, Janine pushed herself up from the bed and stretched the phone line across the room to the sliding glass door. She opened it, stepped onto the tiny balcony and closed the door to the smallest crack that would accommodate the cord. She drew in a deep breath of fresh air—pollen be damned—relieved for a few minutes of freedom from those four suffocating burgundy walls, and from those two captivating brown eyes. Slowly she exhaled, surveying the peaceful scene below her. Except for the fact that the grounds were deserted, and that two uniformed guards stood chatting at the corner of the building, one would never suspect the resort was under quarantine.

"Sis, are you there?"

Janine snapped back to attention. "Yeah, I'm here."

Marie resumed her munching. "You were about to tell me what you and your hunky best man are doing to while away the hours."

She mentally reviewed the day—getting her toe stuck in the bathtub faucet, nearly having a sexual encounter with Derek, discovering she might not be in love with Steve after all... "Not much going on. We've barely interacted, he and I."

"Oooooooooh. Is he the big, strong, silent type?"

"No. He's the big, strong, mind-his-own-business type—hint, hint."

"So he *is* big and strong."

Janine rolled her eyes. "Marie, enough. What's going on out there?"

"Well, you know Mom—she thinks the quarantine is a bad omen. She's been lighting candles like crazy. I took an extra fire extinguisher over there, just in case."

"Thanks for being my buffer, sis. I just can't talk to her right now."

Marie didn't respond, and she'd stopped chewing. Janine waited with dread for her sister's perceptiveness to make itself apparent.

Her sister clucked. "Are you okay, sis?"

She cleared her throat. "Other than a persistent bout of clumsiness, I'm fine."

"What does Steve think about calling off the wedding?"

"Postponing," Janine corrected her sourly.

"Whatever. He's not giving you a hard time, is he?"

Not knowingly. Misery knotted in her stomach. "No, he knows it can't be helped."

"How much longer do you think they'll have the place under quarantine?"

"I don't know. The doctor told Derek worst-case scenario, two weeks."

The announcement obviously stunned her sister into silence. After a few seconds, Marie said, "Well, you asked for something exciting, and you got it—a quarantine, mixed-up rooms, sleeping with a stranger—"

Janine yanked the phone cord tight and hissed, "I am *not* sleeping with him!"

"Easy, sis," Marie murmured, "else I might think that something *is* going on between you and your best man."

Opening her mouth to shout a denial, she realized she was only digging herself deeper into a hole.

"Speaking of which," Marie continued, "where *did* you sleep last night?"

"If you must know, I slept in the bathtub." She held the phone away from her ear until Marie's laughter petered out.

"Whew, that's a good one! So doesn't this guy have any manners?"

"He fell asleep in the bed first, while I was trying to calm down Mother."

"So? You put a pillow in the middle and lie down on the other side."

"Except he was naked."

"Okaaaaaaaay," Marie sang, ever openminded. "And that would be because...?"

"Because he wasn't wearing any clothes."

"Okeydokey," she said in an accepting tone. "Speaking of clothes, what are you doing for them?"

"He loaned me a few things."

"He being Derek?"

"Yes."

"You're wearing the man's clothes?"

"Marie, for God's sake, am I talking to myself here?"

"Is this guy on the up-and-up?"

At least once today, she thought wryly. But she recognized concern in her sister's voice when she heard it, and right now, Marie needed some peace of mind. "He's a decent guy, sis. A little uptight, but decent."

A knock on the sliding glass door spun her around. Derek slid the door open, his expression unreadable as he jerked his thumb over his shoulder. "You might want to see this," he whispered.

She covered the mouth of the phone. "What?"

"It's Steve. He's on television."

CHAPTER THIRTEEN

"WE HAD TO POSTPONE our wedding that was scheduled to take place here at the resort," Steve was saying, looking grim, but perfectly groomed in his country-club casual garb. He stood at a slight angle, the Green Stations Resort sign visible just over his left shoulder.

"So your fiancée is trapped inside the resort?" an off-camera male voice asked.

Steve crossed his arms and nodded gravely. "That's correct."

"And do you know if she's ill, Dr. Larsen?"

"The last time I spoke with her, she was feeling fine, but she's a physician's assistant and could be exposing herself to infected guests even as we speak." He was incredibly photogenic, she acknowledged, his white-blond hair cropped fashionably short on the sides, longer on top. Funny, but she'd never noticed the petulant tug at the corners of his mouth.

"Are other members of your wedding party confined at the resort?"

Steve hesitated for a split second. "My best man."

"Your bride and your best man are locked up together?" The reporter chuckled.

Clearly distressed, Steve held up a hand, as if to stop the man's train of thought. "Not *together* together, as in the same room." He laughed, a soft little snort. "That would be unthinkable."

Guilt plowed through her, leaving a wide, raw furrow. She glanced at Derek and he was looking at her, one eyebrow raised.

"I understand you actually had a room here, sir. How did *you* escape the quarantine?"

He sighed heavily. "I left the property for a medical emergency unrelated to the resort, and when I returned, the quarantine was already under way."

Janine frowned. She'd never known Steve to blatantly lie, although she understood his unwillingness to say he'd been out all night partying. Of course, she'd been lying like a rug herself lately.

The reporter made a sympathetic sound. "I assume you're going to reschedule the wedding as soon as possible."

"Absolutely," Steve said, then looked directly into the camera. "This is for the future Mrs. Steven Larsen. Sweetheart, if you're watching, remember how much I love you." He winked, and her heart scooted sideways.

The camera switched to the reporter. "So, a cruel twist of fate is keeping the fiancée of Dr. Steven Larsen confined with the doctor's best man."

Janine squinted, clutching the hastily hung-up phone.

"As a result, the vice-mayor's son's wedding has been canceled."

"Postponed," Janine muttered.

"Meanwhile, there seems to be no end in sight to the quarantine now in effect at the Green Stations Resort. This is Andy Judge. Now back to you in the studio."

The anchorwoman came on-screen. "Thank you,

Andy. Keep us posted." A small smile played on her face. "Stay with us for continuing coverage of…'The Quarantine Crisis.'" A menacing bass throbbed in the background as the news faded to a commercial.

Janine gaped at the screen.

"Something tells me Steve's father is not going to like this," Derek said.

A knock sounded on the door, kicking up Janine's pulse. In two long strides, Derek reached the door and stooped to look through the keyhole. "It's Dr. Pedro," he said, then stepped back and swung open the door.

"Mr. Stillman, you requested another examination?"

Derek looked in her direction, then back to the doctor. "Janine seems to think I might be suffering from allergies instead of an infection."

Dr. Pedro walked inside and set his bag on the foot of the bed. "Well, let's take a look, shall we?"

She knew she should stay and find out as much about the status of the quarantine as possible, but Janine swept the items Manny had brought her into the shopping bag and escaped to the bathroom to think. She closed the door and dumped the contents of the bag onto the counter, then dropped to the vanity stool, sorting toiletries from souvenir clothes. Bless Manny's heart. In addition to necessities, he'd brought her a single tube of pink lipstick, a nice quality hairbrush and a package of simple cotton underwear.

When the items had been stacked, folded and stored away, Janine sighed and stared at herself in the mirror. Her fingers jumped and twitched involuntarily. Nerves, she knew. Entwining her fingers, she stretched them out and away from her, the first time she'd ever felt compelled to crack her knuckles. One knuckle popped faintly, shooting pain up her hand, and the other fingers emitted a dull crunching sound, which made her a bit light-headed.

She'd never been so scared in her life. Nothing was more terrifying, she realized, than thinking you knew yourself, only to discover an alien had invaded your body and mind. The real Janine Murphy wouldn't be second-guessing her marriage to one of the most eligible men in Atlanta. The real Janine Murphy wouldn't be entertaining kisses from a strange man and allowing his presence to drive her to distraction. The real Janine Murphy wouldn't be lying to practically everyone she knew about her humiliating circumstances.

She squinted, hoping to find answers to her troubling questions somewhere behind her eyes, and found one.

The real Janine Murphy wouldn't be lying to herself.

When she'd seen Steve on the television screen, she'd witnessed a spoiled, polished, self-absorbed man putting on a show for the cameras. Not a single time during Steve's interview had he even mentioned her name, referring to her instead as *Mrs. Steven Larsen.* Granted, his defensive reaction on the phone to her clumsy attempt at intimacy had left a bad taste in her mouth, but she was starting to recognize a disturbing pattern in his behavior that she hadn't seen before— or rather, hadn't wanted to see.

Steve was more interested in her state of womanhood than in her as a woman. For his family name.

For his father's reputation. Heck, maybe even for some kind of deep-seated territorial macho urge. None of which boded well for marital happiness.

From the other room, she heard the sound of the door closing. Dr. Pedro had left, which meant that once again she was alone with Derek. Alone for— how had he put it?—for God only knows how long. A silent groan filled her belly and chest, then lodged in her constricted throat.

She'd have to be dense not to recognize the sexual pull between them. Marie had been telling her stories about electric chemistry, tingly insides and throbbing outsides since they were teenagers, but this was the first time Janine had experienced how a physical attraction could override a person's otherwise good judgment.

A bitter laugh escaped her. Override? More like trample.

Janine's shoulders sagged with resignation because, in the midst of her general confusion, one conclusion suddenly seemed crystal clear: she simply couldn't marry Steve, at least not the way things were between them, not the way things were between her and Derek, even if it was only in her mind.

Regardless of her enigmatic feelings, she wasn't about to drag Derek into the melee. After all, he and Steve were friends long before she came into the picture. Besides, Derek would probably laugh at the notion of her putting so much stock in her physical attraction to him. It was different for men, she realized, but she couldn't help her strong, if quaint, tendency to associate sex with deep emotional feelings. Which was precisely why she found her reaction to Derek so disturbing. If she were truly in love with Steve, she wouldn't have been tempted by Derek's kisses.

Would she?

She heard the room door open and close again, and wondered briefly if Derek had gone to try to set things straight with Maureen the Machine.

A faint rap sounded at the bathroom door. "Janine, our dinner is here."

The split second of relief that he hadn't left the room was squelched by the realization that the sound of his voice had become so, so...welcome. Resolved to be cool and casual, despite her recent revelations, she pushed herself to her feet.

DEREK LEANED against the window next to the desk with one splayed hand holding open the curtain and comparing the vast, sparkling horizon to the south to the sparse, more rural skyline he'd left behind. The remnants of daylight bled pale blue into the distant violet-colored treeline, broken up with splashes of silver and light where progress encroached on the north side of the city. He sipped just-delivered coffee, then winced when the hot liquid burned his tongue.

He deserved it, he decided. For kissing an engaged woman. *Steve's* engaged woman. His pal was a bit on the uppity side, and he questioned his commitment to Janine, but seeing his face on TV, hearing him say he loved her was like a wake-up call to his snoozing sense of honor.

No matter how attracted he was to the woman, he'd simply have to keep his damn hands to himself, and pray that she did the same. She walked up behind him, flip-flops flapping, and he turned slowly, setting his jaw against the onslaught of desire that seemed to accompany every glance at her over the past few hours.

"What did Dr. Pedro have to say—*aarrrrrrrhhhhh!*"

Stumbling over the toe of one of her rubber sandals, Pinky fell forward, clutching the air. Reaching out instinctively, he grabbed her by the upper arm, managing to steady her with one hand before he felt the white sting of hot coffee on his other hand. He sucked in sharply and slammed the cup down on the desk, sending more scalding liquid over his thumb and wrist. He grunted and made a fist against the pain. Before he knew what was happening, Janine had grabbed his forearm and thrust his hand into the partially melted bucket of ice sitting next to their covered food trays.

"Aaaah" he moaned as the fiery sensation gave way to chilling numbness.

"I'm sorry," she gasped. "I'm so sorry!"

"It's okay," he assured her, conjuring up a smile. Truth be known, her body pressed up against his and her fingers curved around his arm were more of a threat to his well-being than the burn. "Really, it'll be fine."

Slowly he withdrew his hand, and Janine leaned in close. "No puckering and no blisters."

"Told you," he said, allowing her to turn his hand this way and that.

Clucking like a mother hen, she reached for the container of honey butter and proceeded to gently douse the reddened areas of his hand.

"That stuff will help?"

She used both her hands to sandwich his, spreading the condiment with feathery strokes that sent an ache to his groin. "The honey will soothe, and the butter will keep the skin moist," she said. "But only after the skin has cooled, else the butter will accelerate the burn, kind of like frying a piece of meat."

"Now there's an image," he said dryly.

"Good," she said, wrapping his hand loosely with a white cloth napkin from one of their trays. "Then you'll remember it the next time you burn yourself."

He bit his tongue to keep from blurting that he normally didn't toss his coffee around.

"Thank you, Derek."

Derek frowned at her bent head. She had braided her hair, and the thick blond plait fell over her shoulder, the ends skimming his arm. "For what?"

"For catching me."

He swallowed and reminded himself of his determination to keep his distance. "I would rather your 'something blue' not be a bruise."

Her hands halted briefly, but she didn't look up. "So what *did* Dr. Pedro have to say?"

"He concurred with your diagnosis," he said, nodding toward sample packets of Benedryl. "My blood tests were negative."

The whisper of a smile curved her pink mouth. "What about the quarantine?"

"Another outbreak today," he said. "Four people in this building, and a half dozen in the golf villas."

"Are the cases serious?" she asked, raising her blue eyes to meet his gaze at last.

A man could lose himself in those eyes, he decided, and he couldn't tear himself away.

"Derek?"

He blinked. "Uh, serious enough to maintain the quarantine."

"There," she said, tucking the end of the cloth into the makeshift bandage. After screwing the lid back on the honey butter, she wiped her hands on the other napkin. "I'll call down for some gauze."

She moved like a dancer, limber and graceful even in his big clothes. With an inward groan, he acknowledged his resolve to ignore her was having the opposite effect—he was more aware of her than ever. When she hung up the phone, she turned back to him, hugging herself, looking small and vulnerable. Her expression was unreadable, and the silence stretched between them. At last she looked away, her gaze landing on a stack of pillows and linens.

"I had those brought up," he said. "I'll sleep on the floor tonight and let you have the bed."

She stared at the linens as if mesmerized. What was going on in her head?

Derek's mind raced, trying to think of something to say to ease the soupy tension between them. Steve's TV interview had shaken her, that much was obvious. Was she worried he was going to tell Steve about their near lapses? That her future with the wealthy Larsen family was in jeopardy?

"I'm starved," he said with a small laugh, gesturing to their covered trays.

Janine walked over and picked up a bottle of springwater. "Go ahead, I'm going to get some air." She practically jogged across the room, escaping to the balcony. Between his company and her claustrophobia, he supposed she was doing the only thing she could under the circumstances.

Derek stared at the tray. Despite the nice aromas escaping from the lid, he discovered he wasn't starved after all. Not even hungry, if truth be known. He poured himself another cup of coffee—an awkward task with his hand wrapped—and mulled over the events of the past twenty-four hours or so. Funny, but he felt as if he'd come to know Janine almost better than he knew Steve.

Of course, he and Steve had never been quarantined in a room together.

The sexual pull between them confounded him. Was it inevitable that a man and a woman in close quarters would be drawn to each other? In a crisis, even a minor one, did age-old instincts kick in, elevating their urge to seek comfort in each other?

Perhaps, he decided with a sigh. But thankfully, humans were distinguished from other animals in the kingdom by their presumably evolved brain that gave them the ability to act counter to their instincts. He snorted in disgust. They were adults—they could talk through this situation. In the event the quarantine was drawn out for several more days, he'd prefer they at least be on speaking terms.

Setting down his coffee mug—better safe than sorry—he crossed to the sliding glass door. When he saw her standing with her back to him, leaning on the railing, he hesitated for only a second before opening the door and stepping outside.

She turned, her eyes wide in the semidarkness. "You shouldn't be out here."

"I thought we should talk."

"But your allergies—"

"Won't kill me," he cut in. Although he was beginning to think that resisting her might. Her pale hair glowed thick and healthy in the moonlight, and he itched to loosen her braid.

"We could go back inside," she offered, her gaze darting behind him as if she were sizing up an emergency exit.

"No, I realize you're more comfortable in an open space. Besides," he said, joining her at the railing, "it's a nice night."

"Uh-huh," she said, turning back to the view, although he noticed she moved farther down the rail, away from him. Suddenly, she emitted a soft cry, reaching over the rail in futility as her plastic bottle of water fell top over end until out of sight. A couple of seconds later, a dull thud sounded as it hit something soft on the ground.

"With my luck lately, that was probably a guard," she whispered.

Derek laughed heartily, glad for the release. When she joined in, he welcomed the slight shift in atmosphere. "I hope you don't take this the wrong way, but you do seem to be a little accident-prone."

"Only recently," she said softly. "I guess I have a lot on my mind."

After a pause, he said, "Tell me about your family." He was intrigued by the upbringing that had shaped her aspirations.

She shrugged. "Not much to tell. My father is a traveling appliance repairman for Sears. My mother gardens. I have a terrific older sister who's a massage therapist. We all love each other."

Very middle-class, he acknowledged. "How did you meet Steve?"

"On the job," she replied, her voice a bit high. "I work at the clinic in the hospital where he performs surgery."

A stark reminder of his friend's career success and Derek's relative failure. At a time when most men his age were hitting their stride, he was struggling to pay the office electricity bill. He cleared his throat. "Steve certainly has a lot going for him. I can see why you're looking forward to marrying him."

She was silent for several seconds, then pointed with her index finger out over the rail. "See those pinkish lights on top of the hill?"

He squinted. "Yeah."

"That's the gazebo where our ceremony was supposed to take place. Tomorrow."

His heart caught at the wistful tone in her voice. "So you'll reschedule. I have a feeling the hotel will bend over backward to accommodate the Larsens when this is all over."

"No."

"Sure they will," he insisted. "Steve's father will—"

"I mean, no, I'm not going to reschedule the wedding."

CHAPTER FOURTEEN

A LOW HUM OF PANIC churned in his stomach. "Wh-what did you say?"

"I said I'm not going to reschedule the wedding. I'm not going to marry Steve."

Adrenaline pumped through his body. "You're not serious," he said, his chest rising and falling hard.

"Yes, I am."

"But why?"

"That's really between me and Steve, isn't it?"

Anger sparked in his stomach. "Not if it has something to do with what happened between us." He'd messed with her mind by not keeping his hands to himself. He'd ruined not only her well-laid plans, but Steve's, too. "Those kisses didn't mean anything, Janine. We were thrown together in an intimate situation. You're a beautiful woman, I'm a red-blooded guy. People do strange things in situations like this. Things happen, but it doesn't have to change the course of our lives."

"Don't blame yourself, Derek. I'm grateful to you, really."

"Grateful?"

"For helping me realize that Steve and I wouldn't be happy."

"I n-never said that," he stammered, desperate to

redirect her thinking. "In fact, you two make a great couple. If you marry Steve, you'll never want for anything."

"Except a kiss like the ones you and I shared," she said, turning to face him.

"Janine," he murmured, his heart falling to his knees. "It was just a kiss, that's all. A friendly little kiss from a best man to the bride." He tried to laugh, but a strangled sound emerged when she touched his arm. "I think you were right about me not being out here," he said, backing into the corner of the railing. "My throat is starting to tingle."

"Kiss me, Derek," she whispered, following him.

His gut clenched. "Janine, I don't think this is a good idea." But even as his mouth protested, he lowered his head to meet her. Their lips came together frantically, as if they were both afraid they might change their minds. He pulled her body against him, groaning with pleasure as her curves molded to fit his angles. She tasted so sweet, he could have bottled her and sold it. His tongue dipped into her mouth, skating over her slick teeth, teasing every surface, savoring every texture. She inhaled, taking his breath, and he lifted her to her toes to claim as much leverage as possible.

Encouraged by her soft moans, Derek slid his good hand under her baggy T-shirt, reveling in the silky texture of the tight skin on her back. He drew away long enough to loosen the tie on his old sweatpants, marveling in the erotic thrill of removing his own clothes from her lithe body. When the pants fell to her ankles, she stepped free of them. The long T-shirt hung to her knees. He pulled her back into a fierce kiss, and realized with a start that she wasn't wearing underwear. Only a skiff of cotton shirt stood between him and her nakedness.

Wild desire flooded his body, swelling his manhood against the fly of his jeans. Impatiently, he tugged on the makeshift bandage to free his hand and tossed down the napkin. He ran his hand along the cleft of her spine, cupping her rear end, rubbing the sticky-slick honey butter from his hand into her smooth skin. Lifting her against him, he slid his fingers down to the backs of her thighs, curving to the inside. His knees weakened slightly when he felt the tickle of soft curly hair against his knuckles, and the wetness of her excitement under his fingers.

He lifted his head, stunned to a moment of sanity. But she met his gaze straight on, her eyes glazed, but unwavering. When she shuddered in his arms, Derek was lost. He lifted her in his arms and somehow managed to get them back into the room, where he set Janine on the bed. She glanced around the room, uncertainty clear in her expression.

Derek ground his teeth, nearly over the edge for her, but he was determined to give her a chance to change her mind. "The lights," she murmured.

He almost buckled in relief that her concern was modesty, but he shook his head. "Lights on, Pinky, I want to see all of you." With slow deliberation, he lifted the black T-shirt over her head, then swept his gaze over her, exhaling in appreciation.

She was slender and fine-boned, as shapely as a sculpted statue, her limbs elongated to elegant proportions. Her long blond braid nestled between perfect breasts, pink-tipped and lifted in invitation. Her slim waist gave way to flaring hips, her taut skin interrupted only by the divot of her navel. A tuft of dark golden hair peeked from the vee of her thighs. Not trusting himself to speak, he gathered her in his arms and kissed the long column of her neck.

Janine arched into him, plowing her fingers through his hair, urging him lower, to her breasts. Her trembling excitement heightened his own desire, which had already spiked higher than he could ever recall. When he pulled a pearled nipple into his mouth, she gasped, a long and needful sound. As he suckled on the peaks alternately, she clawed his shirt up over his back, running her nails over his shoulder blades, making him crazy with lust. He wanted to take his time to give her pleasure, but her enthusiasm overwhelmed him. He'd intended to leave her breasts only long enough for her to remove his shirt, but she continued to tug and pull at his clothes until he was naked, too.

Janine was speechless with wanting him, her body fairly shaking in anticipation of their joining. Derek's body was covered with smooth defined muscle, lightly covered with dark hair, his shoulders breathtakingly wide, his stomach flat, his erection jutting, his thighs powerful. But his eyes were the most captivating part of him.

Softened with desire, his chocolate eyes delivered a promise of tenderness and finesse...all the things she'd dreamed of for her first time. Pushing herself back on the bed, she reclined in what she hoped was an invitation.

It was.

Derek crawled onto the bed with her, stopping short

to kiss her knees, her thighs. Her stomach contracted with expectation, and her muscles tensed as his lips neared the juncture of her thighs. "Derek," she whispered, half terrified, half thrilled.

"Shh," he whispered against her mound as he eased open her legs.

She surrendered to the languid, rubbery feeling in her limbs, lying back in anticipation of…what? She wasn't sure, but only knew that if Derek was offering, she was taking. But she was unprepared for the shocking jolt of pleasure when his tongue dipped to stroke her intimate folds. Her legs fell open as she momentarily lost muscle control. An animal-like groan sounded in the room and she realized the noise had come from her lips.

She'd never known such intense indulgence, such sensual pampering. His tongue moved up and down, evoking spasms each time he stroked the little knob tucked in the midst of her slick petals. A low hum of energy swirled in her body, coming from all directions, but leading to a place deep within her womb. The loose sensations suddenly bundled together, then grew in force, as if they were trying to escape her body. Lulled into the rhythm set by his skillful mouth, she began to move with and against him. The ball of desire rolled faster and faster until she heard herself screaming for release. Then suddenly, a flash of pleasure-pain gripped her body, lifting her to a plateau of shattering ecstasy, then lowering her with numbing slowness back to earth, back to the bed, back to Derek.

Her body had barely stopped convulsing when he drew himself even with her and claimed another kiss. The musky smell of her own desire shocked her, the sharing of it so intimate. She thanked him with her kiss, pressing her sated body next to his, thrilling at the feel of his hard erection stabbing her thigh. Emboldened by his method of pleasing her, she reached down to gently grasp his arousal. His eyes fluttered closed as he groaned his approval, and she was gratified by the moisture that oozed from the tip. Stroking him with long, gentle caresses, she murmured against his neck, "Make love to me, Derek."

He lifted his head, his desire for her clear in his eyes. "Janine, I don't have protection with me."

"In my coat pocket," she said, thankful for Marie's forethought.

After a few seconds' hesitation, he lumbered to his feet, and was back in record time, ripping open a plastic packet with unrestrained vigor. She watched, riveted, as he squeezed the tip of the rubber, then quickly rolled it over his huge erection.

Weak with anticipation, Janine welcomed him back into her arms. They kissed, with fingers entwined, then he rolled her beneath him. Propped on his elbows, he held her hands on either side of her head, pressing them into the soft mattress with his strong fingers. Locking his gaze with hers, he settled between the cradle of her thighs, easily probing her still-wet entrance.

"Janine," he breathed.

A statement? A question? Heavy-lidded, his eyes glittered dark and luxurious. "Now," she whispered.

He entered her with a long, easy thrust, accompanied by their mingled moan of temporary satisfaction. The unbelievable sensation of him filling her overrode the fleeting stab of pain. He moved within her, slowly at first, and from the look of the muscle straining in his neck, with much restraint. But soon she was ready for his rhythm, urging him to a faster tempo with her hips, and clenching little-used internal muscles.

His guttural noises of pleasure banished any doubts she might have had about satisfying him. Content in the knowledge that what felt good to her also felt good to him, she rose to meet his powerful thrusts, sensing his impending release as their bodies met faster and faster. Suddenly he tensed and drove deep, burying his head in her neck, heralding his climax with a throaty growl of completion.

Holding him and holding on, she rocking with him until he quieted, until his manhood stopped pulsing.

She hadn't known, she marveled. Marie had told her. *Cosmo* had told her. Oprah had told her. But she hadn't known how wonderful intimacy could be with a man she truly cared about.

Janine stiffened at the bombshell revelation, her eyes flying open.

Derek lifted himself on one elbow. "Am I hurting you?"

"No," she murmured. But her chest was starting to tighten, and she recognized the warning signs of a panic attack. "But I need to get up."

He carefully withdrew from her body, but instead of rolling over as she'd expected, he sat up and gently pulled her into a sitting position. "Are you okay?"

She nodded, but the tug on her heart when she looked into his concerned eyes spurred her to change the subject, and fast. "I'm hungry now."

A grin climbed his face and he ran his hand through his hair. "Me too. I'll be right with you."

As he strode toward the bathroom, Janine reached for the T-shirt, then backtracked to the balcony for the sweatpants, her mind reeling.

The night air had taken on a sweeter pungency. Her senses seemed honed as she zeroed in on night birds crooning and insects chirping. Everything was louder, fresher, more vibrant. The world hadn't changed in the last hour, she acknowledged, but she certainly had.

She'd never experienced such physical and emotional intimacy with another person, and the intensity of their union frightened her. She felt vulnerable and exposed because she knew the encounter couldn't have meant as much to Derek as it had meant to her. Her heart squeezed when she thought of his face, his smile, his touch, but she quickly pushed aside her inappropriate response.

She didn't really *care* for Derek, she reasoned. She was only fond of him because, after all, she'd given him her virginity. Of course she would feel attached to him in the immediate aftermath of something so momentous in her life.

But try as she might to calm herself, to distract herself, to convince herself otherwise, the tide of emotions continued to churn in her chest. She wasn't in love with Derek, she admonished herself. That would be irrational. Illogical. And highly irregular.

Stunned, Janine forced herself to dress hastily, but could find only one flip-flop in the dark. She leaned over the railing and peered into the dark. Although she didn't see any flashes of yellow, she caught a glimpse of bright white—Derek's napkin-turned-bandage. Her flip-flop was probably down there somewhere, along with her water bottle. Glancing at her hand wrapped around the railing, Janine stifled a cry of alarm. Along with something else?

DEREK CAREFULLY REMOVED the condom, dutifully checking for tears, especially since his orgasm had been so explosive. He frowned at the slight traces of blood, hoping their sex hadn't been uncomfortable for Janine. Masculine pride suddenly welled in his chest. She certainly hadn't *sounded* uncomfortable. Frankly, her eagerness had surprised him, and just remembering her spirited responses made his body twitch. He could get used to her— He stopped, midmotion and gave himself a hard look in the mirror. He could get used to her...kind of enthusiasm. Ignoring the questions niggling at the back of his mind, he returned to the bedroom and pulled on his underwear. Janine had stepped onto the balcony, probably to fetch her clothes. He stuck his head out to check on her, and his heart lurched when her sobs reached his ears.

Remorse stabbed him. Had he hurt her? "Janine, what's wrong?" Panicked, he touched her arm, prepared to repair whatever damage he'd wrought.

"I lost it," she said tearfully.

"Lost what?" he said, then spotted the sole sandal she held. "Your flip-flop? Sweetheart, don't cry, it's just a—"

"Not my shoe," she said, her tone desperate. "I lost my engagement ring."

CHAPTER FIFTEEN

DEREK SWALLOWED. "You lost your engagement ring?"

Janine burst into tears, and leaned on the railing.

"I noticed it was missing," he said lightly, "but I just assumed you'd taken it off on purpose."

"When?" she asked, grasping his arm. "When did you notice it was missing?"

Derek cleared his throat. "When we were, um, in bed."

She tore back into the room and he followed, then stood back as she skimmed her hands across the top of the comforter, then stripped it from the bed and shook it violently.

"Do you see it?" she asked.

He shook his head, guilt galloping through his chest. "Don't worry, we'll find it. You check that side of the room, and I'll start over here."

Janine nodded, emitting a little hiccup, then fell to her knees, patting the parquet floor. Feeling absurdly responsible, he started looking in the opposite corner, patting small areas before moving on, knowing the ring would not stand out against the busy pattern of the wooden floor. Thirty minutes later, they bumped behinds in the middle, both empty-handed.

"It'll turn up somewhere," he assured her.

"Yeah," she said. "In a pawnshop." Sitting back on her heels, Janine covered her face with her hands. A bitter laugh erupted from her throat. An hour ago she was thinking that telling Steve she couldn't *marry* him would be difficult. Now she'd be able to top that tidbit by confessing she'd also lost his grandmother's heirloom ring. The only silver lining was that the ring was a distraction from her revelations concerning Derek. "Oh my God," she whispered, rocking. "Oh my God."

A knock on the door startled her so badly, she jumped. Derek yanked up his jeans and shirt and headed back to the bathroom. Janine dragged herself to the door, but her spirits rose when she saw Manny through the peephole. She swung open the door. "Oh, Manny, thank goodness you're here!"

He held up a roll of gauze. "Is someone in trouble?"

"Big time," she said. She took the gauze, then tossed it on the bed. Janine stepped into the hall, keeping the door barely cracked. She struggled to keep her voice level. "I have to go outside."

Manny sighed. "Janine, I know you're claustrophobic, but—"

"Not because I'm claustrophobic! I dropped something off the balcony, and I have to find it right away."

He held up his radio. "What is it? I'll call a guard to look for it."

"No! I can't risk someone finding it and keeping it."

"What did you drop?"

She puffed out her cheeks, then held up her left hand and wiggled her ring finger.

His eyes bulged. "Your engagement ring?"

She winced and nodded.

He touched a hand to his temple. "Oh good Lord."

"Exactly," she said. "Now you know why I'm so glad to see you."

His eyes narrowed. "I'm not getting a good feeling about this."

"You can sneak me out and I'll find my ring, then you can sneak me back in, and no one will be the wiser." She clapped her hands together under her chin, sniffing back tears.

"Janine, no one is supposed to leave the premises."

"I won't be leaving the premises, I'll just be under the balcony!"

He angled his head at her. "This isn't another pitiful attempt at escape, is it?"

"Cross my heart."

"The most sacred of vows," he noted dryly, but he was wavering.

"Manny, I'm not going to marry Steve Larsen."

His eyes bulged even wider.

"Besides the fact that I don't have enough money to pay for the ring, it's an heirloom. Irreplaceable." She adopted a pleading expression. "Please help me."

At last he sighed. "Okay, but let me do all the talking."

Hope soared in her chest. "You won't regret it."

He shot her a disbelieving look, but a half hour and a half-dozen lies later, they slipped out the side entrance. Flashlight in hand, her feet swimming in a pair of Derek's canvas lace-up tennis shoes, they made their way to the area beneath the balcony—easy to locate since her yellow flip-flop fairly glowed in the moonlight.

"What the heck were you doing up there?" Manny asked, holding up the sandal.

Instead of answering, she snatched the shoe.

"Oh," he said, the solitary word saying it all.

"We're looking for a *ring*," she reminded him, shining her flashlight over the grass.

"Is this yours, too?" He held up the half-empty bottle of water.

She nodded.

A few minutes later he asked, "And this?" The napkin she'd wrapped around Derek's hand waved in the breeze. The honey butter smelled pungent and had left some odd-looking stains on the cloth.

She gave him a tight smile, then took the napkin from him and tucked it in the waistband of her—make that *Derek's*—sweatpants.

He harrumped. "I'm not touching anything else I find unless it's fourteen-carat gold."

"The ring is platinum," she corrected him.

He let out an impressive, sad whistle. "Well, we'd better split up and cover this area systematically. I'll start here and go to the tree, then back to the wall."

With her heart thumping and her fingers crossed, Janine started crisscrossing the area opposite Manny. Taking baby steps in her huge shoes, she stared at the beam of light until her eyeballs felt raw. After only a short while, her neck and shoulders ached. "Manny, have you found it?"

"Yeah, Janine, I found the ring ten minutes ago, but I just like walking humped over in the dark."

She smiled ruefully and shut up. A paper clip, then a foil candy wrapper raised and dashed her hopes.

After an hour, she was blinking back tears. Manny came over to stand next to her, rubbing the back of his neck. "Nothing. Are you sure it fell off your finger when you were on the balcony?"

"I think it did."

He pursed his lips. "You *think* it did? I have two mosquito welts on my face the size of Stone Mountain, and you *think* it did?"

"Well, we couldn't find it in the room, so I just assumed...I mean, we dropped so many things—"

He held up one hand. "I get the picture." Manny shook his head, and chuckled. "Wow, when you mess things up, you mess them up in a big way."

"Well, it's not like I lost the ring on purpose."

"Maybe not consciously."

"What's that supposed to mean?"

"Nothing."

"Something," she prompted.

"Well, it's just that the subconscious can be a powerful force." He splayed one hand. "Did you lose the ring before or after you decided you weren't going to marry Mr. Larsen?"

"After," she said miserably.

He lifted his shoulders in an exaggerated shrug. "Just a thought," he said, then steered her back toward the side entrance.

"What am I going to do?" she asked, blinking back a new wellspring of tears.

"Search the room again," he told her. "And I promise I'll come out myself first thing in the morning with a rake." He smiled, his blue eyes kind. "I might even be able to scare up a metal detector."

"You're the best," she said, giving him a hug.

"So I've heard," he said with a boyish grin. "Try to get some sleep, okay?"

FAT CHANCE, she thought hours later, staring at the bedside clock until it ticked away another thirty minutes. Her tear ducts were swollen and dry. Three o'clock in the morning on what was supposed to be her wedding day, and she lay awake, stiff and sore from the lovemaking of the man sleeping on the floor.

Who just happened *not* to be her fiancé.

But someone who'd become important to her in a shamefully short amount of time. She laughed aloud, but the velvety darkness of the room muffled the noise.

Today she would call Steve and tell him she couldn't marry him, a thought that saddened her. Even though she didn't love him, she was fond of him and his family, and she would always admire his proficiency on the job. She would miss him, along with the promise of a luxurious, if conservative, life.

She sighed. Then after breaking their engagement, she would offer Steve her car, her sole Coach purse and her right arm as a down payment on the lost ring. Now that she thought about it, a hairdresser had once told her he'd give her a hundred dollars for her hair, down to the scalp... Her mother would get used to it eventually. And she could sell her blood every six weeks at the clinic—nobody needed a full ten pints.

Derek murmured something in his sleep. She lifted her head in his direction and saw the pale sheet over him move as he rolled to face her, still sound asleep. Her stomach pitched and rolled when she replayed their passionate encounter in her head. Neither she nor Derek had broached the subject of their lovemaking when she returned from her fruitless search. He'd helped her turn the room upside down, but remained stoic as they stripped the bed and checked underneath. Obviously, the act had been little more than an enjoyable tumble for him, and now he was racked with guilt.

Janine's mouth tightened. He would never know how much their lovemaking had meant to her, not if she could help it. This little triangle she'd created had enough inherent problems without throwing love into the mix.

Love?

Suddenly, the metallic whine of the air conditioner roared in her ears, and the walls seemed to converge on her in the dark. Janine clutched at her chest and gasped for breath, succumbing to a full-fledged panic attack. And why not? she asked herself, grabbing a fistful of sheet. Never before in her life had she had so many good reasons to panic.

"Relax, Janine."

Derek's voice floated to her and she realized he was sitting on the bed, holding her hand. "Take shallow breaths and exhale through your mouth slowly. Close your eyes," he ordered gently, and she obeyed.

"Now breathe, and think about something that makes you happy," he said as if speaking to a child.

His suggestion fell flat, however, because his face kept floating behind her eyelids. She tried to focus, but his touching was so much more appealing.

"Tell me," he said. "Tell me the things that make you happy, Janine."

The concerned note in his voice sent warmth circulating through her chest, making her feel safe. "Peppermint ice cream," she whispered.

The low rumble of his laugh floated around her head. "What else?"

"Red hats...old books...polka music...cotton sheets..."

"Breathe," he reminded her. "Go on."

"Daisies...jawbreakers...bowling...brown eyes..."

Derek's own breath caught in his chest. Did she like *his* brown eyes? His chest ached with the agony of not discussing their impromptu lovemaking. On one hand, he felt compelled to tell her the sex had been a profound experience for him, but on the other hand, she was on the rebound from an engagement to a friend of his, undoubtedly consumed with guilt over sleeping with him *and* losing her priceless engagement ring. For all he knew, the flighty woman might manufacture a story about the ring being stolen and marry Steve after all. He'd be a fool to reveal any of his disturbing feelings to her now, under such volatile circumstances.

He realized her breathing had returned to normal and, eyes closed, she looked like a resting child. Her beauty seemed boundless. The more time he spent with her, the more expressions and mannerisms she revealed, each uniquely Janine, and each riveting. The woman was incredible, and he hoped Steve was smart enough to fight for her love. He hated himself for submitting to his desire for her, for taking advantage of her vulnerability during prewedding jitters. In doing so, he prayed he hadn't jeopardized her chance for happiness.

He started to withdraw his hand, but Janine's fingers closed around his, and her eyes fluttered open. "Stay with me."

Even though everything logical in him shouted not to, he stretched out beside her, careful to leave a few inches between them. Janine turned on her side away from him, then scooted back until they were touching from shoulder to knee. Instinctively, he rolled to his side and spooned her small body against his. A foreign, not completely uncomfortable heat filled his chest, and he suddenly couldn't pull her close enough. She wore a short T-shirt rucked up to her waist, revealing plain white cotton panties. His body responded immediately.

No matter, he thought. She was breathing deeply, probably already asleep and oblivious to his state. He reached up and smoothed the hair back from her face, studying her profile, wishing he knew what made her tick. Unexpectedly, she pressed her rump back against his arousal, and he bit back a groan. Was she merely moving in her sleep, or urging him to intimacy? Janine reached her hand back to hook around his thigh and pulled him so that his sex nestled against hers, settling the question.

Derek buried his face in her hair, then kissed her neck while sliding his hand beneath her shirt to caress her stomach and tuck her body even closer to his. By spreading his fingers, he stroked her breasts, gently tweaking each nipple. He cupped a handful of her firm flesh, rasping his desire for her in her ear. She responded by sliding her hand back and tugging on the waistband of his boxers. He lifted himself just enough to skim the underwear down his legs, then kicked them away. Freed, his erection sought the heat between her thighs, straining against the firm cheeks of her buttocks.

She had shed her T-shirt. With a slide of her hand and a teeth-grating wiggle, the thin panties were pushed down to her knees. Derek throbbed to be inside her, but rolled away long enough to secure a condom. Spooning her close to him again, he reached around to delve into the curls at the apex of her thighs, which were already wet. With great restraint, he inserted only the tip of his bulging erection into her slick channel from behind, and plied her nub of pleasure until she writhed in his arms, moaning his name. On the verge of climax himself, he slid into her fully, thrilling in the extra pressure of their position. Sheer concentration helped him maintain control for several long, slow strokes, then the life fluid burst from him with a force equal to that of a man who might never get to indulge in such sweetness again.

Indeed, Derek thought as his breathing returned to normal, he would never again make love to Janine. He would go back to Kentucky, immerse himself in his work and leave Janine and Steve to work through their problems. Once Steve had singled out a woman to make her his wife, Derek knew he wouldn't easily let her go. The panicky thought sprang to his mind that Janine might be using him to get back at Steve in some way. His stomach twisted. He suspected that Steve was unfaithful to Janine—did she as well?

She sighed and settled back against his chest. With his head full of troubled thoughts and his lungs full of the scent of her hair, he drifted off to sleep.

JANINE STARTED AWAKE, disoriented, but was disturbingly relieved to see Derek's face in the morning light.

"Janine," he whispered, his tone urgent. "Wake up."

"What's wrong?" she asked, looping her arms around his neck and pulling him closer.

"Shh." He pulled away her hands and flung back the covers, sending a chill over her naked body. "Janine, sweetheart, you have to get up. *Now.*"

"Why?" she asked, sitting up grudgingly, wincing at her sore muscles.

An impatient knock sounded at the door, apparently not the first.

"Because," he said, pulling on his underwear, his lowered voice tinged with warning. "Steve's here."

CHAPTER SIXTEEN

SHE SWAYED and Derek grabbed her by the shoulders to steady her. "Steve's here?" she parroted, dazed.

"Yes," he whispered, pulling her to her feet. "Keep your voice down."

Her heart threatened to burst from her chest, and her brain seemed mired in goo. "B-but what's he doing here? How?"

"I don't know," he said, fishing her panties and T-shirt from the covers. "The point is, he can't find *you* here."

Steve banged on the door. "Derek, man, are you awake? I lost my key."

At the sound of Steve's voice, her knees nearly collapsed. She bit down hard on her knuckle, terrified at what might transpire between the men if Steve found out what had happened last night. Twice.

"Give me a minute, Steve," Derek called, pivoting to scan the room. His darting eyes came full circle to rest on the bed. "Get underneath," he said, shoving her clothes into her hands.

"But I—"

"Now, Janine, under the bed!"

Dreading even the thought of being confined in such a tight space, she nonetheless relented, quickly recognizing the lesser of two evils. She shimmied the T-shirt over her head and practically vaulted into her panties. The clothes brought back a flood of erotic memories, and she felt compelled to at least acknowledge their lovemaking.

"Derek, about last night—"

"Janine," he cut in. "We definitely need to talk, but now hardly seems like the time."

Contrite, she nodded, then dropped to her belly and squeezed her way under the bed, giving thanks for her B-cup—a C would've rendered this particular hiding place impossible. Quickly she determined the least uncomfortable position was to lie with her cheek to the dusty floor.

With her heart doing a tap dance against the parquet, she watched Derek's feet move toward the door. The foggy numbness of a panic attack encroached, but she forced herself to focus on breathing. *Please, please, please,* she begged the heavens. *Get me out of this predicament, and I'll behave myself. Really, I will.*

Inhale, exhale. *No more men until I get the ring paid off.*

Inhale, exhale. *No more engagements unless I'm certain the man is right for me.*

Inhale, exhale. *And no more sex until I'm married.*

The door opened and Steve's Cole Haan loafers came into view. Janine bit her lip, certain she was about to be discovered.

"About time, man," Steve said, walking inside.

"Sorry," Derek said, and the door closed. "I was talking to...an important client. What are you doing here?"

"Haven't you heard? The quarantine's been lifted."

She closed her eyes in relief. At least she could get out of here. Away from Derek. Her chest tightened strangely, not surprising considering her present confinement. Inhale, exhale.

"I drove up as soon as I heard," Steve continued. "Here." A paper rattled. "This was sticking half under your door. It says you're a free man." He walked over to the window and flung open the curtains, spilling light over the wooden floor. "This place is like a tomb—it's almost ten o'clock. I thought you were an early riser, man."

Derek grunted. "These damn allergies have me all messed up."

"Are you taking anything for them?"

"Yeah, some over-the-counter stuff."

Steve laughed, a harsh sound. "If Janine were here, she'd be plying you with some cockamamy tea made from crabgrass or something."

She blinked, stung by the cutting sarcasm in his voice.

"Well," Derek said with a small laugh, "she's definitely not here."

"I wonder if she knows about the quarantine being lifted."

"Um, I suspect she does," Derek hedged.

The Cole Haan loafers came closer and closer to the bed, then suddenly, the box springs bounced down, slamming into her shoulder blades and momentarily knocking the breath out of her. While gasping for air, she realized Steve had dropped onto the bed.

"What the hell are you doing?" Derek's angry voice penetrated her wheezing fog.

"What?" Steve sounded confused.

"Take it easy, you'll break the bed!"

Steve laughed. "Relax, man, I'm sure this bed has seen its share of bouncing."

Janine winced. If he only knew.

A long-suffering sigh escaped Steve. "I guess *my* bed-bouncing days are over."

Janine frowned.

"Man, am I going to miss being single. I hate like hell to grow up."

Derek's laugh sounded forced. "I'm sure married life will suit you. From what I've seen of Janine—" he cleared his throat "—she seems like a great gal."

"Yeah, she's a sweetheart. My parents love her."

But not Steve, she realized, shaken that she hadn't noticed sooner how ill-matched they were, how they never really laughed together, shared the intimate details of their everyday life or planned for the future.

"In fact, Janine is the first woman I ever brought home that my mother considered good enough to wear my grandmother's ring."

Her heart skipped a beat.

"An heirloom, eh?" Derek asked. "You probably arranged for her to wear a fake until you're actually married?"

Janine brightened considerably at the possibility.

"Oh, no," Steve said with nonchalance. "Mom insisted she wear the real thing. Pure platinum and flawless diamonds, about forty thousand dollars' worth."

She felt faint.

Derek made a choking sound. "Wow, you must really love this woman."

"She's terrific," he responded, and Janine wondered if Derek realized how evasive his friend was being. "It's funny, though," Steve continued, his voice tinged with regret. "She's never really turned me on physically."

Mortification flowered in her chest. It was just as she'd feared. And in front of Derek, no less.

"Steve," Derek began, his voice echoing her embarrassment, but Steve seemed to be in a talkative mood.

"Oh, she's cute and all, and I have to admit, I'm looking forward to the wedding night."

"That's…great," Derek replied. "Hey, why don't we grab some breakfast?" He walked to the canvas tennis shoes she'd worn last night for her moonlight treasure hunt, and bent to pick up one. Janine grimaced. She'd left them tied so tight, the material was puckered around the eyelets. Even so, she'd still been able to walk right out of them.

The mattress moved again. Steve sat on the edge of the bed for a few seconds, then pushed himself to his feet. "I didn't tell you she's a virgin, did I?"

Janine gasped, and the shoe Derek had picked up fell back to the floor, bouncing once.

"No," Derek said in a brittle tone. "You didn't mention that little tidbit."

"Can you believe it? In this day and age… She's the perfect wife for a politician's family. No skeletons, no baggage."

"Politician, meaning your father, or politician, meaning you?" Derek still sounded a little choked.

"Of course Dad for now, although I don't rule it out for myself sometime in the future."

Another surprise, Janine noted wryly.

"How can you be sure she's a virgin?" Derek asked.

Janine gasped again, then tamped down her anger. After all, she'd acted like a loose goose—her mother's words—around Derek.

"I mean," Derek added with a nervous little laugh, "nothing against Janine, but how's a man really to know?"

"She told me," Steve said simply.

Well, at least he'd believed her.

"And I asked her OB/GYN."

Her body clenched in fury. How *dare* he? Instinctively, she raised her head, which met solidly with a rather inflexible piece of wood. Pain exploded in her crown, and she bit back a string of curses.

"What was that?" Steve asked.

Holding her breath, Janine could feel his eyes boring through the mattress.

"Oh, it's the people in the room below," Derek said, sounding exasperated. "They can't seem to *be still*."

She stuck her tongue out at him.

"Anyway," Steve said, shifting foot to foot, "I need to look for Janine before we eat. The wedding is back on for this evening. Mother has already worked out the details with the hotel. A small miracle, I might add."

Janine swallowed a strangled cry. She needed a miracle, but that wasn't the one she'd had in mind.

"Kind of last minute, don't you think?" Derek asked, walking toward the door.

"My folks think it would make great press, so it'll

be worth it, even if things aren't picture perfect. You have to ride the media wave when it breaks, man."

The door opened and Steve exited first. Derek stepped into the hall, then said, "Oh, I almost forgot. I need to make one more phone call. Why don't you wait for me in the lobby. Maybe you'll run into Janine."

"Good idea," Steve said. "Then the two of you can get to know each other a little better."

Janine closed her eyes, guilt clawing at her chest.

"Uh, yeah," Derek replied. "Give me about fifteen minutes." He walked back inside the room, then closed the door.

Dread enveloped her, a sensation that was beginning to feel alarmingly familiar. She inhaled too deeply, filling her nostrils with dust, then sneezed violently. Before she could recover, strong hands closed around her ankles, and she was sliding across the wooden floor, being pulled out feetfirst. When her head cleared the bed, she lay still, looking up at Derek who stood over her, hands on hips. "Bless you," he said, but his expression was decidedly unsympathetic.

Inside he was seething, although he tried to maintain a certain amount of decorum. The crazy thing was that even in the midst of the frenetic situation, his mind and body paused to register her incredible natural beauty, her pink mouth and blue, blue eyes, her pale braided hair in fuzzy disarray, and long slender limbs, sprawled ridiculously on the floor. He had actually deflowered this lovely creature, destined for the bed of another man. Derek wanted to throw something, but instead he winced and rubbed his eyes with forefinger and thumb.

"You really shouldn't do that."

He opened his eyes. "You really should have told me."

She wet her lips. "Would it have made a difference?"

"Yes," he snapped. He wouldn't have touched her. He ran his hand through his hair, still unable to believe the turn of events. Okay, maybe he still would have touched her, but he would have taken his time, would have tried to make the experience more special for her, which was probably what her fiancé had been planning to do. Remorse racked his chest.

"Yes," he repeated more gently. He leaned over and extended his hand, then eased her to her feet.

"Derek, I can't imagine what you must think of me—"

He stopped her by touching his finger to her full lower lip. "I think we were both a little out of sorts—the proximity, the quarantine, the stress. What happened, happened."

Misery swam in her eyes. "But Steve…"

"Doesn't ever have to know," Derek insisted.

"You're right," she said, nodding. "Telling him would serve no purpose, and I don't want to come between your friendship."

He considered telling her they weren't as close as she might think, but doing so would only confuse the issue. "Good, then we have a pact?"

"Yes," she said with a whisper of a smile.

"And you and Steve will work things out?"

"I'm not sure that—"

"You will," he assured her, forcing cheer. He

clasped her shoulders in what he'd intended to be a friendly gesture, but dropped his hands when the compulsion to kiss her became too great. "You've got a few minutes to get your things together and out of here," he said as he crossed to the door.

"Derek." She swallowed hard and looked as if she might say something, then averted her eyes and murmured, "I don't have much to get together."

He couldn't resist teasing her one last time. "A certain pink number comes to mind."

She blushed, and he decided the picture of her standing barefoot next to the bed, with disheveled hair and wearing her T-shirt inside out would remain in his mind forever.

"I guess I'll see you at the wedding," he said, then left before he could change his mind about walking away. He had problems in Kentucky that needed his full attention immediately, he reminded himself as he rode to the lobby. The sooner he got through the wedding and on a northbound plane, the better. Guilt bound his chest like a vise.

Steve was waiting for him in the lobby, jingling change in the pocket of his tailored slacks, looking every bit the part of a successful plastic surgeon.

"I haven't seen her," Steve said as he walked up, clearly perturbed. "I gave her a pager so I could keep tabs on her, but she never wears it."

Good for her, Derek thought. "Ready to get a bite to eat?"

"Let's hang around in the lobby for a little while, just in case a news camera shows." Steve craned his neck and scanned the massive lobby.

Derek frowned. "Or Janine."

"Huh? Oh, yeah."

Rankled at his seeming indifference, Derek said, "If you don't mind me saying so, you don't seem particularly attached to your fiancée."

Steve shrugged. "What's love got to do with it, right?"

With his attitude of taking things lightly, Derek marveled how the man had made it through medical school. Then the answer hit him—Steve only took *people* lightly. "Well, it matters quite a bit when you consider you'll be spending the rest of your life with someone."

His friend turned back and presented a dismissive wave. "If you're thinking about what I said about her not putting lead in my pencil, don't worry. My surprise wedding gift to Janine is a pair of D's."

Derek frowned. "What?"

"You know—D's." Steve held his hands, palm up, wriggling his fingers in lewd squeezing motions.

Nausea rolled in Derek's stomach. What did Janine see in this guy? Hell, why did he himself call him a friend? He struggled to keep his voice calm. "That's kind of cruel, Steve. And unnecessary, from what I saw of Janine." *And felt, and tasted,* his conscience reminded him.

Steve scoffed. "You always did go for the mousy ones, didn't you, pal?"

So unexpected was Derek's fist that Steve was still smiling when he popped him in the mouth. Steve staggered back, his eyes wide and angry. An expletive rolled out of his bloody mouth, but he kept his distance. "Have you lost your freaking mind?"

"No," Derek said evenly. "But you've lost your best man."

Steve's face twisted as he swept his gaze over Derek. "Fine. I only asked you because Jack let me down."

"You and Jack," Derek said, wiping the traces of blood off his knuckles, "are two of a kind."

"You're jealous," Steve retorted. "You were always jealous of me and Jack."

Derek set his jaw and turned his back on Steve, recognizing the need to walk away. A light from a news camera blinded him, but he didn't stop. At least Steve had gotten his wish—he probably would make the local news.

Steve's spiteful words clung to Derek as he stabbed the elevator button. Jealous, ha. In his opinion, the man had only one thing worth coveting. He stepped into the elevator and leaned heavily against the back wall. A man knew his limits. He'd never competed with Steve or Jack for a woman, and he wasn't about to start now.

But at least he had his memories.

CHAPTER SEVENTEEN

JANINE CLOSED the room door behind her and slung over her shoulder the pillowcase containing her ill-fated costume, her high heels and the items Manny had brought her. She'd managed a quick shower, but didn't have time to dry her hair, so she'd simply slicked it back from her face with gel. The single pair of shorts and the sole T-shirt she had left were so formfitting, she'd decided to wear the coat. Buttoned and belted, admittedly it looked a little weird with the yellow flip-flops, but she didn't care. A hysterical laugh bubbled out. With so many problems, she should be so *lucky* as to have the fashion police haul her away.

Her feet were so heavy, she could barely walk. When she reached the elevator bay, the overhead display showed one car on its way up. For a few seconds, she entertained the idea of waiting for it, then she changed her mind and headed for the stairs. Why tempt another panic attack?

Descending the stairs slowly, she tried to sort out the ugly tasks before her. Marie said she'd be there in an hour, which gave her time to find Manny, and talk to Steve.

Talk to Steve.

Her joints felt loose just thinking about it. Funny,

but in her mind, breaking their engagement seemed anticlimactic compared to confessing she'd somehow misplaced a family heirloom that was worth twice as much as her education had cost. And priceless to his mother, she knew. Her stomach pitched. Oh, well, being in debt was the American way. Some people made thirty years of payments on a house, she'd simply make thirty years of payments on a ring. That she didn't have. And would never truly be able to replace.

After a few requests, and scrupulously avoiding the lobby, she found Manny at a loading dock arguing heatedly with a deliveryman trying to wheel in a cartful of red and white carnations. "Janine! Just the person I needed to see. I wanted to call you, but it's been so crazy now that we're actually back in business." He wagged his finger at the burly man. "Call your boss. She *knows* I strictly forbid carnations for our live arrangements." He clucked. "Smelly weeds." Turning back to Janine, he tugged her inside to some kind of workroom.

"I read on the sheet left in our room that the quarantine was lifted early this morning."

He rolled his eyes. "*Very* early this morning. The CDC traced the bacteria to a bad batch of barbecue *and* a peck of bad stuffed peppers served last Thursday, all from a caterer we sometimes use in a pinch. Past tense, natch."

"Is everyone going to be okay?"

Manny nodded. "All but two guests have been released from the hospital, and those two are recovering well, according to Dr. Pedro."

Starved for good news, she grinned. "Excellent."

"And now for the bad news," he said, his gaze somber.

"You didn't find the ring."

"No, I didn't." Manny pointed to the grass-stained cuffs of his white pants. "I swept the entire area with a metal detector. I found three quarters and a dime, but not what you were looking for." He stroked her hair. "I'm sorry, sweetheart, but I'll keep looking. It'll turn up somewhere, and I have an extremely trustworthy staff. If it's here and we find it, you'll get it back."

"I'm offering a reward," she said, morose. "My firstborn."

He laughed. "I'll put out the word." Then he sobered. "And what's this my catering director tells me about the wedding being back on?"

"He's misinformed," she assured him. "I am *not* marrying Steve Larsen."

"And does he know that?"

She puffed out her cheeks, then exhaled. "I'm on my way to tell him about the wedding…and the ring."

"And about Mr. Stillman?" he probed.

Her heart jerked crazily. "No. Derek and I made a pact."

"To bear children?"

A silly laughed escaped her. "To secrecy. There's nothing between us except a mistake."

He lifted one eyebrow.

"Okay, two mistakes. But that's all."

"You don't have feelings for him?"

She smirked. "Manny, don't you think I have enough problems for now?"

He nodded and relented with a shrug. "I guess I got carried away, what with my perfect record and all."

"I hope this failure isn't going to keep you from getting wings or something," she teased, thinking the silver lining of this black cloud had been making a new friend.

"Don't concern yourself about me," he said. "Now, go." He shooed her toward the door. "Put this dreadful task behind you, then burn that coat, girl."

She threw him a kiss, then made her way toward the lobby, her pulse climbing higher and higher. Every other step she reminded herself to breathe, refusing to have a panic attack now. She'd made her bed, and now she had to lie in it...alone.

Which was, all things considered, better than lying underneath it.

Steve was easy to spot pacing in a conversation area flanked with leather furniture, but she was surprised to find him alone, and apparently agitated. Pausing next to a gray marble column, she observed the man she'd thought to marry, hoping to see some kind of justification for why she had accepted his proposal in the first place.

Steve Larsen was a strikingly handsome man, no doubt. White blond hair, perpetually tanned, with breathtakingly good taste in clothing, housing and transportation. She squinted.

And an ice pack against his mouth?

At that moment he looked up and recognized her. "Janine?"

Summoning courage, she crossed the lobby. "H-hi," she said, feeling as if she were face-to-face with a stranger.

"Hi, yourself," he said with a frown. "Where the devil have you been?"

She blinked. So much for a happy reunion. Tempted to snap back, she reminded herself of the messages she had to deliver. "Collecting my things," she said, indicating her makeshift bag. "And tying up loose ends." Stepping forward, she pulled away the ice pack and gasped at the dried blood and redness beneath. "What on earth happened to your mouth?"

His scowl deepened. "I fell," he said, gesturing to the marble floor. "It's nothing."

"But you might need stitches—"

"I said it's nothing!"

Drawing back at his tone, she averted her eyes, noticing several people were staring.

Steve noticed too, instantly contrite. He bent to kiss her high on the cheek, a gesture she'd once found so romantic. Now she swallowed hard to keep from pushing him away. Her response wasn't fair, she knew. She had made a huge mistake by agreeing to marry him. He bore none of the blame for her naive acceptance.

"Let's sit," she suggested. "I need to talk to you."

Her heart skipped erratically, and her hopes of easing into the conversation were dashed when Steve asked, "Where's my ring?" He grasped her left hand with his free one.

She attempted a smile, but failed. "Um, that's one of the things I have to talk to you about." After clearing her throat, she blurted, "I lost it," and winced.

He lowered the ice pack and stared. A muscle ticked in his clenched jaw. "You...*lost* it?"

Tears sprang to her eyes and she nodded. "Steve, I'm so sorry."

"Where did you lose it?" he demanded. "How?"

She shook her head, her tears falling in earnest now. "I don't know—I've looked everywhere. I'm so, so sorry."

Steve lay his head back against the chair and moved the ice pack to his forehead. "My mother is going to kill me."

Sniffling, she said, "I'll tell Mrs. Larsen it was all my fault, Steve."

He glanced at her out of the corner of his eye. "Except you weren't the one who was supposed to get it insured—I was."

"You didn't get it insured?" she squeaked, then hiccuped.

His eyes bulged from his head, and his face turned crimson. "I didn't think you'd be careless enough to lose it!" He sat forward, his head in his hands. "Oh my God, my mother is going to kill me."

"I'll repay you," she said. "You and your family. Every dime, I promise."

He seemed less than impressed. Looking at her through his fingers, he said, "First of all, it's an heirloom, Janine. It can't be replaced. And second, I find the notion of *you* paying me or my family out of our household money, which will be primarily money *I've* earned, utterly ludicrous."

"Th-that's another thing I want to talk to you about."

"What?"

She looked around to make sure no one was within earshot. "I'm not going to marry you, Steve."

His face took on a mottled look. "You're not going to marry me?"

She nodded.

A purplish color descended over his expression, and he surprised her by laughing. "*You* are not going to marry *me?*" He slapped his knee. "Oh, that's rich. My mother spent all day Thursday calling everyone on the guest list letting them know the ceremony had been canceled, then she spent all this morning calling everyone *again* to tell them the ceremony is on again. And now you're saying she has to call everyone yet again to tell them the wedding is off again?"

Astonishment washed over her. He was more concerned about his mother being imposed upon or embarrassed than about losing her? "All I'm telling you, Steve," she said calmly, "is that I'm not marrying you." She stood and attempted to walk away, but he blocked her retreat.

"Janine, you can't just change your mind—I have plans."

What had she ever seen in him? she wondered as she studied his cold eyes. "We're too different, Steve, I should've never said yes. I'm sorry if this causes you or your parents undue embarrassment. I'd be glad to call every guest personally and accept full blame."

She tried to walk past him, but he grabbed her arm, his chest heaving. "I'm starting to think you didn't lose the ring after all."

"What?"

"Maybe you're planning to sell it."

A chill settled over her heart at the realization that she and Steve didn't know each other at all, but had still planned to marry. "I swear to you, I don't have the ring. And I swear I'll pay you the money it's worth, even if it takes a lifetime. I'm sorry it has to end this way, but we don't love each other. I'm sure we'll both be happier—"

"Will you, Janine?" he asked, still gripping her arm. "Will you be happier going back to your scruffy little old maid existence?"

His hurtful words stunned her to silence.

A little smile curled his battered lip. "Since you'll never be able to repay me for my ring, there is something you can do for me."

"What?" she whispered, frightened at the change in his demeanor.

"I still have my hotel room."

Revulsion rolled through her, and her mind reeled for something to say.

"Mr. Larsen."

They turned, and to Janine's immense relief, Manny stood a few feet away, his hands behind his back, his face completely serene.

"Yes?" Steve asked, easing his grasp on her arm a fraction.

"I'm the general manager of this hotel, and I have something for you."

He frowned. "What is it?"

Manny withdrew one hand from behind him and held up a stopwatch, which he clicked to start. "Ten minutes," he said, his voice casual. "Ten minutes to remove your personal belongings from your room and leave the premises." Then he smiled. "*Without* Ms. Murphy."

Janine suppressed a smile of her own. The general manager had succeeded in shaking Steve enough that he released her arm.

"I don't think you know who I am," Steve said, his chest visibly expanding.

"Sir, I know exactly who and what you are," Manny replied, then glanced at the stopwatch. "Oh, look, nine minutes."

Steve's bravado faded a bit. "I'd like to speak to your supervisor."

"*I* am my supervisor," Manny explained patiently, never taking his eyes off the stopwatch.

Steve looked at her, but she kept her eyes averted to avoid provoking him further.

"I'm going to sue you for the worth of the ring," he hissed.

"Why?" she asked, lifting her gaze. "I don't have anything worth taking."

His feral gaze swept her up and down. "You got that right," he said, then glared at Manny. "Forget the room. There isn't anything in my life that can't be easily replaced." After a dismissive glance in her direction, he wheeled and strode across the lobby toward the revolving door.

She stared dry-eyed until he had disappeared from sight. Then her knees started to knock and she sank onto the pale leather settee.

"Real Prince Charming," Manny muttered, patting her shoulder. "If you can wait another thirty minutes, I'll take you home."

"No, thank you, I have a ride," Janine said, although she didn't recognize her own voice.

"Janine?"

At the sound of Marie's voice, she sprang to her feet and rushed into her sister's arms. "What's going on? I just passed Steve in the parking lot and got the feeling if he'd had a gun, I would have been target practice."

"I broke our engagement."

Marie scoffed. "Is that all? Darling, men are a dime a dozen."

"And I lost my engagement ring."

Marie sucked in a sharp breath. "Oh, now *that* hurts."

Janine pulled back and looked at her sister's pained expression, then laughed in blessed relief. She turned to Manny and mouthed, "Thank you," then she and Marie strolled through the lobby arm in arm. When they passed the reservations desk where Janine had first begged her way up to room 855, she marveled at the changes in her life in a mere forty-eight hours.

She'd lost the man she thought she wanted, and met the man she knew she needed. But when Derek's face swam before her, she quickly squashed the image. She wasn't about to fall into another relationship so soon after her humbling experience with Steve. No matter what she *imagined* her feelings toward Derek to be, frankly, she simply didn't trust her own judgment right now.

On the drive home, she recounted enough details to try to satisfy Marie, while leaving out the more sordid aspects of passing time with Derek.

"So, sis, tell me about this Stillman fellow."

Janine glanced sideways at her sister. No teasing, no innuendo, no insinuation. She frowned. Marie was definitely suspicious. "Um, he's a nice enough guy."

"Nice enough to what?" Marie asked, seemingly preoccupied with a traffic light.

"Nice enough to...say hello to if I ran into him again."

Her sister nodded, presumably satisfied, then said, "I'll call Mom and the whole fam damily when we get home. Again." She grinned. "My gift to you for getting you into this mess in the first place."

"You're the greatest," Janine said.

"I know," Marie replied with a wink. "That's why I'm Mom's favorite."

Janine laughed, then told Marie all about Manny, and by the time they reached their apartment, she was feeling much better. She changed into her ugliest but most comfortable pajamas and holed up the rest of the day in the bedroom, putting her pillow over her head to shut out the sound of the phone ringing incessantly. Marie was a saint to handle it all.

She must have napped, because when she awoke, long shadows filled the room and she was thirsty. Swinging her legs over the side of the bed, she stepped on the empty box she recognized as the one that held the pink bustier and panties that Steve's receptionist, Sandy, had given her for her bachelorette party. The getup was already in the laundry, and once clean, was bound for Marie's closet. Janine would never wear it again. She scooped up the torn box to toss it in the trash on her way to the kitchen. Preoccupied with self-remorse, Janine almost missed the little note that floated out of the box.

Curious, she picked up the tiny card and opened it with her thumb.

Sandy, for Thursday, our last wicked night together.
Steve

Janine read the note again, and once again just for clarification.

Set up by his mistress. Sandy had probably thought Janine would wear the outfit sometime during her honeymoon—her revenge on Steve for marrying someone else? Perhaps. But one thing she was certain of: Steve had been with Sandy, not with the guys when she'd gone to the hotel to throw herself at him.

She should have felt betrayed. She should have felt humiliated. She should have felt manipulated. Instead, she smiled into her fingers, thinking how fitting that Steve had set events into motion that had eventually led to the breakup of his own engagement. She felt... grateful. Because Steve had inadvertently introduced her to a man she *could* love.

From afar.

CHAPTER EIGHTEEN

Honey, I'm home. Derek couldn't turn in any direction in the offices of Stillman & Sons without seeing the new slogan for Phillips—make that *Hannah's*—Honey. Billboard designs, print ads, product labels, website-page mock-ups. He'd outdone himself, easy to admit since he knew his own limitations as an advertising man. Phillips had been bowled over by the concept of using honey for better home health, and had signed an eighteen-month contract. Feeling good about the direction of the business for the first time in a long time, he'd placed an ad in the paper for a graphic artist. Four applicants would be stopping by this afternoon, and it would be good to have someone else in the office for company.

The direction of the business seemed to be back on course, but the direction of his life was another matter entirely.

He sighed and turned the page on his desk calendar. One month. One month was long enough to have purged nagging, accident-prone, virginal Janine Murphy from his mind. After all, she was a married woman. Married to a jerk, but married nonetheless. He had actually considered calling Steve to extend an olive branch, but changed his mind after acknowledging the ploy was a thinly veiled excuse to call on the off chance that Janine would answer the phone. Besides, despite their pact, Janine could have broken down and confessed what had transpired between them—after all, she might have had some explaining to do on her wedding night. If so, neither one of them would welcome his call.

Derek cursed his wandering mind. Jack would get such a kick out of knowing a woman had gotten under his skin.

The bell on the front door rang, breaking into his musings. The first applicant. Glad for the distraction, he stood and buttoned his suit jacket, then made his way to the front. In the hall, he froze. "Well, speak of the devil," he muttered.

"Hi, bro." Wearing a white straw Panama hat, a hideous tropical-print shirt and raggedy cut-off khaki pants, Jack Stillman walked past him, carrying only a brown paper lunch bag. He strolled to his abandoned desk, then whipped off his hat and, with a twirl of his wrist, flipped it onto the hat rack that had sat empty since his departure. After dropping into his well-worn swivel chair, Jack reared back and crossed his big sandaled feet on the corner of his desk. From a deep bottom drawer, he withdrew a can of beer and cracked it open. Then he slowly unrolled the three folds at the top of his lunch bag—their mother was famous for her three perfect folds. The bag produced a pristine white paper napkin, which he tucked into the neck of his ugly shirt, followed by a thick peanut butter and jelly sandwich.

Derek allowed him three full bites of the sandwich, chased by the room-temperature beer, before he spoke. "Care to say where you've been for the past three months?"

Jack shrugged wide, lean shoulders. "Nope, don't care at all—Florida."

"Which explains the tan," Derek noted wryly.

His brother scrutinized his brown arms as if they'd just sprouted this morning. "I suppose."

"I don't guess it would bother you to know that about three weeks ago the agency was a hairbreadth away from turning out the lights."

Jack took a long swallow of beer. "Something good must have happened."

He'd forgotten how infuriating his brother could be. "I landed the Phillips Honey account."

Nodding, Jack scanned the room. "Honey. Works for me." He polished off the rest of the sandwich, drained the beer, then laced his hands together behind his head. "So what the hell else have I missed?"

"Oh, let's see," Derek said pleasantly. "There's tax season, Easter, Mother's Day—"

"Hey, I called Mom."

"—plus Memorial Day, and Steve Larsen's wedding."

Jack frowned and snapped his fingers. "Damn. And I was supposed to be best man, wasn't I?"

"Yes."

"So did you cover for me?"

"Don't I always? When it appeared you'd dropped out of sight, Steve asked me to be best man."

Jack pursed his mouth. "But you and Steve were never that close."

Derek smirked. "I think it's safe to say we still aren't."

"So how was the wedding?"

He averted his gaze. "I have no idea."

"But I thought you said—"

"I went to Atlanta, and got caught up in a quarantine at the hotel."

"No kidding? Did anyone croak?"

Derek gritted his teeth. "Didn't you watch the news while you were gone?"

Jack grinned again. "Not a single day."

Disgusted, Derek waved him off. "Never mind."

"So what's she like?"

"Who?"

"Steve's wife." His long lost brother wadded up his napkin and banked a perfect shot into the trash can.

Derek walked over to his own desk and straightened a pile of papers that didn't need to be straightened. "She's...nice enough, I suppose."

Jack wagged his dark eyebrows. "Nice enough to do what?"

His neck suddenly felt hot. He loosened his tie a fraction, then undid the top button of his shirt. Images of Janine consumed him during the day, and at night he would take long runs to exhaust himself enough to sleep with minimum torment.

"Derek," Jack said lazily, "nice enough to do what?"

The innuendo in his brother's voice ignited a spark of anger in his stomach that he'd kept banked since his argument with Steve. "Just drop it, Jack," he said carefully.

But he'd only managed to pique Jack's interest. "Brunette? Redhead? Blonde?"

"Um, blonde." *Long and silky.*

"Tall, short?"

"Tall...ish." *And graceful.*

"Curves?"

Derek shrugged. "Not enough for Steve, but plenty for—" He stopped, mortified at what he'd been on the verge of saying.

"You?" Jack prompted. Then his jet eyebrows drew together. "You got the hots for this woman or something?"

"Of course not." He shuffled the stack of papers again, but wound up dropping several, then hitting his head on his desk when he retrieved them. Cursing under his breath, he didn't realize that Jack had moved to sit on *his* desk until he pushed himself to his feet.

"Did you sleep with her?"

Derek tossed the papers onto his desk. "What kind of question is that?"

"How many times?"

He looked into the face of the younger brother who could read him like a label, then sighed and dropped into his chair. "Twice."

"And?"

"And what?"

"And it's not the first time you bedded a woman, so there's more to this story."

"Besides the fact that she was Steve's fiancée?"

Jack scratched his head. "Wait a minute, where was Steve when you were breaking in his bride?"

Derek lunged to his feet and pulled Jack close by the collar of his shirt. "Don't say that!"

But Jack didn't even blink. "Oh, hell, she was a *virgin?*"

Stunned, he released him. "Did you pick up mind reading, too?" He wouldn't be a bit surprised.

Jack laughed, clapping him on the back. "Man, you're about as transparent as a wet, white bikini. So you dig this girl?"

"Woman," Derek felt compelled to say.

"Well, yeah, since you deflowered her."

He closed his eyes. "I think it's time to change the subject. She's a married woman, and I don't fool around with married women."

"Just fiancées," Jack said, picking up some of the honey samples sitting on Derek's desk.

"So glad to have you back," Derek said, not bothering to hide his sarcasm. "And don't eat that," he said, swiping the pint of honey butter from beneath Jack's sampling finger. "It hasn't been refrigerated and it might be bad."

"So throw it away," Jack said, moving on to a container of pure honey.

Derek nodded, staring into the container. Jack was right. Why on earth was he keeping it around? Because it reminded him of Janine, he admitted to himself. He swirled his finger on the surface of the honey butter, then flinched when the pad of his finger encountered something sharp, something unexpected. Dipping his finger, he hooked the object and lifted it free of the sticky-slick substance. With his heart in his throat, he removed most of the globs, then held Janine's engagement ring in the palm of his hand. The memories of her treating his burned hand vividly slammed home. She must have lost the bauble in the jar without realizing it.

Jack came over to take a look. "Wow, has Phillips started putting prizes in their packages?"

Already dialing directory assistance, Derek didn't answer. He had to talk to Janine right away, and he didn't want to risk calling her at home—Steve's home. But she'd mentioned she shared an apartment with her sister before, so maybe Janine's name would still be listed under the old number.

The operator gave him a number, which he punched in, his heart thrashing. Jack was holding the ring up to the light. "Put it down!" Derek barked. "That ring belonged to Steve's grandmother and is worth a *lot* of money."

Jack smirked. "No big leap how her engagement ring got into your jar of honey butter."

Derek frowned, then focused on the voice of the person who had answered the phone.

"Hello?"

"Yes, hello, may I speak with Janine Murphy's sister?"

"Speaking," the woman said, sounding wary. "This is Marie Murphy."

"Ms. Murphy, you don't know me. My name is Derek Stillman, and I—"

"I know who you are, Mr. Stillman."

He couldn't tell from her voice whether that was a good or a bad thing. "Okay. Ms. Murphy—"

"Call me Marie."

"Marie. I'd like to get a message to Janine, but it's very important that you not tell her when Steve is around."

"Steve? Steve Larsen?"

"Yes."

"Why would he be around?"

He bit the inside of his cheek. "Maybe I have the wrong number. I'm trying to locate the Janine Murphy who married Steve Larsen."

"Mr. Stillman, my sister was engaged to the jackass at one time, but she didn't marry him."

Derek felt as if every muscle in his body had suddenly atrophied. Impossible. Of course she had married him. She had said they would try to work things out. Steve wasn't the kind of guy who would simply let her walk away.

"What's wrong?" Jack asked.

Derek waved for him to be quiet. His heart was thumping so hard, he could see his own chest moving. "Uh, would you repeat that, please?"

A deep chuckle sounded across the line. "I said my sister was engaged to the jackass at one time, but she did *not* marry him. She canceled the wedding at the last minute."

His heart vaulted. "I see. How…how can I get in touch with her?"

"Well, Mr. Stillman—"

"Call me Derek."

"Derek, it's like this, Janine is juggling three jobs, and she only comes home to sleep."

He looked at his watch, estimating the time he could be in Atlanta. "Where will she be in three hours?"

"She'll be at the clinic this afternoon and evening. Got a pencil?"

Derek grabbed five.

CHAPTER NINETEEN

JANINE JOGGED through the parking lot toward the clinic—late again. Darn the traffic, she was going to be fired for sure if she didn't find a better shortcut. The commute from the urgent-care center to the clinic was always a bit iffy, but she usually made it on time. This week, however, she'd already clocked in late twice.

By the time she reached the entrance steps, she was winded and her feet felt like anvils. She groaned under her breath—another twelve flights of concrete stairs awaited her inside. Well, at least her legs were getting stronger, not to mention her bank account. She'd be able to send Mrs. Larsen a respectable amount for the first payment on the ring.

The woman had been doubly devastated, first by the cancellation of the wedding, then by the loss of her mother's ring. Janine had paid her a visit and they had cried together. Mrs. Larsen blamed Steve to some extent because he hadn't properly insured the ring, but Janine knew exactly where the fault lay. She'd insisted on sending regular payments until the appraisal value had been met…all thirty-seven thousand, four hundred dollars of it.

This first month, she'd be paying off the four hundred. Only thirty-seven thousand to go, and at this rate, she'd have it paid off in a little less than eight years. Mrs. Stillman had graciously suspended any interest, probably because she doubted Janine would even make a dent in the principal.

But she absolutely, positively would not only make a dent, Janine promised herself, she would pay off every penny to rid herself of the psychological obligation to Steve Larsen.

If she lived that long, she thought, stopping to flex her calf muscles, stiff from standing all day, and objecting already to the next eight-hour shift ahead of her. After entering the building, she crossed the lobby, then slowed at the elevator bank, noting how quickly the cars seemed to zip through the floors. Maybe she could take the elevator just this once. Her decision was made when the doors to a car slid open. She was the only one waiting, so she stepped inside and quickly located the door-close button, lest the car fill up with big, pushing bodies.

When the door slid closed, she moved to the rear wall in the center and leaned back, grateful for a few seconds of rest, and blocking out the fact that she was in a small, moving box.

She closed her eyes, and as was customary, Derek's face popped into her mind. In the beginning, fresh from Steve's ugliness and suffering under her own guilt, she had squelched all thoughts of Derek as soon as they entered her head. But gradually, she'd come to realize that remembering their times together made her happy, and darn it, she needed a little happiness in her life. At moments like these, she especially felt like indulging.

His smiling brown eyes, his big, gentle hands, his dry sense of humor. She loved him, a feeling so intense she was embarrassed that she'd imagined herself to be in love with Steve. She wondered if she ever crossed Derek's mind.

Suddenly the car lurched to a halt. Her eyes flew open and her heart fell to her aching feet. She waited for a floor to light up and the door to slide open, but the machinery seemed strangely silent. "Oh no," she whispered, her knees going weak. "Oh, please no."

She stumbled to the control panel and stabbed the door-open button, along with several floor buttons, but none of them lit or produced any kind of movement. Hating the implication, she opened the little door on the box that held a red phone, then picked up the handset. Immediately, the operator answered and assured Janine they would have the elevator moving soon. With her chest heaving, she asked that her supervisor be contacted, and gave the man her name. After hanging up the phone, she shrank to the back wall, forcing herself to stare at the blue-carpeted floor, all too aware of the sickly sweet odor in the air that permeated most medical facilities.

She slid down the wall to sit with her legs sprawled in front of her, and bowed her head to cry—the worst thing a person could do with the onset of a panic attack imminent. But her stupidity, her broken heart and her exhaustion converged into this moment and she recognized her body's need for emotional release.

Burying her head in her folded arms, she let the tears flow and pushed at the black walls that seemed to be collapsing around her. Steel bands wrapped around her chest and began to contract, as if they were alive.

She gasped for air. Inhale, exhale. Her life certainly wasn't horrid—she met seriously ill people every day on her jobs who would gladly trade places with her. But she felt so…so cheated to have fallen in love with a man who would forever remember her as a wanton woman with a penchant for trouble. Most of her life she hadn't been overly concerned about what people thought of her. But worrying and wondering what Derek thought of her kept her awake most nights, even when her body throbbed with fatigue.

She knew Marie was worried about her. After all, she'd lost weight and rarely socialized. Most of her free time to date had been consumed with returning shower gifts with cards of apology. Steve had made one spiteful phone call to her the day after she'd talked to his mother about paying for the ring. He'd told her she'd shamed the family, and he would never forgive her for her outrageous behavior. In response, she had suggested that his receptionist, Sandy, might be a more suitable companion, then proceeded to read him the note the woman had left in the gift he'd given her. Steve hadn't called again.

Derek's connection to Steve presented yet another complication she didn't want to pursue, not in this lifetime. The friendship perplexed her—the two men seemed so different.

Her heart raced. She knew she needed to focus on her breathing, but she felt so weak, physically and mentally. Her throat constricted, forcing her to swallow convulsively for relief. A glance at her watch revealed she'd been at a standstill in the elevator for over twenty minutes. She needed to get out. Now. Struggling to her feet, she pounded on the steel doors with as much energy as she could muster. "Help! Can anyone hear me? I have to get out, please...help...me!"

The phone rang, the peal so loud in the small space that she shrieked. She knelt to pick up the handset, her hand trembling, her lungs quivering. "Please...get me...out of here."

"We're working on it, Pinky."

Her sharp inhale turned into a hiccup. "D-Derek?" she whispered.

"I'm in the lobby, and just in time, it seems. You know, this could be a full-time job, getting you out of scrapes."

"But how—"

"We'll have plenty of time to talk later. Right now, you need to relax and breathe."

Just knowing he was out there made her feel even more trapped. She had to get to him, had to explain how things had gotten so messed up. Her chest pumped up and down, like a bellows sucking the air out of her.

"Breathe, Janine, breathe. They'll have you out of there in no time. Don't think about where you are, just concentrate and breathe. Inhale through your nose, exhale through your mouth."

She did as she was told, content for the moment just to hear his voice. Inhale, exhale. Derek was here. Inhale, exhale. *Why* was Derek here? Inhale, exhale. "What...are you...doing here?"

"Keep breathing. I have some good news. I found that ring you lost."

Sheer elation shot through her. "What? Where?"

"Keep breathing. In that darned jar of honey butter. It must have fallen off when you were tending to my hand. Thank God I didn't throw it away."

Relief flooded her limbs and she tried to laugh, but it came out sounding more like a wheeze. "I can't... believe it." Her joy diminished a fraction at the realization that he'd come back on an errand—albeit a grand one—and not to see her. But at least she'd get to talk to him, to look at him. Inhale, exhale. And she'd be able to return Mrs. Larsen's beloved ring.

"Are you feeling better?" he asked, his voice a caress.

"Yes," she whispered.

"I have more good news," he continued. "Thanks to you, I landed the Phillips Honey account. And you were right about changing the name—sales are up already."

Janine smiled. After all the trouble she'd caused him, she was glad she'd helped him in some small way. "That's wonderful. So your company is back on its feet?"

"Yeah, and my brother finally found his way home, so I'm not alone anymore."

At least she wouldn't worry so much about him.

"Hey, they're getting ready to start the elevator car."

No sooner had the words left his mouth than the car began to descend slowly, the floors ticking by until it halted at the lobby level. She hung up the phone and pushed herself to her feet just as the door opened. A small crowd had gathered and applauded when she walked out on elastic legs. She needed to sit down, but she needed to see Derek worse.

He was hard to miss, jogging toward her, the largest man in the crowd by far. He wore a dark business suit and, if possible, was more handsome than she remembered. Her heart lodged in her throat as he slowed to a walk, then stopped in front of her.

"Hi," he said, his brown eyes shining.

Oh, how she loved this man. "Hi, yourself," she croaked.

"Let's get you to a chair," he said, steering her in the direction of a furniture grouping. She realized she must look a fright—except for the elevator incident, she hadn't stopped all day. The white lab coat she wore over navy slacks and a pink blouse hung loose and rumpled, and her sensible walking shoes weren't even close to being attractive. But, she acknowledged wryly, it seemed silly to fret about her clothing when Derek was intimately acquainted with what lay beneath her clothes.

"Thank you," she murmured as she sank onto a couch. "I was going a little crazy in there."

His smile made her stomach churn with anxiety. "Good timing," he said.

"How did you know where to find me?"

"Your sister told me. I hope you don't mind me coming to your job, but I thought you might want the ring as soon as possible."

She nodded, thinking sadly that by the time she clocked out this evening, he'd be back in Kentucky. Her pulse pounded at his nearness.

"I had it cleaned," he said, withdrawing a ring box from his pocket.

She smiled. How thoughtful. He'd even bought a box.

He handed it to her and she opened the hinged lid. She blinked, then frowned. The ring was platinum all right, but instead of a gaggle of large stones, a single round diamond sparkled back at her. Lifting her gaze to his, she shook her head. "Derek, this isn't the ring that Steve gave me."

His forehead darkened for the briefest of seconds, then he exhaled, looking tentative. "I know it's not as nice as the ring Steve gave you, but I was hoping you would, um—" Derek cleared his throat noisily, then met her gaze "—accept it anyway."

Vapors of happiness fluttered on the periphery of her heart, but she wouldn't allow herself to jump to conclusions, no matter how pleasant. She wet her lips. "What do you mean?"

"I mean," Derek said, his face flushed, "I know we live a few hundred miles apart, and we didn't exactly have an auspicious beginning…but I love you, Janine, and I couldn't bear the thought of returning another man's ring without having one of my own to offer you."

Speechless, she could only stare at him. He loved her? He *loved* her.

Derek winced and scrubbed his hand down his face, then stood and walked around the couch to stare out a floor-to-ceiling window. "Forget it. It was a crazy idea." He laughed. "I let my brother convince me that things were the way I wanted them to be. I have no right to put you on the spot like this." He turned back, his face weary. "I'm sorry."

Carrying the ring, she rose and circled around to join him at the window. With her heart nearly bursting, she asked, "Do you have the other ring?"

He paused a few seconds, then he nodded and pulled a second box from another pocket.

She turned her back to him to hide her smile of jubilation. Janine opened the lid and inspected the dazzling Larsen family ring that now looked to her more like an albatross than a promise.

Derek watched her, dying a slow, agonizing death. What had he been thinking to show up unannounced with an engagement ring after a month of no contact? He could kick himself. Or better yet, Jack. The scheme had seemed like a good one when he and his brother had worked it out, but now he realized he needed Jack's flamboyance to carry it off. In addition to a woman who loved him.

Janine snapped the lid closed, then turned back to him. "Derek, did you know I'm offering a reward for the ring?"

He blinked. A reward? The last thing he wanted was her money. "Janine—" He stopped abruptly when she slid her hands up his chest and looped her arms around his neck.

His body sprang to attention and he swallowed hard. "Um, n-no, I didn't know you were offering a reward. What is it?" He was mesmerized by the love shining in her eyes.

"My firstborn," she whispered, then pulled his mouth down to hers for a long, hungry kiss.

TOO HOT TO SLEEP

CHAPTER ONE

GEORGIA ADAMS GNAWED on her thumbnail as she read aloud the instructions for her new deluxe telephone answering system in hopes the words would make more sense the third time through. "When you select the dial pad mode, you are toggling the live dial pad option. When live dial pad is on, the hands-free option is activated if the auto answer feature was previously selected. See page 38-B, diagram H." Georgia pursed her mouth, then mumbled a curse word that was not in the manual, although she planned to call the company and suggest they include a handy reference page for expletives as soon as she got the bleeping phone working.

After hitting the "clear programming" button, she unplugged all three cords and started over at the beginning of the dog-eared book. Ninety minutes and six fingernails later, she achieved a dial tone and shrieked with success. Doing a victory dance on her sisal area rug, she spiked the instruction manual and gloated when it landed near her VCR that, after three years, still flashed "12:00." Thank goodness her VCR and television had been spared during the electrical storm that had zapped her phone. Positive that any minute she'd mysteriously lose the ability to dial out, she dropped onto her hard couch and dialed her friend Toni's number.

"House of bondage," Toni answered.

"You are terrible," Georgia said, laughing. "What if this had been Dr. Halbert calling you in to work?"

"I'm not going even if he does call. I wouldn't miss this bachelorette party for anything."

Georgia cleared her throat. "About the party—"

"Oh, no you don't, Georgia Arletta Adams! You're not backing out on me."

"How did you find out my middle name?"

"The question is, how many people in the hospital E.R. will I tell if you don't go with me tonight to Bad Boys? Besides, Stacey will be crushed if you don't show."

"Stacey will be smashed and won't care."

"Oh, come on, Georgia, have some fun. Afraid Rob the Blob won't want you ogling naked, sweaty, muscle-bound men?"

Georgia shifted on the firm cushion in a vain attempt to find a comfortable position, then reached to straighten a picture on her side table, one of her photographic creations. "No. Rob's working late and said he didn't mind if I went."

"Good grief, woman, you mean you really asked him?"

Actually, she'd secretly hoped he'd be the slightest bit jealous, especially since she'd yet to see *him* naked after ten months of dating. Instead, he'd sounded surprised, but added that he wasn't the jealous type. He *trusted* her, for heaven's sake—how patronizing. "Asking him was the considerate thing to do."

"It was the pathetic thing to do. The man doesn't own your orgasms."

You're telling me.

"Besides, what the heck else are you going to do tonight?"

Sleep sounded good, but Georgia recognized the early signs of insomnia by now and knew she'd be wide-eyed most of the night. She floundered for a chore that sounded remotely engrossing. "Program numbers into my new phone."

Toni scoffed. "Which will take all of ten minutes."

"Not for the gadgetronically challenged like myself."

"Pshaw. I'll expect you at my place in one hour. Show some skin and bring plenty of one-dollar bills."

Georgia mumbled goodbye, then frowned at the handset, searching for a disconnect button. These new-fangled portable models would make slamming down the phone obsolete. Not that she was the slamming sort, but at thirty, she expected many character-building experiences ahead of her and it seemed prudent to keep relevant props nearby. Fumbling for a button would not have the same impact.

At last she hit the Talk button, surprised when she heard the resulting dial tone. Her confidence bolstered, she pushed the programming button and after a few minutes of jockeying with arrow keys, managed to enter the numbers of the people or places she dialed most often: Rob, Toni, her mother, her sister, the personnel office at the hospital, various friends, the pizza delivery place, the Thai delivery place, the Chinese delivery place and the Mexican delivery place. Then she jotted down the names and corresponding two-digit numbers on the little pullout tablet on the base station, the most impressive doohickey on the entire gizmo, in her opinion.

Georgia wiped the perspiration from her forehead with the hem of her T-shirt. Was it her imagination, or was her apartment the hottest spot north of the equator? From her vantage point, she could see the blasted programmable thermostat in the hall. The building manager had reset it for her three times and the place still felt like a sauna. Oh, well, she'd look for *that* instruction manual tomorrow—she might be on a technological roll, but she didn't want to push her luck tonight. Besides, sweating was good for the pores.

She leaned her head back on a stiff cushion, thinking how much she'd grown to loathe the beige sectional sofa. Two years ago she accepted her registered nurse's position in emergency medicine. When she had first moved to Birmingham, Alabama, leaving behind her mother and sister, she'd bought ultramodern living room furniture for her apartment as a symbol of her newfound independence. Soon, however, she'd come to realize that the harsh lines and drab colors were less than friendly when settling in to watch a classic romantic movie. On the other hand, Rob said he found her furniture a welcome change from the flowery styles preferred by most women.

Georgia smirked, thinking that Rob's preference for furniture could also describe his preference for sex—the man was a minimalist. A heartbeat later, she regretted the thought because Rob Trainer was a hardworking, ambitious accounting consultant and a consummate Southern gentleman. Well, maybe *consummate* was an unfortunate word choice.

An overhead stretch to pull her tired shoulders turned into a full-body yawn. Her insomnia, combined with Rob's gentlemanly ways, was testing her physical endurance, which was precisely why she'd prefer to skip the party at the male strip club. She pulled a hand down over her face, trying to squash the provocative images swirling in her mind, and the quickening in her thighs. She'd never been to a strip club, but she had a bad, bad feeling that such a place would only fuel the flame in her belly she was trying desperately to smother.

She pushed herself to her feet and strolled the perimeter of her living room, opening windows to let in air an nth degree less stagnant than the air inside her tiny third-floor apartment. Thick and pungent, the evening wafted indoors. Street noises rose up to lure her outside—revving engines and bright lights and blaring horns and booming stereos, scantily dressed women laughing and calling to men driving convertibles and straddling motorcycles. Everyone was in search of sex on this hot, southern night.

Including Georgia Arletta Adams.

She sighed and pressed her nose against the window screen. Even people close to her would be shocked if they knew that she, Nurse Goody-Two-Shoes and everybody's little sister, suffered from her own private affliction: a breathing, burning, pulsing, vigorous, distracting, overblown sex drive.

She stopped short of calling herself a nymphomaniac because she wasn't promiscuous. In fact, she had a reputation for being a bit of a prude, which, she'd discovered years ago, was an effective safeguard against a dangerous tendency. She had simply refused to bend to the will of her restless body.

Oh, there'd been a couple of unremarkable encounters with other grad students in college, and one or two brief relationships since. But the men hadn't excited her, hadn't tapped into her secret garden.

Georgia walked to the kitchen and opened the refrigerator door, sighing with relief when the cool air hit her skin. She lifted the tail of her T-shirt to cool her stomach, then removed a banana from the crisper to munch while her refrigerator worked overtime.

She eyed the banana and sighed—everything looked phallic these days. She bit off the end and fanned her shirt. By immersing herself in work, she'd managed for the most part to keep a lid on her powerful urges… until a year ago. Then, triggered by either the surge of hormones most women experience in their early thirties, or years of repression, or this damnable relentless southern heat, her body had launched a quiet rebellion.

Georgia had always assumed she would marry one day, but she'd stepped up her efforts to find Mr. Right, thinking that exploring her fermenting sexuality would at least be safer within the confines of a monogamous relationship. Rob Trainer had seemed like the perfect candidate: handsome and successful, well-mannered and reflective, intelligent and friendly. She liked him immensely. But after investing the past several months in their relationship, she had come to one conclusion: the man had no interest in sleeping with her.

She was ripe for the picking, and he seemed content to walk around the tree.

And, if truth be known, it was more than the sex she craved—it was the closeness, the intimacy generated when two loving people shared sex. The tingly "you complete me" stuff she saw in movies but observed between too few couples these days. If the specter of true love still existed, she wanted it. Matchless love, not the desolate, codependent relationship her parents had passed off as a marriage. She wanted a man who would lower his guard, a man who would make a fool out of himself for her, a man who would cherish her.

Georgia sighed and fanned herself. Meanwhile, that inner rebellion was now reaching cataclysmic proportions. During her nursing studies, she'd read documented cases of spontaneous combustion. At the rate her internal furnace was stoking, and with no end in sight to the scorching summer heat wave, she feared she might be approaching flashpoint.

She finished the banana, and reluctantly closed the refrigerator door, then studied the deep crimson pedicure on which she'd splurged in the feeble hope that Rob nursed a foot fetish. But last night he hadn't even blinked when she'd worn her new strappy high heels. Instead he'd warned her about falling and breaking her neck, then suggested that she double-check her disability insurance coverage and kissed her on the cheek. She'd never thought of herself as the kind of woman who would end a relationship because the guy wouldn't take advantage of her, but she had needs that were clamoring to be met. Somehow she had to find a way to let Rob know she was ready to take the next step, and soon.

   She made a face at her sofa as she passed through the living room on her way to the bedroom. Soon, too, she'd buy a comfortable couch, but for now, school loans and tips for nude dancing men took precedence. Georgia idly lifted her long hair from her moist neck, winding it into a loose knot. She dreaded the evening, and fervently hoped she wasn't about to ignite a blaze Rob might not be able to put out.

EPILOGUE

MANNY OLIVER NOTICED the small brown paper package on his desk when he returned from a particularly grueling staff meeting. When he saw Janine Murphy's name on the return address, he smiled, grateful for a pleasant distraction. His pleasure turned to puzzlement, however, when he unwrapped a black jeweler's box. Intrigued, he opened a small card taped to the top.

My Dearest Manny,

I had these made especially for you by a talented woman I met during my blissful honeymoon. Looking forward to seeing you soon.

Fondly, Janine Murphy Stillman

Stillman? Manny smiled wide and murmured, "All's well that ends well." He carefully opened the hinged box, then threw his head back and laughed a deep belly laugh.

Nestled against the black velvet winked an exquisite pair of gold cuff links fashioned into two tiny sets of angel wings.

* * * * *

CHAPTER TWO

"COME ON, GEORGIA, stop gawking and start squawking!" Toni laughed and dragged Georgia to her feet, then cupped her hands over her mouth and hooted at the gyrating man on stage. The naked bodybuilder wore a headdress and twirled a short stick with fire at both ends, seemingly oblivious of the danger to his lineage. He moved across the stage in little hops to the beat of the calypso music blaring from speakers at deafening decibels. His body was remarkably muscled and proportioned to the point of deformity. Georgia could only stare, and Toni cheered like a woman who'd never before seen a baton.

In fact, the entire room undulated with hundreds of standing women, their hands raised to offer tips, their voices lifted to offer encouragement to the men who performed on the U-shaped runway. Of course, the dancers didn't require much urging to remove every stitch of clothing and wag the audience into a frenzy. The throbbing music and high-pitched screams reached such a staggering crescendo, Georgia was certain the shaking mirrors that flanked the stage would shatter at any moment.

She suddenly swayed and grabbed the back of the chair in front of her for support. Embarrassment rolled over her in waves. Every square inch of her skin tingled. Her breasts felt heavy and, since the room was stifling hot, she couldn't blame their hardened points on the cold. Her stomach swam with dizzying desire.

Georgia held her breath and allowed the atmosphere to consume her. The scent of the performers' body oils, the taste of perspiration on her upper lip, the press of bodies around her, the flashing spotlights that crisscrossed the room, the pulsing music, all swirled around her like a haze of sexually charged ions. It wasn't so much the dancers' naked bodies but the blatant openness that she found so titillating, the fact that the men were proud of their physiques, and that the women weren't afraid to express their appreciation.

Georgia wet her salty lips. It was enough to drive a decent woman to do things she might not ordinarily do.

She fumbled behind her for her untouched rum drink. Curving her hand around the cool glass, she lifted it to her feverish cheek. Georgia glanced at Toni to see if her friend had noticed she was quietly freaking out, but Toni was laughing and waving dollar bills.

Thinking the alcohol might numb her too-keen senses, Georgia gulped the drink. The fire twirler exited in a blaze of glory, only to be replaced by a construction worker with a swaying tool belt. Within minutes, he had stripped down to his hard hat and was taking bids from the women on the perimeter of the stage. Georgia felt a tingling in her thighs and frustration crowded her chest. She tried to project Rob's face onto the body of the dancer, but she couldn't reconcile the two separate images of stability and sensuality.

"Some hammer, huh?" Toni asked, nudging Georgia out of her reverie.

"Hmm?" Georgia scanned the man's considerable attributes. "Oh, yeah, I guess." She drained her glass in another deep swallow.

"Hey, are you okay? I was just teasing about Rob earlier. Did you guys have a fight or something?"

"No."

Toni's eyes narrowed and she jerked her head toward the ladies' room.

Georgia grabbed her purse and followed a bit unsteadily, sensing an inquisition but grateful for the break from the onslaught of erotic cues.

Before the door closed behind them, her friend had lit a menthol cigarette. Georgia frowned, then opened her purse and retrieved a lipstick. "I didn't know you smoked."

Toni exhaled and leaned her rail-thin body against a condom vending machine. "Special occasions only. So, are you having a good time?"

She ran a finger around the collar of the sleeveless white button-up shirt she'd worn tucked into loose black jeans. "Sure."

"Liar. You've been in another world all night."

Her heart pumped the rum through her body, bypassing her empty stomach and sending the alcohol straight to her brain, making her feel floaty and somewhat philosophical. "I have the all-overs."

Toni squinted. "The all-overs? Funny, I don't remember that one from school."

Georgia turned and stared at her flushed reflection in the mirror and talked while she drew an uneven line of mocha lipstick onto her mouth. "I'm restless, fidgety, distracted."

"Horny?"

Leave it to Toni to cut to the chase. She sighed, puffing out her cheeks, liking the way her laugh lines disappeared. "Toni, do you think I would know if Rob was gay?"

Her friend choked, then coughed out a cloud of smoke. "Probably. Why would you think that?"

She blotted the lipstick with a rough paper towel. "I don't really. It's just that I can't figure out his...likes and dislikes."

Toni chortled and dismissed Georgia's concern with a wave. "They all have hang-ups, babe. My old boyfriend liked Aerosmith on the stereo when we made love. Go figure." She pressed fingers to her temples and closed her eyes. "Let me guess. Rob wants the lights off, and his socks *on.*"

Georgia gave her a wry smile. "I wouldn't know."

Her friend's eyes bulged. "You mean the two of you have never had sex?"

"Right."

Toni pursed her lips. "Wow. How far have you gone? Second base? Third?"

Georgia quirked her mouth side to side. "I've never been quite sure what constitutes second and third base."

"You're stalling."

"Okay, we've kissed."

"No uncontrolled groping?"

"No."

"No nipplage?"

"Nada."

"No oral sex?"

She shook her head.

"Damn, no wonder you think he's gay. But I have a lot of homosexual friends, and I'd bet money that Rob is not gay."

Georgia tilted her head and inspected her own reflection. "Which means he doesn't find me sexually attractive."

Toni's face appeared over her shoulder. "Look at you—great hair, great face and great body. I'm telling you, the man is probably intimidated."

She rolled her eyes. "Oh, yeah, that's me, Miss Intimidation. I'm not exactly a siren, Toni."

"Precisely. Most of the time you look like Miss Untouchable." The cigarette bobbed wildly. With a flick of her wrist, she removed the clip that held Georgia's dark hair away from her face, then fluffed the long layers. "And here." Toni removed a cranberry-colored lipstick from her purse. "Toss that brown stuff and try this."

Georgia applied the new color, then frowned. "It's bright."

"Yes, ma'am." She twisted Georgia sideways, then unbuttoned her white shirt until the little pink bow on her bra was exposed. "Do you have to wear the bra?"

"Yes!" Bare skin under thin white cotton? Oi.

"Okay, okay." Toni pulled out Georgia's shirttail and tied the front ends high enough to expose her navel. "There. You just need to loosen up. I'm sure all Rob needs is a signal."

She looked back to her reflection and pursed her mouth. "You think?"

Toni dotted the cranberry lipstick onto Georgia's cheeks, then blended the color with her thumb. Someday her friend would make a wonderfully smothering mother. "Definitely. Do something to shake him up a little. You know, show up at his place wearing nothing but a belt or something like that."

Georgia chewed on her lip. "And what if he turns me down?"

Toni shrugged. "It'll be his loss and then you'll know where you stand. But trust me, he *won't* turn you down."

Her friend had a knack for making things seem so black-and-white. And even as her tongue formed more words of protest, Georgia stared at her new wanton image in the mirror and warmed to the possibilities. She'd worked her way through college and three years of post-graduate work. Every day she handled life-threatening situations at the hospital. So why would she be worried about making a pass at a man she'd been dating for several months? Maybe because it was safer to let him go on thinking she was Miss Modesty than to risk unleashing the passion that boiled beneath the surface. She didn't want to come across as some kind of…well, any of those names her mother had called her father's string of faceless girlfriends.

"Come on," Toni said, snuffing out her cigarette. "Let's buy Stacey a table dance——I saw her eyeing the pirate. Besides," she added with a wink, "we have some planning to do."

Georgia followed her friend, rubbing the headache

forming just behind her ear. While most people had a conscience, her *conscience* had a conscience—a something that reined in her urges, and kept her on her best behavior.

She swallowed. At least so far.

GEORGIA SLIPPED INSIDE her apartment door and swatted at the light switch. Still buzzing slightly from her last drink, she kicked off her shoes next to the couch and glanced at her new phone contraption, but the message light wasn't blinking. How flattering. She removed the portable phone from the base and headed for the bedroom, not the slightest bit sleepy. In fact, her pulse kicked higher with every step.

Over the past few hours, she'd thought about Toni's advice and allowed herself to be carried along on the crest of the erogenous wave rolling through the strip club. She'd decided her friend was right—Rob was waiting for her to make a move. So, during a shared cab ride home, Toni had settled upon the least threatening, yet highly erotic option: phone sex.

Despite that phone sex was a favored fantasy of hers, Georgia felt obligated to protest on behalf of the upstanding girl she was purported to be. Besides, she didn't know how to do it.

Toni had pshawed. "What's to know? You talk, you moan, you hang up."

"But how do I ask him if he wants to?"

"Don't ask, just *do*."

And if Rob were totally offended, Georgia reasoned, she could always move to the Midwest and change her name.

Moving slowly in the dark, she slipped out of her shoes. Could she pull it off? The fact that she'd never participated in phone sex before only heightened her anticipation. Her chest rose and fell more rapidly, her breasts tingled, her thighs grew moist.

She turned on a lamp, then dimmed the illumination to bathe her Verdigris iron bed and the mustard-colored comforter. After stepping out of her jeans and folding them over the padded seat of her vanity table, Georgia sat on the edge of the bed and sank her crimson-tipped toes into a green hooked rug she'd made when she was fifteen—a lifetime ago. At that age she had fantasized of romance and physical bliss, never imagining one element without the other. She had thought by now she would've met a man who could provide a constant supply of both. Could Rob?

She sighed. Well, soon enough she would know if her fantasies would get him off, or scare him off.

Georgia glanced at the clock. One-thirty, Wednesday morning. Rob would be in deep REM sleep. Although if things went to plan, he'd be wide awake within a few seconds. Before she had time to reconsider, she slipped off her white cotton panties and left them lying on the rug. Her hands shook slightly as she held the phone and pushed the button to retrieve Rob's preprogrammed number.

When his phone began to ring, warmth flooded her abdomen. After the third ring, she panicked and started to hang up, but before she could locate the darned Talk button, she heard his sleep-fuzzy voice come over the line.

"Hello?"

Her heart thudded so loudly she could barely hear him. "Hi, Rob, this is Georgia."

"Hmm?"

"D-don't talk," she said, then leaned back against a pile of pillows and lowered her voice to what she hoped was a sexy tone. "Just listen."

CHAPTER THREE

AFTER SIX YEARS on the police force, Officer Ken Medlock should have been used to late-night calls, but he still had trouble focusing on the voice at the other end of the line. He reached for the lamp on the nightstand, but remembered a split second after the sound of the hollow click that he'd forgotten to replace the burned-out bulb.

Did the woman say she was "Georgia"? His mind spun as he tried to place the name—a new dispatcher? Blinking seemed to help clear the cobwebs. One-thirty. Damn, the last time he'd looked at the clock had been less than an hour ago. His intermittent insomnia seemed to have grown worse as the temperature climbed—and now this interruption.

"Rob, I know it's late, but I've been thinking about…us…all evening and I was wondering…that is…" The woman with the sultry voice inhaled and Ken opened his mouth to tell her she had the wrong number.

"I'm not wearing panties."

His mouth snapped shut and his manhood stirred, proving at least one part of his body was processing information.

A small trembling laugh sounded. "I've always wondered if you were a boxer man or a brief man."

What was the mystery woman's intention? Engage in a little late-night dirty talk to entice this Rob guy to come over? "Boxer," Ken blurted, then swallowed and leaned back onto his requisite three-pillow stack. Had he lost his mind? Or more appropriately, had he lost his shame?

"Mmm. Do you sleep in them?"

When I sleep. He couldn't remember such a welcome interruption though—few of his *dreams* were this good. He might have thought his partner was playing another practical joke on him, but even Klone wouldn't go this far. And the woman sounded so sincere, she had to be the real thing. His job required him to make life-and-death split-second judgments, but suddenly he was gripped with indecision—'fess up, hang up, or play up.

His body made the decision by sending a flood of desire to swell his deprived loins. What would be the harm in succumbing to one wild impulse? Before he had time to reconsider, he muttered, "Mmm-hmm." Knowing she might realize her mistake any second, he held the mouthpiece a few inches away from his mouth. On the other hand, if she didn't know what kind of underwear Robbie Boy wore, maybe she'd just met the man. Or maybe she was a prostitute. Ken had lived in the South for most of his adult life, but had never met a woman named Georgia.

"I thought it was time to let you know how I feel."

Or maybe her boyfriend simply didn't know how good he had it. "Okay," he offered.

"But not if this makes you uncomfortable."

He found the crack in her confidence endearing. Did she have any idea how sexy her voice sounded? And the only thing uncomfortable at the moment was his hardening erection. "I'm fine. Um…go on." When silence followed, he was afraid she was onto him.

"Can you shed those boxers?" she whispered.

In for a penny, in for a pound. Ken reached beneath the warmish pilled sheet and slid off his shorts in three seconds flat, not an easy feat in a waterbed while juggling a phone. The TV remote he'd left on the bed crashed to the wood floor. "They're gone. Are—" Ken wet his lips. "Are you undressed?"

"Not yet," she said. "I'm wearing a white button-up blouse and a white bra."

Ken closed his eyes. "Take…take them off," he urged.

From the rustling sounds, he surmised she was stripping. His mind whirled, wondering what this woman who called herself Georgia looked like. Was she redheaded? A brunette? Blonde? Brown eyes? Blue? Hazel? Long hair? Short? Sections of his fantasy woman clicked into place like the tiles in a vertical slot machine. Long, dark hair, blue eyes, a great smile, curvy. And peeling off her clothes.

"They're off."

Ken bit his tongue to keep from asking more questions that might end the phone call. His hand slid beneath the sheet, and he imagined Georgia easing into the bed next to him.

"It's hot over here," she continued, much to his relief. "And I just couldn't sleep after leaving the club. All that nudity affected me."

She was a stripper? That explained the stage name. His conscience eased somewhat. At least she wasn't some innocent lady shedding her modesty for the first time. And she must have an incredible body. Her shadow of an accent didn't belong to a Southern belle, but in his mind, Georgia was as lush and sticky-sweet as her name implied.

"I need to relax," she said, sighing.

Ken could almost feel her breath warming his neck. His answer was a low groan of encouragement.

"Lately I've been hoping we could become more… intimate."

"I never knew," he replied in a low tone. *The truth.*

"We've both been a little shy, but somehow, it's easier to talk about my fantasies on the phone like this."

A hot flush traveled over his skin. "Go on."

"My breasts," she said, her voice suddenly tentative again.

Round? High? Firm?

"Sensitive. *So* sensitive."

Not as visual, but he could make it work. "Mmm-hmm."

She was breathing harder now. "My hair is down and tickling my breasts."

Thank you, thank you, thank you.

"Can you picture me lying next to you?"

Could he? "Uh-huh." She was killing him. Moonlight streamed through a window next to his bed, transforming the tangled sheets into a woman's figure. Her skin was smooth and golden with faint and minuscule tan lines. Beautiful. Their hands tangled as they stroked and caressed each other.

"Touch me lower," she murmured.

His breath caught in his chest.

"Lower," she urged, and he moaned, picturing the dip of her navel and the tangle of dark hair in the vee of her thighs.

"There," she moaned, gratified. "Yes, there."

Ken tensed, moved by the emotion in her voice. "I can't wait much longer."

She was practically panting now. "Yes...now."

He imagined himself ready over her waiting body. Their moans would mingle at the union. She would close around him as he sank deeper and deeper in her warmth.

Her voice reverberated in his head, a stream of soft moans, punctuated with throaty inflection to capture a rhythm he matched without hesitation. He could never tire of her voice. "Talk to me," he begged.

"S-so...good...ohhhhhhhhh...harder...faster..."

Ken obliged, his breathing becoming more ragged with every thrust. "When you're ready," he whispered, "take me with you."

"Yes," she gasped. "Together...now...oh, yes..."

Ken's eyes rolled back as he joined her powerful release. Their voices culminated in staccato cries, then gentled to quiet moans. Satisfied sighs hummed on the line as they both labored to control their breathing.

"That...was...great," he managed between great mouthfuls of air. His body spasmed with residual pleasure and he felt utterly drained.

"Mmm-hmm," she agreed with a silky laugh, then cleared her throat. "I...guess I'd better let you get back to sleep." She'd retreated into shyness. "Good night, Rob. Call me tomorrow." He heard a faint click, then a dial tone.

Ken floundered to sit up and managed to knock the phone and other clutter off the nightstand. He swung his feet to the floor, his heart still recovering from his unexpectedly naughty phone call. He'd seen, done, and heard a lot of things during his years as a beat cop, but this was a first. Unbeknownst to her, the woman had performed a public service.

Today—no, yesterday—had been one of the lousiest days he could remember. No deaths, thank goodness, but he'd answered an excessive number of domestic violence calls, and the criminals seemed to get younger all the time. He became a cop partly because he wanted to pass a safer world on to his nieces and nephews, and partly because he felt law enforcement was the best possible use of his God-given physical strength and mental discipline. He'd simply underestimated the sheer malice with which people treated one another, especially members of their own family.

Every cop experienced times when he simply didn't want to get up and go to work, and Ken had been entertaining such thoughts when he lay down. And although his body now tingled with muscle fatigue, his spirit sang with new vitality. Ken decided he needed to get his priorities in order and find a good woman, then maybe he wouldn't dwell on the misery he encountered every day.

And maybe he wouldn't be tempted to steal an orgasm meant for another man.

His conscience poked at him, but what could he do
now? Nothing, he decided hastily, rising and strid-
ing toward the bathroom. Chalk up the misdirected
phone call as a once-in-a-lifetime experience and let
it be. Tomorrow, Georgia and Rob—whoever they
were—would have a big laugh when they realized
she'd coaxed a wrong number to climax.

Ken leaned against the sink and ran a hand through
his flattened hair, thinking about the sometimes shy
voice of his unwitting partner. What if, instead, she
felt humiliated and kept her secret? What if she worried about the identity of the person with whom she'd
shared such an intimate experience?

Nah.

He splashed his face with handfuls of cool water,
then stumbled back to bed, unable to stop a slow grin
and a wide yawn as he fell onto his pillow. One thing
he did know. His insomnia was cured for tonight.

CHAPTER FOUR

"So how did it go?"

Georgia jumped at the sound of Toni's voice over her shoulder, then smiled sheepishly at her friend. In fact, despite a slight headache and sitting on gum stuck to the bus seat this morning, she'd been gloating ever since her alarm had sounded. She was officially a naughty girl. Life was good.

Toni snapped her fingers in rapid succession. "Come on, you were humming, for Pete's sake."

Georgia glanced at the charts she was working on, then checked her watch. "I'm due a break. Want to get some coffee?"

"Sure."

After letting the admissions clerk know she'd be away for ten minutes, Georgia wrote "break" beside her name on a dry eraser board. "How are things in the nursery?"

Toni looked heavenward. "Please tell me what possessed me to transfer up to the fourth floor."

"You love babies, and you have the hots for the new head of obstetrics."

Her friend frowned. "Oh, yeah."

"And how's that little ploy going, by the way?"

"Well, he calls me 'Terri.'"

"Oh." Georgia hid her smile and led the way into the staff vending room. Two med students sat at a corner table, one studying, one asleep sitting up.

Toni threw up her hands. "My question is, how did the man get through anatomy if he can't remember names?"

Georgia poured them both a paper cup of coffee, then handed Toni a packet of sugar. "He'll come around."

"I hope so. I was planning to have snared a doctor by now. No offense, Georgia—I'm not as enamored with the nursing profession as you are. I'm here to get a husband. A rich husband with talented hands."

Georgia laughed. "Liar. You're a good nurse, Toni. By the way, how was Stacey feeling this morning?"

"Not so good, but she'll recover." After glancing at the med students, she leaned forward. "So I'm dying here. Did you call Rob and...you know?"

Feeling a blush climb her neck, Georgia blew into her cup.

"What, what, *what?*"

"Yes."

Toni squealed. "I knew you could do it if you just let go. Did he like it?"

She pursed her lips, reliving flashes of last night's erotic conversation that still sent stabs of desire to her stomach. His responses had been unexpectedly enthusiastic and sensual—a side of him she'd never seen but had hoped for. "I think so." She lowered her voice and added, "It was fabulous."

Toni grinned. "You vamp, you."

Basking in her awakening, Georgia lifted her chin

and smiled. She'd misbehaved and she hadn't been struck by lightning. She hadn't grown horns. And she hadn't been tempted to ogle strange men on the bus this morning. She had her unfettered hormones perfectly under control.

"I take back what I said about Rob being a bore. The man's obviously a sleeper."

"A sleeper?"

"You know, unassuming. Awakens unexpectedly." Toni wagged her eyebrows.

"Ah."

"When will you see him again?"

"I told him to call me today."

Slurping her coffee, Toni said, "Let's hope he didn't get all Republican at the light of day."

Georgia's smile fizzled. "What do you mean?"

Toni crinkled her nose and pulled an innocent face. "Nothing."

"Oh, no, what do you mean?"

A sigh escaped her friend. "The whole buyer's remorse thing. I just wondered if it was the same with phone sex as it is with real sex. You lose one out of three guys to morning-after malady, you know."

Doubts crowded her previous good cheer. "You mean you think he enjoyed it last night, but he doesn't respect me this morning?"

Toni tossed her half-empty cup into the trash can and wiped her hands together in a "that's that" motion. "Forget I said anything."

She frowned. "I'll try."

"When do you get off?" Then she winked and poked Georgia in the ribs. *"Again?"*

"Oh, you're a riot. I clock out at three."

"Don't worry, he'll call. Ta ta."

Georgia pushed aside her nagging concern and threw herself into the chaos of the afternoon. But every E.R. triage nurse typically experienced at least one day a week during which she questioned her decision to become a nurse in the first place, and today turned out to be hers. Her adolescent dreams of fixing people's bodies—and, thus, their souls—seemed ludicrous in the wake of stomach flus, food poisonings, puncture wounds and other less palatable ailments. No dramatic lifesaving procedures today. She blamed the heat for the elevated tempers. Every patient tested her patience, bickering about the wait, second-guessing the treatments she offered. As her shift progressed, Georgia's anxiety level increased. And as her anxiety level increased, her confidence waned. And as her confidence waned, she felt less and less good about her recent foray into the world of the sexually assertive.

What if Toni were right and Rob had decided her forwardness was uncouth? How would she be able to face him? She'd whipped up a little fudge sauce for their plain vanilla relationship, but had it been too rich for his blood? Since his consulting assignments required that he travel, and due to the nature of her job, they rarely spoke during the day. But after she clocked out, she'd make an exception and call him to gauge his reaction.

"What kind of a nurse are you?" a big, unpleasant-smelling man demanded when she refused to give him a physical for his medical insurance.

Georgia put her hands on her hips. "Sir, this is an emergency room, not your family doctor's office."

"I don't have a family doctor. That's why I came here. I figured it would be faster."

"Get out," she said, jerking her thumb toward the door. "You're taking up room for people who have legitimate emergencies."

Her statement really wasn't true, at least not today, she noted with an irritated grunt as the man stalked out. Almost every person who came through the door had made a mockery of E.R. medicine, a mockery of her childhood aspirations. She woke up every morning, eager to aid those in need, eager to make a real difference in someone's life. But even Nurse Goody-Two-Shoes had her limits. God help the next person who came in to waste her time and the hospital's resources, because she certainly wouldn't.

"Whistling? Man, you must've gotten lucky last night."

Unwrapping a hamburger on his knee, since every square inch of his desk was occupied, Ken cut his gaze toward his partner. "Get your mind out of the gutter, Klone. I slept well, that's all. Damn near forgot what it was like."

The older man grinned and proceeded to talk with his mouth full of club sandwich. "What, no hot number to keep you up all night?"

A *wrong* hot number. "Man, you ask too many questions."

"Job hazard," Klone said, undaunted. "You've been complaining about your insomnia for weeks, but I think you've just been up late womanizing and partying."

"Yeah, my life isn't half as interesting as you lead people to believe."

"Well, then maybe you've been moonlighting."

"Klone, I haven't been moonlighting." Unless he could get paid for working crossword puzzles in the wee hours of the morning.

"Because if you need some extra cash to fund your lifestyle, every business in town is clamoring for cops to direct traffic on their off-hours. If you ask me, the city needs to put up a few more stoplights. Where are you working?"

"Klone, I have not been moonlighting."

"Well, if you ask me, it's high time you find a good woman to settle down with."

"I didn't ask you."

"That's why you're not sleeping, because you're yearning for a soul mate."

Ken grimaced and looked around at their colleagues moving about. "Jesus, keep your voice down. Have you been reading *Cosmo* or something?" He grunted. "I've told you before, marriage isn't for me." He wanted his mind squarely on his job. His first partner out of the academy had been a good-natured fellow, top of his class, with a successful career ahead of him until he met his "soul mate," a woman who messed with his mind so badly, he'd committed grievous errors on the job. The last time Ken had seen him, the guy was unemployed, divorced, and a tad on the bitter side.

Ken's own experiences were somewhat less dramatic, but he'd tired of vapid women who seemed de-

"Sorry, boy," he murmured, aware of a crowd gathering around. One of the dog's legs bent at an odd angle, and he was bleeding badly from the hip. Gathering his wits, Ken looked around and spied the entrance to the County Hospital emergency room less than a half block away. Perhaps someone there could at least stop the bleeding until he could transport the dog to a veterinary clinic.

Decision made, he tied a handkerchief around the dog's muzzle to keep him from biting in his pain, then bundled the dog into the back seat of his squad car. He covered its trembling form with a blanket from the trunk, knowing the gesture probably gave him more comfort that it gave the dog. He hoped against hope he hadn't mortally wounded the poor pooch. Ken slid into his seat, and zeroed in on the emergency room entrance. He'd find help there.

CHAPTER FIVE

"SEE YOU TOMORROW," Georgia called to a coworker as she walked toward the E.R. exit.

What a ghastly day. She removed her name badge and her pace quickened at the thought of talking to Rob. After mulling the matter for hours, she'd decided that he couldn't have feigned his responses last night. She knew abandon when she heard it, and he'd had it in spades. He'd probably already left her a message at home.

The service door next to the stairs burst open and a tall uniformed police officer emerged carrying a small body wrapped in a blanket. "He ran in front of my car," he said, his chest heaving. "He's bleeding, and I think his leg is broken."

Adrenaline and years of training took over and she bolted into action, waving him toward a triage room and yelling ahead as she jogged beside him. "We have a small victim who was struck by a car! Which room is available?"

"Three," the clerk said, handing her a chart as she passed. People parted and Georgia looked for the attending doctor as she led the way into the empty room. "Somebody get Dr. Story," she called before the door closed, then automatically grabbed a pair of surgical gloves from an overflowing box.

She felt a split second of sympathy for the broad-shouldered police officer who lowered his bundle gently onto the examining table. His shirt was blood-stained and his face was creased with worry that pulled at her heart. *This* was the basis of E.R. medicine. *This* was how she could make a difference in the world. She felt an instant bond with the man. He, too, was in the business of saving lives.

"Do you have the victim's name?" she asked, stepping forward.

"No," the officer said, then pulled back the blanket. "He wasn't wearing a collar."

Georgia froze as she surveyed the hairy mass. "It's a dog."

"Yes, ma'am."

His Southern manners aside, exasperation puffed her cheeks as the bond between them vanished with a poof. She stripped off the surgical gloves and strove to keep her voice even. "We treat people here, Officer, not animals."

He frowned. "Can't you make an exception?"

"Absolutely," she said ruefully, "if I wanted to lose my job." She stepped to the door and yelled, "Cancel the call for Dr. Story." Turning back to the dark-haired policeman, she pulled her most professional face. "We have health codes to maintain. You, of all people, should know that."

His dark eyebrows knitted and he adopted a wide-legged stance. "You could at least bandage the cut."

Her heart went out to the poor dog, and she crossed her arms to keep from following her instincts to heal. She also had instincts to eat, pay rent and not default on school loans, which would be difficult to satisfy if she were fired. Even after a year, she was still considered a greenhorn in emergency medicine. Dr. Story watched her like a hawk. A flagrant violation like this one could be the end of her career at County Hospital, a stain on her record. Georgia swallowed and averted her gaze. "I'm sorry—hospital procedures. The veterinary clinic on Sixteenth Street is the closest facility."

The officer's anger was palpable. But instead of leaving, he turned and scanned the shelves of supplies, his big hands touching everything.

"What are you doing?"

"What *you* should be doing," he growled, then yanked a roll of gauze from a box and unrolled several lengths.

She opened her mouth to protest, then realized the futility of arguing with a man twice her size, with three times the determination. Georgia hung back, but as he clumsily wrapped the gauze around the dog's body, something…happened. Unexpected warmth and admiration expanded her chest. The man hadn't a clue what to do, but was driven to act. However misguided, she couldn't help but respect his zeal. When he unwound another twenty feet or so of the gauze, she shook her head. Just like a man to overdo.

"That's enough," she said quietly.

He glanced up, his eyes flashing, ready for battle.

"He won't be able to breathe," she added, then donned more gloves and found tape and scissors. With resignation that she'd probably get written up and reprimanded, if not out-and-out fired, Georgia leaned forward and finished the bandaging, then gave the animal a perfunctory examination. The dog and the cop were wide-eyed and silent, but she could feel the man's anger had dissipated. "Officer—?"

"Medlock," he supplied.

"Officer Medlock, my knowledge of a dog's anatomy is limited, but it appears he does indeed have a broken leg. He might have a broken rib or two as well, but his breathing is good, so I don't believe his lungs were punctured. There's no blood in the mouth, nose, or ears, so if he has internal bleeding, it does not seem to be profuse. And that—" she stepped back and peeled off her gloves "—is absolutely all I can do."

He smiled suddenly and her breath caught in appreciation. Officer Medlock was a great-looking man. Pushy, but great-looking. When she realized she was staring, embarrassment swept over her. Her appreciation of his masculinity was stirred only because of her state of…stirredness.

"Thank you, Dr.—?"

"I'm an R.N.," she said. "Nurse Adams."

"Nurse Adams," he repeated. "Thank you for giving me peace of mind, ma'am."

Her pulse kicked higher under his scrutiny. Few, if any, grown men called her "ma'am." It was kind of… pleasurable. "You're welcome. Now please get out of here while I still have a job."

Ken tried to study the woman's face without appearing to. Her dark blue eyes were heavy-lidded and astonishing, and her mouth… The woman had that fresh-faced, girl-next-door vitality that provoked neighboring boys to buy binoculars. He mentally shook himself, realizing that last night's incognito phone call was behind his heightened awareness. The dog whined, reminding him of his immediate priority. Gently, he rewrapped the animal and lifted the bundle from the table.

The nurse held open the door. "I was just going off duty," she said with the barest hint of a smile. "I'll show you the exit."

"To guarantee I make it out of here?" he asked wryly.

"Something like that."

As he laughed good-naturedly, she removed a leather shoulder bag from behind a counter, then told a clerk she was leaving and ordered an immediate disinfecting of exam room three. As she joined him, he was overwhelmed with the urge to know her, to find out if she were involved with anyone. He scoffed inwardly. Of course someone as beautiful as she would already be involved, maybe married, and probably to a doctor who earned ten times as much as a policeman. Ken tried to keep the dog's head covered as they headed toward the exit so he wouldn't get the woman into trouble, but the poor mutt whined most of the way, raising eyebrows. His unwilling cohort kept her eyes averted and walked swiftly.

"Georgia!"

At the sound of the name that had been on the periphery of his brain all day, Ken halted midstride. The woman next to him hesitated, then kept going.

"Georgia!" someone repeated, louder. He turned to see a plump woman jogging toward them. The comely nurse turned as well.

Ken's feet stopped moving as his brain tried to assimilate the information. This woman's name was

Georgia? He'd never met anyone named Georgia. What were the chances he'd meet two in less than twenty-four hours? He zeroed in on her voice and tried to match hers with the one running through his head. It was possible—he almost laughed—but highly unlikely.

Still, his mind raced for a logical-sounding question that might help him determine if this fabulous-looking woman was the same... No, she simply couldn't be.

"Get out of here," she hissed out of the side of her mouth.

But his feet refused to move.

"Georgia," the woman gasped, lumbering to a halt in front of them. Then she zeroed in on the whining blanket. "Is that a *dog?*"

"Melanie, did you need something?" Nurse Adams asked her, while frowning at him and nodding toward the exit.

The other woman craned her neck, eyes alight with curiosity, then handed his companion a yellow sticky-note. "I almost forgot to give you this message. Rob phoned and said he was called out of town unexpectedly."

Ken swallowed and nearly dropped his patient. *Rob?*

CHAPTER SIX

HIS TONGUE HAD turned to cotton. Ken stared at the woman he'd just met as she read the note in her hand. *This* gorgeous woman was the same silky-throated creature who had roused him from sleep last night? His skin tingled with revelation. He glanced up, expecting a spotlight to be shining on his guilt-ridden head.

"Thank you, Melanie," she said tersely, then proceeded through the door, seemingly lost in thought.

But Ken wasn't ready to let Nurse Georgia Adams walk out of his life. He hurried forward, mindful of the bundle in his arms. "Wait!"

She turned back, but seemed less than thrilled to see him still standing there. "As I said, Officer, the vet clinic is on Sixteenth Street. You don't need an appointment."

He tilted his head, desperate to extend their conversation. "D-don't I know you from somewhere?"

She looked perplexed. "I don't think so. I've never been in trouble with the police."

"Georgia Adams," he murmured to himself, pretending to mull her identity, when in truth, he simply liked the way her name rolled off his tongue. "Georgia Adams…"

"Maybe you've seen me in the halls of the hospital," she offered.

"Wait a minute," he said, improvising. "I know a guy named Rob who dates a woman named Georgia."

She took a half step toward him. "Rob Trainer?"

Ah, the identity of the unwittingly deprived boyfriend. "Um, yes." He shifted the dog's weight to his left side while he extended his right hand. "Ken Medlock."

She hesitated, then placed her soft, healing hand in his. "How do you do, Officer Medlock."

"Ken is fine," he said, reluctantly releasing her hand.

"I'll tell Rob I ran into you when he returns from his business trip."

Uh-oh. "Well, he might not remember me—I've only spoken to him a couple of times...casually." He swallowed. "At the gym?"

"The gym on Arrow Street? Yes, that's where Rob works out." She stroked the dog's ear where the blanket had fallen away. "Poor boy, I hope he's okay."

He could only nod, struck dumb by the serendipity that had brought them together. He wasn't the superstitious type, but it had to be some sort of sign...didn't it?

"Well," she said, lifting her hand in a little wave, "good luck. I'm sure the clinic will fix up your friend like new."

She pivoted on the heels of her sensible white shoes, dragging off a white lab coat to reveal pink scrubs... and a fabulous figure. Her dark hair was pulled into a clasp at the nape of her neck, hanging midway to her back. Nurse Georgia Adams walked thirty feet away to a bus stop, then settled herself onto a wooden bench to wait, just as if she weren't the most beautiful woman on the streets of Birmingham.

Then Ken smiled as a snatch of their conversation returned to him. *I'll tell Rob I ran into you when he returns from his business trip.*

The most beautiful woman on the streets of Birmingham was alone for a few days.

The dog whimpered, yanking his good sense back from the gates of Fantasyland. Ken hurried toward his squad car.

GEORGIA SHIFTED on the hard bench, her cheeks burning with shame. Since Rob had opted to leave her a message at the hospital instead of talking to her in person, he must be upset over their little "session." Toni was right; she'd spooked him by being so forward. She read the note again, wishing the hastily scribbled message had divulged where he was going, or even how long he'd be gone. *Called out of town unexpectedly. Rob.*

The man's communication was nothing if not…economical. But Stacey's wedding was only three days away, and she'd been looking forward to attending it with Rob in the hope that witnessing someone else's lifetime commitment would shed some light on their own aimless path.

She turned her head and watched Officer Ken Medlock's broad back receding. He still held the injured dog in his arms, and when a corner of the blanket fell, he tucked it back in place. Georgia smiled, thinking how few men would have taken the time to aid a wounded animal, especially a big, strapping man.

She'd been surprised to hear that he knew Rob. Officer Ken seemed more...earthy...than Rob's yuppie accountant friends. Of course, he did say they only knew each other from the gym. She frowned just as he rounded the corner and disappeared from view. On the other hand, they must be more than mere acquaintances if Rob had mentioned her name.

Georgia bit into her lower lip, realizing she'd never thought about the kinds of things Rob might say about her to his friends. Would he tell them about the phone sex? She had told Toni, but only because Toni had encouraged her to share her fantasies with Rob in the first place. And she trusted Toni as a confidante.

But the idea of Rob's friends knowing made her extremely uneasy. Almost as uneasy as the fact that she didn't know whether Rob would tell them.

In truth, she really didn't know that much about the habits and acquaintances of the man whom she'd met at the party of a friend of a friend going on ten months ago. They had met over soggy egg rolls and talked about a movie they'd both seen and hated. She hadn't been bowled over, but he was nice and seemed nonpsychotic—a definite bonus in today's singles market.

When Rob Trainer had called a week later to invite her to a Chamber of Commerce cocktail party, she'd said yes, and they'd been seeing each other regularly since. Hectic schedules on both their parts had minimized their dating time to scant weekends and occasional day trips out of Birmingham. Yet even when they were together, Rob wasn't a chatty fellow. His parents were from Cincinnati, but now that she thought about it, she couldn't remember if he'd ever mentioned siblings.

But still waters ran deep. Rob was a handsome, pleasant man with enough ambition for three people. So what if he wasn't always thoughtful and romantic— what man was? An unbidden image of Officer Ken's anxious expression over the injured dog pulled at her heart. Was Rob an animal lover? She doubted it, considering what a neatnik he was. But in her musings, she was starting to realize how few personal details she knew about the man with whom she had initiated phone sex. For all she knew, he could be a serial killer with a low sex drive. Maybe *that* was why he was to familiar Officer Ken.

Then she scoffed at her own silliness. For a straight-laced guy like Rob, a mere parking citation would be tantamount to a public flogging. Rob hadn't been quite as forthcoming with his background as she'd been with hers, but one thing she did know about her boyfriend—he was by the book.

Er, excluding *The Joy of Sex,* that is.

A staccato honk pulled her gaze from the spot she'd last seen the attractive police officer. The bus driver glared at her through the open door. "You comin' or not, lady?"

Georgia jumped to her feet and bounded aboard. If she didn't stop daydreaming, she'd never finish her errands. But even squeezing into a crowded seat among noisy passengers couldn't distract her from the recollection of Ken Medlock's rugged frame. Were Rob's shoulders that wide? She might stop locking her doors if every Birmingham police officer evoked that kind of security.

With a rueful sigh, she acknowledged the only reason she had responded physically to the uniformed man was that her late-night session with Rob had awakened disobedient places within her. Places that— dwelled upon for mere seconds, like now—sprang to life. Her thighs tingled, her breasts tightened, her stomach clenched. Her gaze remained fixed on the back of the seat in front of her. Her focus blurred, and external noises diminished to a static buzz.

Slices of their chance encounter jumped into her brain randomly, like a trailer to a movie. His square jawline, his broad nose, his sincere eyes. *Nurse Adams, thank you for giving me peace of mind.* His smile, his gratitude for her assistance. *D-don't I know you from somewhere?*

Had he felt it too—a connection? An electric physical attraction born of proximity and a common goal?

She admonished herself for thinking sexy thoughts about a man she just met, but something about Officer Ken Medlock seemed familiar. Or maybe his all-American robust good looks just made him seem approachable, as if he were someone she *should* know—like a handsome man in a magazine ad whose eyes reached out to a woman, telling her she was special and if only he could walk off the page, he would make her his. It could happen.

"Town Center Mall!" the driver shouted, yanking her from her schoolgirl fantasies. Georgia disembarked slowly, still suffering from the surreal effects of her musings, and headed in the direction of a shop Toni had recommended to buy a dress for Stacey's wedding. Her friend had described the clothes at Latest & Greatest as "cool duds on the cheap" and insisted Georgia ask for Tom Tom.

But Tom Tom, as it turned out, was *two* men, both named Tom, who were apparently unrelated, yet spoke in tandem.

"Ah, Toni sent you! We have—"

"—exactly what you need for a—"

"—summer afternoon wedding. Won't you—"

"—follow us?"

Georgia's gaze bounced back and forth, then she nodded and followed them to a rack of long filmy dresses. They flipped through the hangers, each whipping out a flowing garment.

"The pink stripe will be beautiful—"

"—with your hair. But the yellow—"

"—will set off your lovely—"

"—complexion. Although the blue floral—"

"—is a perfect complement for your eyes." The men looked at each other, then nodded and said in unison, "The blue floral."

Not her first choice, Georgia acknowledged silently. In fact, floral prints didn't even make her short list; she gravitated to solid-colored clothing. But since her opinion obviously didn't matter, she mutely acquiesced as they shooed her into a dressing room and waited outside, the toes of their pointy shoes tapping. To her surprise, they were right—the blue floral mimicked the indigo of her eyes, and the voluminous fabric fell in feminine folds that skimmed her ankles.

She smiled into the mirror, turning quickly to watch

the delicate hem float on the air. Suddenly, her older sister Fannie came to mind. Georgia had always tagged along to stores and sat in a corner of the dressing room to watch the magical Fannie try on dress after dress for the many dances and parties she attended. She was breathtaking, and possessed an uncanny knack for picking the dress that best showed off her perfect skin and more perfect figure. Their mother would stand behind Fannie in the mirror, beaming as the saleswomen proclaimed Fannie the most beautiful girl they'd ever seen. No one could take their eyes off her, most especially their mother, from whom Fannie had inherited her flashing green eyes and glossy flaxen hair.

Meanwhile, Georgia, being her father's namesake and sporting her father's blue eyes and unremarkable brownish hair, withdrew more and more into the background. Once they'd even left her at a department store by accident. Her father, whom she adored, had come to pick her up and had stopped at a pawnshop on the way home to buy a used 35mm camera. Georgia had been hooked instantly. Photography became her escape, her window on the human condition, and a link to her beloved father. He had died from cancer the summer she turned sixteen. She had just learned to drive, she recalled. Funny, but to this day, she'd never gotten her driver's license.

Her mother loved her; she had simply been preoccupied with Fannie and all that Fannie was. She still was, except now the preoccupation included Fannie's wealthy husband and their two darling daughters. It was a full-time job for her mother, keeping up with the accoutrements of Fannie's charmed life in Denver.

Georgia had been left to her own devices, furthering her photography and attending nursing school. One didn't have to be spectacular looking or musically inclined or a prima ballerina to take pictures, or to be a nurse.

Georgia scrutinized her silhouette and frowned. A darn good thing, too.

"How's it going in there?" one of the Toms called.

She exhaled and emerged nervously to head-nodding and hmm-hmming.

"Darling, you will—"

"—upstage the bride."

She smiled, pleased despite their exaggeration. Then, feeling somewhat like a dressmaker's dummy, she submitted to their tucking and pinning to the tune of snapped fingers and quick sniffs.

"What will your date be wearing?" the taller one asked.

"A suit, I suppose," she said. If he came, that is.

"A *navy* suit?" the other one asked, his voice suspicious. "He simply must wear navy to complement your dress."

She nodded mutely. Being a nice dresser, Rob probably had a navy suit in his closet. Georgia frowned. But why did the image of a navy uniform keep popping into her mind?

Both Toms scribbled on a piece of paper. "Go to the accessories department in Elm's and buy the Derrin straw hat—"

"—with a white band. Then go to footwear and buy the white espadrilles—"

"—with the ankle strap. By the time you get back—"

"—your lovely frock will be ready."

They smiled in unison and recapped their ink pens. Powerless to disagree in the wake of their frighteningly good taste, she took the piece of paper and stopped herself short of a curtsey before she re-donned her scrubs and left the store. Mall merchandising, she suddenly noticed, was all about sex. Loud, pulsing music. Lingerie and skimpy clothing in the windows. Judging from their stiff nipples, even the mannequins were turned on.

Bombarded with erotic cues, she simply couldn't stop thinking about the phone call. And she couldn't stop obsessing over Rob's reaction. Darn Toni for raising the questions in the first place. And darn that Ken Medlock for forcing his way into her impossibly crowded mind. She was suddenly glad she would most likely never see the man again.

As she was told, Georgia headed toward Elm's and, unfamiliar with the upscale store, meandered around until she found the accessories department. Feeling somewhat conspicuous, she glanced all around before trying on hats in the line the men had suggested. *Which* Derrin straw hat with a white band? There were so many. She tried on style after style, then conceded she hadn't enjoyed herself so much in a long time. She even loosened the clasp from her hair, toying with the idea of wearing it down for the wedding. At last she settled on a bowler style, crossing her fingers that Tom Tom wouldn't object to her choice. The espadrilles were fun and comfortable, but a whole heck of a lot more expensive now than when they were first popular a couple of decades ago.

Swinging both bags, she gave in to the rumbling in her stomach and stopped at the food court for a bagel and cream cheese. The mall was a great place to people-watch, a favorite pastime, even without her camera. Take that old man over there reading the paper—priceless. Or the triplets in the combination stroller, all eating ice cream. Or the policeman leaned over, lecturing a group of preteens seated around a table.

Georgia stopped chewing and squinted. Officer Medlock? Her pulse kicked up. What was he doing here at the mall? She watched him send the kids on their way, then glanced at her watch. Ah, the kids were playing hooky. He stood with his hands on his hips and stared after the boys who chanced sullen looks over their shoulders while they shuffled toward the exit.

She wondered how the dog had fared, and decided it was perfectly legitimate for her to ask—she'd put her job on the line, after all. But while she watched, a young woman tottered up to him wearing painted-on clothing, high heels, and exhibiting her mastery of hair-toss. Georgia glanced down at her own institutional clothing and resolved to slink out unnoticed. The officer responded to the young woman's inquiry with a smile that made Georgia swallow a chunk of bagel without chewing.

It promptly lodged in her esophagus, effectively blocking her airway. Georgia clutched her throat. She was choking. She was going to die with last night's tawdry act on her conscience… Her next conversation would be with St. Peter: "Oh, and here's Miss Ring-a-Ding-Ding…"

CHAPTER SEVEN

GEORGIA STOOD and flailed for a few seconds, trying to get the attention of the people around her before conceding she would have to try to administer the Heimlich maneuver on herself—perhaps on the back of a chair?

In the background she heard someone yell, "She's choking!" and before she could fling herself against a solid surface, two strong arms encircled her from behind and applied a quick upthrust below her breastbone. Her feet dangled. On the second thrust, the chunk of bread projected out of her mouth like a torpedo, bouncing off a table a few feet away. People scattered. She gasped for air like a racehorse.

Background applause registered dimly in her oxygen-deprived brain. She was shepherded into a seated position. "Are you all right?" she barely heard.

She blinked a man's face into view. An attractive man. A familiar, attractive man.

"Georgia, are you all right?"

She nodded in abject mortification, realizing that Officer Ken Medlock had saved her life. Didn't that mean he now owned her soul or something? He was kneeling before her, his face creased with the same concern she'd seen when he was carrying the dog. She felt like an idiot.

"How about something to drink?" he asked, his face close to hers.

The man had a cleft in his chin worthy of a super-hero. A strong nose, broad and straight. And she was mesmerized by his serious brown eyes, surrounded by layers of dark lashes and thick eyebrows that were, at the moment, raised. For lack of a better response, she nodded, then tried to clear her head as he reached for her drink. Her skin tingled like menthol—probably because everyone was staring, certainly not because of this man's proximity. She was, however, mindful of his big body. The dark blue uniform was tailor-made to form to his powerful frame.

His fingers dwarfed the paper cup he extended. Georgia noticed he wore a scholarly ring of some kind, but not the married kind.

Not that it mattered. She sipped slowly from the cup of fizzy drink, feeling his gaze bore into her and realizing she must look a fright—muss-haired, flush-faced and teary-eyed from the coughing. Her attempt at laughter came out sounding a little strangled. "You're a regular hero today, aren't you?"

His grin was boyish. "No heroes here, ma'am. Just doing my job."

His dark hair was short, but not short enough to curb the curl on top, highlighted by the sun streaming in from the skylights above them. Amazing how she hadn't known Officer Ken Medlock existed before today, yet their paths had crossed twice in a matter of hours.

"It's a small world, isn't it?" he asked, as if he'd read her mind. That uniform…those eyes…as if he could delve into her psyche, see all her dirty little secrets. She had yet to recover from her episode with Rob, and here she was, lusting after a virtual stranger. Just as she'd feared. Overnight, she had plunged herself into a cesspool of sexuality.

"Looks like you've been having fun up until now," he said lightly, gesturing to her Elm's shopping bags.

In her case, fun always led to misfortune. From now on, fun was her red flag: If fun, then cease and desist.

"Special occasion?" he asked, eyeing the hatbox.

The man had an amazing-looking mouth. Good for…blowing whistles. "A wedding," she croaked.

"Yours?"

From the size of his lopsided grin, he was trying to be funny. As if she couldn't possibly be the bride. Had he been chatting with her mother? She pursed her mouth, suddenly feeling cranky. "No, not mine."

He tilted his head. "Are you sure you're all right, ma'am?"

"Of course," she said, drawing back to massage her side. "That is, if you didn't crack a rib. I'm a registered nurse, Officer Medlock, perfectly capable of administering the Heimlich maneuver to myself."

He gestured vaguely to her chest area. "But you weren't doing it."

She inhaled, indignant. "I was calmly looking for a chair of the proper height."

The man appeared to be immensely amused. "Well, pardon me. Perhaps I should've just watched you turn blue while you looked for the right chair. Or better yet, maybe I should've sent you to a clinic on the other side of town."

Officer Ken was entirely too cocky. Smothering images her unfortunate choice of adjective conjured up, she stood and hurriedly cleared her ill-fated meal.

"Aren't you going to finish eating?"

"No." The two Toms were probably looking for her.

"Maybe you should have a doctor check you over."

And she needed to talk to Rob. "Officer, I think I can make that determination for myself." Georgia stooped to gather her bags and noticed the man had extremely large feet. Oi.

"I'll have to file a report on what happened here," he said. "Should I send you a copy?"

And be reminded of him again? And this spectacle? "No. Goodbye."

He inclined his head. "Ma'am."

His honeyed politeness only fueled her anxiety. She dragged her gaze from him and whirled toward the exit just in time for her conscience to kick in. With a chagrined sigh, Georgia turned back. "By the way, Officer, how's the dog?"

He crossed his arms over his chest, displacing all kinds of muscle. "The vet said he'd be fine."

"G-good," she said.

He nodded, his expression unreadable, although she got the impression he wasn't thinking about the rescued pet.

"Well...thanks."

"You're welcome, ma'am."

She didn't look back as she left the food court, but she could feel Ken Medlock's knowing gaze upon her even after she finished her errands and arrived at her apartment. Between the uniform and his massive frame, the infuriating man packed a powerful punch of sex appeal.

It was a good thing he was so irritating and she was so…fulfilled. Yes, fulfilled.

When she saw the light flashing on her new message recorder, her heartbeat raced. *Rob.* What would he say? Was he excited by the new phase of their relationship, or had she gone too far? After a deep breath, she pushed the Play button, then jumped when a mechanical voice blasted into the stale air of her apartment.

"Thank you for buying this Temeteck product! This is a test message to allow you to adjust the volume. Press '1' if you don't want this message to play again."

Georgia frowned and stabbed the "1" button. Darn it. Oh, well, it was still early. Rob would probably call later. She grabbed a bottle of water and the mail where she'd left it on the table and settled as best she could onto her hard sofa, which she was starting to despise.

Bills, bills, and a letter from her mother. Georgia winced, but decided to get it over with. She slid her finger under the envelope flap, then removed the two pages covered with her mother's familiar script. Same old, same old. She was extending her visit in Denver with Fannie and Fannie's perfect family unit. They needed her, after all.

Which meant that she didn't, of course. Georgia had been their father's child, Fannie their mother's. She didn't begrudge her sister's seemingly charmed life and abiding happiness, but she did resent her mother's implication that Georgia was less of a dutiful daughter for not producing an environment conducive to a visiting, meddling parent.

As expected, the chatty letter ended with:

> *P.S. I lit a candle for you at Mass on Saturday that someday you will find a man who will make you as happy as Albert makes Fannie. How is Bob?*

Georgia closed her eyes and laid her head back on the couch. Fannie had made The American Dream look so easy. She'd slighted her studies in favor of socializing and snared the son of the man who'd created some newfangled racing snow ski, ergo the lodge in Denver big enough to host the winter Olympics. Their wedding had been the social event of the year in Denver. Georgia's bridesmaid gown had cost as much as a semester's tuition. And their mother... Well, *her* happiness was cinched when the star of a nationally syndicated decorating show flew in from Los Angeles just to make the table arrangements.

How was a little sister supposed to follow that act? She wanted all those wonderful things, too, but maybe Fannie had inherited all the husband-hunting genes. Maybe she was destined to be simply a good aunt.

Her phone rang, an alien noise that sounded like a sick pet. *Rob, finally.* She yanked up the portable phone and pressed the Talk button. "Hello?"

"Hey, it's me," Toni said.

"Oh, hi."

"I take it from your depressed tone that Rob hasn't yet called to, um, return the favor?"

She sighed. "He left a message at the hospital saying he was called out of town unexpectedly, and that he would phone, but I haven't heard from him yet."

"He's probably just busy or away from a phone. Hey, what's this about you treating a dog in the E.R.?"

Georgia swallowed. "How much trouble am I in?"

"A lot. What the heck happened?"

She stood and paced the room. "A cop came running in carrying a patient wrapped in a blanket. I didn't find out it was a dog until we were already in an exam room."

"So you booted out the cop, right?"

"I tried. But when I refused to treat the dog, the guy started bandaging him up himself."

"So being the big-hearted person you are, you gave him a hand."

"I didn't have a choice!"

"Uh-huh. Well, I hope the guy was worth the grief you're going to catch tomorrow."

She glowered. "He wasn't."

"Dr. Story is liable to fire you, you know."

"Thank you for giving me something else to obsess about this evening."

"Something else? Oh, you're worried about Rob's reaction."

Georgia gasped. "I was fine until you started talking about buyer's remorse!"

"Well, just in case things don't work out with Rob, is the cop single?"

"I so completely didn't ask."

"Cops are supposed to be great in bed."

She blinked away the image of the man's huge feet.

"I could have sworn we were talking about me being fired."

"Just a little trivia I thought you might be interested in."

Erotic visions skipped through her head—uniforms, frisking, handcuffs. "Well, I'm not."

"Hey, did you find a dress?"

"Yes, the Toms practically flung it on me."

"Aren't they great?"

"I think 'frightening' is the word you're looking for."

"But I'm sure you'll look fabulous for Rob at the wedding."

"I just hope he's back in time to go with me."

"Yeah, you can tell a lot about a guy by how he acts at a wedding. You're lucky that you have the chance to expose him at this point in your relationship."

Georgia sighed. "I'm not so sure that Rob and I have a relationship."

"Well, after last night, he's bound to make a move in one direction or another."

"Yeah, well, thanks again for reminding me how far out on a limb I've climbed."

"Don't worry about Rob. Just try to get to work a few minutes early tomorrow to circumvent Dr. Story's lecture. And dress up."

"I appreciate the warning. See you tomorrow."

She disconnected the call, feeling itchy and restless. What a lousy end to such a promising day. Waiting for Rob to call, the dog episode, the choking incident, her mother's letter. She laughed morosely. Her mother would never have forgiven her if she'd died at the mall—well, maybe in Nordstrom's, but certainly not in the food court.

She closed her eyes, trying to pinpoint her unease, and Ken Medlock's face came to her. Why did the stranger push her buttons? Because he challenged her authority? Because he made her feel inept? Because his intriguing presence mocked her decision to become more intimate with Rob?

Rob. Such a nice man. So…predictable. Nice and predictable. The kind of man a woman could depend on to be faithful. In these days of disposable families, fidelity and trust were high on her list of characteristics in a lasting partner. Rob never looked at other women when they were out together, and he never bragged about a colorful sexual history. He was a gentleman.

She poked her tongue into her cheek. Well, he didn't call her "ma'am" in a rolling Southern tongue, but he was a gentleman nonetheless. Georgia tried not to dwell on the fact that while Rob never flirted with other women, he never flirted with her either. Because after last night, perhaps that part, at least, would change.

She stared at the phone, willing him to call and end the suspense. She counted to one hundred, but it didn't ring. She counted backward from one hundred, but it still didn't ring. Disgusted with herself for literally waiting for the phone to ring, she picked herself up, changed to loose shorts and a T-shirt, then went for a power-walk. Hoping to fatigue her muscles enough to induce sleep, she tried to outstride her plaguing thoughts. Last night she had slept like the dead—the satisfied dead—but tonight looked doubtful.

The exercise provided enough solitude to rehash her sudden and seemingly persistent lapses in judgment—the infamous call, jeopardizing her job, lashing out at a lawman. Around and around her mind spun, dredging up more remorse on each pass. This was why she'd always been a good girl, had always followed the rules. Because she was no good at being naughty. At this age, the most debauchery she could successfully aspire to was exhibiting bad manners.

She returned an hour later, winded and perspiring, to find her apartment almost as warm as the outdoors, and her message light flashing. With fingers crossed ridiculously, she pushed the Play button.

"Thank you for buying this Temeteck product! This is a test message to allow you to adjust the volume. Press '1' if you don't want this message to play again."

She cursed and stabbed the "1" button, then stalked over to her blasted thermostat. "Eighty degrees?" she mumbled. "It's eighty degrees in my apartment." She turned the knob until sixty-eight appeared on the display, but when she released it, the number flashed back to eighty, and there it remained.

Recognizing an impending breaking point, Georgia forced herself to take ten deep breaths of stale, hot air before she called the landlord. Even more irritated at not reaching a live person once she did call, she left an unladylike message about the broken thermostat.

Under the rush of a cool shower, she leaned into the wall and allowed the water to run over her neck and shoulders until she felt somewhat refreshed. More than anything, she needed food in her stomach and a good night's sleep. In the morning, she'd have a better perspective on today's unsettling events.

But when her eyes were still as big as silver dollars at two in the morning, Georgia remembered the old saying about a clear conscience being the softest pillow.

She rolled onto her side and stared at the cordless phone, working her mouth back and forth in thought. Suddenly, the answer came to her. She would call Rob and leave a message of apology on his machine for him to listen to when he arrived home. She'd been too forward, and she'd made them both uncomfortable. They could start over.

Georgia reached for the phone and pressed the speed dial button.

CHAPTER EIGHT

KEN'S BEDROOM was as hot as a boiler room on the sun. The apartment manager had promised his building was next on the list for cooling system repairs, but the entire city was under siege. He threw his legs over the side of the waterbed, then felt his way to the window and propped it open with a book in a futile attempt to catch a breeze.

He hadn't yet slept. His mind kept replaying the events of the past twenty-four hours, which still seemed too fantastic to believe. The only conclusion he'd reached was that his behavior on the phone the previous night had been abominable. The worst part was that he didn't regret it as much as he should, partly because the woman intrigued him, partly because the woman infuriated him.

Ken ran his hand down over his face. But Georgia Adams's crankiness did not exonerate him. He dropped back onto his waterbed—just as the phone rang.

He shot back up, his heart pounding, then relaxed with a laugh. He'd looked up Robert Trainer's listing and discovered their numbers were one digit off from each other's. What were the chances she'd dial it wrong again? Besides, she'd said that Robbie Boy was out of town. It was probably the station dispatcher and, hell, he wasn't sleeping, so why not go on duty a few hours early?

Ken yanked up the phone on the third ring. "Hello?"

"Oh. Hi, it's…me."

He instantly recognized her voice, and his body stirred.

"I didn't expect you to be home," she said quickly. "I was going to leave you a message."

Ken bobbed up and down on his mattress. He could tell her she had the wrong number and hang up. She'd never know it was him. He could do the right thing, right now. The words hovered at the back of his dry throat.

"Wh-when did you get back in town?" she asked.

Or he could do the *compelling* thing, right now.

Ken swallowed and held the phone away from his mouth. "Not long ago. I came back because…because I wasn't feeling well." He pushed down the rising guilt. He'd run a quick info sheet on Rob Trainer today, and uncovered the bare essentials of the man's life—employment, address, background check. Did Georgia know everything about her boyfriend? Her own history was squeaky-clean, including volunteer work with the Red Cross.

"Are your allergies bothering you again?" she asked.

"Um, I guess." He manufactured a cough.

"I thought your voice sounded a little strange," she said, "but I figured it was my new phone. If you're under the weather, though, I'm doubly sorry to wake you. This can wait until you're feeling better."

"No!" he practically shouted. "I mean, um, I was already awake and I'm glad you called."

"Actually, I called to apologize," she murmured.

He wet his chapped lips. "For what?"

"For...disturbing you last night."

He smiled into the phone. "Don't apologize. I...enjoyed it."

"You did?"

"I've been thinking about it all day."

"You have?"

Especially when we were together. "Yes."

"I...was afraid you'd think I was being too forward."

Her little laugh was the breeze he'd been waiting for all night long. Ken closed his eyes. Rob Trainer didn't deserve her. "Not at all. You were wonderful."

She sighed, a silky sound that made him bite back a groan. "I wish you were feeling better," she said, her voice wistful.

Ken sat up straighter, careful to keep the phone away from his mouth. "I feel well...enough."

"Well enough?" She laughed again, and his body hardened. "Well enough for an encore?"

He slid back against the pillows and exhaled. "Absolutely." A protest swam in the recesses of his mind, but desire chased it away. Desire for Georgia Adams. Because as wonderful as his fantasies had been the night before, now he knew what she looked like, how her skin glowed, the way her hands moved. "What are you wearing?"

"Nothing," she whispered. "It's too hot."

He groaned, imagining her lying in bed, arms

stretched overhead, her back arched. She reached for him, bringing him to full erection within seconds. "Georgia, my God, you're so beautiful. Come to me."

"I'm here," she said. "Kiss me...touch me."

"My hands...on your shoulders, arms, stomach."

"Mmmmmm...lower."

"Oh, you're killing me."

"That's it. There."

Her string of telltale moans tested his endurance. When he couldn't stand it any longer, he said, "Wrap your legs around my waist."

"Mmmmmm. Make love to me...now."

The quick sultry request nearly put him over the edge, but he held back, wanting to prolong their encounter. Her hair spilled all around, long and dark against her tangled sheets. Her breasts jutted, her thighs...welcoming. Oh, God help him. "Ahhhhhh," he breathed, easing inside her tight channel. "Oh, yes."

"Mmmm...all the way," she urged. "Yes, deeper... faster."

He obliged, gritting his teeth to match her rhythm without losing total control. "Georgia, I can't...last long. You're too much."

"Oh, I'm almost there...yes..." She gasped, then cried out, a desperately divine sound that drained his energy and his restraint. Ken yielded to her intensity, then matched it, their moans mingling into one song. His muscles bunched, then eased with diminishing spasms.

A comfortable silence stretched between them as they slowly recovered. His eyelids drooped. Georgia's sighs were definitely the cure for his insomnia.

"Are you sleeping?"

He blinked awake. "No." Then he laughed. "Well, almost. That was...incredible."

Her laugh was musical, like a wind chime. "Want to meet for lunch tomorrow in your office building?"

He plummeted back to earth, remembering that she believed she'd just shared an incredible experience with her boyfriend. Her lyrical laughter was meant for Rob. "Um, I think I'll stay home and try to shake this cold."

"I thought you said it was allergies."

"Yes. No. I'm not sure." He coughed as if a lung were in jeopardy.

"You sound terrible. I'll come by tomorrow to check on you."

"No! I mean, I wouldn't want you to catch something. I'll be fine, really."

"Are you sure?"

He felt weak with relief. "I'm sure. Your calls are all the medicine I need. Besides, not seeing each other in person for a few days will make things more...interesting." Was that him talking, purposely perpetuating a fraud?

"But you're still planning to go to Stacey's wedding Saturday afternoon, aren't you?"

When in doubt, dig thyself deeper into a hole. "Well...sure."

"I'm going early to help the bridesmaids dress, so I'll meet you there."

"Okay." He made a mental note to check for a gas leak since he'd obviously lost a few brain cells.

"Meanwhile, I hope you're feeling better soon."

She had the voice of an angel. "I'm feeling better already."

"Good. I'll let you go," she said softly. "Call me when you're back on your feet?"

Ken hesitated. Being on the receiving end of her misdirected phone calls was one thing, but initiating contact and impersonating her boyfriend... "Why don't you call me instead...tomorrow night?"

"Okay," she agreed. "I'll be working the blood drive tomorrow evening at the municipal building, but I'll call you when I get home."

"Great," he said, his mind already leaping ahead.

He kept the phone to his ear until the dial tone sounded, then fumbled around in the dark to replace the handset. He limped to the bathroom and turned on the light, squinting under the harsh illumination. A ten-minute hot shower did little to erase her from his mind. He toweled off quickly, his body still thrumming from their encounter, his ears still ringing with the cries of her release.

Leaning on the sink, he stared at himself in the mirror and rubbed his darkened jaw. Women had called him handsome, even rugged, but all he ever saw in his reflection was a too-big guy whose opportunities had been based more on his brawn than his brain. And, from his conduct of late, he was definitely proving everyone right who believed a big guy couldn't be a mental heavyweight.

Remorse descended on his bare shoulders, bowing them. What was he thinking? He wasn't, of course. He, the man of steel who had vowed never to let his libido get in the way of good sense, had succumbed to a soft voice with an erotic vocabulary.

His watch lay on the sink. Ken smiled wryly. Today was his birthday—thirty-seven. Did men have a biological clock? He laughed. He'd have to ask Klone, who spouted all that touchy-feely stuff when he wasn't playing practical jokes. He winced in the mirror, hoping his partner hadn't planned a birthday surprise. Good old Klone, always trying to set him up with a cousin or a niece of Louise's, although frankly, he hadn't met anyone who piqued his interest and his mind enough to make the rigors of romance worthwhile.

Until now. And as luck would have it, she had no clue how good they were together. In fact, she didn't even like him. And to make matters worse, he was helping to further the *other* guy's cause. A guy who, from Ken's cursory check, had a slightly blemished past.

A whine from his bedroom broke into his perplexing thoughts. He wrapped the towel around his waist and padded to the nook next to the dresser where he'd made a bed for Crash, the pooch he'd accidentally struck. "Can't sleep either, boy?" Poor little guy—he probably missed his owner and was confused about his immobility.

The battered dog gave a little bark in response, then lowered its head.

Ken stroked the spot between Crash's ears that he seemed to like. The ad he'd placed in the newspaper for a found dog wouldn't run for another week. "Until then we're stuck with each other," he murmured. "Hey, remember that lady doc who bandaged you up?"

The dog looked at him with shining eyes.

"Well, besides being gorgeous, she's really hot, but there's this other guy, see, and—" Ken stopped and laughed wryly. "And let's just say if she ever finds out what I've done, I'd be *lucky* to be in the doghouse."

Crash lifted his head and barked his apparent agreement.

CHAPTER NINE

"So NOW when I walk in, Dr. Baxter says 'Here's Nurse Terri who's always very merry,'" Toni boasted of her one-sided romance with the head of obstetrics. "It's so cute."

Georgia lifted an eyebrow. "The man made up a ridiculous rhyme to go with a name that isn't even yours, and you call it progress?"

"Well, you're having phone sex with your boyfriend of ten months and you call *that* progress."

Touché. "Just do me a favor and tell the guy your name, okay?"

"But he'll be humiliated to find out he doesn't know who he's been talking to."

"What about you, the person he's calling by the wrong name?"

Toni sighed. "I just keep hoping he'll glance at my name tag." She focused on something behind Georgia. "Uh-oh, here comes Dr. Story. See ya."

Georgia frowned after her friend who scooted down the hall. Dr. Story, the attending E.R. physician for her shift, did not look pleased, his mouth pinched into a pucker and his glasses low on his nose. And he was making a beeline for her.

"Good morning, Dr. Story."

"Nurse Adams," he acknowledged without moving his lips. "I've been told that you accepted and cared for an animal yesterday in the E.R., but that couldn't possibly be correct because by taking in an animal, you would be putting our entire program in jeopardy, risking jobs, not to mention risking the lives of patients who, in an emergency, would prefer that the nearest facility *not* be closed due to health violations brought on by one willful nurse who is supposed to be setting an example for the entire nursing staff."

If he'd stopped for a breath, she would've defended herself. By the time he finished his tirade, however, she simply apologized and promised that the episode would not happen again.

"If it does," he warned, the end of his nose moving, "you will be fired on the spot."

His eyes qualified his threat—no severance, no letter of recommendation and no farewell party. He turned on his heel and marched away with clicking strides. Georgia swallowed hard. Second chances in this industry were rare, and she wouldn't blow it. At the moment, she resented Officer Medlock intensely for getting her involved with the mongrel—and for popping into her head last night while she and Rob were having…fun.

The memory warmed her still. Maybe Rob *was* the man with whom she could explore her fantasies, all of them. She smiled as she prepared the meds for rounds. Imagine—a man who, much like herself, presented a stoic face to the world, when deep down, he, too, was probably looking for someone to unlock his passions.

How remarkable that they'd found each other. She

kept smiling and nodding to herself, trying to ignore the nagging image of Ken Medlock's face inches from hers after he'd wrapped his big arms around her and squeezed a hunk of bread from her throat. So the man was…obliging. Big deal. Yes, ma'am. No, ma'am. So he'd saved a dog's life and hers in the space of a few hours. Wasn't that the man's job, for heaven's sake? She saved lives every day in the E.R., so if Officer Ken thought she owed him something for that pedestrian procedure he'd performed in the mall, he had another think coming, assuming there was much thinking going on between the big man's ears. She set her jaw and forced his face from her mind.

Thank goodness the day passed with relative ease. Especially nice since she'd be volunteering at the blood drive until late in the evening. She'd be ready to relax with Rob on the phone by the time she arrived home. A wonderful by-product of their sensual sessions was the great sleep afterward, despite the suffocating temperature in her apartment.

Georgia left the hospital around three in the afternoon, emerging in heat so oppressive, she was instantly worried about the turnout for the blood drive. Most people wanted to give, but many looked for a reason to "wait until next time." The heat was keeping people indoors under air conditioners, which had overburdened the power plants to the point of brownouts all over the city. An increasing number of the E.R. patient ailments were heat-related.

She fanned herself with a small notebook she found in her purse, conceding that hormones also rose with the temperature. That might explain why a straight-laced New Englander like herself was behaving strangely, having phone sex with one man while fantasizing about another. If it weren't a felony, it was, at the very least, an extravagant sin.

She aimed for her normal seat on the end of the bus stop bench, but halted in her tracks at the sight of a flapping yellow flyer on the post of a nearby sign. *Lost dog. Mixed breed, male, long multicolored hair. Answers to the name Tralfaz.* Georgia made a face. Tralfaz? No wonder the poor dog ran away.

After writing down the number listed at the bottom of the flyer, she pursed her mouth when a thought came to her. The police station was only a block or so away from the municipal building. Maybe she would drop the number off with Officer Medlock on the way. He'd probably taken the dog to an animal shelter, but she could at least make an effort—but only for the rather cute dog's sake, she told herself during the cramped bus ride.

She had never been inside a police precinct before. Amazing how the mere presence of so many uniformed officers could make one feel so conspicuous, as if within these halls, one's transgressions were as apparent as a swallowed coin in an X-ray. (Her sister had warned her, but she had to try it anyway.)

Inside, the place was chaotic—she hadn't realized so much criminal activity was going on in this adopted city of hers. She waited in line for twenty-five minutes to talk to an imposed-upon middle-aged man with eyebrows so bushy she couldn't help but stare.

"May I help you?" he barked.

"I'm looking for Officer Ken Medlock."

He looked her up and down, then gave her the most curious smile. "Is this about a police matter?"

Georgia glanced down at her white uniform, a fitted skirt and tailored blouse—she'd wanted to look her best this morning for her expected dressing-down from Dr. Story. Her hair was pulled back into a tight, rolled bun. She'd forgotten to remove her stethoscope, but otherwise she failed to see the humor in her appearance. "No, my business is personal."

His remarkable eyebrows climbed. "Oh?" Then his eyes widened. "*Oh*. Just a moment." He picked up the phone and spoke into it, then hung up, grinning. "Right this way."

She followed the man through a maze of hallways and bullpens, but grew increasingly uncomfortable when she realized they were picking up a crowd of officers along the way. What the devil was going on?

"Ken," the man bellowed. "Happy Birthday, man!"

Ken Medlock turned, caught her eye, then unfolded himself slowly from his desk, his face a mask of surprise. Georgia swallowed in dismay—the man was just as attractive as she remembered, darn it. His hair looked as if he'd been running his hands through it. Lucky hands.

"Well?" The bushy-eyebrowed man gestured toward her. "Didn't you bring your own music?"

She squinted at the man. Was he senile?

"What's going on?" Ken asked the people circling around.

"Klone got you a stripper for your birthday!" the man shouted. The group broke into raucous applause and whoops of encouragement.

Georgia froze. A stripper? They thought she was a *stripper?* She glared at Ken, whose eyes bugged, although he clearly wasn't as bothered by the idea as she.

She crossed her arms and mouthed, "Do something."

"Time out, guys," he shouted, T-ing his hands. When everyone quieted, he said, "Miss Adams here is a registered nurse at County."

Shocked silence fell around them. The man who had greeted her mumbled an apology, then melted away with the rest of the shuffling group. Her skin tingled with embarrassment and she was certain her cheeks were scarlet. Were her encounters with this man destined to be awkward?

When they were alone by his desk, he wiped an amused smile from his face with his hand. "Hi."

She was considerably less amused. "Hello."

"Sorry about that, ma'am. The guys around here can get a little carried away. Do you want some coffee or something?"

Oh, that "ma'am" thing was killing her. She wet her lips. "No. I came to give you a phone number."

His grin curled halfway up his handsome face.

"Not mine," she said with a frown. Polite, presumptuous beast. "I saw a flyer advertising a lost dog that sounded like the one you hit."

"Accidentally," he added wryly.

"Whatever," she said, fishing in her purse to retrieve the scrap of paper she'd written on. "Here."

"Thanks."

He didn't look too grateful, though. "Did you take him to the animal shelter?"

"No, I took him home with me."

She blinked in surprise. "Oh. Well. How nice."

"Did I get you in trouble at the hospital?"

"Yes."

"I'm sorry about that, ma'am."

"No, you're not. I told you plainly I wasn't allowed to tend the dog, but you wouldn't leave."

"He might have died."

She shook her head. "Look, I like dogs as much as the next person, but how would you feel if you came into the E.R. with a heart attack and saw a dog lying in the bed next to yours?"

"That depends. Are you my nurse?"

"Goodbye, Officer Medlock."

"Wait. I was about to go on break. Want to grab a bite to eat?"

She did need to eat before going on duty for the blood bank, but she didn't want to eat with him. "No."

"Oh, come on," he cajoled. "No matter what you say, I saved your life yesterday. You owe me a hot dog or something. Besides, it's my birthday."

At the sight of his shining brown eyes, she wavered. He was impossibly appealing, that was certain. And although she could've saved herself yesterday, he *had* stepped in. "Well—"

"Ken," a man behind her yelled. "Happy Birthday, man!"

They were back, the entire crowd, escorting a blonde dressed in a traditional nurse's uniform. If nurses wore white miniskirts, that is. And five-inch heels. But the little cap that secured her bound hair was very convincing, and the black-rimmed glasses made the woman look almost smart enough to wade through the schoolwork necessary to become an R.N.

Georgia shrank back as the woman advanced and set a boom box on his desk, then pressed a button and began to undulate to a stylized version of "Happy Birthday" set to bump and grind music. Georgia's tongue settled into her cheek.

The woman tore off her nurse's cap, releasing her golden hair, swinging it in her customer's face. When the blonde began to unbutton her blouse, Georgia stumbled backward to the entrance, battling an on-slaught of emotion. Some dark side of her wanted to see how the man would respond to the blatant display.

Officer Medlock was loving it. Not in a lecherous, lip-smacking kind of way, but in a good-natured, teas-ing kind of way. The woman was down to bikini top and skirt, wrapping her arms around Ken's neck as she danced around him. Georgia's eyes drooped as she imagined herself in the woman's place, peeling off her clothes for an audience of one.

But for whom?

Her eyes popped open. What was she thinking? When the woman pushed Ken into his chair and climbed onto his lap, she fled.

Georgia was glad to have a block to walk off her discomfiture before reporting for her volunteer work. Her steps were deliberately slow in the cloying heat, and she ducked under awnings whenever possible to escape the intense rays of the sun. But her breathing accelerated when she thought of the scene she'd just left. The *good* thing was that the performer's appearance had spared her Ken Medlock's company. Georgia worked her mouth from side to side.

The *bad* thing was that the performer's appearance had spared her Ken Medlock's company.

She shook herself, dismayed at her train of thought. At the sight of the blonde, he had instantly forgotten his invitation. Georgia pushed down the troubling images of sharing an intimate snack, then grabbed a jumbo pretzel from a street vendor, and hurried into the municipal building in anticipation of occupying her hands and her mind.

Since she'd given him the phone number of the likely owner of the dog, they had no further ties. In fact, Georgia could think of no circumstances whatsoever under which she and Officer Ken Medlock would be speaking in the future.

CHAPTER TEN

"I'D LIKE TO REQUEST Nurse Georgia Adams," Ken told the woman signing in volunteer donors.

She brazenly looked him up and down. "Are you a friend of Georgia's?"

No, but we've had sex. "She and I are acquainted."

The woman's face registered understanding. "Oh, wait. Are you the cop who nearly got her fired?"

He smiled wryly. "Well, I do have other claims to fame."

The woman eyed the nightstick at his side and lifted one thin eyebrow. "I just bet you do. Right this way, Officer Medlock."

He followed the skinny woman, amused that she appeared to know Georgia and Georgia's business. It occurred to him that the woman might be helpful. "Are you the friend of hers who's getting married?"

"Oh, no, that's Stacey Alexander. I'm Toni. Toni Wheeler."

He smiled. "Nice to meet you, Toni."

"Likewise," she said, fluttering her eyelashes.

He saw Georgia before she saw them. She was bandaging the arm of a middle-aged man who'd just finished giving blood. Her face was flushed with a smile as she pointed in the direction of a refreshments table.

Ken experienced a stab of envy—he wanted to be the recipient of that radiant smile. Her profile was classically beautiful, and he asked himself for the umpteenth time why Robbie Boy hadn't slapped a ring on her dialing finger.

"Georgia," Toni said sweetly, "look who stopped by."

She turned her head and her smile dropped.

On the other hand, maybe her mood swings made Robbie Boy dizzy.

"Hi," he said, inclining his head.

"Hello."

Brrr. If the city could bottle that chill, the heat wave would be alleviated.

"Georgia," Toni said in a chiding voice, "you didn't tell me your cop was so cute."

"Is he? I hadn't noticed."

Toni gave Georgia a strange look, then handed her his sign-in sheet and scampered away.

"I'm not cute?" he asked, pulling his best hurt expression.

"What are you doing here?"

He swept his arm over the impromptu clinic. "I came to do my civic duty."

She lifted a sugary smile. "Are you sure your blood isn't too hot after your little birthday celebration?"

Apparently, she hadn't been amused. He squirmed, then grinned sheepishly, holding his hat in both hands. "I'm, uh, sorry about that. My partner gets a little carried away with practical jokes."

She seemed preoccupied with his form. "Hmm."

"Anyway, I tried to find you, um, afterward, but you'd disappeared."

She glanced up. "Look, Officer, I'm a little busy here. If you want to give blood, lie down."

He obeyed, thinking it might be his only chance to be close to her and prone at the same time. She put the blood pressure cuff on his arm, her mouth set in a straight line as she listened with her stethoscope.

He laughed. "From your expression, I must be dead."

"No, but your blood pressure is on the high side of normal. Is that typical?"

"No, it's always been perfect." But then again, his body was now trained to come alive at the sound of Georgia's voice. "Probably the excitement of the day. Can I still give?"

She nodded. "But have your blood pressure checked again in a few days just to be safe. Roll up your sleeve, please."

He unbuttoned the cuff of his blue uniform shirt. "We didn't get to have that hot dog. What time do you get off?" *Besides every time we talk on the phone.*

"Not for a few hours," she said, her expression one of total lack of interest.

The woman would take a scalpel to him if she knew he knew the sounds she made when she climaxed.

"And," she added, "you'll need to eat something as soon as you're finished here."

He didn't push, only because he had the promise of her call again tonight, assuming she hadn't yet figured out she was dialing the wrong number. Besides, the more time they spent together, the more likely she was to recognize his voice. Although, he realized their nightly phone rendezvous were numbered, since her boyfriend would surely call her soon and she'd realize her mistake.

She crossed her killer legs as she made check marks on his form. The woman was infinitely more titillating than that two-bit dancer the guys had hired.

Georgia leaned into him, sharing a whiff of her subtle fragrance, then tied a thick rubber band just above his elbow. She had a European look about her, with flawless skin, sleepy eyes and ultrafull lips. Exotic, in an understated way. Not the kind of woman who would stand out in a room, unless a man were extremely choosy. Her hair was rolled into a dark tight knot on her crown. He longed to see the silky length falling around her shoulders, like it would be tonight when she called.

Her fingers skimmed across his skin with the touch of a butterfly, and to his amazement, he began to grow hard. He slid his hat across his lap as inconspicuously as possible to cover the telltale evidence, but she saw the movement and frowned.

He averted his gaze and whistled tunelessly until he had himself back under control. The woman was addictive.

She turned over his arm and rather painfully flicked her finger against a network of veins at the bend. "There's a good one," she said, the hint of a smile on her mouth.

Of course, when she held up the needle she was going to stick into his arm, he knew why she was smiling.

"Careful, ma'am," he said. "I'm a sensitive—
owwww!"

At last he was the recipient of that radiant smile.
"That didn't hurt now, did it?"

He grimaced as she inserted the tube leading to
a plasma bag into the end of the syringe. "Not much
more than a hot poker in the eye."

"Since your blood pressure is up, you should bleed
quickly," she said cheerfully.

"I suppose that's good?"

She smirked. "Unless you're run down by a police car."

He smirked back. "And brought to you for help?"

"I help any *person* who comes into the E.R.," she
said, "even an impertinent, bossy person."

He wagged his eyebrows. "Oh, but I can be an animal sometimes."

"Just bleed, will you?"

But she seemed pleased that she'd gotten a rise out
of him. The problem was, with all her fidgeting and adjusting, she was getting too much of a rise out of him.
Her phone call tonight couldn't come soon enough.

"Did you find the dog's owner?" she asked.

Her voice sounded not quite friendly but...normal,
at least. "I called, but Crash wasn't their dog."

"Crash?"

He shrugged his free shoulder. "Figured I'd better
name the little fellow seeing as he might be staying at
my place for a while."

She stroked the tube in a pulling motion, facilitating
his blood being drawn into the bag. "Does that pose a
problem spacewise?"

A few seconds passed before he realized she was actually conversing. "Um, no, my place is old, but pretty big. And it's just me living there."

"Oh."

So much for conversing. "Do you live alone?" he asked.

"That's absolutely none of your business."

He'd botched it again. "I meant do you live with your family?"

"No."

Not a chatty Cathy, this one. "Do you have a big family?"

"One sister, two nieces, all in Denver."

He remained silent in hopes she would elaborate.

"My father died several years ago, but I still have my mother. She lives with my sister most of the time."

She looked wistful and Ken thought of all the glad and sad moments in her life he would never have a chance to share, the laughter and tears he would never have a chance to witness. Georgia Adams made him feel proprietary—in a noble way, of course. Well, okay, maybe *all* of his intentions weren't so noble.

"How about you?" she asked.

Ken blinked, so lost in her stunning blue eyes that he'd forgotten what they'd been talking about. "How about me what?"

She sighed as if he were a half-wit. "Do you have a big family?"

"One brother, four sisters, ten nieces and nephews."

"Wow."

He took her monosyllabic response as an invitation to continue. "My folks are alive and well in Virginia.

We kids are scattered, but we try to get together at least once a year."

"That's nice." She checked the bag. "And you're done—in record time, too."

Great. Just when he wanted to spend time with the woman, he'd set a record for bleeding.

She removed the catheter with deft fingers, and gave him a gauze pad to press against the point of entry while she made notes on his form.

"Would you like to have dinner sometime?" he blurted.

At least he had succeeded in getting her attention. He held his breath, but she shook her head. "I can't. Rob and I are...exclusive."

But we're good together, he wanted to shout. *You've been sharing your fantasies with me.* "Did your boyfriend make it back to town?" He knew he was treading on dangerous territory, but he couldn't help himself.

"Yes. But I forgot to mention your name to him."

He squinted. Was she blushing? "Don't worry about it," he murmured, sitting up. He wanted to pull her close for a long kiss, Rob and the crowd be damned. Instead he rolled down his sleeve and fumbled with the button.

Then to his surprise, she stilled his hands. "Let me." He raised his eyebrows, but she simply nodded toward the registration desk. "The line is backing up."

Oh, well, regardless of her motivation, Georgia made buttoning his shirt cuff an erotic act, fingering open the tiny hole and inserting the little gold disc. Ken wiped a film of perspiration from his forehead just watching her nimble fingers and knowing where they'd been.

"There." She gave him a brief smile that stole moisture from his mouth. "Thanks for giving—the blood bank is dangerously low."

"Glad to help. I wish there was more I could do."

"Maybe you could encourage your buddies to come down."

Never one to miss an opportunity, he grinned. "How many pints do you need?"

Her teeth were white, even, glistening. "As many as you can get."

"If I can get one hundred donors down here, will you have dinner with me?"

She bit into her bottom lip. "No. But I'll buy you that hot dog."

His heart fluttered with possibility. "Deal." He pushed himself to his feet. "I hope you have enough blood bags."

Her smile shook him. "Looks like I'll be working late."

He hesitated. Did that mean she wouldn't be calling him tonight? "Did you have plans?"

Georgia shook her head. "I'm supposed to call Rob when I get home is all."

Ken's mouth quirked with smug satisfaction. "Well, when you talk to him tonight, tell him I think he's a lucky man." He put on his hat, then touched the brim. "Ma'am."

CHAPTER ELEVEN

GEORGIA INJECTED a teasing note into her voice, lest Rob think she were interested in the man. "He said to tell you he thinks you're a lucky man."

His laugh was abbreviated. "I don't remember from the gym what this Medlock guy looks like. Should I be jealous?"

She pressed her ear closer to the phone. His head cold had fogged his voice until she could barely hear him. "Of course not. I m-mean, the man isn't repulsive, but he's just not my type."

"Oh?"

"Kind of big and bulky," she said quickly, floundering for words. "And pushy." And he called her "ma'am," as if she were…special.

"Pushy? Well, I guess that's how he was able to get so many policemen down there to give blood."

"I suppose," she said, leaning back on the pillows she'd stacked against her headboard. It *had* been quite a sight, all those blue uniforms standing in line. One hundred and six donors. Ken Medlock seemed determined to get that hot dog—and her attention. Trouble was, he had it. She considered telling Rob about the impromptu deal, but then thought better of it, lest he think she was actually looking forward to spending time with the man.

"Rob," she said quietly, unable to identify the emotions pulling at her. "I know we've been having...fun... on the phone lately, but I was wondering if tonight we could just talk." The way Ken Medlock had wanted to talk today, about family and things that were important. She'd held back with Ken because she hadn't wanted to become invested in a virtual stranger, but she did crave that kind of camaraderie with Rob.

"Talk," he mumbled. "Sure. What do you want to talk about?"

"I don't know," she admitted, casting about for a topic. "How about us?"

"What about...us?"

She smiled and burrowed deeper into the pillows. "Well, what first attracted you to me?"

"That's easy. You're beautiful, smart, beautiful."

A warm, tingly feeling bloomed in her stomach. "That's sweet, but I wasn't fishing for a compliment. What do you think makes us a good couple?"

"Isn't it enough that I'm crazy about you?"

Her grin widened, and she closed her eyes—the words she'd been hoping for, spoken with ringing sincerity. "Are you happy with the way things are going between us?"

"I...guess so. Yes. Yes, I am."

"Good. So am I." Remembering her earlier conversation with Ken, she said, "Tell me more about your family and where you're from."

"I'm from...Cincinnati."

Georgia laughed. "I know that. I mean, what was

your childhood like? I don't even know if you have brothers and sisters."

"Oh, well, you know…I'd rather hear about you."

"What about me?"

"Have you ever told me why you became a nurse?"

She smiled. "I don't think so."

"So tell me."

Georgia squirmed against the pillow at her back as memories flooded over her. Not all bad, not all good. "I guess I was always the family fixer. My father worked a lot." And then there were George Adams's occasional affairs, which she wasn't ready to share. "My sister and my mother were so much alike, they communicated through arguing."

"So you were the peacemaker and the healer."

"I suppose. I was also into photography. When I was seventeen, I came upon a car accident scene and pulled out my camera. But when I developed the pictures, I realized I'd used all my film to capture the paramedics and a nurse who had happened by. They were amazing…selfless."

"There were survivors?"

"Yes," she whispered, the memory keen. "Everyone survived. I decided that the next time I came upon an emergency, I wanted to be able to do more than take a picture. I wanted to make a difference in people's lives."

He was quiet for a few seconds, then said, "You got your wish."

She gave a little scoffing laugh. "If I don't get myself fired for taking care of dogs."

"It was that cop's fault, not yours."

She sighed. "Well, he *was* trying to do a nice thing—he just caught me at a really bad time and put me in an awkward situation. In hindsight, I shouldn't have reacted so...strongly."

"I'm sure he feels the same way. Don't lose sleep over it."

She wouldn't, although the memory of the man hiding his arousal with his hat might make for a bit of sheep-counting.

"Anything else interesting happen today?" he asked.

She liked this change in him. Rob was never much on small talk, but she rather enjoyed sharing the ordinary bits of the day. "Not much happened today. But I did receive a letter from my mother, yesterday."

"Oh?"

"Even living across the country, she has the uncanny ability to make me feel twelve years old."

"Mothers are good that way. Did she give you grief about still being single?"

"W-well, sort of."

"Just doing her job."

She sighed. "I suppose. Is your mother just as bad?"

"Er, aren't they all?"

"When will I get to meet your parents?"

He lapsed into a coughing spasm. "Georgia, I'm suddenly not feeling very well. I think my medicine is wearing off. Could we—" He coughed again, longer and harder. "Could we finish this discussion some other time?"

"Sure," she murmured, sorry for her ill-timing. Darn Ken Medlock for stirring things up inside her.

Feeling awkward, she squirmed against her pillows. "How about—"

"I have to run," he cut in. "Call me tomorrow night?"

"Okay." But he had already hung up. She replaced the phone, chastising herself for being so inconsiderate while he was under the weather. They would have plenty of time to talk on Saturday at the wedding. Georgia noticed the light on her message machine was flashing; someone had called while she was talking to Rob. She pushed the Play button.

"Thank you for buying this Temeteck product! This is a test message to allow you to adjust the volume. Press '1' if you don't want this message to play again."

Georgia groaned and pushed "1." She hated the stupid machine. Maybe something was wrong with it. Hoping a bowl of ice cream would help her go to sleep—in lieu of an orgasm—she walked to the kitchen in T-shirt and panties, stood in front of the open freezer door for a couple of minutes to cool off, then carried the snack to the living room and dropped onto the couch.

An upholstered brick. She had furnished what was supposed to be the most comfortable room in the house with a beige upholstered brick. What on earth did Rob see in this horrid couch? She spooned in the first mouthful of Cherry Garcia, then wondered idly what Rob saw in *her.* He'd said she was beautiful, but did he see the secret side of her that loved to try on hats and eat ice cream in her underwear?

A few days ago, she'd been on the verge of calling it quits with Rob, but now…now she'd discovered this surprisingly erotic and vulnerable side of him. She was anxious to see him on Saturday, to see if he acted differently, more relaxed. Hopefully the phone sex would open other doors of communication; it had so far. Perhaps they would discover they had more in common than their penchant for detail and love of foreign films.

The phone rang, and she reached for the extension. "Hello?"

"You've been holding out on me," Toni accused.

Georgia laughed. "What are you talking about?"

"I'm talking about that big hunky cop who delivered the entire Birmingham city police department to our door. He's gorgeous, and you were so witchy to him!"

"Ken Medlock almost got me fired," Georgia reminded her.

"But he tripled the blood bank reserves single-handedly in a matter of hours."

"He only pulled that stunt so I'd have to buy him a hot dog tomorrow afternoon."

"Oh, how romantic!"

"Toni, the man knows he gets on my nerves, and this is just another way to get on my nerves. I went along with it because it was for a good cause."

"I think he has the hots for you. All that 'yes, ma'am-ing'—Lordy, he's downright fattening."

"Stop it!" She didn't want to think about it. More.

"I'm serious—it's probably all that phone sex."

"Okay, you lost me."

"Vibes! You're giving off sex vibes, Georgia, and the cop is picking up on them. Sex begets sex."

"I thought that to beget is to *have* sex."

"You know what I mean."

"Well, I'm not interested."

"Why not?"

She swirled her spoon in her bowl and frowned. "Because I have Rob, and I think we're finally getting over the emotional plateau we've been on for so long. He's starting to open up."

"That's good...I guess."

"Of course it's good. Why wouldn't it be good?"

"I don't know...the expression on that cop's face. I've never seen Rob look at you that way."

"You mean with ridicule?"

Toni laughed. "If you ask me, I think this Medlock guy is getting you all worked up, and Rob is getting the payout."

Her spoon clanged against the bowl. "That's absurd. And I don't take love advice from a woman who lets a man call her by the wrong name just to spare his ego."

Toni sighed. "I'm going to tell Dr. Baxter tomorrow."

"Good."

"I'm going to tell him I changed my name legally from 'Terri' to 'Toni.'"

"You're hopeless."

"I'd better let you go so you'll be rested up for your date tomorrow with Officer Medlock."

She rolled her eyes. "It's not a date. It's vending food in a public park."

"Did you tell Rob about it?"

She hesitated. "No."

"I rest my case. Night-night."

Georgia frowned at the phone, then, pretending it

was Ken Medlock, bounced it off a stiff cushion. Who was he to barge into her life just when things were starting to go so well with Rob?

CHAPTER TWELVE

ALL MORNING LONG, Ken's moods swung between elation that he'd be seeing Georgia this afternoon for his victory "meal," and self-loathing for carrying the ruse this far. He'd had to cut the conversation short last night because she was venturing into territory that was likely to land him in deep hooey.

Things were getting out of control, namely, his attraction to the woman. Hoping that blockhead Rob had skipped town for good and this mess would somehow resolve itself, he'd called the man's office and was told by a messaging service that Rob was likely to return to Birmingham sometime Sunday. It didn't explain, however, why the man hadn't at least called Georgia from wherever he'd gone. The ingrate.

Still, Rob's loss was his gain, at least until Sunday when the fertilizer would hit the fan. For the next couple of days, he would try to win over Georgia. Maybe with the double whammy of finding out Rob wasn't the man she'd been talking to, and with Ken's unflagging attention, she would break up with the guy.

Ken scratched his temple with the screwdriver he had used to install a box fan in the window of his bedroom. On the other hand, was that the way he wanted to win over Georgia—through embarrassment and by default?

Besides, what the heck would he do with her if he got her? A woman like Georgia probably bought pot-pourri by the truckload. And the most important thing to him right now was being the best cop he could be. Darn it, the woman barely tolerated him and she was already treading on his concentration. How bad would it be if he had unlimited access to her? Bad. Very bad.

Thankfully, Georgia would have no way of tying the phone calls to him even after she discovered she'd been dialing the wrong number. His phone machine featured a mechanical voice with a generic message. As a police officer, his number was unlisted and pro-tected, so it wouldn't show up on caller ID screens or work with those newfangled call-back features.

He sighed. And, as a police officer, his conduct was supposed to be of a higher standard than mere civil-ians. His own loneliness was no excuse for deceiving an innocent woman, even if at first he had thought her to be not so innocent. Sometime, somehow this after-noon he would find a way to tell her the truth.

Georgia (big grin), want to hear something funny?

Georgia (shaking head), you're going to laugh *when I tell you this.*

Georgia (stepping out of striking distance), you're not going to believe this, but...

Who was he kidding? He'd be lucky if the woman didn't filet him. He hadn't broken any written laws, but it didn't take a mental giant to recognize he'd tread upon several unwritten laws.

Geez, Louise, what was he going to do now?

He could simply forget about her, he decided, seeing as how she wasn't keen on him anyway. *He's not my type.* If she called him again accidentally, he could just tell her she had the wrong number and hang up. End of story.

He ran his hand over his face, trying to erase the image of her smiling face, bantering with him last night at the blood drive, maintaining that stern facade. Was he the only man who knew how uninhibited she could be?

From his bed on the floor, Crash barked, reminding Ken that there were more pressing matters than his infatuation with Nurse Georgia Adams. Since he'd pulled an early morning shift for an ill fellow officer, Ken had the rest of the day off to anticipate and dread his afternoon meeting with Georgia. She clocked out at three, so they were scheduled to meet at Herrington Park around three-thirty. He glanced at the clock. An hour from now.

"How about some fresh air?" he asked the dog.

Crash barked twice.

Ken gave the screws on the fan box mount a few more turns, then repacked his toolbox. "Okay, give me a minute to figure out how I can make you mobile, and we'll go to the park. Maybe I can figure out a way to come clean once she gets there." He stopped and appraised the bandaged dog as an idea popped into his head. "And maybe she won't kill me if I look impossibly cute."

"Oh, how cute," Georgia murmured despite herself when she saw Ken coming toward her on the sidewalk.

Not *him,* although he did look surprisingly different and less intimidating in jeans and a navy T-shirt, but the bandaged dog he pulled behind him in the little red wagon. What did Ken say he had named him—Crash?

"Hi," Ken said as they strolled up. "I brought some company, hope you don't mind."

"Not at all," she said, stooping to stroke the dog's fur. "He's a handsome fellow, isn't he?"

"He takes after me," Ken said with a big grin.

She gave him a crooked smile, trying her best to resist his charm. Darn the big man, and his energy pulling at her. In her weakened state, after a night of tossing and turning and a hectic eight-hour shift, she was susceptible. Her immunity to him was lowered, and it scared her. Plus her friend Toni hadn't helped matters by teasing her all day about her "date."

"I was afraid you'd changed your mind," he said.

Georgia gave the dog one last scratch on the head before standing. "No. Last-minute emergency." Of course, she couldn't very well admit the emergency had been her appearance—her hair was flattened by a sterile cap she'd worn most of the day. Her makeup had worn off long ago, and she hadn't brought replacements with her, nor was she about to ask Toni for spares. She'd brought khaki shorts and sandals to change into, but the plain pink shirt she'd hoped to leave on had been compromised by a teenager with food poisoning. Desperate, she'd bought a yellow T-shirt in the gift shop that said Laughter is the best medicine. A nice sentiment, but hardly worth twenty-four dollars.

Ken rubbed his flat stomach, the muscles in his

forearm bunching. "Just gave me more time to work up an appetite."

And she'd bet the man could eat. From her nutrition classes, she estimated his weight, then took into account his probable activity level, and came up with an astronomical amount of calories he needed every day to maintain his build. *One* hot dog? The man could probably eat a dozen.

But he settled for two, loaded with relish, and a plain one for Crash. Georgia ordered another one with relish for herself, but was still rifling for cash when she realized Ken had already paid the vendor for their food and colas. "It was supposed to be my treat," she protested.

"The treat's all mine," he assured her, gathering their food in his arms. "Will you pull Crash?"

Feeling a little foolish, she picked up the handle of the wagon and followed Ken to a picnic table under a sprawling hardwood tree.

"Is this okay?" he asked.

"Sure." Her pulse jerked stupidly—she had no reason to be nervous. It wasn't as if they were on a date or something.

"Are you a photographer too?" he asked, nodding to her camera bag.

She blushed. "Amateur. It's an old manual 35 mm, but it takes decent pictures. I've been wanting to get some shots of the park anyway." She didn't add that a photo shoot also made their little get-together seem like less of a date to her.

"Would you be willing to take one of Crash?" he

asked. "I took out an ad, but I might have a better chance of finding his owner if I had a picture."

She hesitated, only because it would perpetuate their interaction.

"I'd be glad to pay you," he added.

"Nonsense," she said quickly, feeling foolish. "I'd be glad to take a couple if it meant reuniting him with his owner."

His smile was dangerously pleasing. "Thank you, ma'am."

Oh, my. "Are you off duty today?" she asked, gesturing to his clothing.

He nodded, arranging their food so they could sit facing each other. The picnic table gleamed with a fresh coat of forest-green paint. "I pulled early morning duty."

She lowered herself to the cool seat, glad she'd taken the time to pull her hair up and off her neck with a clip. "You must be tired."

He shrugged, sending lots of muscle into motion. She peeled her gaze away as he sat down. "I'm not used to getting much sleep—I have problems with insomnia."

Georgia blinked. "So do I."

He handed her a hot dog on a little paper plate. "It's probably our jobs, weird hours, the stress. You're a nurse—what do you do for yours?"

Georgia choked on her first drink of soda. *I have phone sex with my boyfriend. While I'm thinking about you.* She gulped air. Last week she was a frustrated almost-virgin, this week she was a phone wench.

Ken cocked his head. "Do you have problems swallowing?"

Wiping her mouth with a napkin, she frowned. "Not usually."

"So what about the insomnia?"

She chewed slowly, carefully, then swallowed. "Try to relieve some of the stress in your life."

"I exercise, but it doesn't seem to help."

Georgia fidgeted with her straw. "What about... your personal relationships?"

He stopped chewing. "What about them?"

"Well, do you...have any?"

"If you're asking if I have a girlfriend, I don't."

She tucked the tidbit away in her subconscious, then shook her head. "I mean friends—coworkers, neighbors."

"I know a lot of people, but I'm not sure if I'd call all of them friends."

"Bingo," she said. "You told me you were close to your family and now they're not around. You're probably in need of emotional c-companionship."

He lifted one dark brow.

Squirming on her seat, she spotted the dog and seized the ungraceful way out. "Like Crash. Pets are known to lower blood pressure and to relieve stress."

"It is nice having someone else around the place."

"I've been thinking about buying a pet myself," she admitted. "For the company."

"You don't live with your boyfriend?"

How did the man know every button of hers to push? "No." She was alone, with a couch like a stone.

His brown eyes danced. "So you two aren't that serious?"

"We're not engaged, if that's what you mean." Although if their relationship was progressing as she hoped, perhaps her mother could be reigning over wedding plans sometime in the near future.

"Have you ever been married?" he asked.

"No. You?"

"Absolutely not."

Okay. No ambiguity there. She was wasting the afternoon with a dead-end flirt when she should be consoling her ill boyfriend and exploring the new dimension of their relationship.

Sights and sounds and smells and touches descended all around Georgia, and suddenly she couldn't get out of there fast enough. The blue sky, the cool breeze, the children laughing in the playground—all of it a ploy, to make her think that she was in charmed company. She took another bite of the hot dog, thinking the faster she ate, the sooner she could escape.

"I see a lot of bad domestic situations in my line of work," he said. "I'm sure you do, too."

She nodded, gobbling her food.

"Makes you wonder how the people got together to begin with."

She nodded, washing down a large bite with a deep draw on her soda.

"I mean, of all the people in all of the world, how are you supposed to know when you meet *the* right person?"

She wet her lips. "You just…know, I guess."

"So Rob is the right person for you?"

His words lingered in the air between them. Her first instinct was to tell Ken Medlock that it was none of his ma'am-ing business. But he was so intent, his eyes serious yet alight with friendliness. As if he were…concerned. "I think so," she said, the intimacies she'd shared with Rob so fresh in her mind. If he weren't the right person, what did that make her? Guilt and grease didn't marry well in her stomach.

Ken gave a little laugh. "The story of my life—a day late and a dollar short." He took another bite of his hot dog, just as if they weren't discussing…

What *were* they discussing?

This man, this virtual stranger, threw her off balance, made her feel as if her thoughts and her beliefs were up for negotiation. Such a charming, compelling personality, as large as his muscled body. He reminded her of someone… Her memory ticked backward until… She froze when the match fell into place.

Her father. Good-looking, with a winsome smile. So easy to love, so easy to forgive his faults. Her bedroom had been next to her parents', so she'd overheard their late-night arguments over his infrequent, but hurtful, infidelities. Her mother would cry and be morose for days, but he would bring her gifts and eventually coax a smile from her by whispering sweet things in her ear and kissing her neck.

Georgia stood up. "I have to go."

He wiped his mouth with his napkin. "Already?"

"Yes. Th-thank you for rounding up your comrades last night. Many of them signed up to give regularly."

"That's good," he said. "But I was hoping that you and I might have longer to talk today."

She brushed crumbs from her lap and fed her last bite to Crash. "Sorry, I still have to shop for a wedding gift for tomorrow."

"What about the pictures?"

With hurried hands, she removed the camera and took a couple of shots of Crash from different angles. "I'll mail them to you," she said as she crammed the camera back into the bag.

"I thought you were going to take some photos of the park."

"I changed my mind. Thanks for the hot dog."

"How about dinner?" he asked, standing. "Georgia, I'd like to get to know you better."

Her breath caught in her chest. Ken Medlock was too overwhelming, too...potent. She and Rob were intellectual equals, who now shared a sensual bond as well. She wasn't about to throw all of that away because she was physically attracted to a cocky self-proclaimed bachelor cop.

"I can't," she murmured. "Like I said, I have Rob."

He pursed his mouth.

She swallowed, and her ears popped with the released pressure.

"Did you tell him what I asked you to last night— that I think he's a lucky man?"

Georgia nodded.

"And what did he say?"

She inhaled. "He asked me if he should be jealous."

"And what did you tell him?"

"I told him no, because..."

"Because?"

Best to nip this flirtation in the bud. She exhaled. "Because you're not my type."

He crossed his arms over his chest, a small smile on his lips. "What type am I?"

She chewed on the inside of her cheek.

He leaned forward on the table, his face inches from hers. "Georgia," he said softly, "what type am I?"

Her throat convulsed. The type of man who could set her world on end. Send her spiraling into decadence. His eyes searched hers, and she was afraid of what he saw. She wanted to pull away, but their mouths were like inverse magnets, the attraction growing stronger exponentially as the space between them closed millimeter by millimeter.

Georgia didn't know what she expected, but the electricity of his lips meeting hers was an intoxicating, luxurious feeling of pure indulgence. Like eating white-chocolate-covered cherries while relaxing in a deep, fragrant bath as hot as the body could stand. She opened her mouth to receive him, flicking the tip of her tongue against his teeth in invitation. He accepted with a deep moan that vibrated inside her mouth, sending a stab of desire straight to her belly, and moisture to her—

Georgia pulled back, and covered her mouth with the back of her hand. What had she done?

He remained leaning forward, his mouth open a fraction, his brow furrowed. "Georgia?"

This was sheer lunacy. The man was a player, and she'd fallen for it. Mortified, she stumbled backward, away from the confining picnic table. "You're the type of man...who would kiss a woman who's involved with another man." She wiped at her mouth, breathing hard. "I...I don't like the way you make me feel. I try to be an honest person, Ken, just as I expect the man I'm seeing to be honest with me."

He didn't answer, just stared at her.

"You probably think that's old-fashioned," she said with an awkward but sober laugh. "But trust is very important to me."

A flush darkened his face. Perhaps she'd spoken too vehemently, but the words needed to be said, if only for her own ears. After all, if she were seeing Ken Medlock—not that she would—but if she *were* seeing him, she wouldn't be slinking around kissing some other man in the park.

"Goodbye," she murmured, then grabbed her purse and camera bag and practically ran to the bus stop two blocks away. Cool relief flooded her—she'd managed to disentangle herself from the man without totally dishonoring her relationship with Rob. Close call.

Rob. Remorse sat in her belly. Poor man, he was probably feeling neglected, down with a cold and her playing twenty questions on the phone last night. She'd been so inconsiderate—and she a nurse, for goodness' sake.

When a thought struck her, she chastised herself for not thinking of it before—instead of a clandestine meeting with Ken Medlock, she should be fostering her romance with Rob. She'd stop at Claxton's Deli, pick up a big bowl of their chicken soup and drop by Rob's house.

Georgia turned toward her destination, a decided spring in her step. Rob would be so surprised.

CHAPTER THIRTEEN

ROB'S HOUSE WAS a forty-minute walk from the nearest bus stop, but Georgia didn't mind. The weather was wonderful, if hot, and she had plenty of thinking to do. Ken Medlock's interest in her was flattering, but fleeting, she was sure. She knew Ken's M.O.—the man saw her simply as a challenge, a conquest. Rob, on the other hand, had taken her out regularly for many months now. And they were finally progressing toward the kind of physical relationship she desired. She would be crazy to mess it up now.

Her first thought when she saw Rob's beautiful two-story gray brick home was that she'd never seen his lawn so unkempt. Her second thought was that it must be driving him crazy, lying in bed with a cold while his Bermuda grass went to seed. But at the sight of the newspapers stacked on the stoop, alarm blipped through her. The fact that Rob hadn't been able to retrieve his beloved *Wall Street Journal* meant that he was more ill than he had allowed her to think.

She stepped over the stack of papers, then balanced her purse and the canister of soup to ring the doorbell. After a couple of minutes with no response, she rang it again, perplexed. With no answer, she dug the copy of the door key he'd given her from her wallet and carefully unlocked the front door.

"Rob?" she called in the direction of the upstairs. She walked into the foyer, frowning at the dim lighting. "Rob?"

Concerned now, she set down her purse and the soup, then jogged up the staircase and to the right of the landing into the master suite. Not only was he not in his bed, but the massive four-poster king looked like it hadn't been slept in recently. Rob was nothing if not neat. She'd only been in the suite a handful of times, usually when Rob wanted to show her a new book in his collection of first editions or to retrieve a Band-Aid from the bathroom vanity, but everything appeared to be in place—not even signs of sickness, like medications or boxes of tissues. As always, his surroundings were impeccable.

She checked the other upstairs bedrooms, then descended to the first floor, once again calling his name. Moving quickly from room to room, she scoured the first level, then walked down into the daylight basement, which had been turned into a gaming area and bar, and finally opened the door from the mud room leading to the garage.

A little laugh escaped her. Why hadn't she checked here first? His black Lexus was missing—he'd probably gone to the office, or maybe even driven himself to the drugstore. Relieved, but disappointed to have missed him, she found a pen and a piece of paper to leave a note.

Rob,
I came by to cheer you up with chicken soup and

TLC. Sorry I missed you—hope this means you're feeling better. Left soup in the refrigerator.

Georgia chewed on her lip, conjuring up the nerve to write something more provocative. She inhaled deeply. After what they'd shared together, she could be brave.

Call me tonight if you feel like having a little X-rated fun on the phone. ☺
See you at the wedding tomorrow.
Georgia.

She propped up the note on the black granite counter against a state-of-the-art combination coffee grinder and brewer, moved the newspapers to a table inside the foyer, then locked the door behind her. On the way back to the bus stop, she rubbed the area just beneath her breastbone—that spicy hot dog wouldn't allow her to forget about the little tête-à-tête with Ken Medlock. Everything about the man was an inconvenience.

His face continued to haunt her as she shopped for a wedding gift from Stacey's twenty-seven-page registry at a housewares specialty shop. But she attributed the pesky vision to his wholly improper line of questioning this afternoon.

"Have you ever been married?"

"No, you?"

"Absolutely not."

After hearing a response like that, any sane woman would avoid Ken Medlock at all costs. Why even entertain the thought of being attracted to a man who was cocky enough to issue a warning up front about his commitment capacity?

From the endless selection of delicate china patterns, ringing crystal and mirror-shiny silver services, she chose a large pewter platter with a raised grapevine pattern. She'd read somewhere that people always gave the gifts they wanted for themselves, which was true in this case, she admitted. To her, platters connoted family gatherings and memories made, a blessing she wanted for her friend Stacey…and someday, for herself.

In her mind she pictured a Thanksgiving table featuring a perfectly browned turkey, a dazzling array of impossibly delicious side dishes, and dozens of sweatered arms reaching for more than their share. In-laws, friends…children.

She panned the smiling faces, basking in the warmth of their love. Then she stopped and frowned. What the devil was Ken Medlock doing sitting at the head of her table?

He winked and lifted his hand in a little wave. Presumptuous sod.

She bought the platter and jockeyed it home via the bus, walking into her sauna of an apartment around seven o'clock. She deposited her bags in the living room with a sigh, then smiled at the flashing light on her message machine. Rob had probably called to thank her for the soup. She pressed the Play button.

"Thank you for buying this Temeteck product! This is a test message to allow you to adjust the volume. Press '1' if you don't want this message to play again."

Georgia pressed the "1" button five, ten, twenty times, each time faster and harder than the last. She broke a nail, and her promise to stop cursing aloud. The owner's manual yielded nothing other than a headache and a dent in the wall when she threw it. First thing tomorrow, the blankety-blank phone system was going back to the place where she'd bought it.

She was still grumbling under her breath when the object of her consternation rang. Hoping it was her super telling her the month's rent would be waived due to the unbearable conditions, she snatched it up.

"Hello?"

"Georgia, dear, must you always answer the phone as if you just finished running a marathon?"

Georgia sat on the coffee table, which, she noticed, was more comfortable than the couch. "Nice to hear your voice, too, Mom. Are you having a good time with Fannie?"

"Of course. Her home is *so* luxurious, I feel as if I'm on vacation."

"That's nice. How are the girls?"

"Precious."

"And Fannie?"

"Missing Albert—he's traveling for business. They adore each other, you know."

"Yes, Mom, I know."

"Did you get my letter?"

"Yes, thank you for lighting a candle for me."

"A mother's job."

She frowned. Weren't those Ken's words?

"I saw on the news that Birmingham is under a

dangerous heat wave, and I wanted to see if you were okay."

"It's hot, and my air conditioner isn't working, but I'm surviving."

"Good. Do you and Bob have big plans for the weekend?"

"It's *Rob,* Mom, and as a matter of fact, we're going to a wedding."

She clucked. "Are you getting serious about this young man?"

Georgia reached for a cord to fidget with, then remembered the phone was cordless. "I...don't know. He's...nice." And safe. She frowned. Where had that thought come from?

"Nice? He has his own business and a home—you'd better snap him up."

Her mother saw the world in such simple terms. "But I'm not sure I'm in love with Rob."

"Love?" Her mother made a tsk-tsking sound—she had an entire repertoire of chiding noises. "You're not getting any younger, Georgia."

"Mom, I'm only thirty."

"By the time I was your age, I'd been married for thirteen years."

Georgia bit her tongue to keep from uttering something regrettable—her mother couldn't help that she'd fallen for a smooth-talking philanderer. "Mom, I still have lots of time to settle dow—"

"Oh, there's Fannie, I have to go, dear. Tell Bob I said hello."

She sighed. "Okay, I'll tell him."

"Toodleoo, dear."

"Toodleoo." She disconnected the call, shaking her head. No doubt her poor mother had endured a rocky marriage, although she'd never discussed it with the girls. It was obvious that she was living vicariously through her daughters, mainly Fannie, but Georgia knew she truly wanted them both to be happy.

But she sorely missed her father.

Georgia gave the thermostat a swat as she walked toward the shower, peeling off her clothes. Her earlier thought sprang to mind. Rob was *safe?* Safe wasn't a characteristic, safe was a, a, a...place.

Had she been so affected by her father's indiscretions that she had projected love on to a man who was as opposite from George Adams as was earthly possible?

She stepped under the cool spray and tilted her head back until her hair was saturated and heavy. She sighed as the day's stress began to wash away.

And conversely, had she shunned the interest of the man who reminded her very much of her irresistible father? Ken Medlock's dancing brown eyes mocked her, challenged her.

You did a bad, bad thing, Georgia. You know you want me. I can take you places you've only dreamed of going. Unsafe places.

"I went there with Rob," she murmured.

But you were thinking of me. I was in your mind before you even met me.

She slid the loofah glove over her hand, reveling in the nubby texture and the bulk, the glove resembling a man's hand...a lover's hand...Ken's hand. She resisted the pull of him, his smile, his big body, seemingly built to plague her. Georgia ignored the alarms going off in her head. Perhaps a little fantasy would help get him out of her system. He owed her that much...

Georgia leaned over and began sudsing her feet with the loofah in little therapeutic circles. The water, the rhythmic movement, the aromatic soap. Inch by inch, she rubbed the cleanser into her ankles, calves, thighs, wondering if Ken had a slow hand, or would rush to pleasure her.

Whichever you like, Georgia. I'm at your bidding, ma'am.

He was so earthy, definitely a man in tune with his body. The sheer size of him sent a thrill through her. His mouth... He was a wonderful kisser, strong, firm, insistent. She lifted her head and allowed the water to pulse over her mouth and spill off her chin. She resumed her massage, methodically moving over her thighs, to her buttocks, to her stomach, moving in circles around her navel, triggering a slow grind of her hips.

Happy Birthday, Ken.

She closed her eyes and imagined putting on a show for him alone. He stood outside the shower in his uniform, barred from entry, able only to watch through the fogged glass.

With the loofah, she touched her breasts, outlining their contours, working inward in slow, firm circles.

Do you like?

He could only nod, which made her smile, smug with feminine power. Such a big, strong man. So malleable in her hands.

She moved the glove over her nipples and moaned,

rubbing until they glowed bright pink beneath the white suds. Then she removed the hand-held shower head, turned the water to pulsate, and rinsed the soap from her body, moving slowly from neck to waist, lingering at her thighs before she leaned over seductively to give him a shocking angle while she finished her calves and ankles.

Come out here. I want to touch you.

She turned off the shower and stepped out of the glass stall to towel off slowly and prolong his torture. But when she looked up, he was gone.

The rush of disappointment was keen, overridden quickly by sobriety. She laughed, a hollow little sound in the confines of the tiled room. Of course he was gone. It was her subconscious speaking to her—men like Ken Medlock didn't stick around for long.

But her body still shook from the stimulation, and her breasts fairly ached. She stumbled to the bedroom, longing leadening her limbs. She felt...engorged, ready to come out of her skin.

The light from the bathroom cast just enough illumination for her to find her way to the bed. She fell across the comforter and hugged herself, squeezing her eyes shut against the fantasies that played behind her eyes. Ken Medlock was in her fantasies only because she had seen him so many times over the past couple of days. His face and body were fresh in her mind. She just needed to see Rob, that's all. To be reminded of his blond good looks, his lanky build, his well-shaped hands. She rolled over and stared at the phone in the dark.

Maybe he had called her and wasn't able to leave a message on that fouled-up machine of hers.

Her womb clenched with pent-up desire. It was either call, or fly solo with Ken Medlock's kiss in her head.

She reached for the phone.

CHAPTER FOURTEEN

ALTHOUGH THE BOX FAN had cooled his room somewhat, Ken lay wide awake, his body fatigued but his mind on a treadmill. It had taken all his effort not to go after Georgia today. Never before had a kiss shaken him so. He was falling for the woman, like a big stupid tree. He sighed and pulled a hand down over his face. There was no good ending to this scenario, at least not for him.

When the phone rang, he turned his head on the pillow, stopping short of a prayer. He couldn't very well ask to be led unto temptation, could he? He reached out in the darkness and picked up the phone on the third ring, covering the mouthpiece with a handkerchief, just in case. "Hello?" He held his breath in the silence. One...two...three. "Hello?" he repeated.

"Hi. It's Georgia."

His breath whooshed out in relief. "I'm glad."

She made a happy little noise that clutched at his stomach. "Did you try to call?"

"I...was getting ready to," he said cautiously, wishing he had the nerve to come clean. The woman had already turned him down for a date. What did he have to lose?

Her stolen kisses. Her respect. Her calls.

"I just got out of the shower," she whispered. "It was so hot in here, I had to do something to cool down."

He groaned. Just one last ride, he promised himself. She was so unbelievably sexy, and the fun would end Sunday night when her boyfriend returned, if not sooner.

"Problem is," she said, "I'm still hot."

His erection tented his pale-blue boxers. "It's getting warmer in here by the minute. What are you wearing?"

"A towel."

Lucky, lucky towel.

"What about you?" she asked.

He heard seams splitting as he shed his boxers. "Nothing. God, I haven't been able to get you off my mind."

She murmured her pleasure. "I was wondering… How do you feel about…oral sex?"

He swallowed. "I'm in f-favor of it."

She laughed.

Ken lay back against the pillows and closed his eyes as she uttered erotic words. She knelt over him and took his throbbing rod into that wonderful mouth of hers, flicking her tongue like when he'd kissed her today. Her dark hair fell forward like a feathery curtain, tickling his abdomen. When the ministrations brought him close to the brink however, he instructed her to swing her body around so he could return the favor. He moaned against her musky sex, tonguing the center of her control until she lost it, grandly. His climax followed soon after, quick and intense.

"That was wonderful," he breathed. "I can't imagine anything you would do that I wouldn't love."

She laughed. "I thought the word 'love' wasn't in your vocabulary," she said, her voice breathless and teasing.

Hmm. Rob had never told Georgia that he loved her? "I, um, changed my mind. The last few days…" What? These last few days he'd fallen for her while impersonating her boyfriend?

"Go on," she urged.

He squirmed, not wanting to put words in the man's mouth. "I just feel different about us."

She sighed. "And I was so afraid you wouldn't like this."

"Are you kidding? I can't wait to see you again." That had just slipped out. Ken winced and waited.

"You gave me a scare today," she said.

Ken frowned. "When?"

"When I dropped by your house," she said with a little laugh.

His heart skipped one beat, two beats.

"When I saw the papers stacked up on the stoop, I was worried that you were more ill than you told me. I could just picture you upstairs, withering away in that humongous bed of yours."

Speaking of withering.

"I finally looked in the garage and saw your car was missing. Did you go in to the office?"

His mind raced, trying to keep up with the lies and the half truths. "Um, yes."

"I figured your cold had put you behind," she said. "You sound much better, by the way."

"I'm still a little hoarse," he insisted, then cleared his throat for effect.

"I suppose you got my note." She laughed, then paused expectantly.

He nearly dropped the phone. "I, uh…I—no."

"I left it on the kitchen counter."

"Ah." He cast around for an explanation. "It was dark when I got home and I didn't even turn on a light."

"Oh, well," she said. "I just wanted to let you know I left you soup in the refrigerator."

Ken frowned. "That was nice of you."

"Happy to do it. And I'm glad to hear you're feeling better. I guess this means you'll be at the wedding tomorrow."

He froze. Would Rob be back in time to attend the wedding? "I'm...planning to. If I don't get caught up... at the office."

"Oh," she said, clearly disappointed.

Did Rob disappoint her often?

"Remind me again where the church is," he said in his best guys-will-be-guys voice.

"St. Michael's, silly. Remember, you pulled some strings and got them a deal on printing their invitations?"

"Of course." Ken winced. "Except I don't recall the time."

She sighed. "Three-thirty."

"Right," he said. "Three thirty." Far away, a siren screamed, barely audible over the whir of the fan, but his ears were attuned to the noise of emergency.

Crash scratched against the floor, obviously trying to stand. He barked, several times, ending in a whine—he'd heard the siren, too. Like an idiot, Ken waved his arms to quiet the dog, then bounded into the bathroom and closed the door.

"What was all that noise?" she asked.

"The television," he said, sitting on the edge of the tub. "Some cop show."

"Oh," she said flatly.

"How's work?" he asked, partly to change the subject, and partly because he wanted to know.

"Dr. Story is watching me, waiting for me to make another mistake. He called me in this morning to sign a report he wrote up about that incident with that policeman I told you about."

Ken swallowed guiltily. "Oh?"

"That little stunt he pulled will go on my permanent file."

He was torn between commiserating with her and taking up for himself. "Well, I guess knowing you did the right thing will have to be its own reward."

"Hey, whose side are you on, anyway?" She laughed, and he found himself irritated that she seemed so damnably cheerful around her boyfriend all the time. She yawned, then her laugh tinkled over the line again. "I'm sorry—I'm suddenly so sleepy."

Ken frowned. He wished he could say the same, but he had enough on his mind to keep a dozen men tossing and turning. He didn't want to let her go, but he couldn't very well keep her on the line. "I guess I'd better say good night, then."

"That's funny."

He picked up on an odd note in her voice. "What?"

"You sound so…different."

He adjusted the handkerchief and moved farther away from the mouthpiece. "It's just my cold."

"No," she said, sounding troubled. "I don't mean your voice. I mean…never mind."

"Georgia," he said, overcome with frustration. "I love...talking to you."

She was silent for so long Ken was afraid she had fallen asleep. At last she murmured, "Good night, Rob," and hung up.

GEORGIA HADN'T FELT so thoroughly miserable in recent memory. Her body still pulsed from a release she'd shared with Rob...while she fantasized about another man. And the mind could play devious tricks on a person—she'd even begun to imagine Ken Medlock's voice in Rob's scratchy one.

Was this roiling sensation in her stomach what her father felt when he came home to kiss her mother's neck after a bout of fooling around? Could she even face Rob tomorrow if he showed up for the wedding?

She squeezed a handful of pillow into her fist. Rob didn't deserve this, this...distraction. Not when things were going so well between them. He'd never been so carefree, so vulnerable. For months she'd been hoping for a sign that he was open to exploring a deeper, more intimate relationship. Yet tonight when she'd thought he was going to tell her he loved her, she'd panicked.

"What does that mean?" she whispered aloud in the dark.

It means you're like your father. Never appreciating what you have, always wanting what is out of reach, or things you know are bad. Or wrong. Or hurtful. Willing to sacrifice warm security for hot passion. Self-indulgent. Reckless. Wicked.

Georgia sighed and flung the sheet off her humid body. *And hot.*

CHAPTER FIFTEEN

"WHAT DOES IT MEAN?" Toni repeated over the phone. "I'll tell you what it means—you are falling for the cop."

"No, no, no," Georgia said, shaking her head. "Wrong answer." She sat down on her coffee table and put her feet up on her couch. "Just because I have a couple of harmless little fantasies about the guy doesn't mean I'm falling for him."

"If they were so harmless, then why are you making such a fuss?"

Good question.

"And what about the kiss?"

She was beginning to regret telling her friend everything. "The kiss happened in the heat of the moment—completely unplanned. It meant nothing."

"If it meant nothing, then why are you in such an uproar?"

"Because I feel guilty!"

"If you've done nothing to be ashamed of, you shouldn't feel guilty."

"You aren't Catholic. And I have this fear that Rob will run into Ken in the gym, and Ken will casually mention that we kissed in the park."

"So when you see Rob at the wedding today, tell him about it and let him know it didn't mean anything."

Georgia blinked back sudden tears and made choking sounds.

"It did mean something, though, didn't it?"

She dropped her forehead into her hand. "Maybe," she whispered, sniffing.

"Georgia," Toni said, her voice incredulous. "Meeting someone who makes you feel extraordinary is something to *celebrate,* not cry over."

"But what about Rob? Things were just starting to go so well."

"I think your interest in the cop simply means you're not ready to settle down right now. It's not a crime, and Rob might be hurt, but he'll live."

Georgia lifted her chin. "You're absolutely right."

"So what are you going to do?"

"I have no idea."

"I DON'T KNOW what's wrong with it," Georgia told the clerk, then scooted a box full of the phone, message recorder and wires across the counter. "But the only message I've gotten in a week was the mechanical one about adjusting the volume."

The kid scratched his head and gave her a sullen expression. "You're returning this phone system because no one ever calls you?"

She smiled sweetly—he was the obviously the author of the manual. "*No.* I'm returning this phone system because a friend of mine told me she has left at least two messages I never received."

"Got your receipt, lady?"

She slid it across the counter.

His hand disappeared below the counter to scratch

someplace she couldn't see. "One of our repair guys will have to take a look at it tomorrow. Can we call you?"

She leaned forward, pushed back the straw hat she had bought for today, and enunciated very clearly. "That would be fine, except now I don't *have* a phone. How about you tell me what time tomorrow I can come back."

They negotiated a time, and Georgia exited the store, aware she was garnering a few strange looks because not everyone in the electronics store wore a long sheer dress, a straw hat, and white wedge espadrilles, plus carried a huge wrapped package with a big silver bow.

She caught a bus at the corner of the shopping center, then walked a half block to the church, replaying her conversation with Toni. She was right, of course. If Georgia was so distracted by Ken Medlock, she wasn't making herself wholly available to Rob. It was the pushing and pulling that was making her crazy. The prudent thing to do was to suggest to Rob that they take a break from seeing each other.

She entered the church from the back and followed the sound of raised voices and female laughter down a hallway to the room where the bride and bridesmaids were dressing for their photos. She had never seen so much clutter—clothes, shoes, makeup bags, hair appliances. Stacey looked ethereal in ivory. Her mother fussed with her train while another older woman worked on the bride's chin-length red hair. Toni was one of four bridesmaids dressed in long, straight-skirted gowns in a deep coral color.

"You look beautiful," Georgia said.

Her friend blushed prettily and handed Georgia a curling iron. "Will you curl the back of my hair?"

She helped to arrange Toni in front of a mirror and set to work.

"I don't suppose Rob is here yet?"

Georgia shook her head. "He said he might get hung up at the office since he's so behind from being sick." She couldn't decide whether she wanted to get the breakup over with, or put if off another day.

"You'll look back on this someday and laugh," her friend offered.

"Think so?"

"Yeah, when you and the cop have six kids."

Georgia laughed good-naturedly. What she hadn't told Toni was that while she *was* planning to break off with Rob, she *wasn't* planning to go out with Ken Medlock.

"Too bad you couldn't have broken up with Rob before and asked that yummy uniform to bring you to the wedding."

She gave a noncommittal nod. She was taking a hiatus from men—dating them, even merely *looking* at them, had awakened her dark side. She needed time and space to regain her perspective.

Toni kept glancing in Stacey's direction with a wistful expression. "Think you or I will ever be brides, Georgia?"

An amusing question, since Toni was two years younger. "Probably. Someday. How goes it with Dr. Baxter?"

Toni made a face. "I haven't told him my name yet."

"Toni!"

"I can't help it. He calls me Terri Strawberry now. How cute is that?"

"How *sexist* is that?"

"I know, I know. I'm going to tell him, no matter how embarrassing it is."

"Good."

Georgia finished curling her hair, sliding her own envious glances toward the glowing Stacey—not because the woman was getting married, but because she was marrying someone she was head over heels for. And Neil seemed to be head over heels for her, too. Georgia looked around the room, surveying the happy, fretting women, taking in the buzz of conversation and hair dryers, acknowledging the charge in the air. Excitement. Happiness. Optimism.

She wanted it. She wanted true love and all the trappings of giddiness. And someday she'd have it... if these overactive hormones of hers didn't get in the way.

Georgia smiled and nodded at another bridesmaid who needed an extra hand with her hair. She dreaded the talk with Rob, but she was grateful for one thing— she'd left Ken Medlock yesterday in the park with a stern rejection, and if she mailed the pictures of his dog, she couldn't imagine a reason why she'd ever run into him again.

KEN WALKED PAST the job postings bulletin board a half a dozen times, each time promising himself he would not look. And he didn't. Not until the seventh time. Then, just to satisfy his own morbid curiosity, he quickly scanned the list for churches and businesses in need of traffic control and security for the day.

St. Michael's Church, Janus-Baker wedding, 10:30 a.m. Alexander-Childers wedding, 3:30 p.m. Piper-Matthews wedding, 7:30 p.m. Two officers, two hours for each event.

Georgia would be at the Alexander-Childers wedding in the afternoon. Maybe if he could see Georgia and her boyfriend together, see the way she looked at Trainer, see how the man adored her, he could shake this compulsion to be around Georgia. It was the guilt, he told himself, which triggered a burning need to know how she drank her coffee in the morning, if she left the top off the toothpaste tube, if she painted her toenails.

Telling himself he would bow to Providence and write Georgia Adams out of his life if the jobs were already taken, he walked up to the clerk who assisted in linking off-duty cops with community needs.

"Is St. Michael's all filled up today?" he asked casually.

The young man ran his finger down a grid. "There's one slot left for the evening wedding, seven-thirty. Interested?"

Disappointed beyond words, Ken stood stock still. He'd promised to heed whatever the schedule dictated. He would eventually get Georgia out of his mind. It was just a simple physical attraction, albeit a strong one. Things had worked out for the best—he liked being a bachelor, and she was obviously looking for a more serious relationship.

I try to be an honest person...just as I expect the man I'm seeing to be honest with me.

His track record on honesty took him out of the running anyway, Ken noted wryly.

"Medlock?" the guy asked, waving a hand to recapture his attention. "You want it?"

Disgusted with himself for caring about a woman who'd made it abundantly clear that she wasn't interested in him, he nodded. "I'll take the seven thirty slot. Gratis, for the church."

The clerk pursed his mouth as he made a note. "Mighty nice of you." Then he grinned. "Penance to pay?"

Ken smirked, then grabbed a cup of coffee and returned to his desk, feeling somewhat better. The one upside of not dating Georgia—he would never have to confess that he'd been the man who'd taken the sexual pleasures she'd intended for her boyfriend. He drank deeply of the coffee, still marveling over the week's events. Considering how quickly the situation had snowballed, he should be thanking his lucky stars to have escaped relatively unscathed.

He sat back in his chair with a resigned nod. Yes— lucky, lucky, lucky.

"Hey, Medlock."

Ken turned and jerked his chin up to acknowledge a colleague approaching his desk. "Yeah, Booker?"

"I'm in a bind. I signed up for the three-thirty wedding at St. Michael's, and I just remembered I'm supposed to take my father-in-law golfing. Don't suppose you'd—"

"Absolutely."

CHAPTER SIXTEEN

KEEPING HIS MIND on directing the traffic into the church parking lot from a busy street was difficult when, one, he knew Georgia didn't have a car, and two, he knew that she was planning to arrive early and was undoubtedly already inside. He did, however, keep his eyes peeled for a 1999 black Lexus with a tag number matching the one in his head.

But by the time the wedding was about to be underway, he still hadn't seen one. When the parking lot started crowding, he left the street traffic to the other officer and directed last-minute arrivals into the nearest empty spots. Not the most exciting job, but police work wasn't always exciting. His vital signs did accelerate, however, when he caught a flash of blue darting through the parking lot. Georgia?

He smiled involuntarily. *Georgia.* In a long blue flowery dress that hugged her form, holding an adorable hat on her head so she wouldn't lose it in her haste. She skidded to a halt next to a white car, peered inside, then seemed to be trying every key on a ring. Ken jogged through the rows of cars. "Georgia."

She jerked her head around, and her eyes bugged. "What are you doing here?"

"Volunteer work for the church, ma'am," he said

casually, belying the tattoo of his heart at the sight of her. God, she was beautiful—no, *magnificent* with her shining hair falling around her shoulders. Just as he'd imagined. "Is there a problem?"

She pointed to the car. "The bride wrote her own vows, but left them lying on the front seat. See?"

He nodded.

"But none of these keys seem to work," she said, trying one or two of them again.

"This is a Toyota," he said. "Those look like Ford keys to me."

She squinted. "Stacey gave me the wrong keys!"

He shook his head and pulled out a slim tool. "I'm not supposed to do this for just anybody, but since I know you and since this is an emergency, I'll make an exception."

Her grin when the door popped open was reward enough. "Thank you!" She leaned in to snatch the sheet of paper, giving him a breath-stealing view of her legs as the skirt kicked up. She relocked the door, then swung it shut. "Well…it was nice to see you again," she said, her voice a bit nervous.

He touched the brim of his hat, then watched until she disappeared inside the cathedral. His heart pounded, his body straining forward, compelling him to go after her. Ken forced himself to return to his job, but when his colleague said he would take care of parking the stragglers, Ken removed his hat and ventured inside the cathedral, turning at the staircase and walking up into the balcony, which was empty save for the videographer.

He hung back, scouring the audience below. He

found her hat and enjoyed a leisurely look at her as she
peeked over her shoulder toward the entrance of the
church in anticipation of the ceremony starting—or
maybe of her boyfriend arriving? There was an empty
space next to her on the pew, which irritated him immensely. Rob had obviously known about the wedding
before Ken had promised for him to "do his best to
come." Perhaps the business that had called him out
of town had kept him from returning to Birmingham,
which still didn't explain why the man hadn't at least
called Georgia to say he wouldn't be there.

The organist started playing softly, then the ceremony began. The groomsmen filed in, and Ken studied
the groom, who seemed composed except for rocking back and forth on his heels. Ken felt for him and
couldn't fathom being in his shoes. Taking a vow to
forsake all others for the rest of your life—scary. His
parents had beat the odds, going on forty years of marriage, but these days, things were different. *People*
were different, not as strong, not as dedicated.

His gaze went back to Georgia and he bit down on
the inside of his cheek. Was that why he felt so drawn
to the woman? Because she seemed so complex, this
woman with the face of an angel whose passionate
phone calls would test the devil himself? He squirmed,
his stomach burning with want and guilt and some un-
identifiable urge to find out what made her tick. A hot
flush burned his neck when he realized how he would
seem if someone knew what was going on—watching
a woman from a balcony with whom he'd been having
phone sex without her knowledge.

He swallowed, himself confused by the battery of

emotions pulling at him. He'd never thought of himself as some guy who couldn't take no for an answer. But he had the horrible feeling that something really wonderful was slipping through his fingers. Of all the numbers in Birmingham, why had she called *his* by accident? And why had he responded? And why had they met the following day?

If he gave up now, was he turning his back on fate?

The bridesmaids filed in—he thought one of them was the skinny little friend of Georgia's from the blood drive—and the rest of the wedding party. Then, on the organist's cue, everyone stood as the bride made her way down the aisle. With her back to him, it was easy for Ken to imagine Georgia in the woman's place, approaching the altar with fluid movements. He frowned wryly, projecting Rob's unknown face onto the groom. Was the guy a model type, with spiffy clothes and a fifty-dollar haircut? His ride was expensive enough, and his address put him in a ritzy part of town.

He stole glances at Georgia as the ceremony proceeded. She was rapt, giving solemn attention to the minister's words. Was she foreseeing her own wedding? Would the vows exchanged today either strengthen or weaken her commitment to Robert Trainer?

And the ceremony itself seemed to be going well, with appropriate smiles and nods—until a commotion in the back captured the attention of everyone in the church. Ken couldn't see what was going on directly beneath the balcony, but his instincts kicked in the instant he saw the expressions of panic and horror. He crouched and crept to the front of the balcony, then glanced down through the rails as a man came into view.

"Stacey," the man shouted, his body shaking. "You can't marry him!"

Out of the corner of his eye, Ken noticed the videographer had left his chair and was aiming the camera downward.

"Darren," the bride said, her eyes wide. "You shouldn't be here." Ken could hear the woman's fear.

The groom's face had turned a mottled shade. "How dare you show your face, Haney." Then, as any self-respecting challenged groom would do, he started for the man, his eyes blazing.

But when the man whipped out a knife, the groom stopped short and guests drew back. Involuntarily, Ken's eyes flew to Georgia, who had turned around and looked horrified. Thanks to his crouched position, she hadn't noticed him in the balcony, and neither had anyone else, except for the cameraman.

"Come on," the crazy man shouted at the groom, stabbing the air with his blade. "I told you before that if you're going to marry Stacey, you'll have to get past me first!"

Ken's mind raced, sizing up the situation. The man stood directly beneath him. He could simply announce his presence and draw his weapon, but something about brandishing a gun in church didn't sit well in his gut. His gaze fell upon the metal folding chair the videographer had vacated, and the solution hit him.

GEORGIA'S HEART lodged in her throat. One minute she had pushed aside the hurt of Rob not showing and immersed herself in the unfolding ceremony, and the next a knife-wielding lunatic had taken the church hostage. A memory stirred—Toni mentioning something about Stacey having a creepy ex-boyfriend. She swallowed hard. From his wild-eyed look and the size of that knife, someone was going to get hurt.

A movement in the balcony caught her eye. The videographer was capturing everything on film, and— she gulped—Ken Medlock was holding a folding metal chair over the madman's head. Her heart soared crazily. Then four seconds later, it was all over—the knife fell to the carpet, harmless, and the man lay on his side, moaning, with a bloody gash on his forehead. Several male guests jumped to restrain him.

But at the sight of blood, her own instincts kicked in. She elbowed past the people in her pew and threaded her way through the crowd. "Excuse me, I'm a nurse. Excuse me."

She stepped over the knife, then knelt to scrutinize the man's wound. She sensed, rather than heard, Ken Medlock stride up behind her. The man had such an uncanny knack for being...*around.* And when had she started liking it?

Moving with power and economy of motion, he picked up the knife with a handkerchief and wrapped it. The man emanated quiet authority. "Everyone, step back," he said, waving. He pulled out a set of handcuffs and knelt to the floor. "That means you, too, ma'am," he murmured for her ears only.

She glanced up and was distracted for a split second by his serious brown eyes. "He might have a concussion."

"He also might have a death wish," he said. "And if he tried to hurt you, I'd have to shoot him. So," he added with a little smile, "please step aside until I can cuff him."

She considered a battle, but was moved by the sincerity of his expression. Ken made her feel…grounded. And secure. And very, very aroused. She swallowed, then moved back in concession.

"Will you hold this, ma'am?" he asked, extending the wrapped knife.

She took it gingerly, surprised by its weight, her mind reeling with other possible outcomes of the situation. An incredibly calm hero, Ken cuffed the man's wrists behind him just as the groom, Neil, walked up with a teary-eyed Stacey.

"Thank you, Officer," Neil said, flushed and flustered, Stacey clinging to his arm.

Georgia stepped forward. "Neil Childers and Stacey Alexander, this is Officer Ken Medlock. Ken is…" She looked at him and her heart jerked crazily. "Ken is a friend."

"You're here with Georgia?" the groom asked.

Ken seemed amused. She was sure her cheeks were scarlet as she added, "He's a friend of Rob's."

"I was handling traffic for the church," Ken offered. "I take it you all know this guy?"

They nodded, their faces grim. "Darren Haney and I dated two years ago," Stacey said.

"I still love you, Stacey," the man moaned, his eyes barely open.

"There's a restraining order on him," Neil said, his mouth twisting, his hold on Stacey tight.

"I'll take care of him," Ken said. "You might have to fill out some paperwork later, but I wouldn't let this creep ruin your day. Can you stand?" he asked the man.

"Don't know," the guy moaned.

"Try," Ken said, pulling him to his feet. He looked at Georgia, then nodded toward the vestibule. "Let's take this out in the hall."

She turned to Stacey and gave her an encouraging smile. "Ken's right. If you allow this jerk to ruin your wedding, he'll win."

The bride exchanged questioning glances with her groom, then smiled and nodded. "We'll wait for you to come back in."

"No," Georgia said, shaking her head. "This could take a while. If I'm not here when you come out, I'll see you at the reception."

"Did Rob make it?" Stacey asked.

"I'm afraid not."

"So bring Officer Medlock. We'll save him a bottle of champagne as a small token of thanks." Neil echoed the invitation.

She hesitated, looking over her shoulder. "I'll ask, b-but he seems to be a very b-busy man." The man would probably have to return to the Bat Cave or something.

"Thanks for helping out with this mess," Stacey said. "We'll look for you both at the country club."

Georgia conjured up a reassuring smile and backed out of the chapel, closing the doors behind her. She stared at the knife she held, still incredulous. At the sound of a moan behind her, she turned, donning her professional face.

Ken had deposited the man on a padded bench, lying on his side. She handed the wrapped knife to Ken, then knelt to check the man's pulse, alertness and the extent of the wound.

"He's going to need a few stitches," she said, straightening. "And his vision seems clear, but he probably should have a CAT scan and spend the night under psych observation."

"What the hell did you drop on my head?" the man mumbled.

"A ton of bricks," Ken snapped, "which is apparently what it takes to get the point across that your old girlfriend doesn't want you in her life." He recited the man his rights, then pulled him to his feet. "I'll take the guy to County—it's the closest facility."

"I'll come with you." Georgia blinked. Had she really said that? "I can help arrange a psych consultation once we get there."

"But you'll miss the wedding."

"I told Stacey and Neil that we'd…that I'd catch up with them later," she said with a shrug, astonished to realize that she'd rather ride in a squad car with this man to a place where she already spent too much time, than attend a wedding for which she'd bought a special outfit.

"Won't your boyfriend miss you?"

"He…couldn't make it." Georgia swallowed. Was it immoral to have a pseudo-date with a man before she'd officially broken off with her boyfriend if the only thing preventing her from breaking off with her boyfriend was that he hadn't shown up?

Ken's smile sent a stab of desire to her midsection that banished her thoughts of Rob, guilty or otherwise. "That's too bad," he said, but his decidedly unsympathetic tone gave her a little thrill.

She followed him to his squad car and slid into the front passenger seat when he opened the door for her. After he took the driver's seat, he radioed an apparent partner on the church grounds and informed him of the situation, then called in his arrest of the man and reported his intention to take him to County. She watched him, fascinated by his efficient speech and his professionalism. Her body fairly hummed with awareness of his proximity, the images of the fantasy shower show she'd given him last night ringing in her mind. The man would be shocked if he knew her thoughts.

He replaced the radio handset and started the car. "I'll drop you off at the reception as soon as we're through. With any luck, you'll be there by the time they cut the cake."

She wet her lips as they pulled out of the church parking lot. "Neil and Stacy asked me to invite you to the reception, said they'd save you a bottle of champagne as a token of their gratitude."

"That's not necessary."

"Ken, someone could have been killed," she murmured, not even attempting to hide her admiration for his quick thinking. "You always seem to know exactly what to do."

His profile seemed more serious than the conversation warranted. "No, believe me, I don't always know what to do. But I'm glad in this instance that no one was seriously injured." Then he gestured to his clothing. "Unfortunately, I can't enjoy that champagne while in uniform." He stopped for a red light.

"Do you live in the vicinity of the Arrowood Country Club?"

"About five minutes from there."

"Then why not stop and change first? I don't mind waiting."

His smile of anticipation sent her pulse skyrocketing. He flipped a switch and his blue lights began flashing, the siren wailing. "But I do."

CHAPTER SEVENTEEN

"COME ON UP," Ken said as he shifted into Park. "I'll just be a few minutes and you can say hello to Crash."

Georgia hesitated, then realized she was being silly. Ken Medlock, superhero, was completely trustworthy. Besides, she was curious to see his living space. She followed him up two flights of stairs, then stopped at a nondescript door sporting the number twenty-four. She toyed with her hat, unable to completely ignore the intimate implications of entering his apartment. He, on the other hand, seemed fully at ease as he swung open the door. Georgia wondered briefly if he entertained female guests on a regular basis, then walked inside.

She hadn't expected a tasteful, comfortably decorated, clean apartment with real live plants and pictures of his family studding the built-in bookshelves. "Nice," she said.

"Something to drink?"

She shook her head, suddenly nervous, then fanned herself. "Gee, and I thought *my* apartment was the warmest place in Birmingham."

"Sorry, ma'am," he said with a shrug. "I keep complaining, but this place is still like an oven. By evening it's almost too hot to sleep."

His words sent an erotic thrill through her. Her

thighs quickened. During his bouts of insomnia, did he ever lie awake thinking about her? She couldn't drag her gaze from his thick arms, imagining them around her. The tension hung heavy in the thick air.

"Well," he said, clapping his hands together once. "Why don't you have a seat, and I'll be back in a few." He smiled, then disappeared down a hallway, his shoulders practically spanning its width.

Georgia hugged herself as she wandered around the perimeter of the room, gazing at photos of people who bore such a strong resemblance to Ken, they had to be related. Funny, but now that she thought about it, she couldn't recall ever seeing photos in Rob's house. She hated comparing the two men, but at the moment, it was inevitable.

In the distance a shower kicked on, alerting her to the fact that Ken's muscular body was positioned under running soapy water. Dark skin, dark hair, smooth muscle, long limbs. She pushed away the carnal thoughts and continued her perusal of his apartment.

Instead of leather and glass and chrome, Ken's living room furniture consisted of two big dark-blue denim couches, a blue-and-tan checked recliner, and a low maple coffee table, flanked by a wide-screen TV. She lowered herself to the middle of the nearest couch, her body sighing in appreciation as she sank into cradling cushions. Now *this* was a couch. She closed her eyes and imagined curling up with a bowl of popcorn to watch a movie on the screen, leaning on the shoulder of a large man.

Georgia halted her train of thought, once again aware of the shower going in the background. She was attracted to the man, but attraction was a long way from sharing a remote control. Ken Medlock had made it very clear he wasn't interested in a serious relationship. And she needed to get this bizarre sexual situation with Rob out of her system, this hormonal high that left her feeling so disoriented. The shower shut off.

She jumped to her feet, suddenly wishing she hadn't come up. Ken was simply too physically intense in her current condition. In fact, maybe Rob would show up at the reception and they could talk, leaving Ken to his own devices. Georgia paced the room, tempted to walk out, having horribly provocative visions of Ken emerging in a towel.

At a noise behind her, she practically jumped out of her skin. She turned to find Crash hobbling toward her on a cast, his head dipping with every arduous step. Touched, she crossed the room and sank to the floor to pet him, remembering the day she'd met Ken. Had it been less than a week? In an amazingly short amount of time he had wormed his way into her schedule and into her mind. If she were the suspicious type, she'd be inclined to think he had planned their meetings, but she knew that notion was absurd. How would Ken have known she would be at the mall, the blood drive, or even the wedding today? Even superheroes didn't have ESP.

She scratched the dog's ears, laughing at her far-fetched attempt to find some reason to distrust Ken.

"I think he remembers you from the park," Ken said from the doorway.

She looked up and swallowed hard. He was breathtakingly handsome in dark slacks and a cream-colored shirt. His hair was combed back and lay close to his head. From where she sat, she could detect the woodsy aromas of his cologne and soap. Her senses leapt, her body straining toward his. He walked over and extended his hand to her. His fingers were long and blunt-tipped, sensuous on their own, even if they weren't attached to this man's powerful body.

As if in slow motion, she watched her hand meet his in an intimate clasp, and she allowed him to pull her to her feet. The kiss was inevitable, and perhaps more potent for that reason. Their lips came together with the momentum of two cymbals. She hungrily met his intensity, their bodies molding together. His hands skimmed over her back and she sensed great restraint when he cupped her bottom. He lifted his mouth from hers long enough to rain kisses over her ear, down her neck, whispering her name against her skin. He slid his hands to her rib cage and thumbed the undersides of her breasts through the thin dress. She undulated against him, eliciting a groan.

Crash's sudden bark parted them, and she gasped at the sight of a repairman standing in the door. "Sorry," the guy said sheepishly. "I knocked three times."

Ken put his hands on his hips, his face dark. "Mr. Franks, what can I do for you?"

"Just came to check your air conditioner—everything's supposed to be working. But I can come back."

"We were just leaving," Georgia said quickly, gathering her purse and hat. She sidled by the repairman and waited in the hall until Ken emerged, stuffing his wallet into his back pocket and carrying keys. She didn't trust herself to look him in the eye.

"I'm sorry about that, ma'am," he said in a husky voice.

Oh, that lush accent. "It was as much my fault," she said, still shaken by what could have happened. "We both got carried away."

"I meant I'm sorry that we were *interrupted*."

She tingled under his gaze, but offered no comment. Words really weren't necessary in the universal language of animal lust. Her cheeks burned with shame. Had it been only yesterday that she had rebuked his kiss and told him she was involved with someone? What must he think of her?

"Georgia, say something," he said as they descended the stairs.

"We barely know each other," she murmured. "This isn't right."

He stopped midflight. "Give me a chance. I meant it when I said I want to get to know you."

She shook her head. "This isn't a good time for me."

"Because of your boyfriend?" he asked, an unpleasant expression on his face.

Right now her best defense against giving in to her sexual appetite was to keep hot Ken Medlock at arm's length. "Yes, and I'm sorry if I led you to believe anything different." She continued her descent, then waited for him at the bottom of the stairs.

KEN REMAINED SILENT as he joined her at the bottom of the stairs. He had promised himself he would go slow, dammit, but the entire time he was showering, he kept thinking that the most erotic woman he'd ever known was wrapped up in a beautiful, long-haired package, and sat mere steps away in his living room. By the time he rinsed, he'd had to turn the water to icy cold to get his raging libido under control. He thought he'd succeeded until he walked out and saw her sitting on the floor, petting his dog. She'd been laughing, her cheeks glowing and her eyes sparkling. He couldn't help himself.

"Look, maybe this isn't such a good idea," he said, gesturing vaguely between them.

She stared, her blue eyes luminous. "Maybe."

He sighed. "Why don't I drop you off at the reception? I'll give Mr. and Mrs. Childers my regrets when they come down to file the paperwork on that Haney character."

"Don't be silly," she said. "Stacey and Neil would be disappointed if you didn't come. Besides, after what you did today, you should be there."

"Any cop would have done the same thing."

"But it wasn't *any* cop," she said softly. "It was you." She angled her head at him. "You do have the strangest way of showing up when I least expect it. If I didn't know better, I might think that you…"

He swallowed hard. Think that he what? That he knew more about her than she could ever imagine?

She shook her head. "Never mind. Let's go."

Tingling with remorse, he led her to his gray sport utility vehicle. In response to her raised eyebrows, he gave a little laugh. "You didn't think I drove the cruiser all the time, did you?"

"I suppose I did."

"Well, Miss Adams," he drawled, "I'm full of surprises." *And there's one you'd rather not know about, I'm sure.*

At least he'd managed to coax a smile from her,

and the tension eased a bit. He unlocked the door and helped her climb inside, setting his jaw when he touched her silky skin. The skirt of her filmy dress hung down, in danger of being caught in the closed door. He picked up the hem of the blue dress and, at a loss, handed it to her. The awkwardness and intimacy of the moment caught at his heart, and a lump of frustration lodged in his throat. He wanted to be with her, to access her mind and her body and her dreams, but the distance she maintained, combined with her loyalty to Robert Trainer, compounded by his guilt over the phone calls...

He stepped back and closed the door, struck by how much he could identify with the lunatic who stormed the church this afternoon. The thought of Georgia marrying someone else before they had a chance to explore the possibility of a relationship made him a little nuts. Ken pulled a hand down over his face. *Get a grip, man—you wouldn't crash the wedding wielding a blade.*

No, but he'd be mighty tempted to make a fool of himself somehow.

Practically shaking from powerlessness, he climbed in the driver's seat and proceeded to act as if everything were normal. It was for the best that nothing had happened upstairs, he reminded himself. Because Robert Trainer would be back soon to lay claim on her heart, and the very least he owed her was a confession that would circumvent a rupture in Georgia and Rob's relationship.

I'll tell her at the reception, he told himself, *after a drink for courage.*

CHAPTER EIGHTEEN

"AND A VERY SPECIAL TOAST," Stacey said, lifting her glass, "to our friend and hero, Officer Ken Medlock of the Birmingham City Police Department."

The guests erupted in enthusiastic applause. From across the room, Georgia's heart thumped as he nodded his thanks to the couple, then she drank from her glass. Rob hadn't materialized, so her hope for a buffer from Ken had disintegrated. She'd made herself scarce, moving around the room in an attempt to avoid being alone with Ken. He seemed not to mind, mingling with ease, surrounded by back-patters and hand-shakers who had witnessed the incident at the wedding. And the *women*. Georgia frowned into her half-empty glass. The women were so...*bold* in their body language.

Not that she cared. After all, she'd had her chances. Ken had made no secret of the fact that he wouldn't mind having a physical relationship. And she wanted him, too. But first Rob, now Ken—who would she be lusting after next week? Engaging in sexual games only fed a dangerous appetite. A forbidden boundary was easier to cross the second time, and the activity would have to be progressively more risqué to deliver the same thrill. Where would it end? Not in a committed marriage.

Georgia downed the rest of the champagne and went in search of a phone, thinking she might call Rob to see if they could meet somewhere to talk since she wouldn't get her phone back until tomorrow. She sighed. Although at the time Rob had seemed to enjoy her calls, she'd concluded that he was definitely avoiding her. She wanted to let him off the hook as soon as possible. Literally.

"Georgia."

At the sound of Ken's voice behind her, she closed her eyes briefly, then hurried her steps, scanning the signs on the doors in front of her. When she saw the word *Office* on the second door to the right, she made a beeline for it, despite his rapidly approaching footsteps. His large hand closed around hers on the doorknob, sending her heart into overdrive.

"Georgia," he murmured, "I need to talk to you."

She wished she hadn't drunk that glass of champagne on an empty stomach. She stared at his hand on hers, momentarily mesmerized. "It's not necessary, Ken."

"Believe me, ma'am, it is."

Georgia slowly turned and looked up at the man who was playing havoc with her emotions, and her libido. At soon as she met his gaze, however, she knew she was in trouble. His hand tightened over hers, and his Adam's apple dipped.

I want him, every fiber in her body screamed in unison. His mouth twitched and she felt her lips part. The next instant his mouth was on hers, moving hungrily. He clasped her upper arms with both hands, as if he were afraid she might try to flee. His tongue sought hers, plunging and retreating in a frenzied dance, sending a burn to her thighs. Champagne mingled on their tongues. The friction of skin on skin released the scents of their spicy and sweet colognes. Georgia moaned and jammed her traitorous body against his.

But through the fog of desire, the sound of approaching voices reached her ears. She stiffened and pulled back, recognizing at least one of the voices as a gossipy bridesmaid—if they were seen together, everyone would know, including Rob, that Georgia had been playing Post Office with the man of the hour.

The desperation must have shown on her face, because he said, "In here," and yanked open the door at her back. They ducked inside the dark room and Ken closed the door behind them. They were enveloped in near darkness. The noisy crowd passed by slowly, most of them sounding female, joking and laughing. Someone slipped and almost fell, eliciting a remark about everyone's level of sobriety.

"Did you get a look at that gorgeous cop?" a woman asked. "Whew-we!"

"Wouldn't mind being handcuffed to that guy," another one said, triggering another wave of giggles.

Georgia's entire body pulsed, her senses keened by Ken's kiss and proximity in the darkness. She could hear him breathing, shifting at the group's comments. At last their footsteps and voices faded away.

Relieved that disaster had been avoided, she groped for the doorknob and turned it.

Only it didn't move.

Panic blipped in her heart as she struggled with the doorknob. "It won't open," she hissed.

He made a disbelieving sound. "Let me try."

Georgia yanked her hand back when Ken's touched hers.

He jiggled the knob three times, each attempt more insistent than the last. Then he grunted. "The knob came off."

"Oh, great." Unwilling to accept the possibility that they might be trapped, she turned to inspect their hiding place. Light filtered into the room from a high window on the back wall of the small, narrow room, silhouetting strange shapes that did not resemble an office. She felt along the wall nearest to her for a light switch, but when she found one, the click produced nothing. She flipped it back and forth. Nada. "The light doesn't work," she announced.

"Why were you coming in here in the first place?" he asked, his tone just the tiniest bit accusing.

She bristled. "I was looking for a phone, and I thought the sign on the door said Office." She didn't add that when she heard him behind her, she'd simply wanted to flee, period.

"Looks like some kind of furniture storage closet," he said, his voice angled away from her.

Her eyes had adjusted to the darkness and she could make out old couches, tables and chairs lining the walls, stacked as high as safety allowed. The air was hot and stale, further proof they were in a stockroom. "There has to be a way out," she said, then took one step and promptly tripped over something.

His foot, she realized when he caught her, his hands touching intimate places. Blatant desire shot through her primed body. In the space of five seconds, the atmosphere changed to libidinous. She could barely see him, could barely make out his silhouette, but the electricity between them practically glowed. She couldn't explain the phenomenon that had materialized between them in scant days, but she was powerless to resist it. His hand sought out her jaw, his fingers brushed the back of her neck, and she knew she was lost.

"Let's find the exit later," he murmured, then kissed her thoroughly.

Like a weary soldier, Georgia almost welcomed the moment of defeat. Her limbs were limp with relief, her mind resigned to the inevitable conclusion of their passion. She threw herself into the kiss—if she was going to relinquish her pride to Ken Medlock, she would do it largely.

CHAPTER NINETEEN

GEORGIA'S EYES quickly adjusted to the dim lighting, assisted by the glow of his pale shirt. Their kisses grew more feverish and more promising, tongues dancing, teeth clicking. And the *heat*. The stuffy temperature and the sexual energy combined to create moisture at her pulse points. Her senses were sharp-edged, delivering stabs of desire and pleasure that stole her breath. When Georgia could no longer bear the onslaught, she undid the top button on his shirt. The simple act released a torrent of groans and hurried movements until his shirt and the top of her dress lay open to exploring fingers.

His chest was a wall of firm, smooth muscle covered with a triangle of dark hair. She thumbed his flat, taut nipples, wishing she could see his massive body in full light. His heart thudded beneath her palm, as if the man's hard, insistent erection against her stomach wasn't proof enough that he was alive. He caressed her breasts through her sensible bra, her nipples pearled and aching.

"Harder," she whispered, arching her back.

In answer, he unhooked her bra and released her breasts into his hands, then palmed her flesh and rolled the tips until she cried out. Without warning, he lowered his mouth to her nipple, and the remnants of rational thought fled.

"Ahhhh," she whispered, holding his head against her breast, urging him to draw her deeper into his mouth. He flicked his tongue over the sensitive tip, sending sensations exploding over her in waves, carrying her toward the kind of experience she'd only imagined and now wondered if she could withstand.

It was his touch, she decided, that so aroused her. Firm, yet gentle. Powerful, yet restrained. He caressed her as if she were a special treasure that might break if mishandled. And his voice—or rather, his *noises*— sent a jolt to her thighs. Responsive, expressive, bold. She countered with enthusiasm as he transferred his attention to her other breast, and explored any part of him she could reach. Ken lifted his head and stared into her eyes, then guided her quaking hand to his waistband.

Georgia understood. He wanted her, but he wanted the decision to be hers. And somehow, his tentativeness in juxtaposition to his ragged breathing was even more titillating. She dragged in air through her open mouth and slid her fingers beneath his waistband to feel bare skin, emanating warmth, and the wet tip of his arousal. When he moaned, feminine power welled in her chest, giving her the confidence to be daring. She loosened his fly and clasped his thick erection, then leaned into him, pressing her breasts against his chest.

With a long, guttural moan, he cupped her bottom and undulated against her, then pulled up her skirt, one fistful at a time, until his hands tugged at her cotton panties. Her knees weakened when his fingers delved inside and for a split second, she thought she might be too overcome to reciprocate. But long-forbidden instincts kicked in, causing her to stroke his straining staff. Taking her cues from the rumbling noises he emitted, she squeezed her hand down the considerable length with a slow and firm hand, wondering what it would feel like to have him inside her. The mere thought produced more lubrication for his fingers.

"Georgia," he murmured. "I want you now, right here. Please."

"Yes," she whispered, amazed that he didn't know how much she wanted him in return.

He groaned with anticipation, and bunched the skirt of her dress around her waist. Georgia teased them both by rubbing the tip of his manhood against the front of her panties, and was rewarded when his excitement oozed through the thin fabric. From behind, he skimmed her underwear down to her knees, then picked her up and carried her a few feet, settling her on what appeared to be the back of a couch. She clung to his shoulders, feeling the play of his muscles beneath his shirt as he slid her panties down her legs and nudged open her knees. Georgia felt boneless when his shaft trailed along her inner thigh, leaving a path of moisture. In the back of her mind, a tiny alarm sounded, and at the same instant, he hesitated.

"I have protection," he said, his voice low. She felt foolish for not inquiring sooner, and relieved that he shared her concern. The few seconds that passed as he fumbled in his wallet for the condom and rolled it on seemed agonizingly slow. The scent of her own readiness wafted up to tease her nostrils. She urged him to hurry with her hands and her knees, anxious beyond words for their union. At last, he returned to her, wrapping one arm around her back to steady her as he sought entrance to her threshold. Once, twice, three times he probed her wetness, stroking the tip over the heart of her desire until she writhed with expectation. At last he entered her, taking her breath, then filled her slowly.

The rush of adrenaline rose in her body like the mercury of a thermometer thrust into hot water. Inch by inch, she became engorged with white-hot passion, a helpless but intoxicating feeling that made her limbs loose and her mind languid. When they were fully joined, Ken's head fell forward with a great rasping sigh. He kissed her collarbone and murmured erotic words about how good she felt around him, how much he wanted to give her pleasure.

As if the incredible feeling of him pulsing inside her weren't enough, he began to massage her sensitive nub with his thumb in time to short, jolting thrusts that awakened every nerve center. Her climax broke unexpectedly, shattering around her with the force of a sudden thundershower. She groped at his back, crying out as her ecstasy peaked higher and higher, then emitting a long breathless moan as it drained away. His completion came on the heels of hers, a release that wracked his body with powerful spasms that shook the piece of furniture she rested upon. He gasped her name and gathered her to him, holding her as if she were the source of his energy. Georgia felt utterly desirable and fulfilled, and for the first time, understood the French expression for "orgasm"—*little death*. For one vibrating moment, she wished she could stay locked

in his embrace forever, this man who had proved reality could surpass decadent fantasies.

But as their breathing quieted and their pulses returned to normal, the outside encroached. Voices rose
and fell, and strains of the live band reached their secret hiding place. Georgia became aware of the stickiness of her skin—perspiration and perfume and sex.
And unused muscles in her hips and legs screamed.
She squirmed and he loosened his grip on her, leaving
kisses on her shoulder before he pulled away.

"Are you okay?" he asked as he set her gently on
the floor.

"Yes." As he removed the condom, the shallow light
from the window danced off his powerful frame, sending a new, yet familiar wave of awareness through
her. She averted her gaze, then struggled to right her
clothing while struggling to pinpoint her emotions.
She was at a disadvantage because she wasn't sure
how she was supposed to feel. Grateful? Self-satis-
fied? Awkward? Somehow she had reached the ripe
old age of thirty without the sexual savvy that most
women took for granted.

Her dress billowed at her waist, her bra and
panties were missing and not visible in the darkness.
Ken pulled up his boxers, but otherwise seemed in
no hurry to redress or even to leave, for that matter.

Not that they could leave, since the doorknob had
fallen off. They were going to have to pound on the
door until someone came. She wiped her hand across
her forehead. And how would they explain that they
had both wandered into a dark supply closet? She
closed her eyes and knelt to find her clothing, trying

to cover herself, yet realizing how laughable her modesty must seem at this point. What did he think of her character? Remorse slammed into her with enough power to force her to clutch the back of the couch. What would *she* think of a woman who would have sex in a closet with a man she'd known for mere days?

Not much.

"Here," he said softly, and extended a white object to her in the dark. Her bra.

She turned around to put it on, but he came up behind her and said, "Let me," then fastened the tricky hook for her. After murmuring her thanks, she buttoned her dress hurriedly.

"And here," he said, then extended another white object.

Her panties. Those she could manage on her own. She heard the slide of a zipper and assumed he was repairing his own clothing. Suddenly a dark question darted through her mind: How many closet trysts were on her father's disreputable résumé? Lingering gratification and nagging guilt warred within her. She wouldn't soon forget the physical bliss she'd shared with Ken Medlock, but what kind of place would the world be if everyone went around doing whatever made them feel good? Sex without love was…empty. Disappointing. And, inevitably, destructive.

Her mind reeled. Was it too late to start over with Rob? At least they could build on a foundation of friendship, instead of animal lust. Georgia cast about frantically for a diplomatic way to extricate herself from the lure of Ken Medlock…and her own weakness.

KEN HAD HOPED that their remarkable lovemaking would mark a turning point in their fledgling...*association,* but within seconds Georgia seemed to be slipping out of reach once again.

He cleared his throat, willing words into his head to salvage anything he could out of his abominable lapse in judgment. After all, Georgia wasn't privy to the other facet of their "relationship."

"Georgia, I know what just happened was spontaneous, but I have to admit I've been thinking about it since the first time I saw you." When only silence met his words, he conjured up a small laugh. "In fact, I haven't been able to get you off my mind." He swallowed. "I've been meaning to tell you—"

"Ken, stop." Her voice sounded less than receptive. "I—I don't know what came over me. I know you don't believe this, but I've never done anything like this in my life."

Make love in a closet to a virtual stranger? Or let down your guard and carry your lover with you to the moon?

Her determined sigh was not encouraging. "I think it would be best if we didn't see each other again."

"Georgia—"

"*Ever.* I know these meetings have all been coincidental, but—"

"Georgia—"

"—our paths simply can't keep crossing. There's something—"

"Wonderful?"

"—dangerous about this, this, this—"

"Attraction?"

"Temptation," she amended, and he could hear the frown in her voice. "What just happened was a fluke, a, a, a freak accident."

Apparently the experience hadn't been quite as mindblowing for Georgia. Still, dammit... "Falling in the bathtub and breaking your arm is a freak accident. What happened between us was very deliberate, at least on my part."

She gasped. "You planned this?"

He held up a hand, then realized she probably couldn't see him in the dark. "No, ma'am! I meant once we started kissing..." Ken sighed, knowing he was making an even bigger mess of things, and tried a different tack. "Is this because of your feelings for Trainer?"

She shifted away from him and bumped into something. "Yes," she said finally. "Rob is a good man."

He opened his mouth to tell her what kinds of things Rob was good at, but he stopped short of crossing that line. If Georgia was in love with the man, she probably knew about his past. And if she didn't know, he wouldn't be the one to tell her out of what might be construed as sour grapes.

Besides, he was the first to admit he found the woman irresistible, but what could he really offer her if she broke up with Robbie Boy? He wasn't ready to settle down, to offer her a committed relationship, and certainly not a home in Knox Ridge and a six-figure salary.

"Can we just get out of here, please?" she asked. "I need to find a phone."

Ken recognized yet another opportunity to confess

his deception, before she humiliated herself in front of her boyfriend. But imagining the look on her face when she realized the terrible thing he'd done stopped him. And although her hating him would be the best insulation from the woman's unexplainable appeal, he simply couldn't bear the thought of Georgia Adams hating him.

"Sure thing, ma'am."

She sighed. "Must you call me that?"

"What?"

"Ma'am."

He was at a loss. "It bothers you?"

He thought he heard her sniff. "It makes me feel like a...stranger."

"I'm sorry. I was only being respectful."

"Well...don't."

He clamped his mouth shut, sobered by the abrupt change in atmosphere. Misunderstandings. Awkwardness. Complications. All the reasons he'd avoided becoming involved with a woman. And he was foolish to imagine things would be different with Georgia Adams just because his desire for her had reached unbearable proportions.

Feeling worse than lousy, he picked his way back to the door, sized it up, then listened for foot traffic on the other side. Hearing none, he stepped back and, pretending the door was his own backside, kicked it open.

Georgia strode out, leaving behind the scent of her perfume and her body. Ken realized with a sinking feeling that a peaceful sleep did not appear to be anywhere in his near future.

CHAPTER TWENTY

THE FOLLOWING DAY was Sunday, so Georgia dragged herself from her disheveled bed and attended late morning Mass, fervently hoping to assuage some of her enormous guilt for her behavior at the wedding reception with Ken. And she did—to a tiny degree. But afterward, during the bus ride to the electronics shop to pick up her phone system, she still battled with inappropriate feelings for the man. The trouble was, her body could not so easily forget the way he had made her come alive. Unbidden, images of their lovemaking would pop into her mind, sending warmth to her cheeks and thighs. And when she thought of Rob, she felt even worse.

After Ken had kicked open the supply closet door, she had run like a spooked doe in search of the office. She'd found it, two doors down, and closed herself off from everyone else, but especially from Ken. And although she had picked up the phone to call Rob at his office where he was probably working late, she hadn't finished dialing, partly because she was still so shaken from the closet incident, she was afraid of what she might say, and partly because Rob deserved more than a hurried call or a quick visit while another man's scent was on her body.

So she'd decided to wait until her head was clear and her outlook objective, although judging from the way she felt this morning, that could be some time.

She looked out the window, seeing little of the passing landscape. Ken was Catholic. She'd recognized at least a couple of confirmation ceremonies in the family photos in his apartment. Such a nice-looking family, too—big and smiling, their arms around each other. Just the kind of family she wanted to be a part of, wanted to add to. She wondered briefly why Ken didn't seem to want the same thing for himself. Then she swallowed hard. Perhaps he did want a big family someday, just not with the kind of woman whom she could have in a supply closet.

She closed her eyes, telling herself she deserved the self-derision. Ken Medlock hadn't forced her to do anything against her will. It wasn't his fault that she'd been thinking about him, fantasizing about him since they'd first met. It wasn't his fault that he had been an attractive, convenient outlet for her raging hormones. It wasn't his fault that she was seeking something he couldn't offer.

In fact, Ken had been up-front about the fact that he wasn't looking for a commitment. Georgia sighed. No, she couldn't fault the man's honesty.

When she alighted from the bus, she hadn't yet worked out the emotional dilemma in which she had mired herself. The only thing she knew for certain was that she had to sort things out with Rob, and soon. She'd been hurt when he hadn't shown up for the wedding, but on the other hand, he'd warned her that he might have to work late. She couldn't very well blame her ghastly mistake with Ken on Rob not showing up. The men weren't interchangeable—at least not to a woman with an ounce of self-respect.

She sighed as she pushed her way into the store. The customer service line was already backed up, so she had to stand in line for several long moments before she could talk to the same kid who had taken her phone system for repair the previous day.

"Oh, yeah, I remember you," he said with a little smirk. "You were mad because you didn't have any messages."

"Is my phone ready?" she asked through gritted teeth.

"Got it right here," he said, removing a box from a shelf behind him. "The guys and I had a real laugh over this one."

Georgia worked her mouth from side to side. "And why is that?"

"Because," the kid said, plugging her system into an outlet on the counter. "Turns out this recorder is a little quirky. In addition to pressing the '1' button, you got to adjust the volume in one direction or another to get rid of that welcome message."

"What does that mean?"

He gave her a goofy grin and indicated the flashing light. "It means you got tons of messages, lady." He pressed the button and the mechanical voice announced, "You…have…twelve…messages."

"Twelve?" Concern gripped her stomach. What if she'd missed an important call from the hospital, or from her family?

"Message…one…Tuesday…eight…thirty-four…
p.m."

"Hey, Georgia, it's Rob. Sounds like you got your
new machine. I guess you've already left for the bachelorette party. Wanted to let you know that I've been
called to Columbus, Ohio for a meeting—not sure
how long I'll be gone. I left a message at the hospital today with someone named Melanie, but I wasn't
sure you'd get it. Hope you have a good time tonight
with the girls. I'm on a late flight out tonight. I'll call
you, okay?"

She frowned. Melanie hadn't given her Rob's message until Wednesday. But then again, maybe he hadn't
called the hospital until after she'd left on Tuesday.
Wait a minute. Had Rob just said he was flying out
Tuesday night? That was weird. He'd been home when
she called after coming home from the club.

"Message…two…Wednesday…six…forty…
seven…p.m."

"Georgia, hey, it's Rob again. Just wanted to let you
know it looks like I'm going to be here for a couple
of days. If you need to reach me, call my messaging
service at the office. Sorry I missed you." He laughed.
"Hope you didn't do something crazy last night after
leaving the club."

Georgia frowned. Was Rob so disturbed by her initiating phone sex that he was going to pretend it hadn't
even happened? And he must have fallen ill soon after
he left the message if he'd made it back to Birmingham by the time she'd called him Wednesday night.

"Message…three…Wednesday…seven…twelve…
p.m."

"It's Toni. Just wondering if you've talked to Rob yet about you-know-what and what he had to say. Call me."

Message four was a telemarketer.

"Message...five...Thursday...five...nineteen... p.m."

"Hey, it's Rob. Was hoping to catch you. I see on the news that Birmingham is still under a heat wave, though, so you're probably working overtime in the E.R. I'm still not sure how long I'll be here, but I hope to be back in time to go to Stacey and Neil's wedding. I'll talk to you soon."

Georgia's heart sped up. Something was wrong. Rob didn't sound ill. In fact, he sounded as if he were still in Columbus. She swallowed. But that was impossible—she'd called him at home Wednesday night *and* Thursday night.

"Look, lady," the clerk said. "The line's backing up. Maybe you could finish this at home?"

"Shut up," she said, her mind racing.

Messages six and seven were from telemarketers. Message eight was from the personnel department at the hospital telling her she could pick up a copy of her file update at her earliest convenience—Dr. Story's report on her stint as a veterinarian, no doubt.

Message nine was from her super saying he would try to fix her thermostat, again, on Monday.

"Message...ten...Friday...six...twenty...p.m."

"Hey, Georgia, it's Rob again. Looks like I won't be able to make it back for the wedding. Give Stacey and Neil my best. I'll call you when I get back, probably Sunday afternoon. Looking forward to seeing you."

Her collar had grown moist, and her breathing rapid. The newspapers stacked up on his stoop, his overgrown grass. If she hadn't talked to Rob herself, she'd be tempted to think he was still in Columbus when he made that call. Was he playing some kind of joke? She rubbed one throbbing temple. If he was, it wasn't funny.

"Message...eleven...Friday...ten...sixteen...p.m."

"Georgia, it's Mother. Just wanted to tell you to have a wonderful time at the wedding, dear. And do try to catch the bouquet. Toodleoo."

Georgia closed her eyes briefly, thinking she probably wouldn't tell her mother than when the bouquet was being thrown, she was making animal love in a supply closet to a man who had no intention of ever walking down the aisle.

"Message...twelve...Saturday...eight...forty...a.m."

"It's Rob again." He sounded annoyed, and she wondered where she'd been that she'd missed his call. Probably taking a shower to get ready for the wedding. "I'm starting to get worried since I haven't talked to you for so long. I hope everything's okay."

Her heart lodged firmly in her throat, like that chunk of bagel Ken Medlock had squeezed out of her. *Since I haven't talked to you for so long?*

"Hey, lady," the guy whined. "Give me a break."

"How do you review numbers that are programmed in?" she croaked.

He sighed and pushed a couple of buttons. "You can only see three at a time."

Her gaze flew to the first number she'd programmed: 205-555-6252. It was wrong. Rob's number was 62*25*. She'd been dialing the wrong...

She covered her mouth when the implication hit her. *Oh...my...God.* She grabbed the counter for support.

"Hey, lady, you okay?"

Georgia shook her head dumbly. She'd been having raw, sensual phone sex with a nameless, faceless stranger. She would, quite possibly, never be okay again.

CHAPTER TWENTY-ONE

THE BUS RIDE across town was torturous. Georgia kept replaying the events of the past few days in tandem with the messages left on her machine, frantically searching for some explanation other than the one that left a rock in her stomach, but coming up empty-handed. The implication was nauseating: She was dating one man, having phone sex with another, and having real sex with a third.

When had her life taken such a bizarre twist?

She closed her eyes briefly. When she'd allowed physical needs to override her good judgment. One thing was certain—she had to get to Rob's before he found the little note she'd left about having X-rated fun on the phone. After that, she'd take it one step at a time, assuming there was actually a way to extricate herself from the mess she'd created.

So, dragging the box containing her phone system, she disembarked from the bus and practically trotted the distance to Rob's home. When she saw the local Sunday paper and the *New York Times* lying rolled up on the stoop, she was torn between relief that he hadn't arrived home and dismay that her suspicions were beginning to look horrifically correct.

She set down her box, scooped up the papers, and

fished the door key from her wallet with a hand that shook uncontrollably. She dropped the key altogether when a car horn sounded from the street. When she turned, her heart dove. Rob's black Lexus rolled into the driveway. The note—she had to get the note. The garage door went up and he guided the car inside. She scrambled for the key, thinking she could still beat him to the kitchen even if he entered the house through the mud room. At last she seized the key, then shoved it home and turned it. The dead bolt gave, and she practically fell inside. When she slid into the kitchen, Rob had already spotted her note and was two steps away. She darted in front of him and yanked it out of reach, then gave him a cheerful smile.

"Welcome home."

"Thanks." He gave her a quick peck on the mouth, then his smooth face creased into a quizzical frown. "What's that?"

"What?"

"That piece of paper you just grabbed."

She looked down at her hand. "Oh. This is nothing—just a note I left when I came over the other day to, um, bring in your newspapers."

"Oh. So you did get my messages?"

"Um, yes. Yes, I did."

He smiled. "I was beginning to think there was something wrong with your machine because I couldn't catch you."

Nothing wrong with my machine, just me, she thought miserably. She had hoped for some spark, some sense of excitement at the sight of Rob, but she was merely...sad. Sad that she and Rob both maintained a physical and emotional distance that neither seemed able to pierce, and neither seemed willing to shed. And perhaps neither was to blame—they simply weren't compatible on any level of intensity. In the few days that had passed since she'd last seen him, she had changed too much, had learned things about herself that would alarm and perhaps disgust someone as placid and passionless as Rob Trainer. Still, she owed him some sort of explanation.

"Is something wrong?" he asked. "You look...worried."

The understatement of the year. "Rob, we need to talk."

"Is that Stacey and Neil's wedding?" he blurted, distracted by the Sunday paper that had fallen open on the counter where she'd tossed it. *Local Cop Saves the Wedding Day.* Sure enough, a photo series obviously taken from video stills showed Officer Ken Medlock holding a folding chair over the balcony, the madman being struck down—especially effective since his knife had been knocked from his hand and hung in midair—and another of Ken handcuffing the man. Georgia sighed. Was she destined to be reminded of the man at every turn?

"Yes," she said. "It was a bit of a commotion, but everyone was fine. Um, your friend Ken Medlock saved the day."

His pleasant face folded. "My friend?"

"Officer Ken Medlock. You know, the cop from the gym. I've, um, run into him a few times over the past few days."

Rob squinted at her and his Adam's apple bobbed.

"Your face is all red. Does this have something to do with the cop?"

She tried to will away the flush and clasped her hands together to keep from fidgeting. "Well—"

"Georgia."

She glanced up at his sharp tone, stunned that his expression was a cross between fury and panic.

"I don't appreciate anyone poking around in my past," he said quietly.

Her mouth opened and she shook her head. "But I wasn't—"

"I don't know anyone by the name of Ken Medlock, and I certainly don't know any city cops."

"But he said—"

"I made a mistake," Rob said, smacking his hand on the counter, causing her to jump. "And I served my time."

Georgia backed up a step, stunned by his mood change and the turn of the conversation. He had a record? "Why didn't you tell me?" she asked with as much calm as she could muster.

"Because my past is none of your business," he bit out. "It was one lousy charge of embezzlement— a few thousand dollars to pay off some debts. What is it to you?"

She felt like a fool. Rob had no intention of getting close to her, and deep down, she'd known it from the beginning. She'd perpetuated the relationship because it was safe, because it didn't require her to extend herself or be vulnerable in return. Rob was the kind of man she thought would provide the most stable home for a family, someone to…offset her urges?

"You're right," she murmured. "It's none of my business. I'm leaving."

"Georgia, wait," he said, his expression contrite. "I'm sorry to go off on you like that." He sighed. "It's just not working between us, you know?"

She nodded. "I know."

"But you're such a nice person."

"Thanks, Rob. I feel the same way about you."

"I'd appreciate it if you didn't say anything to anyone about that mess back in Ohio." He smiled sheepishly, and she wondered what she had ever seen in the man.

"I won't." She laid the door key on the counter, then walked out, nearly tripping over the box that held her phone system. All she wanted to do was go home, lie on her hard couch, and have a good, long cry.

TONI SAT in the hard chair that matched the hard couch. "I don't believe it. I just don't believe it."

Georgia lay with her hand over her forehead. "Believe it."

"And you have no idea who this guy is?"

"None whatsoever."

"Wow. How romantic."

She sighed. "I was thinking it was more like something in *Penthouse* Forum."

"Your life is so exciting. Oh! This is just like my situation with Dr. Baxter—he doesn't know who I am, either, but there's this connection, you know?"

"Toni, I don't think it's the same thing at all."

"Well, do you want to find out who this guy is?"

She turned her head. "Of course I do. He could be

some psycho with caller ID who knows my name and number."

"Or some gorgeous single hunk."

"Toni, you're nuts. He's probably married and has kids." Like her father.

"Why don't you call the number now?"

Georgia frowned. "Now?"

"Maybe the guy works during the day and he'll have his machine on, or someone else will answer."

She chewed on the inside of her cheek. "I don't think I want to call the number again."

"I'll do it from my cell phone," Toni offered, reaching for her purse.

Georgia recited the number and sat up as Toni punched it in. "It's ringing," she said excitedly, then handed the phone to Georgia.

She swallowed past the lump in her throat, praying a wife or child wouldn't answer. But after the fourth ring, a voice recorder kicked on with a generic mechanical message. She hung up with a sigh. "Maybe I should just chalk it up to a bad experience. After all, the guy hasn't called me back."

"But that doesn't mean he won't," Toni said. "He could be outside right now, going through your trash, looking for the hair from your brush."

"Oh, now that makes me feel good."

Toni snapped her fingers. "I've got it! A friend of mine told me the police have those reverse phone indexes—they can look up names by the number."

"And what good does that do me?"

All you have to do is ask that big strapping Officer Medlock to do you a favor. Besides—" she wagged her eyebrows "—now that Rob is out of the picture—"

"Don't even say it," Georgia said, holding up her hand. She had enough problems on her plate without getting involved with Ken Medlock. She blinked back hot tears. How utterly stupid she'd been—anyone could have walked in on them, anyone could have seen them coming out of that room. Besides, she'd traded twenty minutes of passion for a lifetime of regret—regret because she knew if given the opportunity, she'd probably do it again. And again. And again.

"You have to admit, he's a hottie," Toni pressed. "When he came charging into the back of the church wearing that uniform, I swear half the women in the church swooned. Rebecca Dooley had her eye on him at the reception, but he disappeared right after the toast."

"Really?" Georgia pressed her palms into her eyes, but snatches of his lovemaking remained so vivid in her mind, her womb clenched and her thighs tingled. God help her, even with everything else going on, she couldn't stop thinking about the man—a clue as to how dangerous he was to her mental well-being.

"He's *interested,* Georgia. You're crazy if you don't go out with him."

"He's a player, Toni. The man told me himself he's not interested in settling down."

"So? You don't have to marry him. Just have a little fun."

She smiled wryly to herself. Just have a little fun? Ken Medlock would be too easy to fall for, and too hard to forget. She had already set into motion events that might haunt her for years. She'd learned her lesson about indulging her darker urges, no matter how tempting.

Toni sighed. "You should go see him, you know. You wouldn't have to give him all the details, just make up something. He owes you one after almost getting you fired and all."

Actually, after their encounter in the closet, they were even, she conceded silently. She'd felt so ashamed for her behavior that she'd even lashed out at him for calling her "ma'am."

I'm sorry. I was only being respectful.

Considering what she had just allowed to transpire, his respectfulness had grated at the time.

Georgia closed her eyes and sighed. The man had only been trying to make the best out of a horribly awkward situation. And Toni was right—the quickest way to find the identity of the guy on the other end of the phone line and to have peace of mind was to go to Ken. She wouldn't have to give him all the details, and she believed he would be discreet. Besides, as far as he knew, she was still dating Rob, so he wouldn't pressure her to see him, not after their discussion in the closet. Indeed, asking for his help would give them a chance to ease the awkwardness of their last parting. And once Ken told her the name of the man who belonged to that phone number, she would be able to put the chaos of the past week to rest.

CHAPTER TWENTY-TWO

KEN JUMPED UP when the hot coffee hit his lap. "Dammit!" He stamped around, swiping at the wetness with a paper towel, then glared at his partner Klone. "What are you looking at?"

From his adjacent desk, Klone lifted an eyebrow. "I'm wondering when someone kidnapped my sweet-tempered partner and left a wounded bear in his place."

He frowned as he dropped back into his seat. "Just having a bad day, that's all."

Klone gestured to the pile of cards and letters that had accumulated throughout the day. "Yeah, it's rough being a freaking hero, ain't it?"

Ken scoffed in the direction of the mail. "My home phone has been ringing off the damn hook." Everyone who had his number had called—his mother, his sisters, his brother, his neighbors, his buddies—everyone except Georgia. And he'd only flipped through the silly cards today on the slim chance that Georgia had sent him a note of some kind.

Why she would, he had no idea, but a man could hope. Since Saturday, he had thought of little but Georgia, wondering if Trainer had made it home, and if she'd discovered she hadn't been talking to her boyfriend when she'd...

Ken rubbed his fists over his scratchy eyes. He hadn't slept much at all the past two nights, and the strong coffee meant to clear his head was making him irritable.

Then he frowned. Okay, his conscience was making him irritable. One foolish split-second decision to selfishly seize the moment had snowballed into an emotional quagmire. Worse, he'd passed up several chances to stop the madness and/or confess the truth. The fact that he'd used a nice, innocent woman led to a troubling state of mind—he was disappointed in himself. Before now he'd always thought of himself as a person of decent character, but one of his father's favorite sayings kept circling in his mind: *It's easy to be a good person if your character is never tested.*

Boy oh boy, he'd failed miserably. He sighed. The answer was painful, but simple: He had to tell Georgia the truth, no matter the consequences.

"Woman trouble?" Klone asked, clamping him on the shoulder.

He looked up. "What the devil makes you think that?"

"Takes a lot to get you discombobulated."

Ken scowled. "Well, it's not a woman." It was what he'd done to her.

Klone shook his head. "You're a bad liar, son."

No, he was a great liar—that was the problem.

"It's that little slip of a nurse who was in here the other day, ain't it?"

"No."

"The one you rounded up all the guys for the blood bank to impress."

"No."

"Well, at least she's an upstanding woman. Might make an honest man out of you."

Ken smacked his hand on the desk. "Dammit, Klone, I'm telling you it's not—" He stopped when he spotted none other than Georgia Adams being led toward his office. A goofy grin hung itself on his face. He stood so abruptly his chair went flying backward. And his stupid heart rolled over like a trained pet.

"Well, lookie there," Klone drawled. "If it ain't the woman who don't have you tied up in knots."

Ken watched her. Her heavy-lidded smoky gaze, the way she moved, the whole of her made his breath catch in his throat. In that moment, he had a revelation. From now on, he would refer to his life in two phases: before he met Georgia Adams, and after.

"Wonder what she wants," Klone muttered.

He didn't care, as long as she was here. One thing he knew for certain—if Rob Trainer wanted Georgia, the man was in for the fight of his life. Unable to stop himself, he met her halfway, grinning like a dolt. "Hi."

"Hi." She smiled and blushed, a great sign that bolstered his mood higher. His imagination took flight. She had broken off with Rob. She was hoping they could get together for a movie or something. She wasn't busy for the next forty years or so. She wouldn't mind having a gimpy dog underfoot.

"I brought the pictures of Crash," she said, handing him an envelope.

"Oh. Thanks."

"And I need a favor," she said, her blue eyes wide and earnest.

He focused on not touching her, not here in front of everyone. "Anything," he said, and meant it. "Come on back to my desk." He pointed the way, then walked behind her a half step, throwing Klone a warning glare as Georgia sat down. The man pursed his mouth and turned back to his own paperwork.

Ken tried not to be distracted by her slim thighs as she crossed her legs. The simple, close-fitting khaki shorts hugged her figure, bringing back gut-clutching memories of her legs around his waist. He cleared his throat. "What can I help you with, Georgia?"

She removed a slip of paper from her purse and extended it to him. "Can you tell me the name of the person who has this local number?"

His heart stopped at the sight of his own phone number written in dainty little numbers, so innocent. Unable to take the slip of paper, he simply stared at it, willing it to go away. His brain clogged, and his vision blurred. What had seemed like the right decision a few moments ago now faded in the wake of losing the chance to win her over.

"Why do you need it?" he heard himself ask in an amazingly calm voice.

Her coloring rose and she squirmed. "Well, I'd rather not go into too much detail. The number has been called from my phone, and I'm just curious as to who is on the other end, that's all." But her smile didn't reach her eyes.

Ken didn't know what to do, so he stalled. "Someone has been using your phone without your permission?"

"N-no."

"So you made the calls."

"Yes, but I dialed the wrong number—this number."

Picking up on her discomfort, he decided that if he pushed her, she might change her mind about wanting the name. "If it was the wrong number, why do you need the name?"

"B-because," she said softly, "I, um, divulged information to this man which was rather personal."

"Information that was meant for someone else?" he pressed.

"Um, yes."

"What purpose would be served by finding this person?"

She averted her eyes and rolled her shoulders. "I'm not sure—"

"Hey, Ken," Klone called from his desk a few feet away, a phone in the crook of his shoulder. "There's a lady up front who wants to talk to you about a lost dog."

A sliver of disappointment cut into him. That mutt was starting to grow on him, and he was halfway hoping no one claimed him. At the same time, he knew someone was probably worried to death about the poor pooch. And he recognized the opportunity to collect his jumbled thoughts. He gave Georgia an apologetic glance. "Do you mind?"

"No, go ahead," she said, standing. "I think I've changed my mind anyway. It's silly, really. I'm sure the man dismissed the incident."

No, he didn't dismiss it, he wanted to say. *He loved it. He might even love you.* Ken straightened, shocked by the direction of his guilty thoughts. "I'm due a break. What would you say to grabbing a bite to eat? I'd like to talk to you, in private." She looked as if she were going to say no, so he added, "Please?"

At last she smiled and nodded. "Okay, but just for a little while."

He grinned. "Great. Sit tight and I'll be right back to get you, okay?"

She nodded and sank back into the chair, looking small and gorgeous and…perfect. He couldn't tell her now, not when that tentative look was starting to leave her eyes. *She'll never know I was the man she was talking to,* he told himself. *And it's better for both of us.*

"I'll hurry," he said, as eager to return as a boomerang.

GEORGIA FELT CONSPICUOUS sitting in Ken's big chair. She glanced around his work environment, thinking it wasn't so different from her own—lots of shared space, a smidgen of private space, loads of camaraderie, a flurry of constant activity. She liked it.

And she liked Ken. A lot. Maybe she had misjudged him. Maybe he wasn't the ladies' man he was reputed to be. Maybe that closet episode was as remarkable for him as it had been for her. Maybe the odd coincidences of their paths crossing meant something special was supposed to happen between them.

She sighed, remembering the reason she'd come to the station in the first place. Ken was right. What would she do with the information if she did get the guy's name? Call him and demand that he not tell anyone that she preferred sleeping in the nude? Chances were the man had an interest in remaining anonymous, and she would probably never know his identity. She conceded, however, that months might pass before she stopped glancing at men on the bus and wondering if *he* were the one.

Whoever the guy was, he was probably having a belly laugh over the desperate woman who had to make the first move with her boyfriend, and who was so distracted she couldn't even tell that the person on the other end wasn't him. She burned with humiliation when she thought of the things she'd told him—intimate things she thought she was sharing with a man who cared about her. If the guy had caller ID, he knew her name. Had he told all of his buddies? Was her name being distributed on the Internet? *For a good time, Georgia Adams will call* you.

"Howdy," said a lumpy-looking middle-aged man who came over to pick up a form from Ken's cluttered desk. "I'm Klone."

"I'm Georgia Adams," she murmured. "You're Ken's partner, aren't you?"

"That I am."

From the twinkle in the man's eyes, she knew he was fond of Ken. "He's spoken of you," she said.

He smiled again. "And I know all about you, too."

She blinked. "Ken has mentioned me?"

"Oh, sure, Ken has mentioned you to just about anyone who'll listen." He leaned forward and dipped his chin. "He thinks you're just about the hottest number in Birmingham."

Guilty heat flooded her face.

A young man walked up, his hands full. "Another stack of cards for Ken," he said, adding to the pile of envelopes overflowing the small desk. He held up a postcard. "As if the man didn't have enough women chasing him, he has to go and make the front page of the paper. Listen to this: 'You can handcuff me to your bed any time. Call me, Barbie.'" He rolled his eyes.

The officers in the vicinity laughed, and Georgia felt uneasy. The man obviously had his pick of women to coax into a closet. Why would he be interested in her?

Klone picked up the slip of paper she'd left lying on Ken's desk and to her surprise, winked broadly as he handed it back to her. "Ken really should get business cards for as often as he's probably passed out this number."

Georgia's mind flooded with confusion. She tried to smile. "Do you...recognize this phone number?"

Klone glanced at the paper again. "Yep— 555-6252—I've sure as hell dialed it enough. It's Ken's home number."

The floor fell out from under her feet, leaving her in a free fall. A week's worth of seemingly disjointed events fell into place with mocking ease, like a pre-schooler's puzzle. Running into him at the hospital, then seemingly at every turn. At the hospital, at the mall, at the blood bank, at the church. He'd looked her up and hunted her down. He'd played her for a fool, an *easy* fool. Scoring in the supply closet. She covered her mouth with her hand to keep from crying out.

"Is something wrong?" the man asked.

Oh, sure, Ken has mentioned you to just about any- one who'll listen. He thinks you're just about the hot- test number in Birmingham.

Georgia lunged to her feet, stumbling backward before she gained her footing. Bile rose in her mouth. "I...have to go," she whispered, then ran blindly toward the exit.

KEN WAS WHISTLING when he walked back to his desk. The woman's lost dog wasn't Crash, and Georgia was waiting for hi—

He frowned at the empty chair, then panned the adjacent area looking for her. "Klone," he called, threading his way through people to their desk area. "Where's Georgia?"

The older man shrugged. "Took off, like someone set her on fire."

"Just like that?" He narrowed his eyes. "Did you say something to her?"

"Maybe a little good-hearted teasing, but nothing to send her off like that. I think she's a little touched in the head."

"You're the only one here touched in the head. Think, man. You had to have said something that upset her."

The man shook his head. "Nope. Cal over there delivered some more mail from your fan club and was cutting up about what a lady killer you are. Then I cracked a joke about you making up business cards so you wouldn't have to write down your phone number so often."

Dread pooled at the top of his head and oozed downward. "My phone number?"

"Yeah, she had it written on a piece of paper. Guess you wore her down for a date?"

He leaned forward and gripped the sides of his desk. "You told her that was *my* phone number written on that piece of paper?"

"Well, wasn't it?"

Ken closed his eyes and swallowed.

"What the hell is going on?" Klone asked.

He straightened. "I'm going on break."

"For how long?"

"I don't know."

Ken jogged to the front of the building and burst through the double doors. A hundred feet away, a city bus had stopped for passengers. He caught the flash of a pink blouse and took off sprinting. But the bus lumbered into motion and pulled away just as he ran up next to it. He searched the windows for her face and when he saw her, his stride broke. Tears streaked her face and she looked at him with such loathing, he was rooted to the spot. He opened his mouth, but knew it was too late for words.

He watched the bus carry her away from him and felt like the piece of trash that lay on the sidewalk at his feet.

CHAPTER TWENTY-THREE

"Maybe I should move to Denver," Georgia said, wiping her nose. "I'm sure my brother-in-law would help me find a job." She tossed the tissue into the garbage can next to the kitchen sink, and grabbed a fresh one for a hearty blow.

For the first time since Georgia had known her, Toni was speechless, and had been since she'd divulged the shocking truth. Her friend could only shake her head, which Georgia feared would come off from all the wagging.

"Jesus, Toni, say something."

"I'll help you load the moving van."

Georgia's face crumpled as a new wave of stinging tears assailed her. Her shoulders shook from abject shame and humiliation and something worse—disappointment. Disappointment that she had started to think that Ken Medlock was a decent guy, maybe even someone she could love. Maybe even someone who could love her back.

Her heart shivered, overcome with sadness.

Toni hugged her, and allowed her to cry for several long moments, then led her to a kitchen chair. "You sit while I fix us something cold to drink. Hmm. Did you know your refrigerator light is burned out?"

Georgia nodded, then sat down heavily. At least the super had honored his word and fixed her programmable thermostat while she was at work this morning. Wouldn't it be nice if she could simply reprogram her heart? Although, with her technical ineptness, she'd probably wind up losing a kidney.

She held her head in her hands, picturing Ken running next to the bus, looking for her. What had driven him to come after her—guilt over his behavior? Fear that she might report him to a superior? Certainly not concern for how she felt being manipulated like a hunk of warm wax.

The things she'd said to him... *Oh, God.*

The phone rang, sending Georgia's heart into her throat. She and Toni exchanged looks, but she allowed it to ring two, three, four times and roll over to the machine. Her own voice invited the caller to leave a brief message, then a beep sounded.

"Georgia, this is Ken." His loud, deep voice penetrated the air, the microphone broadcasting in stereo sound.

Her sob turned into a hiccup. How dare he call her?

"If you're there, please pick up."

She sat rooted to her chair, her eyes narrowed at the machine.

He sighed. "Look, I don't blame you for never wanting to talk to me again. I can imagine what you must think of me. I just wanted to say that...I'm sorry. I'm so sorry, Georgia. It started out as innocent fun, and it got out of hand. Once I got to know you, I wanted to tell you. I *tried* to tell you at the reception before we...well, you know."

Toni shot her a raised-eyebrow look. Georgia closed her eyes.

"I was even trying to think of a way to tell you today—that's why I wanted us to be alone." He grunted. "Although I can't honestly say I would have, because things seemed to be going well between us, and I was hoping…"

Georgia opened one eye. He was hoping?

"I was hoping…"

She opened the other eye. He was hoping?

"I was hoping you wouldn't hate me."

She frowned. Too late.

"I'm sorry I deceived you, but I swear, I meant everything I said when we were on the phone."

Toni pursed her mouth.

After a pause, he said. "Well, I won't bother you again. I just couldn't let things end like this. I'm sorry, Georgia."

The call disconnected and the beep sounded again. She wiped her eyes. Her face and body ached with pent-up emotion.

Toni set two glasses of pink lemonade on the table and sat down in an adjacent chair. "Well," she said, lifting hers for a drink.

Georgia sniffed. "Well, what?"

"Well, he sounded apologetic."

She scoffed. "He's sorry, all right—sorry he got caught."

Toni sipped, then asked, "What was all that about the you-know at the reception?"

She stared into her glass, but knew her face was just about as pink as her drink.

"Georgia?"

She sighed. "We made out in a storage closet."

"Ah. So that's where he disappeared to. I thought you were leaving to call Rob."

"I was," she said miserably. "But he followed me, then we kissed, then we heard someone coming, so we hid in a closet, then one thing led to another." She covered her mouth and breathed through her fingers. "And the whole time, he knew."

Toni put her hand over Georgia's on the table. "Okay, let's break this down. You thought you were calling Rob and dialed Ken's number by mistake."

"Right."

"Then the next day, you met Ken when he came into the E.R. with a dog."

"Right."

"Well, he couldn't have very well planned to hit a dog just to bring him in."

She shook her head. "No, Ken wouldn't do something like that. It was coincidental, I'm sure."

"But when he found out your name, he figured out who you were?"

Georgia bit on her lower lip, trying to remember their initial introduction. "He asked me if he knew me from somewhere, then said he knew a guy named Rob who dated a woman named Georgia, and I asked him if he was talking about Rob Trainer."

"And he said yes?"

She nodded, then her eyes went wide. "I must have called him Rob on the phone. He made up the part about knowing a Rob just to see if I was the person who had called him!"

Toni nodded. "Sounds reasonable."

Georgia smacked herself on the forehead. "The note."

"What note?"

"When I was leaving the hospital that day, Melanie gave me a note and told me that Rob had been called out of town."

"And Ken overheard this conversation?"

She nodded.

"So he knew Rob was out of the picture for a few days."

"But he couldn't have known that Rob wouldn't call, or that my message recorder was fouled up."

Toni shrugged. "I guess he figured he'd take his chances." She grinned. "You must be good."

Georgia blushed. *They* had been good.

"I just think it's amazing that you were torn over breaking up with Rob because you felt like you guys were making headway, when the guy you were really making headway with was the same guy you were lusting and feeling guilty about."

She squinted. "I think I followed that."

"You get the gist."

Georgia sipped her lemonade. "Mmm. What did you put in here?"

"Rum," Toni said, pointing to the bottle on the counter. "Take a big drink. What was Ken referring to when he said he meant everything he said when you all were on the phone?"

She froze.

"What?"

"Well, there was one night—no, never mind."

"What, Georgia?"

"There was one night when I thought Rob was going to tell me that he loved me, and I got all panicky."

"You mean *Ken* was going to tell you."

"Well, at the time I thought it was Rob."

"So why did you get all panicky?"

She swallowed a mouthful of spiked lemonade. "Because…I suppose I knew that I didn't love Rob."

"Because?"

"Because…" She glanced at her friend and sighed. "Because I was falling for Ken."

Toni squeezed her hand. "Then don't you see? This is perfect! He likes you, and you like him."

She shook her head and groaned. "But how could I? I barely know the man."

"So? You knew Rob for ten months and that didn't help. You didn't even know he had a criminal record, for heaven's sake."

But Ken probably did, which could explain why he'd kept asking her about her relationship with Rob. She frowned. There was something honorable buried in the fact that he could have told her, but hadn't, although she couldn't sort it all out at the moment.

"But the man played me for a fool. He knows things about me. Private things."

"And you know private things about him."

True, she conceded. And some deep dark part of her was slightly relieved that at least a third man hadn't been involved in her web of lust. At least she'd had phone sex with a man that she—what?

Cared about? Maybe.

But trusted? Never.

CHAPTER TWENTY-FOUR

KEN STOPPED in front of the E.R. doors to County and rubbed his scratchy eyes. He hadn't gotten a wink of sleep last night, worrying about Georgia, stewing in the misery of what he'd done to her.

Interspersed among the despair, of course, were more positive images. Of her at the mall, flustered after their encounter, laden with shopping bags. Of her taking his blood, then goading him into rallying his buddies for a good cause. Of their kiss in the park, when she'd tasted like sweet relish and fresh air. Of her running through the church parking lot in that filmy blue dress. Of her sitting on the floor of his living room, playing with Crash. Of their frenzied love-making in the dark closet. Of the light of possibilities in her amazing blue eyes when she'd come to the station yesterday seeking his help, never imagining he was the guilty party. Some superhero.

Last night had crawled by, and since Franks had fixed the air conditioning unit, he couldn't blame the temperature. But he'd discovered that the fires of regret could be just as hot as the Southern sun.

Ken took a deep breath for courage. He simply had to see her again, and although he knew her address, he didn't feel comfortable going to her apartment. The woman was already spooked. And the fact that Robert Trainer hadn't contacted him probably meant she hadn't told her boyfriend the truth, which made him feel even worse.

The doors opened automatically, and he walked inside, panning the area for a glimpse of Georgia. His heart pounded in his ears.

"May I help you, Officer?" a woman at the admissions desk asked.

"Nurse Georgia Adams—is she working today?"

The woman pointed behind him.

Ken turned to see Georgia staring at him, hugging herself. At the sight of her sad, heavy eyes, he practically tore the hat he was holding in two. After a hard swallow, he walked toward her and stopped. "Georgia—"

"Why are you here?"

Mindful of the ears all around them, he grasped at the only straw at his disposal. "To have you check my blood pressure." He took the fact that she didn't throw something at him as a good sign and added, "Just as you ordered."

"Anyone can take it," she murmured.

"Please."

She wet her lips, then inhaled and said, "Wendy, I'll be in exam room three."

Her voice was tight, and her body language closed as he followed her. Ken remembered the time he and Klone had entered an apartment building where an armed man had holed up after a bank robbery. What could it mean that he was more afraid now than he'd been then? And that the image of Georgia's tear-streaked face in the bus window had wounded him more than the lead he'd taken in the shoulder when they had rushed the criminal?

"Have a seat," she said, sweeping her arm toward a sterile chair. He recognized the room as the same one in which she'd bandaged Crash. Ken closed the door behind them, then lowered himself onto the small chair.

"Georgia—"

"Your arm, please," she said, holding out a blood pressure cuff.

He lifted his arm so she could fasten it tightly. She refused to look at him as she squeezed the plastic bulb that forced air into the cuff around his arm. When the pressure bordered on pain, she released the air, watching the gauge.

"It's still a little on the high side, but within normal range for a man of your size." She peeled off the device with a rip of Velcro.

"Georgia." He curled his fingers around her wrist loosely.

She looked at him, her eyes moist, then jerked away. "Get out."

He lifted his hands, then stood slowly. "I just wanted to tell you that I'm sorry."

"So you said in your phone message."

"I wanted to tell you in person."

"I thought my lack of response would make it clear that I didn't want to talk to you and certainly didn't want to see you. But," she said, her eyes pooling, her voice straining, "maybe you're the kind of guy who has to be hit with a ton of bricks to get the message."

Her words cut him like the blade of the madman who had rushed the church. She was right. He was no better than that obsessed jerk who wouldn't take no for an answer. That fool was probably also convinced that he was in love.

Ken stopped, mostly because his heartbeat had paused. It was a fair response from his body considering the revelation that had arrested his brain: He loved her.

"Don't make me call security," she whispered, then backed up against the exam table behind her. A solitary tear traveled down her cheek.

He'd never felt more helpless in all of his life. He was the biggest fool in Birmingham, maybe in the entire southeastern United States. A woman like Georgia Adams came along once in a lifetime—maybe. How ironic that he'd spent most of his adult life trying to figure out how to stay out of a relationship, and just when he was thinking about the possibility of maybe sort of trying to picture himself with one woman, she'd slipped through his fingers. No, he'd pushed her away with his games of deceit and manipulation. He didn't blame her for hating him.

He strode out of the room as fast as his long legs would take him. Away from Georgia, so he couldn't hurt her anymore. One thing he knew for certain: She was the hardest lesson he'd ever learned.

Ken had jammed his hat on his head and was nearly out the door when he heard a man calling, "Officer Medlock!"

He turned and conjured up a pleasant expression. "Hello, Dr. Story. Nice to see you again."

The little man looked like an opossum, but he had an excellent reputation in the city. "I just wanted to let you know that after our conversation Saturday morning, I decided to remove the reprimand from Nurse Adams's file."

"Thank you," he said, truly relieved at the one bit of good news.

"From your explanation, I realize she did her best to circumvent the situation."

But as usual, Ken thought, he had pushed until he'd gotten his way, and in the process, had jeopardized the woman's job. What a selfish bastard he'd become. Never opening himself to other people, never considering how his actions might affect others, never putting his own emotions on the line.

"My wife runs the city blood bank," Dr. Story said. "I heard about you rallying your fellow officers to build the reserves. We're indebted to you, Officer Medlock. If there's ever anything I can do for you, just ask."

Ken started to shake his head, then recalled his emotions after the church incident. He'd acknowledged that he could almost identify with the lunatic because if he were about to lose Georgia, he wouldn't wield a weapon, but *he'd be mighty tempted to make a fool of himself somehow.*

Georgia said she wanted an honest man. Well, he'd blown it up to this point, but he could at least be honest about how he felt about her.

Turning a smile toward the good doctor, he said, "As a matter of fact, Doc, there *is* something you can do for me."

GEORGIA LEANED on the exam table, trying to collect herself.

"Hey, are you okay?"

She looked up to see that Toni had poked her head into the room. Georgia sighed and nodded. "What are you doing down here?"

"I had a break and I thought maybe you could use one, too."

"Could I ever." Georgia averted her gaze from her friend's quizzical look as they headed toward the break room.

"Well, I thought you'd be glad to know that I just told Dr. Baxter that my name isn't Terri."

She managed a smile. "Good for you. What did he say?"

Toni grinned. "He said the only way he could remember the name Toni was to think of Italian food—you know, like rigatoni. Oh, and would I like to have dinner with him?"

Despite her own recent romantic disasters, Georgia was happy for her friend. "I knew you'd get your man."

Toni's smile dimmed. "Okay, Georgia, 'fess up. What's wrong?"

Georgia glanced around, then said, "Ken stopped by."

"No kidding? What did he say?"

She grunted. "Same thing—that he was sorry."

"Maybe he is."

"Well, that's not good enough."

"Georgia, what do you want him to say?"

She frowned. "Nothing. I want him to stay away from me."

"Are you sure?"

She fed coins into a soda machine. "After what he did?"

"I'm not taking up for the guy, but anyone can make a mistake."

"Toni, a mistake is adding two numbers wrong. The man has a fundamental character flaw—he's a self-centered jerk who doesn't care about other people." She blinked back a wall of sudden tears. "He certainly doesn't care about me."

A voice she recognized as Dr. Story's came over the intercom. "Please stand by for an important message."

She winced. She'd forgotten to stop by for her personal copy of her official reprimand. What a fun errand *that* would be.

"Georgia, this is Ken."

She missed her mouth and spilled her soda down the front of her scrubs.

Toni stared at her wide-eyed. "He's on the intercom."

"I love you," he said, his voice strong and resonating. "I don't expect this to change your mind, I just wanted you to know."

Georgia dropped the can and allowed Toni to scramble for it while she processed Ken's revelation. She heard muted applause in the halls, and several people walked by the vending room, giving her the thumbs-up.

"What are you going to do?" Toni screeched, jumping up and down.

She shook her head. "He doesn't mean it."

"Are you crazy? The man told you he loved you over the intercom, for heaven's sake!"

"He's just trying to ease his conscience. Men like Ken Medlock will say anything when they're backed into a corner." She should know—she'd seen her father's sugary words and elaborate gifts melt her mother's resolve. Well, she'd rather be alone the rest of her life than submit to a man on whom love would be wasted.

"You're simply going to ignore him?"

Georgia fed more coins into the vending machine, albeit with shakier fingers. "That's right. I'm simply going to ignore him."

At least she would try.

CHAPTER TWENTY-FIVE

GEORGIA STARED at the report in her hand, her official reprimand for "treating a canine in a human health facility." Her own signature looked timid next to Dr. Story's flourishing script.

"Destroy them," Dr. Story had said, handing her both the original that had been bound for her file and a copy. "Officer Medlock came by Saturday morning to explain the situation, and I realize I acted in haste."

She pursed her mouth. Ken's timing surprised her—before their closet encounter, and before she found out about his little "impersonation." Walking to the kitchen trash can, she tore the papers into several pieces before pitching them. She really didn't want to dwell on it too much, though, else she might start thinking Ken Medlock was a good guy after all.

The phone rang, startling her. She was tempted to let it roll over, but decided she wasn't going to allow the possibility of the caller being Ken to influence her phone habits. The sooner her life got back to normal, the boring off she'd be. She frowned. The *better* off she'd be. *Better.*

Ignoring her Freudian slip, she picked up the handset. "Hello?"

She held her breath, and for a split second, God help her, she wanted it to be him.

"Hello, dear, it's Mother."

Shaking her head, she smiled at Arletta Adams's uncanny sense of timing. And absolutely no respect for the time difference from Denver to Birmingham. Not that it mattered, since Georgia couldn't sleep. "Hi, Mom." She dropped onto the couch, no doubt bruising her backside. She wondered vaguely where Ken had gotten his big comfy couches.

"I called to see if you and Bob had fun at the wedding."

She sighed. "Actually, Mom, Bob didn't make it."

"Oh, that's too bad. Why not?"

"It doesn't matter, really. We broke up."

"Oh, honey, I'm sorry. What happened?"

"I realized…that I didn't care for him as much as I thought." She reached for the envelope of photos she'd had developed, and pulled out one she'd taken at the park. Crash was the main focus, his head resting on the side of the wagon, but the lens had captured Ken in the top corner, leaning forward, his cheeks pushed up in a grand smile, his hair slightly ruffled in the wind. The darn viewfinder on the camera was obviously skewed.

"Well, as pretty as you are, you're bound to meet a wonderful man soon. Did you check out the groomsmen?"

She laughed. "No."

Her mother sighed, a musical little sound to the tune of "you missed another chance." "Weddings are a good place to meet eligible men, Georgia."

That smile. She loved that smile. Georgia rubbed her forefinger over his face. Such a nice face. "Now that you mention it, Mom, I did meet someone at the wedding."

By the silence, she knew she had her mother's attention. "Who?"

"His name is Ken," she said before she could stop the words. "Ken Medlock. It's funny, because he reminds me a little of Daddy." Georgia remained stock-still, wondering what her mother's reaction would be.

"That's wonderful, dear."

"Is it, Mom? Is it really?"

Her mother sighed, an earnest one, this time, and Georgia sensed a change in her. "Georgia, your father wasn't perfect, but I loved him. Do I wish things had been different? Of course I do. I wish *I* had been different."

She didn't want to hear her mother accepting blame for her father's shenanigans. "Mom—"

"I hated sex, Georgia."

She swallowed her words, and her eyes bugged. "Oh."

"It was inevitable that your father stray. The few times he did, I didn't like it, but I didn't blame him. And he never stopped loving me."

She clasped a hand to her forehead, stunned at her mother's revelation. "All these years, I thought that he was hurting you."

"Quite the opposite, dear. Your father and I loved each other deeply. He always felt so guilty about his affairs that he brought me gifts. I never doubted his commitment to our family."

In thirty seconds, her entire outlook on sex and relationships had been turned on end. "I don't know what to say."

"Then tell me about this Ken Medlock, dear."

Georgia's mind raced with images of Ken, so many of them jammed into only a few days, and all of them…profound.

"Georgia, what does the man do?"

She pressed the picture of Ken to her heart, and closed her eyes. "He makes me happy, Mom. Can I call you back?"

"Of course, dear."

She hung up and brought her fist to her mouth. Her father had indulged in extra-marital affairs because her mother hated sex. Not because one woman wasn't enough for him. Not because he enjoyed seeing how much he could get away with. Not because he didn't love his family. Her mother had violated her marriage vows first, by not honoring the physical needs of her husband. Georgia had sorely misjudged her father. She sent up a prayer of apology and a smile to the man she'd always adored, but whose situation she had never fully appreciated.

A warm, fuzzy feeling flooded over her, along with a revelation: Perhaps her father had orchestrated the chance meeting with Ken. The sequence of events seemed almost too fantastic for mere mortal coincidence. She smiled. He was still looking out for her. Fannie had Mother, and she had Dad.

So she hadn't inherited dark, lusty, philandering tendencies. Her sex drive had been kicked into overdrive by a man whom she'd been destined to meet. A man who stirred her soul before she even knew him. A man to whom she was drawn both physically and metaphysically.

Georgia counted to ten to calm her pounding heart. She loved Ken. It was impossible, but true. They'd connected so quickly and so intensely that she'd been frightened. Since it seemed too good to be true, she'd been poised for the other shoe to drop. And it had, when she'd found out it was him she'd been talking to on the phone, him she'd been sharing her thoughts and fantasies with. But on some subconscious level, hadn't she wished it were Ken all along?

She was being handed a gift on one of those platters she wanted. She would not turn from love and run.

She looked at the phone and laughed aloud when she realized his number was still programmed in. She pushed the button, then his phone rang once, twice as her heart nearly jumped out of her chest. Was he home? It was awfully late. Was he asleep? Would he be glad to hear from her?

"Hello," he said, and his voice filled her chest with warmth.

"Ken, it's Georgia."

"Hi," he said, sounding glad, but tentative. "It's great to hear your voice. I didn't think—"

"I love you, too."

Strangling sounds came across the line.

"Are you choking?" she asked. "Because I know the Heimlich maneuver."

He laughed. "So you say."

"I was wondering if you know where I live."

"Yes, ma'am, I do."

She smiled wryly. Of course he did. "Well, in that case, I was wondering if you would like to come over."

She heard a loud popping noise, as if the phone had been dropped. "Ken?"

From the rhythmic knocking sound, she realized the handset was dangling and swinging back and forth against something. She laughed into the phone as she heard his door slam.

Georgia hugged herself, hoping that Ken had the cruiser and would turn on the blue lights. She hated to wait.

EPILOGUE

"THE NEXT TIME we get married," Ken whispered against the back of her neck, "pick a wedding gown that has fewer buttons."

"All the better to torture you, my dear," she murmured with a smile, rolling her shoulders in response to the delicious thrill of his tongue. "Ken, I was thinking."

"Hmm?"

She turned in his arms and tugged at the lapels of his black tuxedo jacket. "Since we have the rest of our lives to make love while I'm *not* wearing my wedding gown, why don't we—"

He grabbed her around the waist, grinning. "I like the way you think, Mrs. Medlock."

He carried her to the bed in the luxurious honeymoon suite they'd reserved and set her on the edge. She started to slip off her shoes, but he stopped her, pushing her gently back on the bed. He then removed the satin heels with much ado, and kissed his way up to the top of her white thigh-high stockings.

Just knowing the pleasures that lay ahead had her writhing against the covers. "Blue lights, Ken," she whispered, their private shorthand when one of them could barely wait for the other to love them.

His laugh was throaty as he unfastened his waistband. "I love it when you talk dirty, ma'am."

"Oh, but isn't this better than phone sex?" She moaned as he entered her, swift and hard.

"Is it ever," he breathed against her neck. "I love you, Georgia."

"I love you, too," she panted, meeting his long, filling strokes. Her climax was close, and he knew it.

His face glistened with perspiration as he talked to her, murmuring sizzling, erotic words. Her thighs burned with the need for her release. He drew her knees up and levered himself over her, driving deep, bringing her to the brink, then over, in a rhythmic flood of ecstasy. She cried out his name over and over. His orgasm intensified hers as he expanded and pulsed inside her.

Georgia moaned and smiled to herself as he eased his head down to her shoulder. At this rate, they'd be pregnant by tomorrow. "Ken?"

"Hmm?"

She laughed, fanning herself. "The next time we get married, can it not be in the middle of a heat wave?"

He lifted himself on his elbows, his eyes sensuously glazed. "But since we met in a heat wave, I thought it was only appropriate. Besides," he said, nipping at her neck in preparation for round two, "a heat wave is the best time for lovers."

"Why?"

Ken growled against her neck. "Because it's too hot to sleep."

* * * * *

We hope you enjoyed the

BEST OF TEMPTATION
COLLECTION.

If you liked the stories in this collection, then you will enjoy **Harlequin® Blaze**.

You like it hot! **Harlequin® Blaze** stories sizzle with strong heroines and irresistible heroes playing the game of modern love and lust. They're fun, sexy and always steamy!

Enjoy four *new* stories from **Harlequin® Blaze** every month!

Available wherever books and ebooks are sold.

Riding High

"Caution. Proceeding with it."

"You want to proceed?"

"I do." Her eyes darkened to midnight-blue and her gentle sigh was filled to the brim with surrender as her arms slid around his neck, depositing mud along the way.

As if he gave a damn. His body hummed with anticipation. "Me, too." Slowly he lowered his head and closed his eyes.

"Mistake, though."

He hovered near her mouth, hardly daring to breathe. Had she changed her mind at the last minute? "Why?"

"Tell you later." She brought his head down and made the connection.

And it was as electric as he'd imagined. His blood fizzed as it raced through his body and eventually settled in his groin. Her lips fit perfectly against his from the first moment of contact. It seemed his mouth had been created for kissing Lily, and vice versa.

He tried a different angle, just to test that theory. Still perfect, still high-voltage. Since they were standing in water, it was a wonder they didn't short out. He couldn't speak for her but he'd bet he was glowing. His skin was hot enough to send off sparks.

She moaned and pressed her body closer. She felt amazing in his arms—soft, wet and slippery. He'd never imagined doing it in the mud, but suddenly that seemed like the best idea in the world.

Then she snorted. Odd. Not the reaction he would have expected considering where this seemed to be heading.

He lifted his head and gazed into her flushed face. "Did you just laugh?"

She regarded him with passion-filled eyes. "That wasn't me."

"Then who—"

The snort came again as something bumped the back of his knees. A heavy splash sent water up the back of his legs.

She might not have been laughing before but she was now. "Um, we have company."

Although it didn't matter which pig had interrupted the moment, Regan had his money on Harley. Whichever one had decided to take an after-dinner mud bath, they'd ruined what had been a very promising kiss.

Pick up RIDING HIGH by Vicki Lewis Thompson, available June 2014 wherever Harlequin® Blaze® books are sold!

And don't miss RIDING HARD and RIDING HOME in July and August of 2014!

It feels good to be bad!

Good girl and preacher's daughter Melanie Knowles has lived a sheltered life in Blackfoot Falls, Montana. No one could ever imagine she has a secret thing for bad boys... that is until ex-con Lucas Sloan comes to town.

Don't miss the latest in the
Made in Montana miniseries

Need You Now

by reader-favorite author
Debbi Rawlins

Available June 2014 wherever you buy
Harlequin Blaze books.

HB79805R

Fires aren't all that's sizzling for this smoking-hot firefighter!

Firefighter Dylan Cross, aka Mr. June in the annual "hottie" calendar, is used to risking his life to save others. But he's not about to risk his heart—or his bachelorhood!—when it comes to sexy Cassie Price....

From the reader-favorite miniseries *Last Bachelor Standing*

The Final Score
by Nancy Warren

Available June 2014 wherever you buy
Harlequin Blaze books.

Available now from the
Last Bachelor Standing miniseries by Nancy Warren

Game On
Breakaway

HARLEQUIN®

Blaze®

Red-Hot Reads
www.Harlequin.com

HB79806

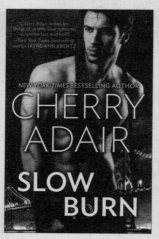